NOKOMIS HOSPITAL

A Jack Kendall Mystery, Book Four

Corruption runs deep at Nokomis Hospital, and those responsible will do anything to hide it.

JAY B. GREENE

Contents

Boketon Press

ISBN (Paperback): 979-8-9942674-5-5
ISBN (eBook): 979-8-9942674-0-0

Book Design by Adam Hay Studio, UK
E-Pub Formatting by Steve Mead Graphic Design

Printed in the United States of America

For my former healthcare sources, coworkers,
family, and friends. They all contributed to
this work, whether they realized it or not.

Acknowledgments
The author would like to express deep gratitude to
the *Sarasota Herald-Tribune* and the Lindsay family
for graciously allowing their names to be used in this
story. I also consulted with several healthcare experts
to develop the technical descriptions for this book.
If there are errors, those are mine, not theirs. Their
contributions in their respective fields have been
significant, enriching the narrative of this book.

Prologue:
Morning Meeting

11 a.m., Saturday, Sept. 8, 1984

Charles McMann knocked on the front door of Mike Lard's mansion on Dona Bay, hoping to finish his talk with his boss about his new growth plan before the hospital party that night.

Stephanie Lard answered. "Oh, hi, Charlie. Mike is by the pool having coffee. You can go right through," she said, letting him in.

McMann, the hospital's chief operating officer, was a slim man in his late forties with thinning sandy blond hair and a meticulously groomed mustache. His sharp, narrow eyes and high cheekbones gave him a calculating appearance.

"Sorry to bother you, but the five-day workweek isn't enough for us to do our business," McMann told her wearily.

"Tell me about it. Mike has already been on the phone most of the morning since we woke up," Stephanie said.

"How was your night?" McMann asked as he walked through the living room with her.

"Mike drank too much as usual, but he woke up at 7 a.m., just like always," Stephanie said. "You know Mike."

A bleached blonde with blue eyes, Stephanie met Mike five years before at a bar in Venice. Ten years younger than Mike, she had been divorced from her previous spouse, just like him, for cheating.

"Go ahead and interrupt him if he's on the phone. Can I get you coffee?" Stephanie asked.

"No, ma'am. I won't be staying that long," McMann said as he walked out through the back door.

Mike Lard's pool patio was extravagance distilled—a turquoise glass pool edged in smooth travertine, palm trees lit from below, and designer teak loungers arranged like a resort spread. A marble-topped outdoor bar gleamed beside a chef's grill, and soft ambient lighting reflected off the bay just beyond the seawall. Everything about the space whispered money and intention.

"Hi, Mike," said McMann. "Hope you don't mind that I stopped by."

Lard was stretched out on a teak lounger with thick white cushions, glancing up from his newspaper. Short and stocky, with a fading hairline and a deep, sunbaked tan, he looked more like a man on permanent vacation than the CEO of a struggling hospital.

"Not at all. What's on your mind?" he asked.

"I want to tell you about the rest of my plan before the party," McMann said.

"Sure. What did you say about buying buildings?"

"We do that now," McMann replied, "but I propose doing it on a much larger scale."

"Why doesn't Carl want to manage these?" Lard asked,

his eyes narrowing. "He does everything else we ask him."

"Carl flatly told me he wouldn't get involved in any more of our deals. You could talk with him tonight, but if Carl doesn't reconsider, I think our new person should be on our payroll, an employee," McMann said.

"I see. I'll talk to Carl, but I have someone in mind in case Carl is out," Lard said, shaking his head. "Tell me your idea."

"I have my eye on a vacant office building we could buy for $70,000. It's not listed yet. I know the agent. For a 10% kickback, he would work with us," McMann said.

"Go on."

"Once we purchase it, we could sell it to the hospital for $200,000, get somebody to convert it into physician offices, charge the hospital an inflated rate, and secure kickbacks from that."

"Once he takes the kickback, he's ours, just like the trustees and Carl Billingly," Lard said with a devilish grin.

"I know Johnny, the agent. Believe me, he won't talk," McMann insisted.

"So, you 're saying we could clear $130,000, minus a 10% kickback for the agent and 10% for the contractor, so that's $90,000 for us?" asked Lard.

"Approximately."

"Perfect. We probably need three more buildings like this to generate the profits we need," Lard replied.

"Yes, no problem. It would provide us with another source of revenue to spend or invest in other ventures. The advantage of this plan is that the hospital would also gain revenue from the doctors' rent, potentially another $50,000 annually. It all would help alleviate some of our deficit. We need to run this past Brophy for a financial review," McMann said.

"I like that. Some trustees have started asking too many questions. Can the building sales be connected to us?"

"No chance, unless they conduct a deep audit, which the board won't approve since the chair and several trustees are now taking cuts," McMann said with a grin.

"I don't see why Carl won't participate. He's managing the other fictitious company," Lard remarked.

"He doesn't have a problem with the one building, but he doesn't want to manage the multiple buildings you want. It will be an easy sell to the trustees. We know Medicare and private payers are shifting inpatient care to outpatient, so we have built-in justifications to purchase the buildings," McMann said.

"The board is another issue. What exactly did Carl tell you?" Lard pressed.

"You should discuss it with him, but he said the IRS began an audit of his 1983 taxes. I don't think his accountant is as good as ours."

"I'll talk to him at the party tonight," Lard said. "We can't have him getting in trouble."

"About the party...did you know David convinced Christine McVay to join the board?"

Lard smiled. Over the past five years, he had carefully recruited board members in close partnership with Board Chairman David Royster. They appointed trustees based on their willingness to defer to management's instructions or based on business kickback arrangements.

"I asked him to talk to her," Lard said.

"You told David that Chris wants to become a partner at her accounting firm. David convinced her that joining the board would help her career," McMann said. "She's very ambitious, and David told me she will do anything to get ahead."

"Is he sure? I haven't spoken with her about my expectations of board members."

"David thinks so, but maybe you should talk to her."

"I'll feel her out at the party and offer her the finance chair position," Lard said. "If she agrees, we'll know, and once she signs those falsified bond documents, she'll be on the hook, and we'll have another trustee in our pocket."

"She did enjoy our party last week," McMann said with a hearty laugh. "Who knew she liked cocaine?"

"That was a good sign to me," Lard said. "I'm going to push her along. We have some major decisions ahead, and I want to secure a majority of trustees."

"We're almost at the point for the big votes," McMann pointed out. "Six of our 15 trustees are financially benefiting or actively taking side payments. Two others either don't know or don't care what we're doing. We need two more on our side to be sure, and then we'll have a super-majority."

"I'm still working on Dr. O'Neal, but I think Manfred Lords, the newest trustee, will be the one."

"Isn't Lords married to Dr. Melissa Lords, our new pediatrician?"

"Yes. When Dr. Lords moved to Venice and applied for medical staff privileges with us, her husband approached me for a job. He recently got his general contractor's license," Lard explained.

"Won't Dr. Lords be upset when we close the maternity unit?" McMann asked. "Manfred won't vote for it if it'll upset his wife. Have you seen her? She's a knockout."

"She's attractive, no doubt. But she'll help convince her husband."

"How's that?"

"I'm going to offer her the job of vice president of pediatrics, which includes free office space and staffing." Lard laughed. "She won't say no."

"Did you run the free office space by Gus Lessem? He still refuses to take our bribes, but he negotiates the best compensation package of any hospital lawyer in 100 miles, and he's been turning a blind eye to the number of freebies you've granted to employed and recruited doctors the past year. He says it violates anti-kickback and fraud laws. He's right, of course," McMann said.

"I'm not worried. The feds won't pay attention to a 200-bed hospital, especially with a pro-business Republican in the White House," Lard said.

"Well, if you're not worried, I'm not either," McMann said. "Those doctors getting free rent and support staff have increased admissions and services directed to us. They are 25% higher than those of other doctors. This helps maintain our admission rates above 80%, which should be good enough."

"You keep coming up with these money-making schemes for us, and I'll move the chess pieces around. By the way, I offered Manfred Lords a contract to handle my boathouse," Lard said. "I also mentioned we might have other work for him. He's in dire need of employment."

"Wait until he discovers he'll be paid from the executive account," McMann responded. "Once he gets the first bonus check, he'll be one of us."

"Like all the rest. Wait, it just occurred to me: If Riggles won't run our new bogus company for medical offices, imaging centers, and pediatric centers, I'll ask Lords," Lard mused.

"Mike, won't it look like a conflict of interest for Lords to be on the board if he also runs our phony company?"

"I'll talk to Steve about how to set it up, but you're right, he can't be a direct employee. He'd have to be a contractor like Riggles. The phony company would pay him before the transfers to us," Lard explained.

"Then he'd be a trustee in our pocket, whether he likes it or not."

"Well, we probably will need one more definite vote, and I don't think Dr. O'Neal will be it," Lard remarked.

"I get the same impression. O'Neal has been asking a whole lot of questions in medical staff meetings and at the last board meeting," McMann observed.

"We need to slow down our information exchange with Dr. O'Neal. When I recruited him for the board, he said he would do it if it meant more business for his group and, in return, give us preferential treatment," Lard said. "He isn't living up to that agreement. We are giving him additional business—maybe not as much as he wanted—but I'm facing some pushback now."

"I am getting the same feeling," McMann said. "We could replace him."

"I'll talk with David about it. O'Neal's been hesitant so far to take free rent and a cut on his office buildings. I told him it would make up for the overall drop in heart admissions," Lard explained.

"He won't do it even though he's upset Sarasota Memorial and National Healthcare are taking some of our cardiology business with their new advertising and primary care referral network strategy," McMann replied.

"Don't remind me," Lard said. "Is that all for today?"

"Yes, sir. I just wanted to brief you before the party."

"Sounds good. I'm going for a swim now," Lard said as he stood and headed toward the pool.

McMann watched him dive cleanly into the eight-foot end. He had always loved coming here, especially at night when the underwater lights shifted the water from aqua to sapphire to a soft violet glow. Mike rarely entertained, preferring to have his parties at the hospital, but when he did, the place felt like a private resort.

Standing in such luxury always made Charles's own lifestyle seem dull. He desired more. His $300,000 home—up from the $210,000 he paid in 1977—felt second-rate by comparison. He owned a comfortable house, a product of Sarasota County's explosive rise during the 1970s and '80s as the region transformed from a quiet coastal town into one of Florida's most desirable enclaves. Cultural attractions, warm winters, and world-class beaches had driven a wave of growth that sent property values soaring.

But even in that booming market, his place couldn't compete with Mike's. Lard's $1 million mansion wasn't just larger—it was curated, illuminated, and engineered to impress.

You couldn't stand on that patio without understanding one thing immediately: Mike Lard wasn't just the CEO of Nokomis Hospital; he was the ruler of this mile-long stretch of the bay. And he had built himself a palace as proof.

Chapter 1:
Dinner in Nokomis

7 p.m., Friday, Sept. 7, 1984

Jack Kendall parked his Mustang GT at the Tillis home and looked over at Bobbie, her hand resting on her bulging tummy.

"You ready?" he asked.

"The babies and I are always ready to eat," Bobbie said with a tired grin. "I hope Keith serves his famous chocolate cake for dessert."

Jack smiled. Keith was an old high school friend who played on he football team, and Jack had known him since grammar school. He had a knack for baking chocolate cake.

As they approached the 1950s-style lodge house just off U.S. 41 in north Nokomis, Keith greeted them at the front door with a welcoming smile and his usual quip.

"Hey, look at you two—a married couple with a Pulitzer Prize, twins on the way, and still finding time to get tangled up in murder investigations," Keith teased.

An accountant with a penchant for cracking dry jokes, Keith gave Jack a firm handshake and patted Bobbie's shoulder.

Barbara, a petite brunette who also went to high school with Jack, rolled her eyes. "Ignore him. He reads all your articles and pesters me about how you survive these insane situations."

Jack chuckled, taking a seat at the dining table. "Survival is the name of the game in journalism these days."

Keith chuckled. "Journalism, ha! That's what you call it? Now I know what 'deadline' really means!"

Jack glanced at Bobbie. "Jokes aside, I've got good people watching my back, and I am very lucky to have this one."

Barbara smiled. "You two seem happy."

"We are," Bobbie said, lacing her fingers through Jack's. "It took us long enough to get here."

"C'mon in. We've got some catching up to do," said Keith, showing them inside their house. "Jack, would you like wine, beer, or your old favorite, the Vesper martini? I know what Bobbie is having."

"I'll just take a Heineken," said Jack, sitting on the living room sofa.

"Be right back," Keith said as he left for the kitchen.

"So, how are you, Bobbie, carrying twins?" Barbara asked, sitting down next to her. "I've been anxious to talk with you. We haven't spoken in months. We've got two kids, but I didn't have them all at once."

Bobbie exhaled. "I've been feeling exhausted lately. If it worsens, I've been thinking I might take an early maternity leave."

"Why don't you?" Barbara asked. "Isn't your due date next

month?"

"Yes, but I don't know. I'm torn. I've got a lot of work at the newspaper and enjoy staying busy," Bobbie said. "Besides, Jack needs looking after."

Jack shook his head and raised an eyebrow. "Bogotá again? I'll never hear the end of that disaster," he said with a sly smile.

As Barbara eyed Bobbie curiously, Keith returned with a beer for Jack and a big glass of water for Bobbie.

"I heard that. I'd like to know how you survived that shootout with Gordon Gecht in Bogotá!" exclaimed Keith.

Jack instinctively rubbed his shoulder. "Yeah, he nicked me, but I got him, too."

Barbara shuddered. "That man gives me nightmares. Was he the same guy who worked for that drug dealer at the High Seas?"

Jack's jaw tightened. "Yeah, the same. But the real nightmare was what Becky went through in Bogotá."

Bobbie squeezed his hand, sensing the shift in his mood.

Silence hung in the room momentarily before Keith took a deep breath. "Man...and I thought my job was stressful."

Jack smiled. "Accounting audits don't usually involve shootouts."

"You've never told us the whole story," Keith said, sitting down. "Do you mind? First, I'd like to know how the hell you didn't get yourself killed exposing Robert Mackey's cocaine empire at the High Seas?"

Bobbie shifted in her seat. "Jack, do you have to?"

Jack exhaled. "I shouldn't, but I'd like to explain to Keith and Barbara."

"All right, but keep it short. You know how I don't like to relive those times," Bobbie said.

"That bastard, Gordon Gecht, tried to kill me on Mackey's orders to shut me up about my investigation into the High Seas trafficking ring," Jack said. "Gecht and his flunky, Steve Ferro, knocked me out and injected me with crack cocaine to make it look like I overdosed."

"You still reported on the High Seas, didn't you? Closed it down?" Barbara interjected.

· "Not me personally, but Bobbie and I wrote articles about what the FBI, the Sarasota Police Department, and Chief Tom Bagley did to shut down that coke factory at the High Seas," Jack said.

"That was after Gecht nearly killed you," Keith said, remembering Jack's stories.

"Yeah, I got impatient and followed Gecht from the High Seas to Mackey's Siesta Key house," said Jack. "I thought Becky might be there."

"As usual, taking unnecessary risks," Bobbie said.

"Maybe, but I'd do it again because I followed a tip and my instincts. Besides, I survived, and the clues pointed me to Jamaica, where I found her," Jack said.

"Then you went there with your brother and that girl from the hospital," Keith recalled.

"Sarah. Yes," said Jack, exhaling. "Long story, but Becky and Michelle Talley escaped to Bogotá."

"I hate to say it, Jack, but I never liked Becky," said Barbara. "She was beautiful and charming, granted, but she knew you had come for her, and what did she do? She took off for Colombia to split that five million in drug money that Michelle Talley's fiancé left her."

Keith frowned. "Now, Barbara, we know what Becky meant to Jack and how her death affected him," he said calmly. "By the way, that was a beautiful eulogy you delivered at her wake."

Jack nodded, his voice quieter now. "Thank you, Keith. Bobbie was kind enough to accompany me to Bogotá to investigate what happened. Although she didn't initially agree with the idea, we persuaded the Colombian police to set a trap for him. It all culminated in that gunfight at the warehouse in a rundown section of Bogotá."

"And that's when you got shot," Barbara added.

"He could have been killed," Bobbie whispered. "If it weren't for Lieutenant Morales following us to the warehouse and calling the ambulance..."

Jack nodded. "Morales was a detective in the Bogotá Police Department," he explained. "I got lucky. He arrived just after Gecht and I shot each other."

"Please, Jack, enough," pleaded Bobbie, tired from the exchange.

"May I get you something, dear?" asked Barbara.

"No, I've got this water. Jack likes to tell these stories, but he almost died. I sat next to him on the floor, pressing on his shoulder to keep his blood from pouring out," said Bobbie, taking another sip of water.

"I'm sorry, Bobbie. That must have been terrible," Barbara said.

An awkward silence enveloped the room, and then Keith interjected.

"Let's talk about your last big investigation—the one involving that corrupt phosphate company," Keith said. "That's how you won a Pulitzer Prize. Congratulations!"

Jack nodded. "Thanks. Bobbie and I won it, yeah. Granger Phosphate. They murdered James Brewster to cover up illegally dumping toxic sludge into Terra Ceia and Tampa Bay."

Keith came over and patted Jack on the back. "You exposed the whole scheme. It was beautiful, man."

"Thanks, but the story almost got quashed. When I started investigating Granger, they threatened to sue the *Herald-Tribune* for libel to shut me up," Jack said, pausing. "The delay cost James Brewster his life."

Bobbie touched his arm and turned to the Tillis couple. "Jack still blames himself for James's death even though he did all he could to protect him."

Jack said in frustration, "If we had published that story on Friday, he wouldn't have died, his sister wouldn't be serving a life sentence, and those four corrupt phosphate executives would be the ones serving time instead of being dead."

"We all agree on that, but Elizabeth would have lost it some other way," Bobbie softly said. "Her schizoaffective disorder was worsening. Jack, Gecht's dead. It's over. Just drop it."

"That was unfortunate. But after Brewster was killed, you didn't back off. You kept pushing," Keith said, grinning. "Reminds me of high school. We'd get in trouble, apologize, and figure out a way not to get caught the next time."

Jack chuckled. "Yeah, we thought we were so smart. Looking back, the principal and teachers were aware of what we were doing. They just didn't know how to stop us."

Barbara looked at Bobbie. "Has Jack told you those high school stories? We were always getting into trouble."

Bobbie smiled weakly. "You were involved in those?"

"Sometimes," Barbara admitted.

"Okay, okay, enough about high school. We've grown up a little since then," Jack said.

"Yes, but you still like to fight against bullies and try to right wrongs," Barbara said. "Those criminals you went after—

Robert Mackey, Pierre Grousland, and Gecht. You stopped them."

"They all ran businesses that killed people," Jack said with disgust. "I hate that. It makes my blood boil. Mackey sold cocaine to people and destroyed many lives; Granger polluted the environment, hired Gecht to kill James, then tried to kill his sister, Elizabeth, plus Bobbie and me."

"I loved how you exposed their lies and..." said Keith, hesitating.

Jack interrupted. "You mean how I avenged Becky's death?"

"Yes, I'm sorry to keep mentioning it," Keith said.

"It's all right. It's been nearly two years now, and I am very happy with Bobbie," Jack said, leaning over to kiss her. "But, yeah, they thought they could scare me off. But we had a trap ready for Gecht, and it worked."

Keith shook his head in disbelief. "You must have a death wish, Jack, getting so deep in your investigations."

"I like to call it persistence," Jack said.

Barbara noticed Bobbie had closed her eyes. She shifted the conversation. "You're about to become a father, Jack. How do you feel about that?"

Jack glanced at Bobbie, who had opened her eyes a little at the mention of her pregnancy. "I feel excited and nervous. Mostly, I want to be the same kind of father I had, just with a longer life."

Keith raised his glass. "To fatherhood!"

Jack and Barbara raised their drinks, and then Keith snickered, "And if you survive your next investigation, you'll become a great father."

As they clinked glasses, Bobbie winced and pressed her hand to her temple.

"My head hurts," she murmured. A moment later, her vision blurred, and she looked around in confusion.

"Bobbie, what's wrong?" Jack asked, standing up and moving over toward her.

She shook her head and blinked. "I...I don't know where we are," she murmured, her voice trembling. Tears welled up, spilling down her cheeks. "Can we go home?"

Barbara, sitting next to Bobbie, gasped and moved closer. "Jack, look at her," she said, placing a hand on Bobbie's forehead. "She's hot, and she's clammy. Her face is so pale."

Jack didn't hesitate. His heart pounding, he guessed what it was—and it wasn't a headache.

"The nurse at Lamaze class warned us that headache and vision loss could mean eclampsia," said Jack as he considered what to do. "That's it. This is an emergency. We're going to the hospital. Now." Jack reached to help Bobbie up.

Barbara placed a steadying hand on Bobbie's shoulder. "Let me grab my keys..."

Jack shook his head. "I've got her. Keith, give me a hand."

Keith took one of Bobbie's arms. Jack held the other. Barbara opened the front door, and they helped Bobbie into the car.

"Do you want me to go with you?" Keith quickly asked.

Jack shook his head, maintaining a focused gaze on Bobbie.

"Call me as soon as you know something!" Keith shouted as Jack ran around to the driver's side, started up his GT, and pulled out of the driveway.

It was a five-minute drive to Nokomis Hospital.

Chapter 2:
Friday Night in the ER

7:30 p.m., Friday, Sept. 7, 1984

Jack sped south on U.S. 41, crossing the Dona Bay Bridge, and raced toward Nokomis Hospital on the peninsula between Dona and Roberts Bays.

Bobbie sat slumped in the passenger seat, breathing heavily. Her skin was slick with sweat.

Jack's GT was hitting 75 mph on the Tamiami Trail. He glanced over as he approached the turn, and Bobbie suddenly tensed. Her body jerked violently—her arms and legs convulsed as a seizure overtook her.

"Bobbie!" Jack shouted as he sharply turned off the highway. He accelerated again down the five-block street leading to the hospital.

Thirty seconds later, as he made the final turn into the ER entrance, he slammed on the brakes and honked the horn for attention inside. Jumping out of the car, he rushed to the passenger's side, opened the door, and leaned in, shaking her gently.

"Bobbie, wake up." No response. He felt her forehead—hot and clammy.

Heart pounding, he sprinted inside. "I need help!" he yelled. "My wife is pregnant and unconscious in my car—somebody help, now!"

On Friday nights, the ER was packed. A security guard rushed over to give Jack a hand. Together, they ran back to the car.

"She was fine fifteen minutes ago!" Jack exclaimed.

At that moment, a doctor and a nurse burst through the doors with a gurney. They carefully lifted Bobbie out of the car and onto the stretcher.

"I'm Dr. Rashad," the ER doctor introduced himself as they wheeled Bobbie inside. "Tell me what happened."

"She's pregnant with twins," Jack said, his pulse racing. "We were sitting down for dinner when she said her head hurt, and she couldn't see clearly. Then, she had a seizure on the way here. It all happened in under fifteen minutes."

"We need to take her blood pressure and start an IV," Dr. Rashad calmly said.

Jack followed them into the examination room. He looked around. The ER seemed disorganized and chaotic, and the staff appeared overwhelmed by the number of patients.

"Her BP is extremely high at 160 over 110," Dr. Rashad observed with a concerned look. "Nurse, we need a CBC and a catheter for a urine sample."

Jack knew from his healthcare reporting that CBC meant complete blood count, a fairly standard test, but the urine sample meant something else.

"She had a seizure in the car. Is this eclampsia?" Jack worriedly asked. "Her OB-GYN advised us to monitor her blood pressure."

"Could be. I need an ultrasound and a fetal monitor. We need more help in here!" Dr. Rashad said louder.

A few seconds later, a second nurse entered the room. "We are looking for the ultrasound cart," she said.

"You can't find one?" asked Jack, growing more worried.

"We've been busy, and tonight we are understaffed," Dr. Rashad explained, continuing his examination.

Five minutes later, an older woman, who appeared to be a volunteer, pushed in a cart with a portable ultrasound and fetal monitor.

"Where do you want it?" she asked.

"Right here. Thanks, Mrs. Brodsky," Dr. Rashad said as he quickly applied the scanning gel to Bobbie and passed the electronic wand over her belly. The results appeared on the small screen.

"You are right, Mr. Kendall. You have twins. They appear normal and without distress. But I am not waiting for further test results. Nurse, get me the magnesium sulfate," Dr. Rashad said.

As the nurse rushed out of the room, Jack nervously asked, "What's happening now?"

"We need to stabilize her," Dr. Rashad said. "Nurse!" the young doctor yelled again.

"Where is she?" Jack asked.

"Probably looking for the IV bag. We are a little short on supplies. As soon as she gets back with it, I will stabilize your wife and have our on-call OB-GYN examine her," he said.

"Is this normal, the lack of equipment and supplies?" Jack asked. "What's going on?"

"It's been getting worse the past few weeks. We should be okay once they sign the new vendor contract," Dr. Rashad said.

"This is due to a contractual dispute with vendors?" Jack asked incredulously. "All this? Short staffing, lack of supplies and equipment? It's hard to believe."

"That's what we've been told. Meanwhile, we're doing our best," Dr. Rashad said. "Oh, here comes the IV."

The nurse hurried in with a bag of magnesium sulfate. She inserted the needle into a vein in Bobbie's arm, and the fluid began to refresh her.

Jack stood there in disbelief. Only one hour ago, Bobbie had seemed as normal as a woman nearly eight months pregnant with twins could be.

They had been so careful with the pregnancy. Bobbie had cut down on her workload, and Jack helped her make all her prenatal appointments. Her blood pressure was higher than usual and fluctuated during the day, but everything was going well with her pregnancy.

Bobbie took the recommended prenatal vitamins and got plenty of sleep. She was slightly diabetic but well within normal ranges. However, her OB-GYN warned of the dangers of high blood pressure and the possibility of preeclampsia.

After a 20-minute dose, Bobbie stabilized and awoke.

"How are you feeling?" Jack asked.

"My head hurts," Bobbie said, her voice hoarse and strained. "How long was I out?"

"About 45 minutes," said Jack. "The ER doctor said an OB-GYN is coming."

"What is this thing in my arm?" Bobbie groggily asked.

"It's an intravenous drip. They are giving you magnesium sulfate to stabilize you," Jack replied.

"Where am I?" Bobbie asked, looking around confused.

"I brought you to Nokomis Hospital. The doctor is treating you for eclampsia."

"Where is the doctor?" Bobbie asked, coughing. "I don't feel good."

"He left. The doctors and nurses are understaffed here. They told me to watch the monitors and call out if you had any problems," said Jack.

Bobbie shook her head. "I don't understand. Are the babies all right?"

"So far, so good. Dr. Rashad, the ER doctor, didn't say too much other than that the babies are doing well and that you have eclampsia. You passed out in the car. I was afraid you might slip into a coma. He said to wait for the OB-GYN. Something is going on at this hospital."

"What do you mean?" asked Bobbie, still groggy.

"They seem short-staffed and overwhelmed, and they don't have supplies," Jack said. "Right now, all that matters is you. I'll find out later what's wrong here at the hospital."

"I don't feel good, Jack," Bobbie said, closing her eyes as tears rose.

"Bobbie, stay awake. The doctor will be here in a minute," he said.

Jack looked at the monitors, and Bobbie's blood pressure rose again. The fetal monitor showed steady beats, but Bobbie seemed to be worsening.

Chapter 3:
Surgery

8 p.m., Friday, Sept. 7, 1984

As Jack turned to leave the room, a middle-aged female doctor nearly ran into him as she hurried in.

"Excuse me. Are you the OB-GYN?" Jack asked.

"Yes. Dr. Rashad asked me to come in and take a look," said Dr. Jennifer Chastain, a 40-year-old obstetrician on weekend emergency call.

"She woke up, said she wasn't feeling well, and fell back asleep. What's wrong with her?" Jack asked.

Dr. Chastain looked over at Bobbie, who appeared asleep and breathing deeply.

"I need to do some tests. You can stay, but please let us do our work. What is the patient's name?" Dr. Chastain asked.

"Bobbie Kendall. I'm Jack Kendall. Do you want me to tell you what happened?" Jack asked.

"Dr. Rashad briefed me," she said.

"She is receiving magnesium sulfate. Does that mean she has preeclampsia or eclampsia?" Jack asked.

"Eclampsia. She's having seizures. Dr. Rashad's quick thinking in giving her the magnesium sulfate probably prevented a coma, but she had a large seizure in your car, and she'll most likely have some small ones if we don't act," Dr. Chastain said as she looked over the ER notes of Bobbie's treatment.

"That's what I thought, but she woke up confused and groggy. Her voice sounds different," Jack said in an anxious tone.

"She has high blood pressure, and the urine test revealed elevated protein levels. I can see that her face is puffy. The ultrasound shows some pulmonary edema. I'll need to take another," Dr. Chastain said. "What week of pregnancy is she in?"

"The 32nd week?" Jack said. "Maybe 33rd? What does pulmonary edema mean?"

"Fluid in the lungs caused her voice to sound strained. We need to stop the fluids now. Mr. Kendall, Bobbie is stable now, but I recommend we take her to surgery immediately," Dr. Chastain urged.

"Surgery?" Jack asked.

"She needs a C-section. We need to deliver these twins as soon as possible," she insisted.

"Yes, but what does this mean?" Jack asked again.

"We're doing everything we can for Bobbie, but I won't sugarcoat it—eclampsia is a serious condition and very unpredictable, especially for a woman expecting twins. We're taking all necessary steps right now to ensure her survival," Dr. Chastain stated.

"Survival?" Jack gasped. "She woke up and seemed to be improving. How are the babies? They are so small."

"Mr. Kendall, we can't delay. It's best to go ahead and deliver the babies and then treat your wife."

"Go, do it," Jack said.

"Nurse, call surgery. Tell them we are bringing Bobbie Kendall in for an emergency C-section," Dr. Chastain ordered.

"Yes, Doctor," the nurse replied.

"Would you like to come up with me? We have a waiting room," Dr. Chastain offered.

Jack followed the obstetrician to the elevator. While they waited, he asked her about the hospital.

"You know, Doctor, I should tell you that I am the healthcare reporter at the *Herald-Tribune*. I noticed the ER seemed to be a chaotic mess. I was told the hospital is understaffed. What's going on?" Jack asked.

"A lot, but we still have an excellent surgery team," Dr. Chastain replied. "Don't worry."

The elevator opened, and they entered.

"I trust you will do an excellent job with her C-section, but we had to wait for an ultrasound cart and magnesium sulfate bag in the ER. It could have been a lot worse for her. What's wrong at this hospital?" Jack pressed.

"Financial problems, I heard, but let's talk about it later," Dr. Chastain said with a frown. "I want to focus on Bobbie and your babies."

"Yes, Bobbie is the priority, but I will hold you to that promise to tell me what you know," said Jack with a smile. "So, have you performed many C-sections on women with eclampsia?"

"Yes, you'd be surprised at how far we've come in preventing serious complications and postpartum side effects," she replied.

"What kinds of complications?"

"Several, but we will keep an eye on her. Once we deliver the babies, we can give Bobbie more medicine," Dr. Chastain said.

"Will that reduce her blood pressure?" Jack asked.

"We'll be monitoring her closely after delivery. High blood pressure can persist, and other issues could arise."

"Like what? You forget I am a reporter."

"I realize that," she said with a slight smile, "but the most immediate concern is stabilizing Bobbie's blood pressure. It was high before we gave her the medicine. She is better now, but we must remain vigilant. We have a dedicated team that will provide her with the best care possible. Just let us do our job."

The elevator stopped on the third floor, and Jack followed Dr. Chastain to the swinging doors leading into surgery.

"Over there is the waiting room. We will keep you informed as we move along. Try to remain calm," she reassured.

"How long will it take?" Jack asked.

"It's hard to say, Mr. Kendall. We'll keep you informed throughout the process. She is being prepped right now."

Just then, Dr. Chastain's pager beeped.

"I need to go," she said. "Wait here. I'll talk with you soon."

As Jack sat in the surgery department waiting room, he thought about how lucky he was to be near a hospital. Bobbie had passed out and was barely breathing when Dr. Rashad and the nurse wheeled her into the ER.

While Venice Hospital was only eight miles away, Sarasota was further—15 miles away.

As Jack waited, he reflected on what Dr. Rashad had told him and what Dr. Chastain had confirmed. Something was wrong at Nokomis Hospital; it was evident that the facility was understaffed. He recalled the two patients lying on stretchers in the halls. They appeared stable—the one bandaged was scowling while the other was sleeping.

Jack had visited many hospitals before. Bags of trash piled in corners and carts full of dirty gowns were unusual sights. Did the hospital lack enough staff to clean the ER and care for its patients? He needed to learn more about Nokomis Hospital, not just to satisfy his journalistic curiosity but also for Bobbie's sake.

During the past 18 months, Jack spent much of his time covering Sarasota Memorial Hospital, Doctors Hospital, and Venice Hospital in Sarasota County, as well as the ownership changes at Manatee Memorial Hospital and Blake Hospital in Bradenton.

He realized he hadn't written any articles on Nokomis since several "superstar" cardiologists were hired over a year ago.

At least Bobbie was receiving care, and Dr. Chastain seemed competent, but he didn't know her as well as he knew Dr. Rafferty at Sarasota Memorial.

Sitting there, lost in a thousand thoughts, he called Keith, his brother Ed, and his mother, Laura. He quickly informed them that Bobbie was at Nokomis Hospital, receiving treatment for eclampsia and undergoing a C-section to deliver the babies. He also left a message for Dr. Rafferty.

What else should he do? He thought about Bobbie. He reflected on how lucky he was to have married her after Becky was killed. He had always wanted children, but Becky never shared that wish.

Now, with Bobbie in surgery, he could only wait and pray—actions he famously lacked—for the children he always wanted.

Chapter 4:
Bobbie Delivers

9 p.m., Friday, Sept. 7, 1984

Dr. Chastain left the surgery department and walked over to Jack in the waiting room. She was smiling.

"Mr. Kendall, congratulations on the birth of your twins. They each weigh slightly more than four pounds. They are small, but they are fighters," Dr. Chastain said proudly.

"Thank goodness. How is Bobbie?" Jack nervously asked.

"Your wife did well. She awoke and remained alert throughout. We'll be monitoring them all closely and providing the best care possible," she said.

"I am so happy to hear that," Jack said. "When can I see her and the twins?"

"She's still in post-op, and we are monitoring her condition. The babies have been taken to the NICU. You can go over there and look at them through the glass window. They should be in there shortly," Dr. Chastain said.

"Are they healthy?" Jack asked.

" I mentioned, they are fighters, but preemies can face issues. Yours are eight weeks premature. As a precaution, we placed them in incubators to keep them warm," she said.

"Is that normal?" Jack asked.

"For preemies, yes. Their body temperatures are slightly low, and their breathing is a bit shallow," Dr. Chastain said. "Overall, there are no concerns. Every measure is within the normal range for their size and age."

Jack furrowed his brow, his expression questioning.

"We will know more in a few hours as they adjust to the world," she added.

Jack felt relieved. "Thank you, thank you," he said as Dr. Chastain smiled and started to leave.

"Wait, I want to say that you did a great job. Now, this may sound ungrateful, but when can we transfer them to Sarasota Memorial?" Jack asked. "It's where we planned to have the twins with Dr. Rafferty."

"I wouldn't recommend that now," Dr. Chastain said, her face showing surprise. "Dr. Lords is the neonatologist on staff. I am sure she would agree that we should not move them for several days. We need to continue to monitor Bobbie for at least a week to make sure her blood pressure doesn't spike again."

"I mentioned this before. I was confident in your surgery team, but I am concerned about the condition of the hospital," Jack said.

"I understand your concerns, but we have a top team in the obstetrics department and NICU," she said. "As I said, we are swamped tonight."

"It's more than that. I've been to hospitals on Friday nights before. Something is wrong with this one. You were in the ER.

The place is a mess with trash and dirty linen in the halls. This isn't normal," Jack said.

Dr. Chastain didn't respond. Jack noticed in her eyes that she didn't want to discuss the hospital. He looked around and saw several employees and visitors walking through the halls.

"Maybe this isn't the best time to talk, but you said you'd discuss the hospital later," Jack said plainly. "If you don't mind, please tell me what's wrong. I'll keep asking everyone I see. You don't know me well yet, but as a reporter, I will find out."

"I can imagine, but I can't talk with you right now," said Dr. Chastain in a whisper. "I'm on call and am busy myself. Maybe later. Call my office, and we can meet somewhere else. I need to get back to Bobbie. She is safe and in good hands. I will make sure the nurses understand."

"If you think the understaffing, lack of supplies, and trash and linens in the halls won't affect her care, I will go along with keeping Bobbie here tonight," Jack said.

Dr. Chastain stood there, contemplating how to respond.

"Doctor, Bobbie is the most important thing right now. I am worried because I have never seen such a chaotic mess in the ER. You did a great job with the C-section. I just…I just need to know more," Jack said, pausing, then adding, "I'm going to look for Nicole. How long will Bobbie be in post-op?"

"It is hard to say. Mr. Kendall—Jack—after you talk with Nicole, come back to the surgery waiting room. I'll find you," she said.

"I appreciate it, Dr. Chastain," said Jack as he turned to leave.

He took off in search of Nicole McIntosh, the well-liked vice president of nursing. He wanted to know more about the supply shortages and any additional information she could provide.

He had a little time before meeting Bobbie and the twins, and he was worried and nervous about their situation. To keep his mind occupied, he went back to the ER and found the security guard who had assisted him earlier.

"Excuse me. I'm Jack Kendall. You helped me carry my wife in earlier. What's your name?" Jack asked.

"I'm Josh Lucas. Is your wife all right?"

"Yes, she just gave birth to our twins. I have some time before I can see them, and I thought I would look for an old friend who works here. Do you know where I can find Nicole McIntosh?" he asked.

"Nicole? She's probably off-duty. I haven't seen her tonight," Lucas said. "She usually works days."

"Of course. What am I thinking? It's Friday night. I can't believe it."

"I'm sure you're upside down now, but your wife is good, and you have twins. Congratulations," Josh said with a big smile.

"Thanks. Would you mind if I asked you about the hospital? The ER is a mess, and I was told there have been supply shortages. What's wrong?" Jack asked.

"I shouldn't say, but it's been like this for two months—even longer, if I told the truth. I suspect they are having financial problems," Josh said. "I used to work directly for the hospital. Last year, they laid off everyone in security and contracted out the service. We have fewer people doing the same jobs, and some are not as experienced."

"By the way, I'm Jack Kendall with the *Herald-Tribune*. This was background, but I may want to discuss this with you on the record later, if that's all right," said Jack, handing Josh his newspaper card.

"I'd love to talk. Give me a call. We'll see."

"Thanks, Josh," said Jack as he walked to the elevator that would take him to the surgery department's waiting room.

* * *

Thirty minutes later, Jack was pacing in the surgery department's waiting room when he saw Dr. Chastain approaching him.

"Your wife remains stable," she said. "You can go up and see her in the maternity ward."

"Is she awake?" Jack asked.

"Yes, just don't stay long."

"Thanks, Dr. Chastain," Jack said.

"Just remember, she's been through a lot."

"Is there anything I should know?"

"You should be there to support her emotionally," she advised. "We're doing everything medically possible, and your presence will mean a great deal to Bobbie. Let's take this one step at a time, Mr. Kendall."

"Thanks," Jack said, breathing a sigh of relief.

* * *

As Jack entered Bobbie's hospital room, he saw her resting on a bed with an intravenous needle in her arm and monitors connected to her head and chest. He was full of relief as he approached her bedside.

"Bobbie, you made it. The doctor said you and the twins are going to be fine."

Bobbie smiled weakly, her eyes filled with gratitude. "I

am so tired. All I want to do is sleep. I can't believe we did it. Have you seen the babies? Are they okay?"

Jack nodded. "We have a healthy baby boy and girl. Dr. Chastain said they are doing well, but I haven't seen them yet. I wanted to make sure you're safe."

Bobbie's eyes filled with tears. "I can't wait to see them, to hold them."

Jack gently took Bobbie's hand and kissed it. "I'm so proud of you."

"I don't remember what happened. I wouldn't be here without you. You kept me and the babies safe," Bobbie said, looking at him with admiration.

Jack smiled. "I knew something was wrong when you started crying at Keith's house. You had a sudden headache, and you weren't yourself."

"I don't remember that at all," Bobbie said, looking at Jack, her eyes filled with overwhelming emotion—a mix of gratitude and love.

"Jack, thank you for being there with me. I can't believe we have our little boy and girl," Bobbie beamed.

"The doctor said our babies are preemies. They are in incubators to keep them warm and protect them from infection. We need to let them get cared for before we can hold them. It would be best to stay in the hospital for a few days before you go home," Jack said.

"I can't wait to hold them," she murmured. "Now I want to sleep."

Jack reached over and kissed Bobbie's forehead again.

"Close your eyes. I'll go check on the babies and be back soon," he whispered.

Chapter 5:
Jane Willoughby
10 p.m., Friday, Sept. 7, 1984

Jack walked to the preemie ward, thinking about Bobbie, his newborns, and how he could uncover the dysfunction at the hospital. Along the way, he saw Dr. Chastain reviewing a chart.

"Dr. Chastain. Bobbie went back to sleep. She's exhausted. Her hands were shaking. Is that normal?" Jack asked.

"Quite normal. As I said before, eclampsia can be challenging to predict, even in healthy pregnancies. It's more common in first-time pregnancies, and while Bobbie is in good health, it can sometimes occur without clear warning signs. But she is doing well."

"Good. I'm going to see the babies. How are they doing?" Jack asked.

"They are doing well for four-pound babies and scored at the top of the Apgar tests," Dr. Chastain said. "If you visit them, ask for Dr. Lords. She is the pediatrician in charge. I'm going home now. You can call me on Sunday about the hospital."

"Thanks, I'll do that," said Jack.

When Jack got to the preemie ward, a nurse stopped him.

"Can I help you?" she said.

"Yes, I am Jack Kendall, Bobbie's husband. Are our twins here?"

"Hi, Mr. Kendall. We just received them. You can't go in, but we have a window where you can see them," the nurse said. "Come with me."

Jack walked past the door and saw the large, 10-by-20-foot plate-glass window.

"Wow, this is big. There are so many babies in there. How many?" Jack asked.

"We have ten, including your two. Have you named your twins yet?" the nurse said.

"We have a few ideas. I want to talk with Bobbie before we make a final decision," Jack said.

"Right now, they are Kendall Girl A and Kendall Boy B. See, there they are," said the nurse, pointing toward the back right side.

"The girl was born first?" Jack asked.

"Yes, by 30 seconds," the nurse replied with a smile.

Jack looked at the babies in the incubators. They both had fetal monitors hooked to their little chests and arms. The baby boy had jet-black, bushy hair, and the baby girl had light, reddish-blonde frizz on her head.

"It will be easy to tell them apart, at least right now," Jack said.

The nurse smiled. "They are so cute and doing well for what they have been through," she said. "It's fortunate that you encountered this problem now."

"Now? What do you mean?" Jack asked.

"You're Jack Kendall, the healthcare reporter at the *Tribune*, aren't you?"

"Yes."

"You are a reporter, and you don't know what's happening here?"

"Not yet, but I want to know what's wrong. I see it's understaffed in the ER, with piles of trash and carts of dirty linen in every department. Dr. Chastain said your department is good except for the dirty linen," Jack said. "I've been told there are supply problems, and security has been outsourced."

"That's just a few of our problems, but I don't want to be quoted if you are doing a story," the nurse replied.

"I will certainly do a story. I need people to go on the record. Maybe I should talk with Dr. Lords?" Jack asked.

"She isn't here now, and Dr. Lords won't talk anyway. She's on management's side, and her husband's on the board. Don't ask her anything unless you want to hear the company line. Anyway, I'd like to tell you some things if you want to hear them."

"On the record, with your name?"

"Not on the record, at least now."

"Okay. Whatever you say is off the record and not for publication. "If I ask you to go on the record later and you agree, I will use it in a story," Jack said. "I sense something is wrong here."

"There is. I heard you and your wife were at the hospital, and I expected to see you. I am glad you are here. I am Jane Willoughby, director of maternity and NICU services. This is my unit."

"I'm happy to meet you. What can you tell me about the condition of this hospital?" Jack asked. "You said, 'We were fortunate to have encountered this problem now.' That sounds ominous. What did you mean?"

"First, you should ask our CEO why he wants to close our maternity unit and lay off our maternal-fetal staff," the director said. "I'm so mad. We have been delivering babies and staffing the neonatal intensive care unit where your twins are now since this hospital opened nearly 20 years ago."

"Closing the maternity department? Why?" asked Jack.

"Good question. Lard says it's due to Medicare and private payer cuts. I think it isn't a profit center for them, and their mismanagement is causing all this cost-cutting," she said. "It's just my suspicion, but I think I'm right."

Jack was stunned by the news. Dr. Chastain said the babies would be all right at the hospital, but he wondered if he should discuss transferring them with Dr. Lords as soon as possible.

"But how could Nokomis be losing money?" Jack asked. "You're part of a thriving, vibrant community near Venice and Sarasota."

"We shouldn't be losing money. We have an occupancy rate of more than 85%. I have my opinions. The board is considering eliminating inpatient obstetrics and mental health and selling its ambulance service," the director said. "There is also a rumor that the hospital may be sold."

"Sold? To Sarasota Memorial? Or to National Healthcare, the for-profit company buying all the hospitals from here to Naples?" Jack asked.

"I don't know who, but if it's National, they'll cut more than Lard has, or maybe Lard is cutting because they're telling him to. Either way, the cuts will devastate patients and employees in the area, and it won't be good for the community," she said.

"Maternity, mental health, and emergency. Those are all

critical services. They want to do this to save money?" Jack asked. "I don't understand."

"None of us understands. You should speak with other people and ask the CEO," Willoughby insisted. "Lard says the hospital has short-term financial problems related to the new Medicare payment system, but some of these issues have been going on for years, and other problems are also occurring."

"Like what?" Jack asked.

"I shouldn't say anymore. Someone might overhear. Let me give you my card. Call me at home," she said, writing down her home phone number. "I will tell you what I know if you protect me. You need to write a story. Perhaps getting the word out to the public will stop them."

Jack nodded.

"Now, enjoy your twins. You probably won't be able to hold them until tomorrow," Willoughby advised.

"One more thing. Does Nicole McIntosh know all this?" Jack asked.

"You know her?" she asked.

"Yes. I've been looking for her," Jack replied.

"I trust you will keep this a secret. Nicole knows a lot about the executives."

"Let her know I'll be here all weekend with my wife and want to talk with her as well."

"I will. Now I'd better get back inside," Willoughby said.

"Thanks for your help. I'll talk with you later," said Jack, looking back at his two babies with wonder and concern.

After 10 minutes, Jack decided to get a coffee in the cafeteria and make a few calls: his mother, Bobbie's parents, Keith and Ed. He'd let them know the babies had been born and Bobbie was safe and resting.

Walking to the cafeteria, he knew he had to get to the bottom of what was happening at Nokomis Hospital. However, Bobbie was his top priority at the moment.

Chapter 6:
Cocaine in the C-suite

7 p.m., Saturday, Sept. 8, 1984

Charles McMann arrived late at Nokomis Hospital's fifth-floor penthouse suite with the box of expensive foreign wine and cocaine.

He was upset about having to perform this task, especially after the liquor store in Venice refused to deliver to the hospital due to unpaid bills. He had to pay cash and pick up the bottles himself.

Then he also had to scrounge up the coke because Harry Goldfarb, the director of environmental services, was nowhere to be found. Bringing the cocaine to the party was usually his responsibility.

By 7 p.m., the party was already in full swing. Softly in the background, the small jazz band played "So What" by Miles Davis.

Mike Lard was the first to greet McMann. He was dressed in his trademark Hawaiian shirt, which he always wore on Saturdays.

"Hey, Charlie. What took you so long? We missed you. Let me help you with that box," Lard said as he opened the top and pulled out two bottles.

"Don't even ask," McMann said, frowning. "I want a big glass of red."

Lard didn't pay attention. He held up two bottles of $100 wine and made an announcement. "People, tonight we have Mendoza from Argentina and Château Latour–Pauillac! I'm opening now!" Lard roared.

He turned to Charlie and whispered, "You get the coke?"

"That's what took me so long. Harry was supposed to bring 10 grams to the hospital this afternoon. He left work early, and nobody saw him. I called him, and he didn't answer. I drove over there at 5 p.m., and nobody was home," Charlie said.

"He's probably bingeing again. Well, let's not worry about it now," Lard said. "How much do you have?"

"Only five grams, my stash. Do you have any in your office?" Charlie asked.

"I have some. I am sure we have enough for tonight if we pool our resources," Lard said.

Cora Billingly approached the two men, her face wild. She was notorious for mixing quaaludes with wine and could quickly get intoxicated.

"Where's my glass of wine, darling Mike? You promised me something expensive," she slurred.

"My dear Cora. Did Carl let you out of his sight again? Come with me. I will pour you a big glass," Lard said as he moved toward the bar table.

Lard was proud of his newly designed entertainment room. It was located on the main hospital's penthouse floor, providing it with additional privacy from the rest of the hospital.

Bathed in natural light during the day and offering breathtaking coastline views at sunset, the entertainment room spared no expense to present an air of sophistication and indulgence. Upon entering the room, guests were welcomed by a spacious, tastefully decorated living area with plush sofas, designer chairs, and stylish décor. Floor-to-ceiling windows lined the walls, offering a complete view of the blue-green water overlooking Roberts Bay and the Gulf of Mexico to the west, a tall, scrubby jungle to the south, and growing subdivisions on the other two sides.

Lard hired a bartender and a gourmet chef to serve his guests. They worked with a fully stocked bar, but the liquor selection was running low due to vendor payment issues.

As the guests arrived, Chef Gustav was busy preparing tasty hors d'oeuvres, including sliced roast beef, scalloped potatoes, shrimp cocktails, smoked trout croquettes, jalapeno poppers, and stuffed mushrooms. Many vegetables adorned the serving tables.

At almost every Saturday night party, Lard made sure that cocaine and liquor circulated freely as hospital executives and managers entertained business associates and carefully vetted employees, donors, board members, and potential property or service buyers. He invited a mix of like-minded and discreet conspirators, along with their wives or girlfriends. No specific business was discussed, but he believed it created opportunities to casually present money-making ideas.

Once a month, on Wednesdays, Mike Lard held exclusive poker parties, inviting a select group of men and a few women.

These smaller, more intimate gatherings served as a cover for more decadent activities, as Lard mainly limited the guests to men, specifically to entertain them with "special guests"—strippers and prostitutes.

"Mike, when you have a minute, I'd like to update you on the warehouse plan," Brophy said, clearly reluctant about the plan but feeling the need to bring it up.

"Can't it wait? Cora needs another drink," Lard replied, dismissing the concern with a wave. He turned to Carl's wife, a forced smile on his face. "Don't you, sweetie?"

"But Mike, we also need to discuss the number of vendors putting credit holds on our supplies," Brophy said.

"Not now," Mike said as he rubbed Cora's thigh. She sexily smiled at him.

"Mike, your wife is watching us, and so is Carl," Brophy said.

"Go flirt with her," he curtly said, dismissing Brophy.

Steve Brophy shrugged and left. Mike could even be rude to his friends when he didn't want to do something, even when he was hyped on coke and scotch.

"He's in one of those moods," Steve told Carl and Stephanie Lard.

"Cora will need a room and a bed in about 15 minutes to sleep it off," Carl said, unconcerned about what had happened. "She won't remember a thing in the morning."

"Mike is such an asshole sometimes," said Stephanie. "He does that on purpose just to annoy me."

"I wanted to talk with Mike about a business deal, but I think he is off the rails tonight," Steve said.

"He's also not getting any sex from me tonight," Stephanie said with a laugh.

Carl and Steve chuckled. They knew Stephanie, and they

knew that when Mike flirted with wives, strippers or hookers, she usually responded with wild sex. At least, that's what Mike told them.

Suddenly, Cora slipped and fell on the floor. Mike started laughing and couldn't stop.

"Cora, did my joke knock you out?" Mike said as he stared at her prone body on the carpet.

"Stephanie, can you help Cora to the bedroom? She must have taken two vitamin Qs. I want to talk with Steve for a minute," Carl said.

"I'll try. Maybe Mike can help me. He gave her the drinks," said Stephanie as she strolled over to help a fallen Cora.

"Steve, I talked with Charles about the outpatient peds and imaging center and the new company under which you wanted to put it. It sounds like a good plan, but I can't manage it," Carl said. "My tax attorney told me the first company could raise questions with the IRS. You should create a fictitious corporate name with somebody else."

"Charles told me about your concerns. I was going to speak with Mike about it tonight, but he doesn't want to be bothered," Steve said. "Maybe you can talk with him."

"I will. Mike is getting frisky with Cora again. He can't control himself when coked and scotched up. I'd better go see how she's doing," Carl said.

Steve nodded, took another sip of his drink, and looked for Charles McMann and his cocaine. He wasn't in the room, which meant he was down the hall in Mike's office, where he and the others must've been partaking.

Mike's office was two doors down in the C-suite, next to the boardroom. Before Steve left the party, he filled his wine glass and glanced around the room. He thought it was the same old scene, except Mary wasn't there.

The 20 guests were drinking, talking, and laughing. Six couples danced as the jazz band played Duke Ellington's "Take the A Train."

It was a good time for Steve to leave. He hadn't danced since Mary left him last December, right before Christmas. She'd confronted him about his involvement in the crimes at Nokomis Hospital. Wanting no more part of it, she'd given him a year to get out of it, or she would file for divorce.

He put the bad memory out of his mind and strolled to Mike's office. He needed a snort of cocaine to take away the depression that suddenly burdened his thoughts.

The door was closed. A light shone from the crack by the floor. He tapped at the door and pushed it in.

The four men sat in chairs around a small card table to the side of the room. Two gram-sized containers of white powder, along with their drinks and cards, rested on the table.

They were playing poker. Harry talked, and Charles— along with construction firm contractor John Riggles and his employee, Delman Palmer—laughed.

Brophy didn't like Palmer, who was supposedly a carpenter on Riggle's construction crew. He didn't know what Palmer, a New Yorker, did for Riggles, but he'd never seen the man swing a hammer.

They didn't notice as Brophy entered the room.

"So, there you are," Brophy said to Harry. "Where did you go this afternoon? I called and went to your house, but you weren't anywhere."

"Everything is cool. I was at my house. I didn't hear you knocking. My wife was out shopping, and I needed to take a nap," Harry said.

The rest of the guys laughed.

"Steve, I already jumped on him for being MIA," Charles McMann said.

The others laughed again.

"Is this Mike's stash?" Brophy asked.

"No, I brought it," Harry said.

"Move over, guys—I need a couple of lines," said Brophy as he pulled over his chair and sat down.

"How goes the party?" asked Riggles, owner of a successful construction company, even before he started submitting inflated building contract bids to Nokomis Hospital. The board blindly approved Lard and McMann's recommendations.

During the past four years, Lard, Brophy, and McMann had split over $2 million in kickbacks with Riggles for a medical office building adjacent to the hospital, an outpatient imaging center, and renovations to the penthouse suite and emergency department. Upcoming construction plans called for a cardiology office for new board member Dr. O'Neal and a lease for a second supply warehouse.

"Cora passed out, Mike is drinking a lot, and everyone else is either dancing or chatting," Brophy said.

"I missed that?" Riggles asked with a chuckle.

"When she takes those disco biscuits and drinks wine, she is the life of the party for like 10 minutes," Palmer said.

"Harry, you'd better go talk with Mike and let him know you are still with the living," Brophy said.

"One more toot, then I need a martini," Harry replied as he took his straw and sucked in a thick line of cocaine. "I'll be back in a few minutes."

Brophy snorted several more lines as the others continued playing cards and gossiping about Cora, the board members, and wealthy donors.

Harry wasn't feeling well. He stopped at the restroom before he entered the party room. Looking in the mirror, he was surprised to see redness in his left eye and a puffy face. His head throbbed.

He wondered if he should have stayed at home after injecting the crack cocaine, but at the time, he'd thought he needed to appear at the party to avoid questions. Despite his weakness, he slowly entered the party room and looked for the bartender.

* * *

Donald Tusk, the hospital's biggest donor, strolled over to the bartender about the same time.

"What's your best drink, Leroy?" Tusk asked.

"My name isn't Leroy, sir. It's Jose," the Cuban bartender, a long-time hospital employee, replied respectfully.

"Whatever, Jasper. Get me a King's Blues Tonic," Tusk commanded.

"I'm sorry, sir, but I can't. We don't have it."

"Never mind. Make me a Manhattan, light on the bitters," Tusk sighed dejectedly.

"Yes, sir," Jose said, quickly turning to make the drink.

Just then, Jimmy Giles, a longtime board member and general contractor, noticed Tusk at the bar and approached him. "What are you drinking tonight, Donald?"

Leroy didn't know how to make King's Blues, so he's making me a Manhattan," Tusk said.

"Donald, you've been at this party once a month for the past year, and you know Jose doesn't have King's Blues," Jimmy said.

"Well, he should, and I'm going to call him Leroy or Jasper or whatever the hell I want until he fixes me one," Tusk loudly said.

"Jose, did you hear that? See if you can order a bottle of King's Blues liquor for Mr. Tusk," Jimmy said.

"I'll try again. I asked for two bottles in June, but our orders have been delayed. The vendors haven't been filling them," Jose said.

"What's that you say?" Tusk bellowed. "The vendors won't deliver?"

"Donald, let's go over here and talk," said Jimmy as he picked up his glass and walked to the nearest high-top table next to the bar.

"Wait, what is this about the vendors?" Tusk asked angrily.

"The hospital's having cash flow problems," Jimmy said. "You'll have to talk with Mike about it. Jose is just an employee. Come with me."

"I'll get to the bottom of this," Tusk promised.

"Before you talk with Mike, let me tell you this first. Do you know what Mike is planning?" Jimmy asked, his face filled with worry.

"Mike is always planning something," Tusk said. "What do I care? He builds something, and I give him money to put my name, my son's name, or my daughter's name on it. That's all I care about."

"Did you know he wants to join National Healthcare?" Jimmy said. "I read a draft memo to the board."

"Like a merger?" Tusk asked.

"Yes. I know about it, but Mike hasn't told the board."

"Why are you telling me, you little rat?"

"I just thought you should know about it ahead of time.

The hospital is also losing a ton of money. Do you know about that? You should. That's why Mike can't order your precious King's Blues. You give the foundation a lot of money, and it's going down the drain," Jimmy blurted.

Tusk stared at Jimmy in disbelief. "What are you doing? You are drunk. Get away from me, you disgusting piece of crap," he said as he walked over to talk with Lard.

Jimmy stood there, dumbfounded, as Tusk dismissed and even criticized him. He hadn't thought that passing critical inside information about the hospital would go that way. He hoped Tusk would appreciate the info and reward him later if things went sideways.

He always did whatever Lard asked him to do. However, the financial losses and the withholding of annual reports to the IRS made him worry that the elaborate fraud he had participated in would soon turn into a house of cards that would collapse.

Jimmy watched as Tusk reached Lard, then turned away. Lard had just approached Christine McVay.

He chuckled as he saw Tusk go past Lard and McVay and walk over to talk with the three strippers/prostitutes Lard regularly hired for parties.

* * *

Lard had wanted to have a deep conversation with McVay for several weeks. Tonight was the night. He was confident that if he could persuade her to join the board, she would be a valuable asset to the management team. She was a rising star at Beloit Associates, an emerging accounting and consulting firm in Venice.

"How's everything, Chris?" Mike inquired in his most courteous tone.

McVay sipped a glass of wine as she talked with board chair David Royster.

"Everything is fine, Mike. David and I are talking about me joining the board and what I should expect," McVay said.

"We talked briefly about that last Saturday, remember?" Mike said with a sarcastic chuckle. "You were more interested in the toot."

"Of course, these parties can get crazy, and I got carried away last week," she said. "Tonight, I'm going to turn down the dial. I hadn't drunk or done so many other things since my sorority days."

"Feel free to cut loose any way you want. We have a few special benefits for our friends, and what happens at the party stays at the party," Mike said, chuckling. "Believe me, I've been there."

McVay blushed.

"Follow me. Let's get some fresh air. Do you mind if I take this lovely lady from you, David?" Mike said.

"No, go right ahead. I see Donald talking with our special guests. I'll join him. I've been meaning to talk with Jasmine," David said as he headed for the three women.

"Chris, come with me," Mike instructed as he led McVay to the expansive outdoor terrace. "Do you like it? I designed it."

The terrace boasted comfortable seating and a bubbling hot tub in the northwest corner. A half mile away was the Gulf of Mexico, past hospital-owned, undeveloped property. A gentle sea breeze and the rhythmic sound of waves crashing against the shore created a serene ambiance ideal for Mike's intimate conversation.

"Chris, I want to personally invite you to the board. David speaks highly of your financial skills. We have many growth plans in the future. The key is speed. You may not have heard, but National is buying up hospitals south of us and has made an inquiry about Nokomis," Lard explained, pausing to see if McVay reacted.

She looked carefully at him to see if there was a question.

He continued, "Obviously, we haven't presented anything to the board yet, so you haven't missed anything, but management is considering it."

McVay stared ahead, closely scrutinizing Lard.

"As a finance expert, you understand the value of size and scale. National's master contracts with vendors could reduce our medical and equipment supply, staffing, medication, and labor expenses by more than 25%, a number that an astute CPA like yourself can appreciate."

"That's a lot. Suppliers must overcharge smaller hospitals a pretty penny," McVay said. "I'd like to examine this issue more closely. I'm new to the hospital business, and I'd hoped to go slow before having to weigh in on such a huge deal."

"We will brief you fully. We want to give you time, but many important decisions are coming in the next few months, and we'd like to bring you up to speed," Lard said.

McVay raised her eyebrows. She'd been considering the offer to join the board, but she believed she would have enough time to review the hospital's audited financial statements from the past five years before deciding.

"Cutting expenses is one reason we would like to lease a warehouse a few miles away to bulk store our supplies. We have limited space at the hospital," Lard said. "Through our strategic planning process, we have identified a building to lease, and we are hoping for your vote to approve it at our next meeting."

"Mike, I'm not sure this is the place to discuss pending hospital business, especially since I'm not officially on the board," said McVay. "I appreciate what you're saying, and I would consider any plan very carefully."

"Of course, Chris. Let me change the subject. I want to make you an offer. Once you're officially on the board, would you be willing to become our finance committee chair? It might require a few extra sessions and reviewing reports before meetings," said Lard. "It also would include a $1,000 monthly expense account."

"One thousand? I don't understand. Anyway, isn't Frank Burns the finance chair?"

"He's getting ready to step down. He's been the finance chair for five years, and we like to rotate chairs to keep everyone fresh. He will remain vice chair of the board," Mike said. "I will keep the position open until you accept."

"One question. What is the thousand-dollar expense account for?" McVay asked.

"Whatever you want it for. Call it a monthly stipend or honorarium."

"Well, we can discuss this. As we address the hospital's business, I wanted to ask you about the financial reports. I was told all you give the board are summaries, one or two pages. As an accountant, I'd insist on seeing the full reports," she said.

"We try not to burden our board members with too much information," Lard said. "These reports are 20 to 30 pages long. Let me discuss with Steve Brophy the possibility of providing you with longer summaries. He's responsible for the reports."

"If I become finance chair, I must see the full reports. Also, I would love to meet with Steve before I accept anything," McVay said. "You realize—or maybe Chairman Royster hasn't told you—confidentially, I am interested in joining the board to make partner at my firm. I have a full work schedule over there."

"Yes, David told me. Becoming the finance committee chair would be a feather in your cap, and you don't need more work. Let us handle that for you. We've had a great track record of building this hospital to the success it now enjoys. We don't want to change now," Lard said.

"Thanks, Mike. Let me think about it."

"Sure, why don't you spend a few minutes out here under the starry sky. Think about my offer. We run the hospital, and the board raises money and approves our actions. You will have a good position on the board until you make a partner; then you can rotate off if you want," Lard said with a smile. "It's not the worst way to get ahead."

McVay stared at him without giving away her surprise. Then she looked out toward the black waters of the intercoastal waterway, Casey Key, and the gulf beyond. Hundreds of stars twinkled in the sky, and a half-moon was low on the horizon. The view was magnificent.

Could she accept Mike's offer? It didn't seem right, but it was what she needed.

Chapter 7:
Uninvited Guest

Midnight, Saturday, Sept. 8, 1984

It was almost midnight. Jack was dozing in an oversized chair. Bobbie lay sleeping with an IV attached to her arm. It had been a long day, but she was recovering well.

A squeaking sound in the hallway drew Jack's attention. Half asleep, he dimly saw a housekeeper peeking her head into the room. She motioned for him to come outside.

"Are you Jack Kendall, the newspaper reporter?" she sheepishly whispered in a heavily accented voice.

Jack nodded, stood up, looked at Bobbie—who hadn't stirred—and silently stepped toward the door. The housekeeper motioned for him to follow her past the nurse's station near the maintenance room.

"What is it?" Jack asked.

"Can I tell you things about the hospital? You are asking questions all day?" she asked meekly.

"That's right. Who are you?" Jack asked.

"Valentina Rubenko," said the mid-20s, blonde housekeeper in broken English. "I work here three years. There is talk of layoffs. We need more workers. They increase our work to 10 hours with no more pay."

"I'm sorry to hear that," said Jack. "It's been a long 24 hours for me. My wife had a C-section last night, and she has been sleeping on and off all day."

"We wish her to recover well, and your babies have good health. You write newspaper story to help us?" Valentina asked.

"Yes, I will when I return to the paper next week," Jack said. "Do you know something about why this is happening?"

"They say hospital losing money. But they have parties every Saturday night. I clean up after I finish my night shift. They spend money like nothing. So much waste with food," Valentina said with disgust.

"A party? Now? Where is it?"

"Fifth-floor office."

"How can I get there?" asked Jack. He looked back at Bobby's room and decided he could take a quick look. It seemed like a good opportunity to learn more about what Jane had told him regarding the hospital's wasteful spending and plans to make service cuts.

"You can't go up there on your own. Executives have offices on the fifth floor. There's a boardroom with a private elevator. The stairway door to get up there is always locked," she said.

Jack gave her a disappointed look.

"But I have master key," she added with a confident smile. "Come with me."

Chapter 8:
"We Have An Emergency"

After Midnight, Sunday, Sept. 9, 1984

As the Saturday penthouse suite party wound down, Carl noticed that Cora was still sleeping in the quiet room, which executives used during the day to meditate, rest, or relieve stress. Often, on Saturdays or during the weeknight parties, intoxicated guests used it to recover.

"I'd better go get her. Time for us to go," Carl said, setting his drink down.

"Say, where's Harry?" Charles said. "I haven't seen him for a while."

"He went to rest in the quiet room a while ago. He complained about having a headache and wanted to lie down," Stephanie said.

Charles was alarmed because he knew Harry was prone to overindulging with cocaine and whiskey. He followed Carl into the quiet room.

The scene shocked Carl and Charles. Cora and Harry were both on the floor, passed out. Vomit coated their shirts and puddled on the floor.

"Call down to the ER. This is serious," said Charles as he checked Harry's pulse. It was faint.

"Honey, wake up. It's time to go," Carl said as he bent over and whispered to Cora, wiping the vomit from her mouth with his handkerchief. Her face was sunken and pale, and she wasn't moving.

Stephanie entered the room and saw the two on the floor. "Carl, what are you doing? Cora needs help," she said, picking up the phone to dial the ER.

"This is Mrs. Lard. We have an emergency in the penthouse entertainment room. Cora Billingly and Harry Goldfarb have overdosed," Stephanie said.

Mike Lard saw Carl, Charles, and Stephanie enter the quiet room. He burst in and heard his wife talking on the phone.

"Overdosed? No, it can't be. They just had too much to drink. Let's help them stand up and walk around. They will be fine," Mike said offhandedly.

"No, look at them. They've vomited on the floor. It's on their clothes," Stephanie said. "They're barely breathing. They need medical attention. I called downstairs. They're coming."

Just then, Harry's body began to shake with convulsions. Cora appeared to be in a coma.

"You might be right, dear. We need to handle this confidentially," Mike said, quickly transitioning to damage control. "Let's gather our team here. I don't want this to become a source of gossip on Monday."

"Mike, let's just hope that is the least of our problems," Charles replied.

* * *

Jack gazed through the glass doors of the entertainment room on the fifth-floor executive penthouse suite while standing in the hall, drawn by the commotion inside. He was trying to identify who was at the party.

But something strange started to happen. The band paused in the middle of a song, and he heard loud voices. Suddenly, several people in the main room hurried into a smaller room. Then the elevator began making mechanical noises, and he heard beeping from the floors below. Someone was coming up.

Jack scampered toward the executive office across the hall as the elevator doors began to open. He pushed the door open and rushed inside just as a doctor and three nurses entered with gurneys.

Behind the door, Jack peered through the glass opening. He saw Dr. Rashad—who had treated Bobbie—and a nurse in blue scrubs, wheeling a gurney into the entertainment room. Two other nurses pushed a second gurney into the room.

There was no doubt this was an emergency. Jack had to document what was happening. He reached into his backpack and pulled out his Nikon camera. He had brought it into the hospital to take photos of Bobbie and the newborns. He was grateful to have it because now he was covering a news story. He quickly changed his film from 400 to 800 speed, a faster film for the lower-light conditions.

* * *

Inside the quiet room, Dr. Rashad saw Cora and Harry on the floor. He asked one of the nurses to check on Cora, who seemed to be responding slightly to Carl's soothing talk. He moved closer to Harry, who was still convulsing.

"Has Harry been doing cocaine again?" Dr. Rashad asked. "How long has he been like this?"

Charles hesitated, but Stephanie nudged him to speak.

"He went home sick today. He could have been doing cocaine earlier," Charles said. "He complained of a headache two hours ago and came here to rest."

"Nurse, I need the tPA. He's having an ischemic stroke," Dr. Rashad said. "We need to get him to the ER immediately for blood and urine tests."

"Will he be all right?" Stephanie asked.

"We won't know until we get an MRI. He should have been seen earlier. What was going on all night when he was stroking?" Dr. Rashad asked.

"We were just talking and dancing," Stephanie said. "Everyone was having a good time, and we just didn't think there was a problem."

"How is Cora?" Dr. Rashad said.

"Her heartbeat is slow," Nurse Betty replied.

"What was she doing? Cocaine?" Dr. Rashad asked.

"I don't think so. She took a quaalude to calm her nerves before the party. She may have had two and probably drank too much wine and mixed drinks," said Carl.

"With Cora taking quaaludes and Harry using cocaine, we need a tox screen on both of them, and we need to pump Cora's stomach," Dr. Rashad said. "Let's get them downstairs immediately."

* * *

Jack heard more noises coming from outside in the hall near the entertainment room. He needed a better view and a clear line of sight to take pictures. He hesitated. What if someone saw him? What excuse could he give for being there, hiding in the executive suite waiting room? Valentina Rubenko, the helpful housekeeper who had let him up the stairs, would definitely be fired if anyone caught sight of him.

He broke into a light sweat. He hadn't thought twice about sneaking up to spy on the party, but he suddenly realized his actions could get him in trouble. There was more going on than he expected. He hadn't broken in, but he wasn't supposed to be there. The thrill of seeing for himself what the executives were doing after hours while the hospital was falling apart was too tempting.

However, he was there, and he had to strike a balance between caution and gathering information to expose what was going on.

As he contemplated his situation, Jack heard voices from the other side of the executive suite. He swiftly moved away from behind the suite's door and hid behind a large brown sofa. He quietly took a tape recorder from his backpack and turned it on.

"All I'm saying is that Lard throws these parties almost every Saturday. He funds them by funneling private insurance and Medicare payments into a special executive payroll account," said a boisterous deep voice.

"He's got balls. I'll give him credit for that," said a voice in a punchy New York City accent.

Jack didn't know either voice.

"You don't know the half of it. Lard is a genius. He and McMann concocted a scam to buy buildings and then sell them to the hospital at inflated prices," the deep voice offered.

Jack overheard that and needed to find out who said it. The conversation was very incriminating. He checked his recorder to make sure it was working, then peeked around the corner of the sofa for a look. He had to identify them later.

* * *

"Is that how they pay your kickbacks?" asked Delman Palmer, the New Yorker.

"Yes, one way. I get paid through multiple channels. They have board members in their pockets. Take the entertainment room. Do you know Lard got the board to approve $3 million in renovations? It cost me $1 million to do the job. We split the other $2 million," said John Riggles, the deep-voiced man, laughing.

"No wonder you can afford to contract with me for $10,000 a month, plus expenses," Palmer said. "By the way, the boss in Miami wants me back in two months."

Boss in Miami? Jack thought. *Who could that be?*

"He told me. I've got some special assignments for you based on our local needs," Riggles said.

Just then, Riggles heard some commotion in the hall and looked out the glass window in the door. "Something is going on at the party," he said, looking out the window by the suite's front door.

"John, let's just go. I've stayed too long and done too much coke here. I want to go to that all-night bottle club and find some girls," Palmer said. "The strippers in Lard's party are a little too tame for me."

"We will, Delman, just wait a minute. A doctor is coming

out with a nurse holding an IV. That's Harry Goldfarb. He's out cold. Must have OD'd," Riggles said.

"What a fool. I told him not to mix crack with ludes and alcohol," said Palmer, peering over past Riggles to take a look.

"Here comes another wheeled stretcher. It's Cora Billingly. She's out, too. Probably gave the ludes to Harry," Riggles said, shaking his head.

"Ms. Disco Biscuit herself. Rank amateur," Palmer said with disdain.

Riggles watched in amazement as a doctor and three nurses pushed the two gurneys into the elevator. "Wait, here they come," he said. "Mike, Carl, Charles, Stephanie, and Donald Tusk, the rich jackass donor. What are they doing?" He sounded bewildered. "Let's go find out."

* * *

As they left the room, Jack risked being caught and quickly took several pictures of the men as they turned to leave the C-suite waiting room. Once the door closed, he carefully approached it, placed his tape recorder down, and snapped several more photos of the group gathering in the hall through the glass window. No one seemed to notice him, as all attention was on the medical emergency.

He retreated to his hiding spot behind the sofa and leaned against it, hoping the photos were clear enough to show recognizable faces. His recorder was still running by the door. He could hear the conversation in the hall.

* * *

"Why is Harry using so much goddamn cocaine?" Mike asked Charles. "That idiot's lost control."

"I've told him to take it easy. He just laughed at me, " Charles said.

"And Carl, how could you allow Cora to become so careless?" Mike angrily asked.

"She's been under a lot of stress lately, and everything we're doing to make money seems to be affecting her," Carl honestly said. "That's another reason why I want to reduce these illegal deals with you and the hospital."

"I wanted to talk with you about cutting back. We need you, but it's more important for you to get Cora straightened out. I can't have people talking about these things at the hospital—not now," Mike said. "We're at a critical point with the merger talks with National."

"Mike, you shouldn't be discussing that now. You haven't even briefed the board," Stephanie said.

"I heard that," said Tusk. "Lard, you'd better talk to me about what I've heard tonight. I don't like my money going into a black hole."

"Whatever you heard is hospital business. We have it under control," Mike replied. "I'll talk with you about this later."

"You'd better have a good story. I'm leaving now. This party is over. I'm not sure I'll be back unless you control your people, and I expect full answers to my questions next week," Tusk said, glaring at Lard.

* * *

Jack heard the elevator door beep as it opened. Tusk, Riggles, Palmer, and other partygoers entered the elevator and descended. Several more groups exited the entertainment room.

A few minutes later, Jack saw that the hall was empty. He felt safe enough to sneak out of the suite. He glanced at the entertainment room, where Valentina and another housekeeper were cleaning up. After snapping a few more pictures, he went downstairs.

It was nearly 1 a.m., and as he cautiously returned to Bobbie's room, he reflected on everything he'd discovered that night about the hospital. Drugs, alcohol, and overdoses at a party in the executive suite? Insurance scams, kickbacks, construction bribes, a possible merger with National Healthcare, and a shadowy New Yorker hired by the hospital for two months. For what purpose?

The same hospital where he had heard executives running scams, embezzling funds, and mismanaging resources?

He quietly made his way to Bobbie's room without being noticed. As he entered, he tried to stay as quiet as possible. She was still asleep, and he needed some rest too. It had been a long day, and he had a list of things to check on in the morning, including his wife and newborns.

Chapter 9:

Recovery and Discovery

Morning, Sunday, Sept. 9, 1984

Bobbie was resting in her maternity unit room when Dr. Chastain entered.

"Good morning, Bobbie. How are you today?" the obstetrician asked.

"I've been better, doctor. How are my babies?" Bobbie asked as she opened her eyes.

"Your twins are doing very well. They are considered preemies at four pounds each, but they are in good care."

"Oh, so small!"

"We'll closely monitor their development and provide specialized care to ensure they gain weight and strength," Dr. Chastain explained. "It's normal to feel concerned, but we have the expertise and resources to support their growth and development. We'll work together to give them the best possible start in life."

"Where are they? Why aren't they here with me?" Bobbie asked.

"They are in incubator cribs in the NICU to keep them warm and prevent them from contracting infections."

"But when can I see them?"

"Because they are so small, premature infants often require specialized care and monitoring," Dr. Chastain said. "I will meet with Dr. Lords later this morning, and we will devise a plan."

"I feel so tired. Yesterday was a blur. I slept most of Saturday. What happened to me?" Bobbie asked. "I don't remember much."

"We're closely monitoring your condition. You developed eclampsia. Do you know what that is?"

"Yes, Dr. Rafferty warned us about it."

"It can be serious, but it's manageable with prompt treatment. Right now, our priority is your health and safety, and the well-being of your twins. You are receiving treatment to control your blood pressure and prevent seizures. Any questions?"

"What are these medications you are giving me?" Bobbie asked.

"Fluids and magnesium sulfate to lower blood pressure and prevent seizures," Dr. Chastain said. "Have you talked with Jack?"

"Yes, he told me, but I wanted to hear it from you."

"If you don't have any more questions, I will talk with Dr. Lords about when you can see your twins."

"Jack went to see if they could be brought into my room."

"He did? Maybe you can see them this afternoon. If you continue to improve, I will write an order to allow it," Dr.

Chastain said. "By the way, I spoke with Dr. Rafferty at Sarasota Memorial. She is thrilled to hear about the twins and looks forward to seeing you after you are discharged."

"Thanks for passing on the news," Bobbie said. "I look forward to taking care of my babies at home. How long do you think I'll be here?"

"It's too early to say, but it will probably be at least a few days. We'll keep an eye on your blood pressure. It is stable now, but your condition can change, and we want to continue your treatment and track your progress," Dr. Chastain said.

"What about the twins? When can they go home?"

"Dr. Lords can be more specific, but generally, preemies can go home when they breathe on their own, eat by mouth, and maintain their body temperature and weight," she said. "It could be five days or a week...longer if they develop complications."

"Oh, I just hope I can see them today, but now I want to take another nap," Bobbie said, closing her eyes.

"You get as much rest as you need," Dr. Lords said before leaving the room.

*   *   *

Jack was standing behind the glass window in the NICU, watching the twins, when Dr. Lords approached.

"I understand you wanted to talk with me?" she asked.

"Yes. What can you tell me about them? They look so small," Jack said.

"They are doing fine. If Dr. Chastain is agreeable, Bobbie can visit the twins this afternoon."

"That's good. She will be delighted. She's been asking

72

about them all morning," Jack said. "She hasn't even seen them through the window."

"Oh? I would have thought by now. How is she doing?" Dr. Lords asked.

"She's still got her monitors and IV drip, but she got a lot of rest last night and is feeling 100% better."

"Do you have any questions?" she asked.

"I'm sure Bobbie will ask a million, so I'll wait for her to take the lead," said Jack. He looked directly at Dr. Lords with a serious expression. "I'd like to ask about something else. Do you know the hospital's plan to close the maternity department and NICU?"

"I know you're a reporter, and I don't want to swear you to secrecy, so I will just say this: until it happens, we're doing our jobs," Dr. Lords said.

"Okay. Let me ask you this. Would you oppose my request to transfer the twins and Bobbie to Sarasota Memorial? And when would be the soonest we could do it?"

"There is no reason to transfer them. We're caring for them just as well as Sarasota Memorial could," Dr. Lords said. "And a transfer adds unnecessary risks."

"Hypothetically, when is the soonest it could be done?" Jack asked.

"One week," Dr. Lords said with a frown.

Noticing the doctor's change in demeanor, Jack explained, "Thanks. Good to know, just in case. It's no reflection on you. We live closer to Memorial, and it's what we planned."

Jack paused. "I will talk with Dr. Chastain, and if it's all right with her, I will bring Bobbie to see the babies this afternoon."

Dr. Lords nodded and walked away. Jack watched her curiously. She was an odd one.

Then he exited the NICU office and entered the preemie ward. He gazed through the glass window once more with amazement as he watched his newborns sleep. It was incredible that he had twins. He wondered what it would be like to be a father and who his babies would grow up to be.

As he stood there, palms pressed lightly against the glass, a warm ache filled his chest. Jack had always dreamed of having a son someday—someone to teach, to guide, to toss a baseball with.

But now, fate had doubled the gift. A son *and* a daughter. Two tiny lives depending on him. Two futures he was suddenly responsible for helping shape. The thought humbled him, steadied him, and thrilled him all at once. Whatever storms he faced in his work, whatever dangers lurked in his reporting, he knew this: being their father would be the most important story he'd ever be part of.

*　*　*

Nicole McIntosh spotted him before he noticed her. She moved down the hallway with her usual purposeful stride, the kind born from long shifts and constant decisions. Her warm, expressive face—bright eyes, high cheekbones, and an approachable smile that softened even the worst hospital days—stood out in the muted light of the maternity floor. A neat, chin-length bob framed her face, smooth and tucked behind her ears, giving her a polished but easygoing look. Lean and athletic, with the upright posture of someone who led from the front, she stopped beside Jack just as he was marveling at his newborn twins through the glass.

"There you are," Nicole said gently. "Congratulations on

the arrival of your beautiful babies."

"Hi, Nicole. I still can't believe it. They're healthy, but I'm a little worried about Bobbie. She had a close call," Jack replied.

"I'm sure she's getting fantastic care. The maternity wing has some of our best nurses," Nicole assured him. "I heard from them that you were looking for me."

"Thanks for finding me," Jack said. "I've got a lot of questions about what I've seen at the hospital and what's going on here."

"And what do you think is going on here?" she asked carefully.

"What I think isn't as important as what *you* think."

Nicole hesitated. "I'm not sure I should say anything right now. You've got newborns. Shouldn't you be thinking of them and your wife?"

"I'm sure Bobbie will mention that once she recovers," Jack said, his tone firm but not unkind. "But Nicole, we've known each other a while. You know I can't ignore what's in front of me. I was told you were off today. Did you come in on a Sunday morning to talk with me, or is there something else going on?"

She held his gaze for a moment, then exhaled. "All right. Once I heard you were here, I didn't think it would take long for you to start asking questions."

"Yes, so..." Jack encouraged.

"This is off the record for now," she said quietly, "but the hospital faces financial problems affecting the availability of supplies and vendor services. I'm trying to get more information."

Jack nodded slowly. "I thought so. But financial problems? How can that be? You have a large endowment, and the last financial statement I saw, in 1981, showed profits of over five million dollars. In a growing community like this, you should have all the resources you need."

"That was three years ago. Things have changed," Nicole admitted. "I was told we lost ten million dollars in the last two years and another seven million so far this year, but that is a heavily guarded secret."

"Not anymore," Jack muttered as he wrote the numbers down. "What else?"

"I was also told the losses were covered by transferring money from the foundation."

"Seventeen million transferred from your charitable foundation!" Jack exclaimed, stunned. "How did I miss that?"

"Shh—don't be so loud," she warned.

Jack leaned closer. "How can that be happening?" he whispered. "Every other hospital is making money."

Nicole took a steadying breath. Jack could see she was fighting to understand it herself. "Don't worry," he said quietly. "You don't have to say anything more now. I'm going to look into this."

He already knew charitable donations couldn't legally be used to cover operational losses—particularly if they were designated funds. Jane's comments, the supply shortages, the closed units, and now Nicole's revelations were forming a dark and undeniable pattern.

"There's more to it, Jack," Nicole whispered. "I can't go on the record yet. We're still trying to get proof before we take it to the board."

Based on what Jack saw and heard in the executive suite the night before, he wouldn't be surprised if the problems were worse than she feared—criminal, even. Lard and the other executives had looked unhinged, sloppy, reckless.

"I heard some talk late Saturday night about Lard, Brophy, and several others involved in insurance fraud—diverting Medicare payments into a special executive payroll account," Jack said. "Do you know who in management is involved in what amounts to embezzlement?"

"All I have are suspicions," Nicole replied. "But Charles McMann is likely involved. A friend told me he suspects Steve Brophy, Carl Billingly, John Riggles, and Harry Goldfarb, too."

"I know the CFO, Brophy. Who are the others?" Jack asked.

"McMann is the COO, Billingly is a general contractor, Riggles runs a construction crew, and Harry is vice president of environmental services. They're all close to Lard."

"I heard a few other names… Donald Tusk, Cora, and Delman Palmer?"

"You should know Tusk—he's a major benefactor. Palmer works for Riggles, but I don't know what he actually does. Cora is Carl Billingly's wife." She narrowed her eyes. "Say, do you know about the Saturday parties in the C-suite?"

"I was there last night," Jack said. "Long story, but it's where I heard Riggles and Palmer talking. We can go over the party later. Several newsworthy things happened."

He paused, then asked, "Can you get me the hospital's financial statements for the past two years and memos from department heads asking for supplies?"

"I'm working on gathering documents, but it's difficult. Financial statements are tightly guarded," Nicole said. "What else?"

"Oh—pictures. Billingly, Riggles, Palmer, Harry, Cora, Tusk. Anyone you can find."

"I think so. Why?"

"They were all there last night. I need to be sure who's who. I took photographs of the party. I'll share them after my photographer develops them."

"All right," Nicole said. "I'll get the pictures and mail them to your office. I can help you identify the C-suite party photos."

"Thanks. What else can I do?"

"Talk to people. Obstetrics, mental health, housekeeping, dietary, emergency, ambulance services. And Jane—she can tell you more about the rumor that they want to close labor and delivery."

"Jane told me as much as she knows," Jack replied. "She suggested I talk with you."

"I'll try to get you the financial statements," Nicole said. "I have someone helping. You should also interview Lard and the board chair. And talk with Dr. Joel O'Neal. He's on the board now and suspicious about what's going on. I've spoken with him."

"Can you ask him to call me?"

"You'll need to talk to him yourself," she said. "I can't expose myself unnecessarily. And don't tell him you talked with me."

Jack hesitated, then said, "Nicole, can I give you some advice?"

"What is it?"

"Talk with a lawyer about becoming a federal whistleblower. They can protect you."

"That's what my husband says. He's a lawyer," Nicole answered. "But I need to investigate further. If I involve the authorities, it has to be at the right moment. Whistleblowing has consequences. I'm not sure how I'm going to handle this yet."

Jack nodded. She wasn't wrong to be cautious. Now he had two managers and possibly one doctor ready to confirm the worst rumors about the hospital.

"It sounds like you just want to do what's right—for the hospital, the staff, and the patients," Jack said.

"It's the only reason I'm sticking my neck out," she replied. "What the executives are doing is affecting our ability to provide care for the community."

"I promise I'll look into this," Jack said.

"I know you will. We'll get to the bottom of it," Nicole said softly before turning and walking away.

Jack watched her go. Despite his happiness over the twins' safe arrival, the conversation left a weight on his chest. Something was deeply wrong at Nokomis Hospital—and now he had no choice but to uncover the truth.

He sensed Bobbie would feel the same way. Still, he was worried that his investigation into hospital corruption might cause Bobbie to question how committed he truly was to her and their twins, even though she understood the unpredictability of journalism and the importance of a breaking story.

He took another look at his newborns, smiled at them, nodded, and then went to the nurse's station to call his detective brother, Ed.

"Excuse me, nurse. Do you have a phone I can use for a few minutes?" Jack asked.

"Hi, Mr. Kendall. Director Willoughby told me to do whatever I could to help you. You can use the phone behind me. Come around," said Cathy Leesay, the charge nurse for the neonatal unit. "We need your help. There's something seriously wrong here."

"I know," Jack said. "Jane told me management might

close your department and convert the space to outpatient pediatric care. Could you talk with me?"

"We've heard a rumor. It's not official yet. The board has to vote on it. What do you need to know?" the pediatric nurse asked.

"What do you know about the financial losses?" Jack asked.

"I can tell you this. A lot of people suspect the top executives are misusing funds."

"How so?"

Cathy looked around, then said quietly, "They're hosting late-night parties, spending a significant amount of money that could be allocated to patient care."

Jack moved closer, encouraging her to continue.

"Then they claim they're broke and say we can't afford to pay vendors to handle linen and daily trash removal," she whispered, looking down the hall. "It piles up. You've seen it."

"Yes. I imagine if the Joint Commission were to come in for an inspection, the hospital would likely get cited," Jack said, hoping she'd divulge more information.

"They will. We've already reported them. The commission should be here soon. When they do, more nurses will come forward."

"Will you call me when they arrive?"

"I certainly will."

Jack handed her his business card and wrote his home number on the back.

"Do you have a few more minutes?" Jack asked.

"All right, but let's move toward the back of the station to be safe. Your twins, by the way, are doing so great," Cathy said with a smile.

"Thank you. We're praying they get stronger," Jack replied.

He took a deep breath. "Do you think I can bring Bobbie to see them soon?"

"I think so, but Dr. Lords will have to approve."

"Of course. Now, you mentioned late-night parties. What can you tell me about them?"

"Well, I've never been, of course, but one of my young male nurses got invited to a mid-week party a few months ago," she said. "He said everyone was drunk, and there was cocaine, marijuana, and other drugs being used. Later, just before he left, four strippers came in and were doing lap dances for some of the men."

"Is that right? Did he say who was there?" Jack asked.

"He recognized Mike Lard, Charles McMann, several managers, doctors, and donors. He saw several board members were there as well."

"Were there any women or wives present?"

"Not on Wednesdays," Cathy said. "He told me he'd been to several parties on Saturdays where the wives were there, drinking, doing drugs, dancing, and so on. However, the strippers were only there on Wednesdays, although he might have seen one or two on Saturdays. They didn't strip when the wives were there—for obvious reasons—but several were in attendance."

"The wives know about the strippers?" Jack asked incredulously.

"Of course. The wives are told they're there for the rich donors, doctors, and business associates—but that's not all. The wives have no choice. It's sad," Cathy said wistfully.

"I know about the weekend parties. Did you hear what happened Saturday night?" Jack asked.

"No, but I can check with a friend in the ER who worked

that night," she said. "What happened?"

"Two people overdosed. A woman named Cora and Harry Goldfarb. If you find out how they are—or anything else—let me know. I'll be here for the next week, but you can call me at the newspaper or at home any time after we leave."

"I'll find out later today when she comes in and let you know."

Jack gave her his card, thanked her and walked over to the phone to call Ed. He needed to tap into his brother's detective agency for help.

"Hey, I've got an assignment for you," Jack whispered. "I want you to get all the financial documents you can find on Nokomis Hospital—IRS 990 forms, bond documents, credit rating documents, and bank loans. See if any suppliers to Nokomis Hospital are willing to discuss billing issues. Anything you can think of related to Nokomis?"

"Wow, this'll use up a bit of your monthly retainer fee," Ed said with a chuckle. "What's going on there?"

"Everything. I've never heard of such corruption and degenerate behavior from hospital executives. Nokomis is losing money hand over fist when they should be fat and happy. We need more evidence, but it looks like the executives are committing fraud and holding parties with cocaine, drugs, strippers, and prostitutes," Jack explained.

"Strippers? At Nokomis Hospital? I thought that was a boring retirement beach town hospital," Ed opined.

"You and me both. They are in a sleepy town right between Sarasota and Venice, and the executives apparently think they can get away with anything."

"Is this going to be another major investigation?" Ed asked. Jack could hear his pen jotting down notes.

"I'll have a big surprise for them when I crack this story. I can't tell you more right now. If you need to reach me on Monday, call Bobbie's room. I'll be there, or she can take a message," Jack said.

"I'll put Francis on it. He used to work at a hospital and knows about all these things. How's Bobbie?" Ed asked. "I mean, aren't you there to have babies?"

"I am, but she's doing fine. They are taking good care of her. She's sleeping a lot, which gives me time to snoop around, but we may be here for several more days."

"Eclampsia? What are they doing for that?" asked Ed.

"Everything. They gave her lots of fluids in the beginning; now they're giving her medication to lower her blood pressure. It keeps going up and down. I don't like it," Jack said.

"Why don't you transfer her to Sarasota Memorial?" Ed suggested. "I'm sure she'd get better care there, and with a lot less stress."

"I asked and was told maybe in a week," Jack replied. "She's getting good care now because they know I'm here and watching them. I have to go. Let me know about the financial records."

"I will. Do you need a change of clothes or anything from your house? I could come with Mom on Monday. She's been asking."

"Oh, I forgot to call her today with all that's going on. Let her know you've spoken to me, and that she can come with you. Bring me something casual. Thanks. Talk later."

Chapter 10:
Lard Confronts Jack

Noon, Monday, Sept. 10, 1984

Mike Lard stormed angrily to the maternity ward. Every time he went there, he thought about how much money he lost because of its neonatal intensive care services. Once started as a loss leader, it was now draining valuable revenue at a rate he considered unsustainable.

Lard had heard that Jack Kendall was at the hospital with his wife and had been seen talking with employees all weekend. He wanted to see for himself if the rumors were true. If they were, Lard would put a stop to it. He didn't need a reporter snooping around for a story.

Just before lunch, Jack was in Bobbie's room, reading a book. He had just returned from discussing the rumor that the outpatient mental health unit would be shuttered to cut costs.

Lard didn't like that Jack seemed to have free rein of the hospital. He was annoyed that Kendall was asking questions instead of coming to him, and now he wanted to set the record straight.

"Mr. Kendall," said Lard as he entered the private room. "I understand you have some questions about the hospital. I wish you had approached me instead of interrupting my workers during their shifts."

Jack heard Lard's booming voice, looked up from his book, and stood up. He glanced at Bobbie, who had her eyes closed.

"I'm only here to be with my wife and newborns," said Jack, speaking softly, trying not to disturb Bobbie. "Did you hear what happened the other night?"

Lard's expression hardened. He assumed Jack was referring to the party where two guests had overdosed.

"What do you mean? What happened Saturday night?" he shot back defensively.

"I meant Friday night—sorry," Jack corrected himself. "The past 24 hours have been a blur."

But Jack had already caught Lard's reaction. He hadn't been asking about the overdoses, but Lard thought he was.

"You'd better explain, Kendall," Lard growled, his tone laced with suspicion.

"You didn't hear? We came into the ER on Friday night after Bobbie collapsed during dinner. Dr. Rashad and Dr. Chastain diagnosed her with eclampsia. By the way, they saved her life, and our twins are doing great. We hope to go home this week," Jack cheerfully said.

"I'm happy for you, but why have you been wandering around asking questions?" Lard asked.

"Sorry, but you know that I'm a reporter, and I saw with

my own eyes how messy and disorganized the ER was. Trash and dirty linens in the halls. Short-staffed. I am surprised the Joint Commission hasn't cited you for infection control problems. Or have they?" Jack asked.

"Is that a question?" Lard shot back.

Bobbie opened her eyes. "Jack, can you and Mr. Lard discuss this outside?"

"Mike, I'd like to hear your side. Can we talk somewhere else? I don't want to disturb my wife further," said Jack, turning to Bobbie. "Are you all right?"

"Yes, just talk with him somewhere else," she weakly said, her eyes half open.

"Follow me," said Lard, leading him into the hallway. "I want to answer your questions."

"I need your answers on the record. Would you like to do that in your office? I can meet you there in 15 minutes with my notebook," Jack said.

So, I'm right. You're gathering information for a story," Lard said accusingly.

"I didn't intend to do a story, but after seeing the trash and linen in the halls and talking with employees, I realized I haven't done anything on Nokomis in more than a year, so yes, I am going to do a story," Jack acknowledged.

Lard winced. He had to play this right. "Kendall, I will see if our CFO can sit with us. I want to clear up any misconceptions you may have about our transition."

"Transition? To what?" Jack asked, pausing for a reaction. He decided not to ask him about the potential merger with National Healthcare Corp. or the rumored closures of maternity and mental health services yet.

The CEO gave him a blank stare.

"All right, I'll be there," Jack added.

Lard turned and walked away. As he left the maternity unit, he passed several nurses and rooms with patients and their families without acknowledging or looking at them.

The nurses acted as if they didn't see him as he walked by. Once he did, they gave him icy stares.

Jack watched the scene unfold. He saw a hospital administrator who showed no concern for patients and employees who disrespected their boss. Seeing Lard's demeanor was so unlike anything he knew about healthcare executives, most of whom cared deeply about people and employees.

But Mike Lard was different. He didn't seem to care about the patients at his hospital—maybe because he had already decided to cut maternity services and felt guilty about it. Or, maybe he didn't care.

Jack knew he needed to prepare for the interview with Lard. But without solid facts about the hospital's finances, he felt at a disadvantage. He had to ask direct questions and seek straightforward answers. After Ed got the hospital's financial records, he could verify Lard's statements during a second interview.

Before doing anything else, Jack went back to Bobbie's room to call Rick Wiseman. He hadn't spoken directly with his news editor since the emergency and the babies' delivery. He also wanted to thank Rick and the *Herald-Tribune* for the flower bouquet he and Bobbie received that morning.

He strolled into the room and noticed Bobbie was awake. "How are you, darling?" Jack asked.

"I slept a lot this morning. I feel groggy and hungry. I hope they bring in lunch soon."

"I saw the lunch carts in the hall. Won't be long. Say, I

hope you don't mind. I need to call Rick. Can I do it here?"

"Jack, when you're finished, I'd like to talk with you about what you're doing," Bobbie said softly.

"What do you mean? My investigation of what's happening here?" Jack asked.

"Yes, but go ahead and call Rick. Try not to be too loud like your usual self," she warned.

Jack nodded. He picked up the phone and dialed the *Herald-Tribune* city desk.

"Hi Rick, Jack here. First, we got the flowers, and they are fantastic. They brightened up the room and lifted Bobbie's spirits. Thanks so much," Jack said.

"We're all pulling for you and Bobbie. How is everyone doing?" Rick asked.

"Everything is going well here. Bobbie is receiving good care. Her blood pressure continues to fluctuate, so the doctor wants her to stay for a few more days. We can't transfer everyone anyway because the twins are in the NICU," Jack said.

"Well, take as much time as you like. Give Bobbie my best wishes, and tell her that Katie is taking care of her beat and not to worry," Rick said.

"10-4 to that. Say, I got a story here," Jack said, glancing over to Bobbie, who stared at him with a frown.

"You don't say?" Rick chuckled. "What is it? You interviewed everyone you talked to at the hospital, and let me guess, you want to write a feature story on efficient healthcare services?"

"No, just the opposite," Jack laughed. "Nokomis lost $10 million over the past two years under cost-plus reimbursement, and another $7 million so far this year. Several sources here think top executives are embezzling."

"Wow. That's big!" exclaimed Rick.

"Do you know how much Sarasota Memorial reported they made in previous years?" Jack asked.

"Thirty million in 1980 and 1981," said Rick, remembering Jack's story from last year about regional hospital profits in the years before the Medicare prospective payment system went into effect.

"Right. There could be a financial cover-up. In addition, the CEO, Mike Lard, plans to cut maternity services, mental health, and the alcohol and drug rehabilitation program to balance the books," Jack said.

"You've been as busy as Bobbie," Rick quipped.

"Hardly. By the way, I witnessed a wild party Saturday night in the executive suite, where a hospital manager and the wife of a construction company owner OD'd on cocaine, quaaludes, and alcohol," Jack whispered.

"You saw what? How?" Rick asked incredulously. "You were supposed to be helping your wife deliver twins."

"It happened later, around midnight, when Bobbie was resting, and the twins were in the ICU. Listen, many hospital employees tell me about the issues here. It's a longer story to explain the coke party in the C-suite, but I'm interviewing Mike Lard in 10 minutes," Jack recounted.

Bobbie's body slumped, and her face reflected sadness as she understood that Jack wouldn't have time to talk about how his reporting on Nokomis was upsetting her.

"I suppose I shouldn't be surprised you're finding time to work even as your wife is resting in the maternity unit," said Rick sarcastically.

Jack let the rib pass. "Rick, I will give you a full briefing later on what I have. By the way, I'm planning this for the Sunday issue. I hope to obtain the hospital's financial records and other relevant documents, which will take some time. I also need to interview the board chair and get several doctors and managers to go on the record."

"All right, all right," Rick said. "Do what you need to do. I'll give you plenty of space for Sunday. And try to enjoy yourself. You're a new dad."

"I am. I don't feel any different—yet," Jack said.

"Believe me, you'll feel very different once they come home, and you have to change diapers 24/7," said Rick, a father with a wife and two young children.

"I'll keep you posted on the story. Later," Jack said as he hung up and turned to Bobbie.

"Everyone says hi and get well soon," Jack said cheerfully.

"I heard," Bobbie whispered, trying to hide her disappointment.

Jack noticed her mood shift and moved beside her as she lay on the bed. He took her hand.

"I've got to go now. I'll be back in a bit, and then we will have time to talk and be together all afternoon. Dr. Lords should be in soon to let us know what time I can take you to visit the twins in the NICU."

"All right, but I don't know why it's taking them so long to let us go see them."

"It is a combination of you and the twins getting strong enough," Jack said. "Well, I'd better go. I don't want to keep Lard waiting."

"Don't be too long. I want to talk," Bobbie said, reminding him of his promise.

Jack nodded, kissed her, then turned to grab his backpack with his camera, tape recorder, notepads, and pens, before quickly leaving the room.

The walk to the C-suite was nearly the same as the night before, when he'd followed Valentina Rubenko and spied on the party. This time, however, he took the elevator, and the button to the fifth floor worked.

He walked into the executive office waiting room, a familiar sight with the long, brown leather sofa he had hidden behind the night before.

Another difference was that a secretary greeted him. "May I help you?" she said.

"I'm Jack Kendall with the *Herald-Tribune*. Mike Lard wanted to see me."

"Good morning. Mr. Lard is waiting for you. Follow me," she said.

Jack walked down the hallway to Lard's office. She knocked on the door.

"Come in," Lard said.

The secretary opened the door. "Mr. Lard, Jack Kendall," she said.

Jack walked into the room. Lard sat behind his desk with Steve Brophy and Tonya Creating, the hospital's public relations director, sitting in chairs around him.

"Have a seat, Mr. Kendall. I think you know Mr. Brophy and Ms. Creating," Lard said bluntly. "We're here to answer your questions about how the Medicare cuts have affected hospital operations. I believe you have the wrong impression and have been misled."

Jack took out his tape recorder and notepad. "Do you mind if I tape our interview?" he asked.

"We are taping as well," Lard replied.

"Fine. As you know, I brought Bobbie to the ER Friday night at about 7 p.m. She gave birth to twins in a successful emergency C-section at 8:30 p.m. Everyone is fine, although Bobbie is being treated for eclampsia, and the doctors recommend she stay in the hospital for at least one week with the twins," Jack said.

"We're very happy for you," Tonya said. "What's your problem?"

"Nothing with the hospital staff. They have been wonderful. Many have expressed concern about proposed changes in several departments, lack of supplies, vendor service delays, and, frankly, worries that management isn't fully committed to them," Jack said.

Lard shook his head in disagreement. "Mr. Kendall, hospitals across the country face similar challenges because of Medicare's new DRG payment system. We have seen a 60% drop in Medicare revenue in the program's first seven months, and we are considering changes because of it."

"Has the drop in revenue from Medicare caused supply shortages?" asked Jack.

"What supply shortages?" Lard asked.

Jack blinked. "Mike, the consensus among nurses, doctors, housekeepers, and janitors is that a range of items are in short supply or missing."

Lard's eyes blazed with fury. "You've been meddling with my employees, getting them to tell you things that aren't true."

"I've seen these shortages with my own eyes," Jack calmly said.

Lard exclaimed, "Impossible. You are making this up to sell newspapers!"

"Hardly. Why would I do that when my wife is here to

have babies?" Jack questioned. "Mike, did you know that departments have to barter for basic supplies like bandages, dressings, gloves, needles, syringes, IV tubing and bags, catheters, gauze, and sponges?"

"You're exaggerating," Lard said.

"Not at all. Do you know that some medications in the pharmacy department are in limited supply or unavailable?"

"We're renegotiating vendor and supplier contracts," Lard said. "We're aware of some shortages and are working to increase supplies."

"You mentioned vendor contracts. I was told certain vendors—namely, equipment maintenance, sanitation, laundry, housekeeping, and food service—are withholding supplies and services until they receive past-due payments," Jack said.

"A few are, but we're on top of this and expect to rectify the issue in the next two months," Lard explained.

"How? Sale of the hospital?" Jack asked, deciding to be direct about the merger tip.

"Who told you that, or did you make it up? We're not going to sell our community hospital," Lard thundered.

"Just asking. Lots of hospitals are for sale or looking to merge due to the new payment system, and I heard that National Healthcare Corp. has made some inquiries. Is that true?" Jack asked.

"We get inquiries all the time. As I told you at the beginning, Medicare cuts have forced us to make difficult choices about how we spend our money. Every hospital is going through this process," Lard said. "This is just a blip, and certain disgruntled employees are using it as an excuse to complain to the press. You are a far better reporter than to be taken in by their whining."

"Okay. Prove it to me. Shut me up. Give me your audited financial statements for 1981, 1982, and 1983, and the unaudited first half of this year," Jack suggested, hoping Lard would take the bait.

"I can't release those without board approval," Lard said, leaning back on his chair and looking over at his CFO.

"What about IRS 990 Forms for those same years?" Jack asked. "You are required by law to make them available to the public upon request.

"We haven't filed them yet. Steve, can you explain?" Lard asked.

"We filed for extensions because the new forms are so different from how we normally record revenue and expenses," Brophy said. "We will file them by next March."

"Fine. Steve, you've seen your financial statements. Could you please provide the hospital's gross revenue, net patient revenue, net income, and operating income for the past two years, 1982 and 1983? I'll write them down, and based on these numbers, we can discuss the impact of the Medicare cuts, as you call them, for this year," Jack said, holding his pen and looking at his notebook as he waited for a response.

"Again, I can't release that information without board approval," Lard insisted.

"How long will it take you to get board approval?" Jack asked.

Lard said, "Our next board meeting is in October. I can ask."

Jack looked at Lard, then at Brophy and Creating. They all had stone-cold faces. He wasn't going to get anything from them.

"Several employees told me that the hospital lost $10 million in fiscal year 1982 and 1983, with an average total revenue of

$40 million annually. Is this information correct?" Jack asked, pressing Lard for numbers again.

"How would they know? It's not true. We've made money—not as much as before because of the Medicare cuts, but we're by no means losing money," Lard said flatly.

"Is this accurate, Steve?" Jack asked.

"It is. We have net positive cash flow," Brophy replied.

"You're making money on operations?" Jack asked. "I want to be crystal clear about what you're saying."

"Correct," Lard said, interrupting Brophy. "I don't know who told you we're losing money, but it is a bald-faced lie."

"Odd, I heard the hospital has lost $7 million so far this year. Is that true?" Jack pressed.

"Absolutely not true," Lard said, looking over at Brophy. "Any more dumb questions?"

"Did the hospital transfer money from the 501(c)3 Nokomis Hospital Foundation to cover operational losses?" Jack asked.

"Where did you get this information?" Lard said. "I just told you, we don't have operational losses."

"I can't reveal my sources, but multiple people have told me this," Jack replied. "If you used restricted charitable donations to fund hospital operations, you may have violated IRS and Florida law."

"Mr. Kendall, I think this interview has gotten off track. You are taking the word of disgruntled employees over that of the hospital's CEO and CFO," Tonya said.

"I have been at the hospital less than 48 hours, and I have seen things on my own that lead me to conclude there is something wrong. Yes, I'm concerned about what I see and hear from some employees," Jack said. "The situation seems much different than when I interviewed you, Mike, early last year."

"As I told you before, we are adjusting to the new Medicare reimbursement changes. We discussed this after you attended our public board meeting," Lard reminded Jack.

"Yes, but I need more than just your assurances. I need documents to support your claims. Could you possibly discuss my request for financial records with Chairman Royster?" Jack asked forcefully. "He has the authority to release them to me without full board approval."

"I will ask Chairman Royster, but I believe he will side with my recommendation not to release unaudited statements for a newspaper story," Lard said.

"Please ask him. Now, what about maternity services? Does management have a plan to eliminate maternity services, and if so, when will it happen?" Jack asked.

"We have discussed this. It will be an agenda item at our October meeting, which you are welcome to attend. We cannot discuss it in more detail before the meeting," Lard replied.

"Is it true you may cut this vital community service because NICU loses money? And labor and delivery is low margin?" Jack asked.

"I cannot get into details, but it's a well-known fact that maternity services at many hospitals lose money, just like ERs and burn units," Brophy said.

Lard raised his hand. "Now wait a minute, Kendall. We are going through a transition, as I said before, but we also plan to expand services such as cardiovascular surgery, invasive cardiology, orthopedics, neurosurgery, and gastroenterology."

"I see," said Jack. "Mike, isn't it true that those services make hospitals the highest profit margins?"

"Are you a hospital financial expert?" Lard said, standing up and waving his arms. "For your information, with our growing retirement community, these services are in high demand. Our patients need them."

"What about the mental health, alcohol, and drug abuse program? Aren't those programs in high demand with a war on drugs underway?" Jack asked. "Aren't these departments under review to cut?"

"No further comment, Mr. Kendall. You have an agenda here," said Lard, looking at Tonya for help.

Tonya started to talk, then Jack interrupted. "You invited me here to answer my questions. Am I wrong? These are my questions. Do you plan to eliminate your maternity services and mental health departments and lay off more than 150 workers?"

"Mr. Kendall. I think this interview is over," Tonya said.

Jack raised his voice. "Did you transfer $10 million from your foundation to cover the expected operational losses for the previous two years, and plan to transfer more for this year?"

The executives stood up, signaling the end of the conversation.

"Will you answer my question? Are you refusing to answer these questions?" Jack continued to press Lard.

"You have some nerve, coming up here and demanding answers to questions that haven't been decided yet," Lard said, walking around the desk toward Jack in a threatening manner. "Kendall, I do not want you talking with any employees, period," Lard said, adding, "Stay in your room. Do you understand?"

"I'm not sure you can do that. There's something called the First Amendment and freedom of the press," Jack said calmly.

"This is my hospital!" Lard roared. "I make the rules!"

Jack stared at Lard in disbelief. "What are you afraid of? Your employees? The truth?"

"Smartass. Get out of my sight," Lard snapped.

"Mr. Kendall, follow me. I'll walk you back to your wife's room," Tonya said.

Jack didn't move. "Before I go, I'd like to be guaranteed another interview after I review the financial records I requested," he said as Tonya pulled on his arm to leave.

Jack stood up, his full 6-foot-4-inch frame towering over the others. "Mr. Lard, I will write a story. I'll give you three days to contact Chairman Royster about my request and for you and Steve to reconsider your answers."

"Three days, he says? Out!" Lard yelled.

"Sure, but the gossip among employees won't go away. The trash in the halls, the dirty linen, and the undelivered medications and supplies won't just disappear because you refuse to talk about them!" Jack shouted as Tonya led him from the room.

Lard moved back behind his desk, boiling with anger. He tried to stay calm, but Kendall got under his skin. He hated reporters. They asked too many questions, especially the ones he didn't want to answer.

As Jack stood at the door with Tonya still tugging on his arm, he stared at Lard, hoping for a response. Lard glared back.

After a few seconds, Jack broke the silence and said, "All right. I will let Tonya know my deadline to give you another chance to comment."

Lard waved him away. Jack turned to leave with Tonya, a faint smile on his face.

Chapter 11:
House of Cards

1 p.m., Monday, Sept. 10, 1984

Lard continued boiling after Kendall left. The tension in his office was thick, and McMann and Brophy prepared for the inevitable explosion.

A nosy reporter snooping around the hospital and talking to employees was annoying enough. But now, with several lucrative schemes underway, the last thing they needed was scrutiny.

"I want Kendall derailed. Do what you must, but stop him," Lard growled as he stood up, walked over to the mini-bar, and poured himself a scotch and water.

Lard took a quick sip, then looked back at his lieutenants.

"Maybe relying on him not to talk with employees won't work. He's stubborn. I should limit him to maternity and NICU and have a security guard posted outside his room," Lard said, taking a long sip.

"I want him watched closely, and ask Dr. Lords to discharge

his wife and babies as soon as possible," he added.

"Yes, sir," McMann responded instantly.

"Report to me after you talk with her," Lard said.

"Until they can be discharged, we can make Kendall and his wife so uncomfortable that he'll want to leave," McMann grinned.

Uncomfortable, Lard muttered to himself. *Make Kendall uncomfortable*, he thought, a vengeful smile slowly forming on his face. Kendall was a nuisance—no, more than that, he was a problem. It suddenly occurred to him that there might be another way to get rid of a problem like Kendall.

* * *

Michael J. Lard began his career as a real estate salesman in 1954. He recognized a promising future in healthcare, went to college, and earned a master's degree in healthcare administration in 1966. With Medicare expanding the revenue opportunities, he saw plenty of chances to take a share of the profits.

When several northern millionaires decided to build Nokomis Hospital in 1965, they took advantage of the introduction of Medicare, which offered millions of seniors low-cost healthcare services.

Once hired as CEO by Nokomis in 1972, he convinced wealthy donors to pay hefty "recruitment fees" to attract top doctors from nearby Venice and Sarasota.

Initially successful, Lard started hiring lieutenants he knew were willing to bend and break laws, regulations, and ethical rules governing nonprofit hospitals.

In the early days, the huge profits earned by Nokomis

Hospital gave him opportunities ripe for embezzlement.

Lard, Brophy, and McMann had mastered the art of siphoning funds from the hospital. Months before Jack and Bobby's arrival, they purchased a warehouse and used it to store medical and surgical supplies that were secretly bought with money embezzled from the hospital.

Then, they leased it to the hospital under a false company name, effectively creating a new revenue stream. They sold the supplies at a substantial markup and kept the profits. The scheme worked so well that they planned to buy a second warehouse and sell it to the hospital at an inflated price.

That was just the most recent of their money-making ventures. They were a few days away from transferring the supplies to Nokomis to make up for the shortages they had caused when Kendall arrived with his sick and pregnant wife.

For years, theft was simple. No one was watching their backs. Not the board, the government, or local law enforcement. Considering the scale of the crimes, Lard realized he had become too comfortable with the risks he was taking.

He knew investigative reporter Jack Kendall was at the *Herald-Tribune*. But Kendall had been busy investigating the corrupt phosphate fertilizer plant at Granger Station and the murders by the psychopath Elizabeth Brewster in the Sarasota-Bradenton area. Before that, he also thought the murder of Becky, Kendall's wife, by Gordon Gecht would've occupied the reporter's mind.

Why would Kendall bother with a 200-bed hospital in south Sarasota County? Still, Lard couldn't have predicted that Jack's new wife would need treatment for eclampsia in his ER. What could he do now to hide his crimes?

Over the past decade, they had siphoned off more

than $30 million through embezzlement, fraud, and quiet laundering schemes. Hospital funds meant for patient care were spent on luxury condos, weekend trips to the Bahamas, golf memberships, and gifts for their wives, girlfriends, and anyone else they wanted to keep happy.

Rumors drifted through the hospital corridors, but most of the 15-member volunteer board of trustees had no idea how deep the rot ran. They didn't know the hospital had bled $10 million in just two years—nor that it was now losing more than half a million dollars *every* month.

Some trustees had inklings, but Lard had a way of neutralizing them—turning on the charm, feeding them half-truths, or burying them in financial jargon until their eyes glazed over. The few who understood enough to be dangerous also understood how little appetite the others had for confrontation. These were retirees enjoying their final chapters in South Sarasota County—a place they chose for its climate, golf courses, and peace and quiet. The last thing they wanted was a scandal that could damage their reputation.

For Lard and his circle, stealing the money had been the easy part. Hiding the growing financial crater was getting harder.

The new Medicare prospective payment system had wrecked their profitable little scam. Under the old cost-plus model, they could spend freely and get reimbursed. Now, Medicare rewarded efficiency—and efficiency was not Lard's strong suit.

To cover the gaps, Lard instructed Brophy to secretly transfer $17 million from the hospital foundation into the hospital accounts over the past two and a half years, hiding the transfer in reports to both boards. The issue was that much of the money came from restricted donations—funds legally required to be used for specific programs. There weren't enough unrestricted funds to replace it.

Those trustees who knew about the transfers asked when the foundation would be repaid. Lard's answer disappointed them—and some of them sensed he didn't have a real plan.

The losses pushed Lard to accelerate merger talks with National Health Care Corp., a fast-growing for-profit chain eager to expand into Florida. National had two things Lard desperately needed: sophisticated billing systems that could squeeze every penny from the new Medicare rules, and deep enough pockets to cover the $17 million foundation gap before anyone smelled trouble.

He rehearsed the pitch in his mind: a prime hospital location, a booming market, and the chance to lure high-revenue physicians by selling them shares in outpatient ventures. All true. But underneath it all, he needed one thing more than anything else—National's quiet agreement to fill the financial hole he'd dug before any auditors came poking around.

If he pulled it off, the merger would be a jackpot. A seven-figure compensation package, stock options, guaranteed contracts for himself, Brophy, and McMann, and generous golden parachutes waiting whenever they wanted to walk away.

But there was one threat he hadn't anticipated, one problem he couldn't charm or bluff his way past: Jack Kendall.

What if Kendall put the pieces together? What if National got cold feet because of something Kendall wrote? Then the entire scheme—every lie, every theft—would come spilling into the light.

Lard felt that fear tightening around him every time Kendall's name came up.

He couldn't let that happen. Kendall couldn't be allowed to expose them.

No—Kendall had to be silenced.

Chapter 12:
Family Visits

4 p.m., Monday, Sept. 10, 1984

It was late in the afternoon. Jack and Bobbie were finally allowed to enter the NICU to see their twins up close in their clear, enclosed incubators.

Bobbie thought it was a dream because they were sleeping in plastic cribs with heart rate monitors, wires attached to their chests, and breathing tubes in their mouths.

Dr. Lords said the monitors were mainly a precaution. They were small yet sturdy. She aimed to prevent common complications like heart and lung problems, brain bleeds, low blood sugar, feeding issues, jaundice, and infections.

"We want to encourage you both to visit as often as you want. For infants, admission to the NICU can be a psychologically and physically distressing event," she said. "Research shows that preterm infants suffer from higher rates of depression and anxiety in childhood, adolescence, and adulthood, likely, at least in part, related to the experiences they have in the NICU."

"I'll come as much as I can," said Jack.

"Can these incubators be wheeled to my room? I want to be close to them," Bobbie said.

"We can't do that, but I'll see if you can be transferred to one of our maternity beds nearer to the NICU," Dr. Lords said. "They're filled right now."

"Doctor, you have the sensors on them. What are you monitoring?" asked Jack.

"Apnea and bradycardia," Dr. Lords said. "They're called the A's and B's. Apnea is the temporary or complete cessation of breathing. Bradycardia is abnormally slow heart action. If a baby stops breathing, an alarm will begin beeping."

"Everything is normal?" Bobbie asked.

"Both are doing very well. The twins are getting stronger every hour," Dr. Lords said.

"Jack, I'm getting tired, and my head feels heavy. Can we go back to my room?" Bobbie asked.

"Sure. I'll take you now. Dr. Lords, we'll be back later with my mother and brother," Jack said.

* * *

As Bobbie napped, Jack reviewed his notes from the interview with Lard when Ed popped his head into the room.

"Hi, strangers. I heard this is the maternity suite for Mr. and Mrs. Kendall," Ed said with a smile.

Mrs. Laura Kendall followed Ed into the room. "Oh, such beautiful flowers," she said. "Who got them for you?"

"Well, the big rose bouquet from the first Mrs. Kendall came in this morning. Hi, Mom," said Jack warmly.

"How are you both? Bobbie, I am so proud of you. And

you have twins! A boy and a girl. You both are blessed," said Laura, gazing at Bobbie with admiration and empathy.

"I'm doing better, but I'm still sleeping a lot. Jack and the nurses are taking good care of me," said Bobbie, holding Jack's hand as he stood next to her. "The heart monitor and IV drip make it look worse than it is. I can't wait to show you little Ella and Eli."

"Ella and Eli? Are those their names?" Ed asked.

"Not officially. Bobbie likes those names. I like Laurel and Hardy, but I can't decide which is the boy or the girl." Jack laughed.

"Stop joking. Ella and Eli sound very nice. I would very much like to see them when you are ready," Laura said.

"Let's go. The babes are just down the hall," Jack said, moving toward the door.

Ed came up to Jack and handed him a thick brown envelope.

"What's this?" Jack asked.

"What you asked for. Financial statements, reports, market share studies, and recent lawsuits against Nokomis Hospital," Ed said.

"You got it so soon? Who gave you this?" asked Jack as he opened the large envelope.

"Francis. His source at Sarasota Memorial was more than happy to talk about Nokomis—all off the record. They apparently have excellent market research," Ed said with a sly grin. "Francis told me you should call the CEO for an interview. He doesn't like Lard and is ready to rip into him."

Chapter 13:
Terry Myles

Monday, Sept. 10, 1984

At work early that morning, Terry sat in his office staring blankly at a spreadsheet. The columns of numbers—meant to represent patient census, projected reimbursements, and equipment depreciation—blurred into nonsense. But the one that stood out, clear and damning, was "Net Loss YTD." It flashed like a warning light he could no longer ignore.

Terry Myles had the lean, disciplined look of a man who once lived a different life and was still learning how to inhabit this new one. In his early thirties, he carried himself with quiet restraint, his straight posture and long, angular limbs hinting at strength he no longer believed he possessed.

His face was sharply defined—high cheekbones, a squared jaw, and steady, deep-set eyes that revealed more sorrow than he ever admitted aloud. His dark hair was kept cropped close, practical and unfussy, and there was a stillness about him, a contained energy, as if every movement was measured to avoid stirring up memories he wasn't ready to confront. Even in casual clothes, he looked slightly out of place in his own skin, the loss of his wife and two children etched into the worn edges of his expression.

Yet beneath that grief was something steadier—a decency Nicole had noticed immediately, the reason she believed he could help her expose what was happening inside Nokomis Hospital.

The phone rang. It startled him. He picked it up.

"Hi. How was your weekend?" Nicole's voice was soft, familiar.

"The usual. Home. Dinner with the folks," Terry said softly.

"And?" she teased gently.

"Nothing else. Still unpacking."

"You know I'll keep asking. The offer still stands: Saturday night dinner with Pete and me. You can also meet my friend, Della. I think you'd like her. She's curious, and she's available, Terry."

"I'm not ready for anything like that, but... thanks for thinking of me," he said, his voice low, his words careful.

"It's just a dinner. She'd be good for you. She's been through a lot as well." Nicole paused. "I'll keep asking... Listen, Terry, I didn't call just for that. Can you meet me in the cafeteria for coffee?"

He looked at the spreadsheet, then glanced around the office and sighed. He wasn't getting much done anyway.

"Yeah," he said. "Give me five minutes."

* * *

The cafeteria was only half full, the quiet clatter of breakfast trays, glasses, and plates echoing through the tiled space.

Nicole waited at a corner table, a coffee already in hand. She waved him over, then motioned toward a quieter table by the wall.

"I saw Jack Kendall on Sunday," she said as soon as they sat down. "His wife had twins Saturday night."

Terry shot her a quizzical look. "Who's he?"

"You know. Jack Kendall is the *Herald-Tribune* reporter. Didn't I tell you about him?" Nicole replied slowly.

Terry knew where this was headed. "You want to ask again about the financials, don't you? I already gave you the bottom-line numbers for the past two years."

Nicole smiled softly. "Lard called me into his office to accuse me of leaking that information to Kendall."

"What did you tell him?" Terry asked excitedly.

"I said I'd spoken to him, yes, but only about the supply and nursing shortages. That's all. Nothing about the financials." Nicole leaned in. "I need more help."

Terry didn't answer right away. He stared into his coffee, stirring it with the flimsy plastic stick.

"You've been a good friend since I came here," he finally said. "I told you what I suspect because I don't like what Lard and his cronies are doing to this place."

"Will you talk with Jack Kendall about the financial losses?" Nicole asked.

"He's a reporter. I don't want to get involved like that."

"He's good, and he's honest and trustworthy. He'll cite you anonymously."

"I really don't want to get involved," he repeated, his head down.

Nicole pressed. "Terry, Kendall is the reporter who exposed the phosphate company in Manatee County that dumped radioactive slime in the bay. Won a Pulitzer for his hurricane coverage, too."

"I remember hearing about it. So that's him."

"He's not just after a scoop. He's trying to help," Nicole reassuringly explained. "I told him what I knew, but I haven't said a word about you. I promised him some staff memos. You don't have to talk to him, but I'd like to share the documents you said you could get."

"Let me think about it," Terry said cautiously.

"You told me you've seen the most recent numbers. Can you get copies?"

He hesitated. "I don't know. I've been getting these headaches again."

"I told you—see Dr. Barkley. It could be migraines," she advised.

"I will," Terry muttered.

"Terry...patients are suffering. Nurses are overwhelmed. You saw what happened in the ER Saturday night. Bobbie Kendall could've died. Her twins, too."

Terry exhaled slowly. "I'll try. If Brophy lets me, I think I can get a draft of the nine-month report. It's for the board's October meeting."

Nicole's face lit up. "What's in it?"

"Shows a slight profit. But it's fake. The foundation covered another $7 million in losses."

"Is that on top of the $5 million they shifted last year?" Nicole asked.

"Yes. This time, they didn't even bother disguising it. I've been reviewing the financials for the past couple of years. Last year, they moved money between restricted and unrestricted accounts first. This time, just straight from the foundation."

"Were there any footnotes or supplemental documents in the report?"

"Not in the draft, but I know where they are. I might be able to get them next week when Lard and Brophy go on that trip with Chairman Royster, Riggles, Palmer, and Giles to the Bahamas," Terry whispered.

"Please be careful."

"I will. I'll drop the financials at your house afterward."

"Great. Pete will be home this week before he goes out of town for a meeting. Maybe you can play a round of golf with him the following weekend?"

"Maybe," Terry said with a slight grin, revealing a hint of his once cheerful personality.

"You don't mind if I give the documents to Jack?" Nicole asked.

Terry shook his head. "I don't want to know what you do with it. I'm doing this for you and the patients."

"I won't say a word, but you'll see how they'll be used if you read the *Herald-Tribune*," Nicole said with a smile.

Terry nodded. They talked quietly for a few more minutes, then Nicole excused herself to start her shift.

"See you tonight," she added as she stood up and turned to leave. On her way out, she noticed Dr. Wickman, chief of radiology, was sitting at a nearby table. She smiled as she passed, then looked back at Terry, wondering if Wickman had overheard anything.

Terry remained seated, his head down, fingers tracing the rim of his empty cup. The cafeteria had gotten noisier. A couple of nurses from pediatrics were laughing at a nearby table. Someone wheeled a squeaky cart past him.

Nicole realized they needed to be more careful and find

other ways to talk. She watched as Terry leaned back and stared at the ceiling. He looked so sad, so lost. She hated pushing him to speak with Kendall, but she felt obligated to stop Lard.

Terry regretted not telling Nicole more about the familiar heaviness creeping into his head during their conversation, a warning sign that a migraine might be coming on. But this time, it felt different. The pressure behind his eyes wasn't just from stress; it was something more personal. The weight of what he was being asked to do—help Nicole expose Lard's corruption—was cracking open a door he tried hard to keep shut.

Grief, raw and unrelenting, began to rise inside him, dragging him back toward that awful day six months ago. The memory of losing his family pressed against his chest like a tide he couldn't hold back. It wasn't just a headache. It was the beginning of another wave—a flashback, a reckoning, a reminder that no matter how far he'd run, the past was always close behind.

CHICAGO, HFMA CONFERENCE
Friday, February 3, 1984

Terry was back at the Healthcare Financial Management Association conference at the Sheraton Towers. He remembered the mustard-colored carpet and the way the keynote speaker droned on about capital cost allowances. He remembered the vibration in his coat pocket and the sound of his pager.

CALL PHILADELPHIA FIRE DEPT—URGENT.

A strange chill passed through him. The words didn't make sense. Fire department? He walked briskly out of the ballroom, passed a few milling hospital finance folks chatting about DRGs and capex budgets, and found a house phone near the elevators.

As he dialed, he thought the page had to be a mistake. Then, the call connected. A deep voice answered on the other end.

"This is Deputy Chief Lawrence, Philadelphia Fire Department. Is this Mr. Myles?"

"Yes..."

"I'm sorry to inform you. There was a fire at your home this morning. Your wife...Jill...and your children...Jonathan and Elise...were inside."

"Wait—what?" he whispered. "Are they... are they okay?"

Another pause.

"No, sir. I'm very sorry. The fire spread quickly. We believe it was electrical—possibly the living room heater. They didn't make it out."

Terry said nothing. He couldn't. His throat tightened like a vise, and his vision narrowed. The world suddenly didn't feel real. The patterned carpet, the fake ferns, the sound of a fax machine behind the front desk—they all seemed impossibly distant.

He dropped the phone. A woman in a blue HFMA lanyard turned her head, concerned.

"I need...I need to get back home," Terry muttered. His voice was ragged and broken.

He stumbled into the men's room down the hall, locked the far stall, and collapsed onto the closed toilet seat. That's when the sobs came—harsh, sudden, uncontrollable. His hands shook as he covered his face.

His family. Gone.

Just the night before, Jill had called him from home, describing how Jonathan had spilled spaghetti all over his school uniform and worried he'd get in trouble, and laughing about how Elise had drawn a picture of Terry giving a speech in front of "a million boring people." He promised to bring Elise back a souvenir snow globe and Jonathan a Bears football jersey. He said he'd be home on Friday. Jill told him not to forget the gifts.

He asked her what she wanted.

"Silly," she said to him, "only you."

Now...nothing.

When he finally emerged from the restroom, his face blotchy and red, he passed the ballroom again. The same Kansas CFO was still droning on about Medicaid audits. The projector clicked. Someone coughed.

He rushed home. The house was unrecognizable—a charred skeleton. The smell of smoke lingered for days. No furniture. No toys. No bedtime stories. All their memories and dreams were gone.

Without a home or a family, he packed up what belongings he had and left Philadelphia for Venice, where his parents had moved two years earlier. A month later, he was hired for a job as an accountant at nearby Nokomis Hospital.

Everyone told him the sunshine would help. He wasn't sure it ever would.

* * *

Back in the cafeteria, Terry blinked, pulled back to the present by the clang of a tray.

He thought about Karen, his therapist from those early days after the loss of his family and his move to Florida. Karen always asked him the same thing when he hesitated:

"What's the right thing to do, Terry?"

She was right then. She was right now.

He looked out the cafeteria window toward the main entrance of the hospital. Nicole was right, too. Patients were suffering. Good nurses were quitting. And Lard was lining the books as if nothing mattered.

Terry Myles had lost everything once. He couldn't save Jill. He couldn't protect Jonathan and Elise. He couldn't save his own family.

Maybe it wasn't too late to help someone else.

Nicole was right.

He stood up, smoothed his tie, and walked out. It was time to act.

Time to do the right thing.

Chapter 14:
Nicole McIntosh

Late Afternoon, Tuesday, Sept. 11, 1984

Nicole's shift was nearly over. It had been a long day: ten emergency department admissions, four transfers from nursing homes, three code blues, and one unruly patient who wanted to be discharged against medical advice, all with too few staff and not enough supplies and medications.

She carried herself with the calm, purposeful confidence that had become her hallmark over fifteen years at Nokomis Hospital—a quiet poise developed from balancing compassion with unyielding resolve. Even now, moving briskly down the corridor, she maintained that upright, assured posture that reassured staff and patients alike.

Over the past few weeks, medical units had been forced to borrow and trade supplies. Nicole, who had risen from bedside nurse to vice president of nursing not for power but to protect the people who relied on her, did her best to ensure care didn't suffer.

Still, the staff kept asking questions and was losing patience. Her warm, attentive eyes—usually a source of comfort—were now clouded with concern every time another nurse approached her asking where the next shipment of gauze or tubing had gone.

In all her years working at Nokomis Hospital, she had never seen such disorganization. Where were the supply deliveries? Bandages, gauze, syringes, IV tubing, and even cleaning liquids were running low. And that was just the beginning. More items were added to the shortage list every day. She hated this version of leadership—the kind that made her feel like she was protecting her staff from those above her, rather than supporting them.

McMann had promised to fix the vendor and supply problems. However, Nicole knew from quiet, tense conversations with purchasing that vendors weren't getting paid on time and were limiting their orders. She was a grounded, practical leader—someone who still leaned over charts with the practiced ease of a bedside nurse—and she didn't tolerate evasiveness well. The ethical backbone that defined her refused to bend to the excuses she was getting from upstairs.

Nicole wasn't concerned about her nursing and support staff. They were excellent, dedicated, hardworking, and always found ways to keep going. But she could sense their morale slipping. They watched *her*, too—her posture, her tone, her eyes—to see how worried they should be.

What worried her far more was what Dr. Joel O'Neal had told her: Lard, Brophy, and McMann were diverting revenues from operations with the help of four or five other managers. Nearly half the board was on the take or complicit by doing nothing. The thought of administrators profiting from sick people felt like a personal violation of everything she believed in, everything she had worked for.

Married, devoted to her husband, anchored by a strong ethical core, Nicole had always believed that her role—her purpose—was to protect both her staff and the community they served.

Dr. O'Neal had also hinted at more bad news he'd heard about maternity services. She wondered if Jane knew. She had to tell her, but not until later. She had an appointment to talk with Dr. O'Neal after the meeting with Terry. Getting both of them to help was a priority.

As Nicole headed to Jane Willougby's office to meet with Terry, she considered the motivations of those responsible. She honestly didn't understand how executives could justify profiting from the suffering of others, prioritizing investors over employees and patients. Nicole became a nurse to help sick people, not to watch leaders manipulate finances while beds sat short of supplies. Providing inferior care to boost profits and maintain high bond ratings—this was a world she had never trained for.

It also wasn't part of her nature. She enjoyed hands-on nursing. She only became vice president of nursing to be an advocate for employees and patients. Unfortunately, she now saw her job as protecting them from management. She dressed with understated professionalism—clean lines, practical elegance—but beneath that polish lived a woman who would never willingly bend her ethics to accommodate greed.

She had once believed that management could improve patient care. But here, according to Dr. O'Neal, management was the problem. Were Lard, Brophy, McMann, and others taking money from the hospital, short-changing employees and patients? That was the big question.

She hoped Terry could confirm what Dr. O'Neal had told her and shed light on other things. Nicole opened the door to Jane's office. Terry and Jane were waiting for her.

"Hi, Nicole. Terry and I have been chatting about how he's getting along in Florida. He told me you've been inviting him over for dinner, and he feels bad he hasn't had the time," Jane said.

"Terry knows he has an open invitation," Nicole said, raising her eyebrows at him. Turning to Jane, "How has your day gone?"

"I'm fine," Jane said, glancing at the young executive, who had a serious expression. "Terry has something to tell you."

"I reviewed the hospital's financial statements from 1980 and the draft budget report for the first nine months of fiscal 1984," Terry explained. "It was odd because Brophy left the locked file cabinet open where the most recent financial documents are stored. I still need more information, but I have more than I did when we spoke last week."

"I know you don't want to get involved, but we must understand what is happening at the hospital. You see what is going on around us," Nicole said.

"Yes, but I only did this for you, Nicole," Terry said.

Nicole nodded. "I appreciate it, but I'm worried about our financial situation. How bad is it?"

"The new Medicare payment system has impacted our revenue this year, but it will get worse if we do nothing. However, that isn't the problem," Terry said.

"No? Seems a lot to me," Jane commented.

"Revenue from Medicare is only 10% lower than three years ago, so that's not the main issue. Private health insurance payments have risen by 5%, and we have minimal uninsured and charity care because of our affluent community."

"So, what's the problem, then? We can't seem to pay our bills, and vendors are withholding supplies. It's getting worse," Nicole said, her voice full of desperation.

"We don't have the cash. The problem is on the expense side. Our total expenses have increased by 25% over the past two years, primarily due to higher costs for administrative, medical, and support services, mostly through outsourced contracts, as well as for supplies," Terry explained.

"Supplies that don't make it to our nursing floors?" Nicole asked sarcastically.

"Some vendors have stopped delivering because we haven't paid them, but we are buying more supplies than are actually reaching us; that's the strange part," Terry said, shaking his head. "Normally, we would ask the COO about missing inventory."

"McMann," said Nicole. "He's in deep with Lard. I've got to confront them again."

Jane touched Nicole's arm. "Be careful. Those men are dangerous."

"Terry, what else have you found?" Nicole asked.

"Focusing on expenses, employee compensation costs have remained stable or decreased over the past two years due to a hiring freeze and outsourcing. However, top management and external management contracts have surged as we've relied on them to fill gaps."

"So, rising management expenses are our problem?" Jane asked.

"Yes. More precisely, the real problem, from what I can tell, is that mismanagement and potential corruption have caused significant operational losses," Terry said.

"Corruption—that's what Dr. O'Neal hinted at. And mismanagement, which doesn't surprise me," said Nicole. "Do you know where it's coming from?"

"Mismanagement is easy to identify, but corruption? Not yet; I don't have the current supporting financial data or the audits with the footnotes," said Terry, his voice trailing. "I'd rather not get into that, if you don't mind, until I investigate further."

Nicole wanted everything, but she didn't want to pressure Terry, at least not yet. He somehow had just gained access to additional financial documents and needed more time to review the numbers.

"But *are* you going to investigate further?" asked Nicole. "You've done really well getting us this."

"I'm helping," he said.

Nicole smiled warmly. "You are, and we know you are doing your best. Relax, tell us what you know."

Jane stood up and walked around the desk behind Terry.

"What about the new DRG system? Paying us flat fees for Medicare procedures and services? Lard and Brophy talk about that all the time as a problem. How has that impacted us? Do you see anything about that in those reports?" Jane asked.

Terry nodded. "It's true. Medicare's shift to the inpatient prospective payment system with diagnostic-rate group reimbursement last October changed everything."

He shook his head. "But if you're asking me if that caused the problem as Lard describes? No, that's not as much of a problem as they would have you think."

"Not a problem? We haven't been told anything like what you've told us, except that we are being paid less for what we do," Nicole said.

"Well, that is true, up to a point," Terry said. "Do you want me to try and explain the DRG prospective payment system?"

Jane and Nicole looked at each other and rolled their eyes.

"Can you make it simple for a couple of nurses?" Jane pleaded.

"All right. Instead of paying hospitals under a cost-plus-profit formula, which is based on their historic costs plus, say, 2%, they now pay a flat DRG rate for nearly 600 inpatient procedures.

"Go on," Jane said.

"This new payment system is meant to encourage cost-efficient medical care management," Terry explained. "Since we are in year one, I'm not sure how that is affecting us yet, but I've been told it's beneficial now for many hospitals six months in, so it's hard to understand the losses."

"But is Lard correct?" Nicole asked. "We are paid less? And that has caused our problems?"

"Well, partially. It's complex. But, as I said, payer revenue is not our problem. Something is missing from the expense reports. I don't know what yet. It's as if unaccounted-for expenses or money are being diverted to other uses. We need a forensic audit to find out where it's going," Terry said.

"This is what Dr. O'Neal believes," Nicole said. "He's not an accountant or auditor and can't track the money. You are our only hope."

Nicole gazed at him with pleading eyes. Terry looked away, feeling the pressure to respond.

"I hear you. I'm trying, but what I don't understand is why

Lard, Brophy, and McMann haven't done more to prepare the hospital for the efficiencies required under the DRG system," Terry said. "Brophy should know better. He's the CFO."

"Doctors tell me that Brophy and Lard keep telling them to discharge patients based on their DRG payments, not on their conditions, and to run tests as long as we are paid for them, at least for the inpatients," Nicole said. "Why?"

"Dr. O'Neal knows that's backwards and poor patient care," Terry said. "At my former hospital, we started discharge planning early and used multidisciplinary teams to coordinate care. Too many hospitals hold patients longer than necessary because they aren't prepared to discharge them."

Terry stood up and raised his voice. "We have no plan here. I've asked Steve why, and he tells me they are working on it. I should be involved; he knows I was part of the team at Philadelphia Medical Center that prepped for DRGs, and he hasn't asked me for help."

For the first time, Nicole saw Terry's passion, something she sensed he had been hiding or suppressing because of his grief over losing his family. It was as if he were waking up from a long sleep.

Jane also noticed that something had changed in Terry. She didn't want to ask what it was. She was thankful he seemed motivated to help them rather than being reluctantly helpful.

"They should ask you for advice. Instead, Lard wants more admissions to compensate for fewer paid days per stay," Jane observed.

"Correct," Terry said.

Nicole interjected, "That reminds me. One of my nursing management friends at Sarasota Memorial mentioned that total Medicare revenue and profits have increased for hospitals in Florida and across the nation during the first half of 1984, based on surveys by the American Hospital Association."

"Is this true?" Jane asked.

"It is. Many hospitals, including Memorial, are making record profits so far this year by quickly adapting to the new reimbursement model," Terry said. "Hospital management publications like *Modern Healthcare* have reported that successful hospitals have streamlined operations, reduced unnecessary procedures, and improved efficiency. *Modern* quoted many CEOs who said hospitals can make money on Medicare if you are smart about it."

"I see *Modern* on your desk all the time," Nicole said admiringly. "I've heard Lard joke about not wasting his time on it."

"*Modern* has many good case studies of successful hospitals. At my previous job, we respected *Modern*. Our CEO would encourage us to call hospital managers we thought were doing a good job to learn from them," Terry said with a smile.

"It's absolutely true that by controlling costs while providing necessary care, there are many hospitals under DRGs that are making money—in some cases, more money, in fact, despite what Lard says."

"Why can't we do that?" Nicole asked.

"Laziness? I don't know why. Brophy is smart. He should know better. They must have other priorities that I don't understand," Terry said.

"Like what?" asked Jane.

"Greed, especially Lard and McMann. With Steve Brophy, I sense he wants me to know things. He hired me, knowing where I worked. We were profiled in *Modern* for our cutting-edge financial practices and successful management."

"What are you saying?" asked Jane.

"Hmm, what am I saying?" Terry said, thinking for a moment.

"There could be three reasons. The first is that they haven't a clue, which I don't believe. The second is they are losing money on purpose," Terry said.

"On purpose?" Jane asked.

"Yes, just think about it. We are aware of the rumors that National wants to buy Nokomis. What if Lard is purposefully making the hospital look bad so National can swoop in and buy it for a song?" Terry speculated.

Nicole stood up, her face red with anger. "That could explain it."

"Wait, Nicole, there is a third possibility," Terry said.

"I can't wait to hear this one," Jane encouraged.

"Steve hired me, and from what I have heard, without Lard's knowledge. He knew my track record. He knew I would see how poorly run this hospital is.

"Maybe he wants me to figure out what's really going on. He tells me not to worry about the financials, but he doesn't stop me from accessing the records. I'm pretty sure Lard would be upset if he knew Steve had been slowly allowing me access to the real financial records."

"I wondered how you could get those numbers," Nicole said. "So Lard doesn't know what Brophy is doing? You think Brophy could be helping us expose what's happening here?"

"I don't know why he would; he's in as deep as the others. Just don't say anything to anyone about Steve," Terry said. "I've talked with him about instituting these practices, but he is hesitant, not overtly opposed. He tells me the time isn't right."

"I don't understand what you're saying," Jane said. "Could

Steve Brophy save our hospital?"

Terry stopped talking and sat down. "We shouldn't get our hopes up. If there is corruption, Steve is just as involved as Mike, Charles, and the rest of them."

"What are you going to do?" asked Nicole.

"All I know is there is something else going on that is increasing expenses. I've looked at all the financial files I can find. Unless Steve leaves open another locked drawer and leaves a file on my desk, there are missing audits and other contract documents that could probably give me the answers."

"Oh, Terry, if you could look into it, we might be able to save this hospital," Nicole said, her voice full of desperation.

Terry hesitated. "I'm trying to help," he said, looking down. "You know what I'm going through. I'm stressed out enough just talking about it with you two."

Nicole nodded. "I know. I hate pushing you like this, but you have the knowledge and access to information that we and the community need."

Terry winced. He knew how much what he could discover meant to Nicole, Jane, and everyone. He also felt an obligation to do the right thing.

"You also have strength, Terry. I've seen it today," said Nicole, looking at Jane, who nodded. "You can do it, for all of us."

Terry nodded. "If Jill were with me, I could."

"She would want you to help us, I know she would. She believed in you. We believe in you," Jane said.

"Under normal circumstances, I could do this," said Terry, pausing before taking a deep breath. "All right. I think I know where these documents might be."

He stopped himself. Nicole and Jane waited.

"But if I do this," said Terry, looking at the two women intensely, "it has to be on my timetable."

Nicole nodded. "We trust you'll do the right thing. Thanks, Terry. We probably should end this meeting now. Please let us know what you find."

She turned to Jane. "I'll call you tonight. I need to visit Dr. O'Neal before I head home. Ready? Okay, let's leave separately. I'll go first."

Chapter 15:
Dr. O'Neal

6 p.m., Tuesday, Sept. 11, 1984

After work, Nicole drove to Dr. Joel O'Neal's medical group's office building, hoping he could finally shed light on the rumors floating around the hospital.

She pulled into the quiet parking lot, the sun already dipping low, and parked near the entrance. The glass doors were dark. When she tried the handle, it didn't budge—it was after hours.

Nicole knocked, unsure if he was still inside. After a few minutes, footsteps approached, and the door cracked open. Dr. O'Neal appeared, loosening the collar of his white coat, looking tired but cordial.

"Nicole," he said warmly. "Come on in."

He held the door for her and then led her down the dim hallway to his office at the back of the suite. Once inside, he motioned for her to sit. Files, board packets, and medical charts were stacked neatly on his desk—order within chaos.

He closed the door and lowered his voice.

Over the next twenty minutes, he vented his frustrations. He had been on the board for about a year, yet the trustees were given only polished summaries—never raw numbers, never full financials.

"Nicole, they give us headlines, basically, and ask us to vote on them for million-dollar projects," Dr. O'Neal said with disgust. "There is no discussion or explanation. I've been to three meetings last year and two meetings this year, and this is how it goes."

"Incredibly, Lard or McMann presents the issue, and Chairman Royster immediately calls for a vote. Immediately!

"Jimmy Giles usually makes the motion; it's seconded by Vice Chair Frank Burns and approved in an 11-3 or 10-4 vote. I can tell at least three or four members don't want to vote to approve these things, but they seem helpless and just go along with it."

"Is there a meeting in October?" Nicole asked.

"Yes. I was told we are going to vote on several things, including a supply warehouse, a second one," Dr. O'Neal said in disbelief.

Nicole was flabbergasted. "Another? For what? We don't have enough supplies inside the hospital. Why do they need another building to store non-existent supplies?"

Dr. O'Neal shook his head. "I asked Chris McVay, our newly appointed finance chair. She's the accountant with Beloit Associates. Do you know her?"

"I haven't met her. What did she say?"

"Chris told me she wanted a discussion about this, but Lard and Brophy wouldn't permit it," Dr. O'Neal said, frustration evident in his voice. "I like Chris, but she's holding back information and voting on things for reasons I can't understand. She said that the hospital would be resupplied if we approved the lease. I don't know how or why, but she said that."

"That doesn't make sense...unless Lard is purposefully withholding supplies to get the board to vote on things they want," Nicole mused. "I've been told Lard may be making the hospital look worse and cutting programs to pave the way for a merger with National Healthcare, but all that is speculation."

"Oh, really? I may have more to say about that shortly," Dr. O'Neal said.

"You'll let me know?"

"Call me in a few days."

"What else did Chris McVay say?"

"Very little. However, she said we also could vote next meeting on closing the maternity unit and the alcohol and drug rehabilitation program," Dr. O'Neal said.

"We've heard that talk," said Nicole glumly. "Do you think it will happen?"

"I have evidence. Besides, if this comes before the board, like Chris said it could, it's because Mike Lard wants it to happen."

"What do you make of it all?" Nicole asked.

"I tell you what—I joined the board to get a doctor's voice into decision-making. We have enough doctors on salary, and I was promised that future capital expenditures would be directed to my group and additional physician office space. Still, I didn't sign up to be a rubber stamp for corrupt hospital executives," said Dr. O'Neal.

"Corrupt? You told me that before. Do you know something more?"

"That's all I'll say now. I should have more information soon. Let's talk another time. I'm nearing the end of my patience," Dr. O'Neal said, wiping his brow. "Here, take this copy of a draft memo I was able to get from the board secretary. You didn't talk with me or get it from me. Understand?"

Nicole nodded.

Dr. O'Neal handed her an undated memo from Mike Lard to David Royster, the board chair. "I've got to call it a day now. We'll talk soon."

Nicole stared at it, stunned. Evidence. Real evidence.

"Be careful with that," O'Neal said quietly. "This wasn't meant for us to see."

She nodded, her pulse racing. "Thank you, Joel. Truly."

He stood to walk her out, giving her a look that mixed concern with resignation—as if he already knew the board would never act.

As she followed him down the hallway to the front door, she glanced at the memo with her mouth open. This was the first formal proof that the rumors were true: Lard wanted to terminate maternity and inpatient mental health services.

At the door, she shook Dr. O'Neal's hand. No words were spoken. She walked to her car with a heavy heart. Everything she feared was coming true.

Still, Nicole didn't want to believe it. She had worked with Mike Lard, Steve Brophy, and Charles McMann for more than half of her career. They'd been good to her in the beginning, but in the last several years, they had changed—and for the worse.

But the internal board memo Dr. O'Neal shared confirmed her darkest suspicions. It detailed management's proposal to the board to close the inpatient obstetrics unit, including labor and delivery, the neonatal ICU, and maternal-fetal medicine.

Nicole folded the memo and slipped it into her purse, her hands trembling only once before she steadied them. For years, she'd trusted Lard, Brophy, and McMann, believing they still cared about patients as much as profits. That illusion was gone.

The memo in her bag wasn't just proof of a bad decision—it was a map of their betrayal. She couldn't take this to the board. Lard had planned the rubber-stamp vote well.

If the hospital were to survive, she would have to gather every shred of evidence, hope Terry has the strength to finish the job, and trust Jack Kendall to expose everything.

She had no choice: she would risk her job, maybe more, but she couldn't let them destroy the place she considered a lifeline to the community.

Nicole stepped into the evening air, clutching the memo as if it were a live wire. She unlocked her car, slid into the driver's seat, and sat there for a moment, gathering herself before heading home—knowing that whatever happened next, nothing at Nokomis Hospital would ever be the same.

Chapter 16:

Cocaine and Silver Bars

Wednesday, Sept. 12, 1984

Charles McMann sat behind his large, heavy oak desk, waiting for his weekly silver shipment. He tapped his fingers on the desk and looked at his watch.

Dr. Stan Wickman was late. McMann, the hospital's tough-minded chief operating officer, didn't like people being behind schedule. It was nearly 6 p.m., and he needed to be home shortly to take his wife to the opera.

Denise McMann didn't like being late either. The opera was the one thing they had in common besides their love for money. Another reason was that Denise wanted to appear proper to people. She didn't want anyone talking or gossiping about her or Charles.

McMann popped a pill into his mouth. He was feeling especially stressed today because his wife kept asking more questions about the hospital. She was close to Mary Brophy and upset that she had left Steve for reasons she wouldn't share.

A knock on the door drew a smile from McMann. "You're ten minutes late," he said.

"I know," said Dr. Wickman, handing over six bars of silver.

"I'll take them," McMann said. "Here, this is yours."

"Thanks," said Dr. Wickman, taking a thick envelope stuffed with $20 bills. "This is my last delivery."

"We're not finished," McMann growled. "You understood our arrangement."

"Yeah, but things have changed," Dr. Wickman said flatly. "I'm done. I quit."

"I'll double your payment to $500 per bar," McMann offered.

"It's not the money. We've been discovered."

"What?" McMann exclaimed.

"I overheard a conversation between Nicole McIntosh and the new accountant Steve hired," the radiologist replied, his voice hushed.

"Terry Myles?"

"That's him. They know something is wrong."

"You'd better explain a little more, doctor," McMann said. "You're in just as deep as the rest of us."

"They were in the cafeteria early this morning. I was getting some coffee when I saw them. I took a table near them and heard Nicole tell Terry she talked with the *Herald-Tribune* reporter, Jack Kendall, about the deficit the past two years," Dr. Wickman relayed.

"What the hell is Terry doing?" McMann demanded.

"I don't know, but did you know Kendall is here? His wife had a baby Friday night in an emergency C-section," Dr. Wickman said.

"Yes, we are aware, and Mike knows he's talking with our employees," McMann said, disgusted. "We are handling that. What else did you hear?"

"Myles told her he suspects we are misappropriating hospital funds and haven't implemented cost-containment programs like Sarasota Memorial and other hospitals," Dr. Wickman said. "Nicole asked him to tell Kendall what he knows. He is hesitant, but if he speaks, the reporter will have a lot of ammunition to hurt us. We could be exposed. This is why I want out now."

"I am glad you gave me this information, Dr. Wickman. You are right, we have a serious problem. Mike already told Nicole and Terry not to talk. At least for now, save all the used X-ray film and let your intermediary know we are pausing this operation," McMann instructed.

"I hope Mike knows how to handle this," Dr. Wickman said. "I don't want to lose my medical license or go to jail for getting involved with you for a few measly thousand dollars."

"You're forgetting the coke and prostitutes," McMann said. "Your wife won't like hearing about that."

Chapter 17:
The Real Mike

Afternoon, Wednesday, Sept. 12, 1984

Mike Lard was speechless when McMann described his conversation with Dr. Wickman.

He sat at his desk, contemplating how to present the latest plan to revitalize the hospital and hide the crimes that had contributed to its issues, while preparing for the upcoming board meeting.

As McMann started to speak, "Mike, I…" Lard cut him off, saying, "Shut up, I'm thinking."

Lard got up from his desk, walked over to the mini-bar, poured himself a scotch, drank it, filled another half-glass, and stood there, staring at McMann.

"Wickman heard Myles tell McIntosh we are misappropriating funds? He said this? I thought he wanted to get away from trouble, not cause it for himself," Lard growled.

McMann nodded, keeping quiet while Lard vented.

"And McIntosh—what a bitch. We've been good to her for

nine years, and she tells Myles to talk with Kendall? After I told her to keep her mouth shut?"

"That's what Dr. Wickman said," McMann gloomily recounted, walking over to the mini-bar to pour himself a drink.

"I ought to fire them both today," Lard mumbled, adding, "but that might be too good for them."

"Dr. Wickman heard everything and is frightened. He wants to stop melting down the silver. I hope you agree with me. I told him we are pausing that operation," McMann said.

"That's fine. We have other sources to cover the cost of the cocaine and the parties. We can divert the proceeds from our new leasing plan. That doesn't worry me," Lard said.

"What does? Myles and McIntosh?"

"It's Jack Kendall. If he talks with McIntosh or Myles or gets our financial statements, he'll know that everything I told him about why the hospital is losing money is a lie," Lard said. "We won't be able to finish this merger with National. Once we get the merger completed, it won't matter if Kendall fact-checks us or not."

"No, it'll be National's problem. Should I have a word with Kendall?"

"No. When he calls back for an interview, I'll let him talk with Brophy. He can explain how the financial statements don't tell the whole story."

"You think that will satisfy Kendall?" McMann asked.

"No, he's going to write something," Lard said, taking another sip. "We need to minimize the damage. Medicare is already reviewing infection control in our sterile processing department, and the Joint Commission has sent a letter regarding a site visit scheduled for the next two weeks. I don't want the IRS looking at our finances."

"What should we do about Terry and Nicole?"

"I'm going to lay the hammer on them tomorrow. You tell Palmer to investigate them and find out exactly what they are doing."

"What do you want done?" McMann asked.

"Nothing physical for now. Tell Palmer to find out everything he can and report to me," Lard said. "Wait, tell Palmer to make his presence known to them. I want them to sweat. Meanwhile, I'm going to tell Terry and Nicole that we are onto them, and they should contact Kendall and retract everything."

"What if they refuse?"

"Tell them if a story comes out with anything about the hospital's finances, we will fire them and destroy their careers."

"Right. What about Kendall?" McMann asked.

"Is his wife still in the hospital?" Lard asked.

"Yes, Kendall has been here every day," McMann replied.

"I thought I ordered you to discharge his damn wife. Why hasn't that been done?" Lard demanded.

"We asked Dr. Lords and Dr. Chastain to discharge the wife, but both refused," McMann said. "They said it was too dangerous for her and the babies until next week."

"What about Kendall. Is he still wandering around, talking with employees?" Lard asked.

"He hasn't gone too far, and when he does, I've assigned a security guard to follow him and take names of anyone he talks with," McMann said.

"I want him isolated in his wife's room. He can only check on their babies in NICU," Lard said.

"I checked with our attorney about that. Lessem advised against doing anything like that. He said that would give Kendall another story to make us look bad."

"I don't care. The situation has gotten much worse. Tell the security guard to make sure Kendall stays in his wife's room and doesn't wander," Lard said. "Explain our visitor rules to him. He is not allowed to speak to or interview employees, period. He cannot leave the room except to leave the hospital or go to the NICU. He will be removed from the hospital if he leaves the room without permission. We have rights too."

"Won't that be like admitting our guilt?" McMann asked.

"He already thinks we're guilty. I don't want him talking with anyone else," said Lard, raising his voice. "Goddamn reporters. They think the world revolves around them."

Chapter 18:
"You Will Be Fired if You Talk with Kendall"

Morning, Thursday, Sept. 13, 1984

Nicole McIntosh rode the elevator to the fifth-floor executive suite for a meeting with Mike Lard. On the way, she decided to confront him about the supply shortage.

She was about to demand changes. She wasn't concerned about getting fired. He needed her there with the inspections approaching. Besides, she felt the timing was right to stand up for the hospital, its patients, and its staff.

With that in mind, she opened the door to the C-suite offices and prepared herself for what she believed would be her last chance to fix things from within the system before revealing everything to Jack Kendall. She had no idea that Dr. Wickman had reported her previous conversation with the journalist.

"McIntosh, I've been told some very troubling things about you. You have been a naughty girl. Very bad. Sit down," scolded Lard in a demeaning way.

"Mike, what is this?" she asked, sitting down, clearly offended.

"Did you get the confidential financial statements of this hospital from Terry Myles and pass them on to Jack Kendall?" he asked harshly.

"No, I didn't do that," said Nicole, telling a partial truth because she hadn't given Jack the financial statements—yet.

"I told you before not to talk to Kendall. Did you?" Mike demanded.

"I congratulated him on his twins and asked how his wife is. You know I've done interviews with him before," she said nervously.

"I understand. That's why I will say this just once: I want you to tell Kendall you retract everything you said to him. Tell him you misspoke, that it was all a misunderstanding. After that, it's 'no comment' if he calls or approaches you for information. Then, if you talk with him again, consider yourself fired. Do you understand?"

"Yes, Mike," Nicole replied meekly.

"Now, get back to your work," Mike growled.

Nicole sat there looking at him behind his big oak desk. She was almost speechless. *Gather yourself*, she thought. *This is your only chance. Tell him what you think about the hospital.*

She stood up. "Mike, you think I don't care about this hospital, but I do. We have serious problems that need to be fixed. You must address the supply shortage. It has worsened over the past two weeks. Do you know that departments are trading with each other to keep going?

Mike stared at her, saying nothing.

"Let me tell you. Kendall isn't an idiot. You tell me not to talk to him. He already knows what's happening at this hospital because he can see it," she said, stepping forward toward his desk. "Did you know nurses are bringing bedsheets home to wash them because we lack clean linens? Nursing assistants are taking out the trash to the dumpster because housekeeping and janitorial services have been cut to the bare minimum."

Mike shook his head. His face reddened with anger.

"And do you realize we will fail the Joint Commission's inspection? Have you thought about what that means? What are you going to do?" Nicole asked as forcefully as she could.

Lard stood, still silent, shaking with emotion. "Are you finished?" he asked angrily.

"No," she flatly replied. "When will we get our supplies? When will you fully staff the housekeeping, laundry, food, security, and janitorial service departments?"

She hesitated, then decided to let it all out. "And when will you stop wasting money on those Wednesday and Saturday night parties? Nursing and patient care could use more investment!" she shouted. "Everyone knows, and it's giving the hospital a bad reputation!"

Lard had heard enough. "Do you want to be fired this very moment? And when I fire you, I will make damn sure I give you such a negative reference that you'll be lucky to find another job as a bedpan washer! Now, get out, and stop talking to Myles and Kendall." He pointed a finger toward the door.

With tears in her eyes, Nicole turned and hurried into the hall. Several people heard her shouting and stepped out of their offices. She was visibly trembling, but after a few seconds, she smiled, having told Lard precisely what she thought of him.

She didn't pause to exchange pleasantries or explanations with coworkers. She had no time for that. This wasn't over, not by a long shot. If Lard thought he could intimidate her into silence, he had chosen the wrong woman.

Nicole marched straight to Terry Myles's office, her pulse racing. He had to know what had just happened. Moreover, she must convince him to speak with Jack Kendall.

Today, she would make sure both of those things happened.

Chapter 19:
Confined

Late Morning, Tuesday, Sept. 13, 1984

The door to Bobbie's room slowly opened, and Charles McMann entered, his hospital ID swinging slightly against his chest. His eyes first glanced at Bobbie, then shifted to Jack, who was sitting in the chair closest to her bed, a legal pad resting on his knee.

"Jack," McMann began in that careful, measured voice administrators use when they want to sound polite while delivering bad news. "I need to make you aware of some restrictions."

Bobbie shifted under the thin blanket, sensing that something was wrong.

McMann moved closer, keeping his tone neutral. "From this point forward, your access is limited to the maternity unit and the PICU. You'll be issued a visitor badge that includes your name, destination, and date. Security will be posted on the floor to make sure there are no misunderstandings."

Jack set his pen down slowly. "I'm here for my wife and my children."

"And you're welcome to be here," McMann said quickly. "But hospital policy is clear. Patient privacy and well-being come first. We must limit unnecessary disturbances. Certain areas, such as intensive care, operating rooms, and research labs, are restricted. Visitors are granted access only where needed, and you are no exception."

Bobbie's brow tightened. "What's this about? He's not bothering anyone."

McMann gave her a gentle smile. "Mrs. Kendall, we're simply following procedure. The visitor management system requires registration at each visit. The badge we issue will be programmed—figuratively speaking—to match your authorized areas. It's the same for everyone here. Your husband will have all the access he needs to see you and the babies, but not beyond."

Jack didn't raise his voice. He didn't need to. "Charles, I plan on writing a story about this hospital. Isolating me won't stop that."

McMann's smile thinned, but he didn't take the bait. "The maternity staff and PICU employees have been instructed to limit conversation to subjects involving your wife and the twins' care. That's for their protection as well as yours."

Bobbie looked like she wanted to argue, but Jack caught her eye and gave the slightest shake of his head. He wouldn't push this restriction. He needed to finish his story and didn't want any more distractions, neither for his snooping nor for Bobbie.

McMann offered a final polite nod. "Enjoy your time with your family, Jack. Security will be in the hall if you need anything."

When the door closed, Bobbie exhaled hard. "They're treating you like a criminal, an enemy."

Jack forced a smile. "They're treating me like a reporter."

He rose from his chair, walked over, and kissed her forehead. "Get some rest. I'll check in on the twins. Keep an eye on my notebook and briefcase."

Jack placed his briefcase with his notes near Bobbie's bed and headed for the door. He glanced at the security guard standing outside like a sentry, protecting company secrets.

"Hi, Officer Brody," said Jack, catching the nameplate on the man's uniform. "Walk with me. I'm heading to neonatal to check on my babies."

A 20-something security guard, Brody straightened himself, a bit too eager to show he was on duty, and fell in line behind Jack. The soft squeak of his shoes echoed down the hallway, each step a reminder that Jack was on a short leash.

* * *

Thirty minutes later, Jack returned to Bobbie's room, a visitor badge clipped to his shirt. She had fallen asleep, so he opened his briefcase and took out his new Tandy TRS-80 Model 100, its small LCD screen faintly glowing under the overhead lights.

The quiet hum of the hospital filled the background: monitors pulsing their electronic beats, soft wheels squeaking down the hall, nurses murmuring over charts. Jack shut it all out.

He started organizing his thoughts and notes, assembling them like puzzle pieces—supply shortages, staff complaints, whispered warnings, and the financial irregularities Nicole had hinted at. His fingers moved carefully, each word bringing him closer to the truth.

If McMann thought a badge and a few security guards could fence him in, he misunderstood the reach of a reporter armed with a portable computer and something worth chasing.

Jack paused, staring at the blinking cursor. One piece of the puzzle still sat just out of reach—Terry Myles. Nicole swore he would uncover something about Mike Lard that could blow the story open. He wondered what Terry knew. His lips tightened.

He knew the real challenge wasn't chasing paper trails or decoding ledgers; it was convincing a man he'd never met to risk everything and go on the record. Until he reached Myles, the whole truth about Mike Lard and the corruption inside Nokomis could stay locked behind the hospital's walls.

Chapter 20:
Terry's Grief

Morning, Thursday, Sept. 13, 1984

For Terry Myles, weekday mornings were the worst. They stretched on like a prison sentence he didn't deserve. No wife to talk to over coffee, no children to herd toward school. Just a kitchen too quiet and a calendar without purpose. He had thought once about getting a dog—something to feed, to walk, to look forward to at the end of the day—but the thought of losing another living thing felt like setting a timer on more grief.

His nights were no better. He'd come home, make a simple dinner, watch television—which he barely remembered afterward—maybe skim through a few finance journals before going to bed early.

Weekends weren't much different. On Saturdays, he usually visited his parents, staying for dinner and sometimes a movie before heading back to his silent house. His father often invited him to golf—just like they had in Philadelphia before the move—but Terry wasn't ready for anything that resembled normal.

He still missed his wife and young children. He would always miss them. Tears came to his eyes when he thought of the plans he and his wife, Jill, had for their lives. Children were just the beginning. Next was building their careers together. Like him, she was a CPA, and they planned to start their own small business when the children grew older.

But all those plans fell apart in a terrible night filled with smoke and fire. He often dreamed about that night, struggling to get home but unable to do so. And he always felt powerless to save them.

* * *

A light tap on his office door pulled him out of his repetitive thoughts. Nicole McIntosh stepped into his office and quietly shut the door behind her.

"Terry, can I talk to you? I just came from a meeting with Mike," she explained, still visibly shaken from her encounter with Lard. She tried to compose herself to avoid upsetting Terry.

"Sure," he said, pleased to see her, but wondering why she was breathless and her eyes puffy and red. "Are you okay?"

"I think so," Nicole said. "Mike called me into his office this morning and threatened me. He was rude and told me to stop talking to Jack Kendall. I told him if he'd give us the supplies we need and stop laying off good people, Kendall wouldn't have anything to write about."

"Yeah," Terry said. "He gave me the same speech. Told me to retract anything I might've said to you or Kendall. And that he'd be watching."

She gave a brief, grim nod. "Then we need to be smarter. No more hallway conversations. If you'd like to meet, please leave a note on my car tire in the garage. I'll do the same."

"Makes sense," Terry said. "So what's the next move?"

"I don't know if you've thought about our talk on Monday," Nicole said evenly, "but this conversation with Mike was the last straw. I'm not stopping. I'm going to keep doing what I've been doing—advocating for this community and our people."

Terry rose from his chair and walked to the window, staring out at the parking lot. "Then you should know," he said quietly, "I've looked closer at the last few years' financials—just like you asked."

Her voice sharpened. "What did you find?"

"You want the short version?"

"Please. I can't stay in here long."

"We've talked about how Lard blames Medicare for reducing patient income. But the reality is that revenue has only dropped by 5%. Admissions and patient days have increased each year, along with the local population. By July, losses had surpassed half a million, totaling $17 million over the past 31 months. We are close to defaulting on twenty-five million in tax-exempt bonds."

"Does the board know?"

"Doesn't look like it. Lard and Brophy keep pointing to Medicare, bad debt, and charity care as the culprits."

"So what's causing it?"

"My opinion? Operational losses. Mismanagement. And corruption," Terry whispered.

"Just what you thought. You have to tell Kendall. And give him copies of everything," Nicole urged.

Terry shook his head. "I made the copies, but it's not that simple. I told you, Lard said I'm being watched, and I bet you are, too."

She glanced toward the door. "Then let's be careful. This should be our last office meeting. We need to meet at my house. I'll let you know when. Bye."

Terry nodded as she departed. He had to decide. He leaned back on his chair, eyes fixed on the spreadsheets scattered across his desk. The numbers didn't lie.

Even if there was fraud, Nokomis Hospital should still be making money. Medicare length of stay had dropped by only 2% since January, while American Hospital Association data for the month showed a 4% decline.

On the other hand, admissions increased by 8%, well above the national average of 4.7%. Those numbers should have meant financial stability, maybe even a surplus. Instead, the place was bleeding $500,000 a month.

He had suggested to Brophy that management and the medical staff work together to streamline the discharge process, making it more efficient for patients to leave. Collaboration with doctors to reduce waste was also necessary.

He also told Brophy that they should standardize purchasing to eliminate redundancies, select the best products based on clinical value, and obtain the best prices on supplies, medical devices, and pharmaceuticals.

There was also no meaningful collaboration with doctors to reduce healthcare waste, share data on costs and outcomes, and standardize practices based on evidence.

But Terry could guess why none of that was done. Lard didn't want anyone looking too deeply into the books. It was one of the reasons he thought Brophy, who seemed like a good guy, might be avoiding making changes. Brophy wasn't ignorant. He was one of the sharpest finance men Terry had ever met, which made his silence all the more damning.

Other hospitals had adapted quickly to the new DRG payment model. They streamlined operations, reduced waste, and improved discharge times.

But at Nokomis, inefficiency wasn't a flaw—it was the business strategy. Extra tests, padded stays, inflated billing codes...and a leadership team willing to let the hospital edge toward insolvency while they blamed Washington.

Terry rubbed his temples. This wasn't just poor management. This was fraud. And he had the numbers to back it up. He had no other choice but to get the evidence he needed, and there was only one place to look: Lard's office.

* * *

Before leaving for the night, he called Nicole's home number and waited for the beep. "Tell Kendall I'll meet with him Monday night," he said, voice low. "Tell him I'll bring what I've got. I'll drop what I have off with you Sunday night."

He set the receiver down and sat there for a moment, looking out his window and watching the parking lot empty in the fading light. He'd already lost everything that mattered once. Helping bring the truth to light wouldn't get his family back—but maybe it would keep someone else from losing theirs.

Chapter 21:
First Story

Morning, Friday, Sept. 14, 1984

Jack stood by Bobbie's bedside for a moment, watching her eyes flutter open. The soft morning light filtered through the hospital curtains, casting a warm glow on her pale face.

"I need to get to the paper," Jack whispered.

Bobbie smiled weakly. "You don't have to rush."

"I know. But I've got to talk with Rick, make a few phone calls, and type my story into Atex," Jack said.

She reached out and squeezed his hand. "You know I've been wanting to talk with you about our new family and us, but I know now how important this story is to the people who work here."

"I understand, and I'm sorry. There's a lot going on right now. We'll have more time to talk later," Jack assured her. "You know I love you and those incredible little munchkins. Just keep focusing on getting stronger."

"I know. I will. I wanted to tell you it's okay. I've met several nurses, housekeepers like Valentina, respiratory therapists and technicians. It's sad what management has done here. I want you to nail them and expose everything."

"I'm glad you feel the same way I do," Jack said, bending over to kiss her forehead.

"Write a great story and don't worry about me. I'm feeling better, and I see the twins are getting stronger every day."

Jack nodded. "You're right. Eli's breathing problem is improving. He's off the ventilator now."

Dr. Chastain told me. I'll visit them while you're gone so I won't be lonely," she whispered.

Jack stood up to leave, squeezing her hand once more. "I'll be back tonight, after we put the story to bed. Call me at the paper if anything comes up."

Bobbie smiled and watched him turn, walk out the door, and stop for a second to blow her a kiss.

* * *

Jack breezed into the *Herald-Tribune* office. He saw Kathy, the receptionist, busy as usual answering the phone and helping people waiting for appointments. He nodded to Curtis Nettles, a security guard, who motioned him over.

"Jack! I heard the news—congrats, my friend. Twins, huh?" said Curtis, a teammate from the newspaper bowling league. "You missed Wednesday's game, but I guess delivering twins is a pretty good excuse."

Jack smiled and tapped him on the shoulder. "I may be out for a few weeks. Your handicap should keep us in the mix until I get back."

Curtis gave a hearty laugh and waved him goodbye. Jack

walked up to the elevator, pressed the fifth-floor button, and rode it to the top of the building.

Entering the newsroom, he heard the familiar clicking of keyboards, phones ringing, and people engaged in various conversations.

He saw his old friend, Tom Justice, the state government political reporter, at his desk, wrapping up a phone call.

Tom spotted him. "Morning, Jack. How's Bobbie and the babies?"

Jack smiled. "Better than I deserve, given the circumstances of the last week."

"I got the details from Rick and Katie. She's been helping out on Bobbie's beat, but I'm sure you'll hear all about it," Tom said. "Are you here to work or just to check in with everyone?"

"I've got a story to write. Can we catch up later? Maybe for lunch. I don't know what I have going yet," Jack said.

"Sure, let me know," Tom said as he picked up the phone again.

Jack headed to the city desk. Rick Wise glanced up as he got closer.

"Hey, stranger. Got a minute?" Rick asked.

"That's what I'm here for," Jack replied with a grin.

Rick slid a freshly printed schedule across the desk. "Sunday's front page. Your story's top of the fold."

Jack sank into the chair beside him, picking up the Sunday budget line, noticing the story jumped to the inside local section with room for a sidebar.

"Fifty inches for the main bar? That's generous. How long can I go with the sidebar?" Jack asked.

"I'm not sure. What do you have? How are other hospitals doing under Medicare? A first-person story about Bobbie and the twins?" Rick asked.

"You mean it's up to me?" Jack teased.

"I've learned to trust your instincts," Rick said without a hint of sarcasm.

"I have several ideas. Let me get back to you after I've made a few calls," said Jack, standing up. "So that you know, this is just the first of many stories."

"Right-o," Rick replied with a big smile. "As I said, I trust you. Go blow them away."

Jack nodded with a chuckle. "I've got the material this time." He turned and headed to his desk.

Katie North, a young reporter assigned to cover Bobbie's police beat—at least temporarily—saw Jack sitting down and approached.

"Hi, Jack. How are you and Bobbie? And the twins?" she asked softly.

Jack smiled tiredly. "Hi, Katie. Better. Thanks for asking. And thanks for helping with Bobbie's beat."

Katie nodded. "She's a hard act to follow. Everybody loves her. Let me know if you need an extra set of eyes or someone to chase leads."

Jack appreciated the offer. "You're doing great. I'm on deadline today. Let's talk next week about it. I'm sure Bobbie will be out for at least a month."

As Katie walked away, Jack looked at his desk and saw a pile of phone messages. Usually, Kathy gave them to him when he arrived in the mornings. But he had been out for nearly a week, so she must have brought them up. He sifted through the pile and pulled out a message from Nicole McIntosh. The message included a phone number to call Terry Myles on Monday to set up an interview for that night.

Jack grinned and quickly typed a reminder message into his VDT computer, for he knew what that meant. Terry had agreed to tell him everything he had found out. He then grabbed the phone and dialed Ed.

"Hey, I'm back at the paper. Did you learn anything more about the talks between Lard and National Healthcare?" Jack asked.

"Francis spoke with his source at Sarasota Memorial. He got an off-the-record confirmation that Lard is pressing to move this merger along very quickly," Ed said.

"I see. Well, that's helpful. Anything else?" Jack asked.

"Yeah. I'm looking over Francis's report on the scuttlebutt compiled by Memorial's marketing people about Nokomis. All this is for background, not attribution. I will get it to you this afternoon," Ed said.

"I'm going to call Memorial's CEO, Stacy King, right after lunch. Can you get that report to me this morning?" Jack asked.

"Sure, I'll drop it by shortly. Listen, Francis said that King will talk with you. I take it King doesn't like Lard much."

"I'll set up the interview. Thanks, and keep me posted," Jack said, hanging up.

Jack dialed Memorial's efficient and friendly PR director, Susan Swartz, to get on King's schedule. "Hi Susan, how are things at the big hospital?"

"Saving lives every day. How are you?" she happily replied.

"You heard about Bobbie and Nokomis?" Jack asked in a grave voice.

"I'd like to hear it from you when you have time," Susan asked.

"Not now, but maybe lunch soon. Lots going on. Say, a little birdie told me Stacy could talk with me about Nokomis and Medicare finances. Is he available over the phone about one today?"

"I'm sure he will, but let me check. Will 15 minutes be enough? He's pretty busy on Fridays," she said.

"Sure, let me know. Thanks, talk soon," said Jack, hanging up.

His third call was to Rose Blatt, a healthcare professor at the University of South Florida in Tampa. She had valuable insight into hospital finance that would help him improve the story's narrative.

"Rose, it's Jack Kendall with the *Herald-Tribune*. I'd like a quick comment about the financial losses at Nokomis Hospital. CEO Mike Lard blames Medicare's new prospective payment system that pays flat fees per procedure. Is there truth to that?"

Blatt exhaled audibly. "That's an easy excuse. Many Florida hospitals have actually improved margins under the system by streamlining operations. Sarasota Memorial, Tampa General, and even smaller community hospitals are profiting from Medicare. Nokomis's problem isn't the payment system. It's that they've layered debt and overhead onto a structure that can't support it."

Jack scribbled notes quickly. "So that's why they're losing half a million a month?"

"Could be. Rising supply costs play a role, yes, but you don't get to that kind of deficit without reckless spending."

Jack asked the obvious next question. "What about the rumored merger with National Healthcare?"

"That's not about saving the hospital," Blatt said firmly. "That's about saving executives. For-profit systems like National will come in, cut services, sell off assets, and walk away with profits. And if the rumors are true—that Lard wants a golden parachute—then the merger is more about protecting him and his circle than about protecting patients."

"Thanks, Rose. That really helps explain the big picture," Jack said, jotting down her points.

* * *

Curtis dropped off the marketing report Sarasota Memorial had compiled on Nokomis at 11:30 a.m. Jack was looking it over when Tom Justice stopped by. "Can you have an early lunch?"

Jack shook his head. "I've got to read over this report and interview Memorial's CEO."

Tom nodded. Before he walked away, he said, "I should have known better to ask. Let me know when you're free."

"Maybe in a month," Jack said with a chuckle as he looked back at the report, jotting down notes and questions.

He was amazed at the marketing study on a competing hospital. It read like a spy novel of a foreign government. The report provided data and analysis on Nokomis's market share, service offerings, and patient perception, broken down by department and service line.

That made sense, but then Jack read a section titled "SWOT Analysis." He had never heard of that. He pulled out his Hospital Administration Terminology reference book. The SWOT analysis outlined Nokomis's strengths, weaknesses, opportunities, and threats to Sarasota Memorial.

Under "weaknesses," several items stood out: "management ethics," "financial instability," "insufficient staffing," "medical errors," and "poor patient satisfaction."

No surprise there. Then, under "threats," one phrase caught

Jack's attention: "Likely merger with National Healthcare Corp."

Unfortunately, there was a stamp on top that read, "Not for Publication." At least Jack had substantiated everything he had heard so far from Rose, Nicole, Jane, and Cathy.

Something made him look up at the wall clock. It was already nearly 1 p.m. Ninety minutes had swiftly gone by. Jack pushed back his chair, took a breath, and dialed Memorial's executive office line. A few minutes later, Stacy King came on the phone.

"Hi, Stacy. Thanks for taking my call. I've just been reading a very interesting market report on a nearby hospital," Jack observed.

"Jack," King began cautiously, "you can't quote from the report, but I can talk about it generally. I can also tell you what I think about Nokomis, but I can't speak officially about the merger discussions."

"I get it. Tell me what you can."

"Between us, there are fairly substantial rumors that Nokomis is shopping for a buyer," King said.

"How are you hearing this?"

"Consultants and insiders talk. People are always looking for their next job," King confessed.

"Why a merger?"

"We hear Lard wants someone who'll give him a golden parachute and reimburse the foundation for the 'loans' it's made to the hospital. National Healthcare's name keeps surfacing," King said. "Of course you can't quote me on that."

Jack leaned forward, typing notes into the computer. "But National Healthcare? Why would they be interested in a hospital that's projected to lose more than $7 million this year and lost $10 million the previous two years?"

King paused before answering. "Because Mike Lard knows how to sweeten the pot. This has to be on background as well. He's cutting money-losing services, laying off personnel in those departments, maternity, alcohol and drug abuse, and even emergency, while beefing up outpatient services, all things that National wants done so they can maximize profits once they take over. You can draw your own conclusions on what that will do to the community in South County."

Jack tapped loudly on the last sentence on his keyboard. "Can we go on the record now? They've been telling the press that Medicare cuts are killing them. Is there truth to that?"

King let out a brief, controlled laugh. "On the record, that's a convenient excuse. The truth is, hospitals that adapt and streamline are making money on Medicare. We are. So are others in Florida. The federal rules aren't perfect, but they reward efficiency, quality, and, finally, legitimate volume. If you run your operation smartly, you come out ahead. Nokomis isn't doing any of those things."

Jack frowned. "So the half-a-million-dollar-a-month loss isn't about reimbursements?"

"No," King said firmly. "Medicare's the scapegoat. Let me be clear. The real reason a hospital loses money is due to mismanagement, waste, inefficient contracts, and a board... this is off the record, a board that hasn't been asking the right questions for years, and is either asleep at the wheel or willfully blind."

King paused briefly. "I'm back on the record. There are ongoing stories about loans between the hospital and its foundation. I won't speculate if these rumors are true, but if those loans exist, they're...unusual and potentially improper, at the very least."

Jack typed furiously. "Some might say these loans look like self-dealing?"

"The feds would have to say that, not me," King said.

"What about the talk that Lard wants a buyer to make the foundation whole?"

Another pause. "Off the record, that's the whisper, yes. If true, it would tidy things up for certain people. Whether it benefits the community is another matter."

Jack let the silence stretch. Finally, he asked, "Stacy, why share this with me?"

"Because," King said carefully, "the public deserves to know what's at stake before deals are signed in back rooms. Be careful, Jack. You poke at Lard and his crew too hard, you'll find they know how to poke back."

"What do you mean?"

"Off the record. Ask Sheriff Bagley. Our hospital security team tells me that Bagley has information that Lard hired some muscle from Miami to enforce his contracts and to get this National deal over the finish line," King said.

"Lard must be desperate to buy protection," Jack said, jotting down a note to ask his hospital sources about it.

"Jack, I've got to go. I hope you have what you need."

"I do. You're always a big help. Don't ever leave Sarasota," Jack teased King.

"Call anytime," he said.

The call ended with a quiet click. Jack whistled as he set down the phone, staring at the notes on the computer screen. The pieces were lining up—greed, mismanagement, and a hospital being bled from the inside out. Stacy King certainly doesn't like Lard and Co. Few did.

Now it was time to call Lard. He reached for the phone and dialed the executive office number, identified himself, and asked to speak with Mike Lard.

After a brief pause, the receptionist returned. "Mr. Kendall. I'm sorry, but Mr. Lard, Mr. Brophy, Mr. McMann, and several others left for the Bahamas at noon for a board retreat."

Jack frowned. "Is there anyone who can comment on my story?"

"Sorry, sir. You can try Tonya. No one else is available at this time."

Jack asked the secretary to leave a message for Tonya and Lard, noting the time and stating that he was on deadline and calling to get a comment about his story, which was to be published on Sunday.

He gradually lowered the receiver, wondering whether he should have asked the secretary to contact Lard at his hotel. He decided to check if she was still there.

"Hello, I've changed my mind. Are you still there?" Jack asked. "Miss?"

The secretary had hung up. In his imagination, Jack could hear Mike Lard complain about not getting a chance to tell his side of the story. His story was coming together, but the players were already slipping away.

He picked up the phone again and redialed.

"Hello, this is Jack Kendall again from the *Herald-Tribune*. Could you leave a message at the hotel where Mike is staying in the Bahamas? Tell him to call Jack Kendall immediately. I'm writing my story, and I'm on deadline tonight. I need to run a few things by him," Jack blurted out.

"I was leaving a message for Tonya to call you back. I can call the hotel for Mr. Lard, but I can't guarantee anything.

Mike is usually very busy on these retreats."

Jack held back a sarcastic remark. He was sure Lard and Co. had flown to the Bahamas for a weekend of gambling, golfing, drugs, and women.

"I understand. Just tell them both it's urgent. I'm here at my desk writing the story."

He turned back to his typewriter, fingers quickly flying as he finished the Sunday story. It was time to tell the truth about Nokomis Hospital.

Chapter 22:
Infiltration

Early Morning, Sunday, Sept. 16, 1984

Terry Myles felt nervous as he slid the master key into the lock on the stairway door that led to the fifth-floor penthouse suite. Even though Nicole had told him that no one would be in the executive offices on Sunday at 7 a.m., he wasn't used to violating company rules, let alone breaking the law.

While the nine-month financial statements he gave Nicole showed the hospital had operating losses, they didn't provide evidence of the crimes he believed Lard committed. What he needed to find was the departmental operational budgets, which would give more information to enable a thorough evaluation of the hospital's monthly revenue and expenses.

Ultimately, though, Terry understood that Nokomis Hospital would require a forensic audit to uncover potential financial misconduct, such as fraud, mismanagement, or regulatory violations. He hoped to find evidence of embezzlement, believing it was the only explanation for what was happening at the hospital.

As he climbed the stairs to the executive floor, he put on a pair of blue surgical gloves. He took a deep breath and then opened the door to the darkened suite, lit only by a few pilot lights from the security panels. The silence of the place felt unnatural, as if the expensive carpet itself muffled his footsteps. He shivered and took another deep breath, for there was no turning back now.

He switched on his flashlight and went inside. He had only been in Mike Lard's office once—the day he'd been hired—and that memory brought no comfort. Another shiver ran down his spine as he opened the largest of the six rooms in the C-suite.

Closing the door carefully behind him, he reached for the wall switch. The room flooded with brightness, making the space seem surreal and hostile at once.

The space was designed to impress: a massive mahogany pedestal desk gleamed like polished stone, flanked by a dark brown leather rocking chair that looked more like a throne than office seating. Behind it, a plate-glass window stretched across the wall, the black silhouette of Dona Bay outlined faintly by scattered boat lights.

Off to the side, a matching leather sofa and two wingback chairs gathered around a glass-topped coffee table, the kind of setup meant for discreet, powerful conversations.

Terry's pulse quickened. He moved swiftly behind the desk. He didn't have much time.

The middle drawer swung open first. Inside, a hospital checkbook and register were neatly arranged. He noted the account number and the bank's name: Citizens Bank. Strange; it wasn't Nokomis's usual bank. He flipped through the register—and froze.

The names jumped out immediately: Mike Lard, Steve Brophy, Charles McMann, Carl Billingly. Several others were unfamiliar. The amounts, though, were staggering: entries of $3,000, $7,500, $10,000—payments funneled like clockwork.

He set the checkbook aside and examined it more closely. Several handwritten notes described what appeared to be an "investment" in a supply warehouse. However, the numbers didn't add up—the purchase price was three times the market value. Why would the hospital buy a warehouse when there were supply shortages?

Next, he found a black leather notebook filled with ledger entries. He caught his breath as he traced the columns. The executives had established a covert system of revenue diversions and payouts, diverting hospital funds into private accounts. It read like a playbook of white-collar crime.

Reading closely, he found that the hospital's top executives misappropriated revenue for personal luxuries, including building luxury homes, purchasing diamond rings, taking expensive vacations, and overpaying for outpatient service facilities.

Even worse were the notations in the margins—reminders about "rings," "house lot transfers," "Bahamas condo." They weren't just stealing money; they were living off it.

His hands trembled as he spread open the register, notebook, and documents on the desk. Taking out his small camera, he began snapping photo after photo. He hoped he had enough film. He paused between clicks, each one sounding louder in his ears than it should have, as though the shutter might summon security.

He kept glancing at the door, half expecting Lard's heavy

frame to fill the doorway, his face twisted in rage. But Lard was in the Bahamas and not due back until 7 p.m. Terry reminded himself of that—again and again.

When the camera whirred at the end of its roll, he cursed softly, fumbling to reload. He hoped the shots he'd taken would be enough. After taking thirty-six pictures, he realized he was making a mistake.

He needed to make photocopies of the documents. He gathered the papers and hurried into the hallway, where the Xerox machine was. He turned it on but then impatiently returned to Lard's office while it warmed up.

He moved to the right-side drawers. In the bottom one, underneath some scattered stationery and a brass paperweight, he discovered something unfamiliar: a small glass vial with a powdery residue. Cocaine. He took another photo, his heart pounding. He knew about Lard's Saturday night "gatherings." Here was the proof. Should he take it? It probably bore Lard's fingerprints. He set it aside.

He heard the Xerox machine beep and hurried back to start photocopying. The machine was loud, and he broke into a sweat. He was too involved to stop now. After a few minutes, he finished, gathered the pages, and went back into the office and carefully replaced the originals.

Something made him pause. He looked at the other side cabinet drawer. He reached to pull it open, but it was locked. Where was the key? Maybe inside the center drawer? He looked carefully inside again, then paused once more.

Think. Where would it be?

Something made him feel the top of the drawer. What was it he felt? Taped to the top was a small key. He tore it out and unlocked the side drawer. He pulled it open. Inside were several thick files. One was marked "**New Warehouse Project**."

He flipped it open. This wasn't about a warehouse. It was a secret ledger—a shadow set of records used to track the real money trail. Terry's trained CPA eye deciphered the meaning of each page. It was spelled out in black ink:

Kickbacks from construction firms disguised as "consulting fees."

- Money laundering through shell vendors that billed for equipment and supplies never delivered.
- Phony companies—names that meant nothing, yet showed up repeatedly in the hospital's accounts payable.
- Inflated expenses tied to renovations and service contracts.
- Revenue skims from outpatient centers that were grossly overvalued.
- Transfers routed through Bahamian banks under thinly veiled "investment returns."

Terry's heart was throbbing; the beats hammered in his ears. He felt stressed. No, he couldn't be getting a migraine. Not now. He ignored the feeling. He couldn't stop.

He reached deeper into the drawer and pulled out another folder: "**Department Budgets, A & B**." This was the missing piece. It contained two sets of hospital departmental budgets.

The first set of budgets appeared to be the "official" version—what was presented to the board and auditors—that showed moderate expenses and tight margins. He was somewhat familiar with the numbers.

But the "real" version, buried here in the secret file, revealed the truth: entire departments gutted, revenues siphoned off, expenses inflated by millions. The cardiology budget alone showed a $750,000 difference between the fake and real numbers. Pediatrics, surgery, oncology—every department had been hollowed out to bankroll the executive circle.

When he reached the back of the file, he found more handwritten notes in Lard's scrawl: names, dollar amounts, and coded initials that hinted at kickback percentages. It was undcniable.

He placed the files on the desk. The stack of evidence looked damning. He forced himself to stay methodical. He needed to photocopy the most incriminating ledgers in the files.

Terry rushed back to the Xerox machine, copying everything page by page. He felt more at ease as he placed each document flat on the glass, pressed the start button, and the whirring noise broke the office's silence.

Finally, he was done. He carefully closed the drawer and glanced at the top of the desk where the vial of cocaine sat. He felt uneasy doing it, but he quickly placed it in a small plastic bag and slipped it into his pocket.

He stepped back to ensure he left everything as he had found it. He had what he needed. All that remained was to get the film developed, make copies of the documents, and hand everything over to Nicole.

What she decided to do with it would determine the future of Nokomis Hospital—and the men who had been ripping it off.

Chapter 23:
Investigations
Late Morning, Sunday, Sept. 16, 1984

When Jack's story came out on Sunday, residents of Sarasota County were shocked to learn that Nokomis Hospital planned to cut maternity services and had used charitable donations to cover financial losses.

Many hospital employees were pleased that the plan had been exposed, hoping it would put pressure on the board to halt it.

When Lard got home from the Bahamas later that day, he read the story and was furious. He knew Jack would publish a story, but he didn't know how convincing it would look in black and white.

He was also steamed because Kendall made him look like a fool. His denials of financial and operational problems rang hollow, and his comments about employee concerns seemed insincere.

The fallout came rapidly. Instantly, Lard and his management cronies had made enemies of the hospital's most prominent donors, including Donald Tusk and Dr. Valeri Paremi.

NOKOMIS HOSPITAL DIVERTS CHARITABLE DONATIONS TO COVER MOUNTING LOSSES; PLANS MATERNITY SERVICE CUTS

Jack Kendall
Herald-Tribune Staff Writer

Once a jewel of Florida's Gulf Coast, Nokomis Hospital now finds itself mired in financial distress, diverting millions of dollars in charitable donations to keep its doors open—a move that experts say may violate federal law.

To offset operating losses in the past two years, the 200-bed nonprofit hospital transferred more than $10 million from its tax-exempt foundation, according to internal financial statements obtained by the *Herald-Tribune*. The practice, legal analysts say, raises questions about whether the hospital improperly tapped donations that the Internal Revenue Service restricts for specific purposes.

An IRS spokesperson declined to comment on Friday.

Hospital executives defended the transfers. "Everything we did was legal," said Michael Lard, Nokomis's president and chief executive officer. He blamed Medicare's new prospective payment system,

173

which assigns flat reimbursements for patient stays, for the hospital's financial woes. "Like many hospitals, we've been hit with large Medicare cuts. It has caused us to look for alternative revenue streams."

Board Chairman David Royster echoed the defense. "We trust and believe in management. We wouldn't do anything that would hurt the hospital," he said. Asked when the board formally voted to authorize the transfer of restricted donations, Royster declined to answer. "On the advice of counsel, I cannot comment."

But at least one board member disputes that version of events.

"I have reviewed all the board secretary's meeting notes for the past three and a half years—all fourteen meetings," said Dr. Joel O'Neal, a cardiologist who joined the board earlier this year. "No discussion or vote was taken to use restricted donor money to fund hospital operations."

Two other trustees contacted by the *Herald-Tribune* declined comment.

A HOSPITAL IN DECLINE

Nokomis, which reported net patient revenue of $40 million in 1983, lost nearly $5 million that year. A $5 million transfer from its foundation turned what would have been a catastrophic deficit into a modest surplus on paper. Through the first half of 1984, the hospital reported another $7 million operating loss, again offset by a foundation transfer of equal size.

Despite the patchwork fixes, conditions inside Nokomis have deteriorated. According to more than a half-dozen employees who spoke on the condition of anonymity, the hospital faces chronic shortages of basic medical supplies—bandages, gloves, catheters, even toilet paper.

"A shortage of these supplies can significantly impact the hospital's ability to provide quality patient care," Dr.

O'Neal said. "It also indicates potential mismanagement."

Vendors have begun withholding services until past-due bills are paid, employees said. Maintenance crews, laundry services, and food vendors have all curtailed operations. "Creditors won't come in to fix things because the hospital owes them money," said one department manager. "Then we suffer, and the patients suffer."

LOOMING CUTS, ANGRY DONORS

Behind closed doors, Lard has floated proposals to shutter entire service lines. In a draft memo obtained by the *Herald-Tribune*, he recommended closing the hospital's maternity unit—a move that could eliminate 100 jobs.

Dr. O'Neal said Lard justified the cuts by telling him, "We lose too much money. Families can go elsewhere." Lard denied making those remarks.

For donors, the revelation that their contributions are being used to cover routine losses has been galling. "Something is rotten in Denmark, and it's not the fish," said Donald Tusk, a retired New Jersey businessman and Nokomis's largest benefactor. "I was under the impression donations were given for specific capital projects or uncompensated care, not to offset mismanagement or blatant theft."

BLAME AND COUNTER-BLAME

Lard insists Nokomis is a victim of federal policy. He said 80 percent of the hospital's revenue comes from Medicare and Medicaid. "When government payments are cut, we must reduce expenses in other areas," he said.

But rivals say the problem lies closer to home. "Most well-run hospitals still make money on Medicare," said Stacy King, chief executive of Sarasota Memorial

Hospital. "We knew two years in advance what each diagnostic group would pay and adjusted expenses accordingly." Sarasota Memorial expects margins of more than 10 percent this year.

Employees at Nokomis say management has avoided sacrifice. Executive salaries, bonuses, and perks remain unchanged or even increased, while frontline staff face shortages. "When I was a cardiology fellow at Beaumont Hospital in Royal Oak, Michigan, our executives took 25 percent pay cuts to keep the hospital solvent," Dr. O'Neal recalled. "It was called shared sacrifice. There is none of that here."

A PATTERN OF NONPAYMENT

Nokomis's refusal to pay vendors has led to lawsuits from lenders, staffing agencies, and service providers. In one case, a laundry contractor accused the hospital of routinely switching vendors to avoid payment and bouncing checks, calling it "a deliberate cash management process."

Lard dismissed such claims as exaggerated. "It's a cost of doing business," he said. "Hospitals operate on 3 percent margins, while suppliers gouge us at 10 or 20 percent."

But for patients, the impact is not abstract. A nurse call system in one unit has been broken for over a year because the repair company refuses to return without payment. In the emergency department, doctors say they sometimes lack reagents needed to confirm heart attacks.

"It's crazy," said one emergency physician. "We have patients' lives in our hands, and we're arguing over unpaid invoices."

Nokomis Hospital's future now rests with its board, which is scheduled to meet on October 10 to decide whether to close its maternity services. For employees and patients alike, the decision will signal whether the hospital can survive at all—or whether its decline is too far gone to reverse.

Chapter 24:
Conspirators at Work

Morning, Monday, Sept. 17, 1984

Mike Lard arrived at the office earlier than usual, still slightly hungover and tired from a weekend of cocaine, booze, golf, and gambling in the Bahamas. He had read Kendall's story the night before and hardly slept.

During the flight home, he made several decisions that needed his immediate attention on Monday morning. However, Kendall's story required new and urgent action.

"June, bring Gus Lessem and Charles McMann in here for a meeting at 10 a.m., and tell them they'd better have no excuses for being late.

"Yes, Mike," she said.

"And tell Charlie I need him to stay for a 10:30 meeting with Steve and John Riggles," Mike said.

"Yes, Mike," she said.

Lard knew Nicole McIntosh was right. He should have started preparing for the Joint Commission inspection as soon as he heard they would be coming last week. He was lucky they didn't conduct a surprise inspection, so at least he had some time to get ready.

However, he had been busy discussing the merger with National Healthcare, which he wanted the board to vote on at the October meeting. He also had to handle Cora and Harry's overdoses and Kendall's hospital stay.

Sure, he had other things on his mind. Now, he had no choice.

Kendall had written a story about the hospital's financial losses. While it was embarrassing, Lard knew that 25% of the nation's hospitals were expected to lose money in 1983, the first year of Medicare's new prospective payment system. The losses wouldn't get him in trouble.

What bothered him was that Kendall had found out the Nokomis Foundation had transferred $17 million in restricted charitable donations to the hospital over the past two and a half years.

The IRS would ask questions, and Lard needed to assure them the transfers were a mistake and would be repaid. He would also have to answer questions from the FBI and other state and federal agencies about other irregularities that Kendall uncovered. He had to find a way, however, to avoid an audit at all costs.

"Mike, Gus and Charlie are here," June announced.

Glumly, Lard began the meeting.

"First, Gus, I want you to get Dr. Lords to discharge Bobbie Kendall. Don't take another 'no' from her. Get her and her damned husband out of here," Mike said flatly.

"Any reason in particular? We usually don't interfere with medical decisions," Gus said.

"Tell Dr. Lords they have worn out their welcome. No, use your lawyerly skills to strongly suggest I want them out and that it is in their best interests to do so," Lard said.

"It's short notice, but I could ask her to find a medical reason to send Mrs. Kendall home. Maybe tell her the hospital will be very busy with the Joint Commission coming," Gus said.

"Remind Dr. Lords that her husband is on the board and that she is in line to head our new pediatric outpatient center," Lard said.

"I'll get on that right away. Did you need me for anything else?" asked Gus, who always tried to avoid getting too involved in hospital matters for plausible deniability.

"Hold on. Three things. Is there anything in that newspaper article that Kendall wrote that we could sue him over?" Lard asked. "There were several anonymous sources."

"I read it very carefully, and unless you tell me there are errors, everything I read that Kendall wrote is true," Gus said.

"Second, I want McIntosh and Myles fired. They directly disobeyed my orders not to give Kendall financial data or inside information," Lard said.

"Mike, we don't have any proof they did anything. Do you have evidence we can cite?" Gus asked.

"They used confidential financial data right from Brophy's files. Where would Kendall have gotten that unless Myles stole it and gave it to him?" Lard asked angrily.

"We need evidence, maybe a confession from him. You can fire him, of course—both of them—but that won't keep them quiet," Gus said. "They may even feel freer to talk on the record. We don't have any confidentiality agreements

179

with them, unfortunately."

Lard poured himself a glass of water, broke open an Alka-Seltzer, let it fizz, then gulped it down. He wiped his lips on his shirt and bowed his head in defeat.

"Three, the foundation transfers that Kendall reported. How bad will that hurt us?" Lard asked, his voice cracking.

Nokomis General Counsel Gus Lessem coughed, then cleared his voice. "They didn't waste time. We've been contacted by the Florida Attorney General's Office, the FBI, the IRS, and the U.S. Department of Health and Human Services."

Lard sat down, stunned. "Already?"

"If they have hard evidence, I believe this will likely lead to investigations for healthcare and insurance fraud," Lessem said.

"Enough, Gus. You can leave. Let me know when the Kendalls are gone," Lard said, belching.

Turning to McMann, Lard asked, "Charlie, we need to prepare for the Commission. Can you hire a quality improvement company today to get us ready for that inspection?"

"This is short notice to hire them. I've spoken with Premier Consultants, who can do it, but it won't come cheap. They quoted $10,000 per day," McMann said.

"Are they good? Better, will they do what we want?"

"They know what they're doing, but it's a tall order. I don't need to tell you that we're a mess right now. We're a week or two away from purchasing the supplies from our Chinese vendor for our warehouse, and then we can restock our hospital," McMann said.

"At this point, I just want to minimize the damage," Lard said. "They need to start by 6 a.m. Thursday to get done by early next week, which is when my source told me the inspections would start, but he couldn't be sure."

"I will call them, and they can send some teams over as soon as possible," McMann said.

"Now, I also want you to call Baxter and have them deliver all the supplies that are on backorder," Lard said.

"They'll want checks upfront and no discount. They knew we were going to bypass them from Shenzhen Supply Co.," McMann said.

"Fill those damn shelves," Lard yelled. "Tell accounting to cut those checks for $50,000."

"The total bill for all this could be more than $100,000," McMann cautiously said. "I'm not sure we have that in our cash accounts."

"Tell Steve. He'll know where to get the money," Lard said. "We've got to do this. Now, go ahead and make the calls. Come back here when you're done. Steve and John should be here soon."

Lard checked the clock. It was 10:30 a.m. Brophy and Riggles would arrive soon, so he headed to his liquor cabinet and poured himself a tall, neat Dewar's.

He had been drinking more in the mornings lately, and he was also snorting more cocaine at the start of the day. He reached into his drawer to grab his coke stash. It wasn't there. Where had he put it? Was he paranoid, or had someone moved it?

Just then, June rang. "Steve and John are here."

"Call Charlie and tell him to join us when he's done, then send them in," Mike said, still wondering what happened to his coke vial.

Brophy and Riggles entered Mike's office. They sat in chairs by the desk, waiting for him to speak. They knew he was upset over Kendall's article.

"Gus told us there is nothing we can do about McIntosh and Myles ratting on us, at least now," Lard said. "Maybe not legally, but John, I want Palmer to ratchet up his investigation, find out how they're sharing information and what they are giving Kendall. Gus said if we have evidence, we can fire them for cause. I will ruin their careers, and nobody will believe their stories about us."

"Palmer has been tailing them and keeping notes, but he will love doing more on this assignment. He hasn't had much to do since you asked him to come up from Miami," said Riggles, whose mob connections were crucial in protecting their scams.

"I believed we needed him for this merger and to handle any board issues. I didn't expect to find traitors among us. I'm glad I urged him to come early, though I wanted him to meet everyone," Lard said.

"You also wanted to start cashing in on the cut you've been paying the Cubans monthly for protection," Riggles said. "I told you the investment would be worth it. They've helped my business tremendously by sabotaging the work of my competitors."

The phone rang. "Charlie is coming in now," June said.

"Mike, everything's ready. The company will send some consultants this afternoon, and the full crew will arrive tomorrow morning. They will inspect every department and do what they can to prepare for the inspections," McMann said.

"Tell them to concentrate on sterile processing. We know we've had issues since we outsourced," Lard said.

"The surgeons and the nurses will talk about the canceled surgeries and the dirty instruments," McMann said.

"Make sure the company throws away those reports and substitutes ones that provide better explanations," Lard demanded.

"I already explained our problems. That is one reason their price is so high," McMann said. "They will do what they can to hide the problems."

"Now, let's talk about the National merger," Lard said. "They're in on the deal. They will assume our debt and liabilities and pledge $25 million to the foundation to help support charity care and improve our technology."

"What about the transfer of the foundation money?" Brophy said. "That was illegal. We knew it then, but for obvious reasons, we didn't want to inform the board and include it in the financial statements."

"They agreed to donate another $20 million to the foundation to cover those losses over the last three years," Lard said.

"It must be done carefully, as the FTC and the DOJ now will review the merger closely, especially since everyone has read Kendall's article," Brophy said. "And if we get a bad inspection, the scrutiny will increase."

"I know. I know. That's why I want the board to approve the letter of intent. I'll write a memo to the board promoting this merger. I expect you both to persuade the board members that this is a good deal," Lard said.

"Right, boss," McMann said.

Lard glanced at Brophy, who nodded.

"Now, we need to meet again soon once Palmer finds out what Terry and Nicole are telling Kendall," Lard said. "We may have to take more drastic action."

Chapter 25:
Newborns Go Home

11 a.m., Monday, Sept 17, 1984

The morning after the *Herald-Tribune* published the hospital finances story on the front page of the Sunday paper, Dr. Lords marched into Bobbie's room without knocking.

"We have decided you're well enough to be discharged," she said briskly. "Can you be ready in an hour?"

Surprised, Bobbie could hardly speak. "I've been saying I'd like to go home soon, but you said yesterday that I might be here another week?"

"You've been here nine days. We think you should go. Your husband has asked me to transfer you to Sarasota Memorial, and we believe you can go home today and see Dr. Rafferty in the morning," Dr. Lords said.

Bobbie felt much better and was ready to go home, but the decision still seemed rushed. "Did you talk with Dr. Chastain about this?" she asked.

"No, but I'm sure it will be all right with her as long as you see Dr. Rafferty in Sarasota," Dr. Lords said.

"Are you *sure* the babies are all right to leave?" Bobbie asked, her voice full of concern.

"I will fill out the discharge forms," said Dr. Lords as she left the room.

A nurse entered a moment later with a chart in her hands. "Well, looks like you're going home," she said with a frown. "How are you feeling?"

"Fine, I suppose. I'm just stunned by how sudden this is," Bobbie said. "Do you know what's going on?"

"No. I was just told to get you ready, but both babies have been doing great. Eli's been a little sleepy this morning, but his breathing's steady. Ella's alert as usual. I'll print your discharge papers."

Another nurse peeked in and added, "We'll miss you all. You've been one of the quietest rooms on the floor...at least for now."

Truth be told, Bobbie wanted to spend the rest of her maternity leave at home.

Still confused about Dr. Lords's change of plans, Bobbie called Jack at the newspaper, where he had been working since last Friday morning. The plan this week was for him to work mornings, then drive to Nokomis after lunch to visit Bobbie and the twins for a couple of hours, then return to the paper.

"That's odd. We're not entirely ready for you to come home. Did you talk about your discharge with Dr. Chastain?" Jack asked.

"Not yet. Dr. Lords told me I could go, but acted strangely about it. She advised me to see Dr. Rafferty immediately. I got the impression someone wants us out," Bobbie grumbled. "I think they read your Sunday story. You shook things up, as usual."

"I have much more, but I first wanted to call Lard's bluff about Medicare being to blame for everything," Jack explained. "I'm sure the IRS and maybe the FBI will be interested in the money transfers to the foundation."

"It's probably all right. At least the twins are healthy. I want to bring them home. What's ready?" Bobbie asked.

"We have the basics: cribs, changing table, and most importantly, diapers," Jack said with a laugh. "I can call my mom and ask her to prepare the house for you and the babies. When are your parents coming?"

"Probably not until next week. They want to wait until we're settled. Dad doesn't like to do much, and Mom can't disagree with him."

"Before we leave, I'll call Dr. Chastain about your discharge and Dr. Rafferty at Sarasota Memorial to see if they know anything about this quick discharge decision," Jack said.

"That's a good idea. I'll feel better away from here. There's a lot of stress at this hospital. You can feel it in the air," Bobbie said.

"I'll make the calls and drive down to help you prepare. Just take your time. No need to rush, and don't let them discharge you before I get there," Jack said.

"I'm not so sure. Dr. Lords acted like she wanted me out immediately."

"All right. Just wait until I get there before you do anything."

"I will. By the way, I love you," Bobbie said.

"I love you too," Jack replied.

Jack opened his wallet to find Dr. Chastain's number. He

dialed it and got her answering service. "This is Jack Kendall. Leave a message for Dr. Chastain that Dr. Lords has discharged Bobbie Jackson—err, Bobbie Kendall."

Jack hung up and dialed Dr. Rafferty's phone number. A secretary answered.

"Hi, this is Jack Kendall calling about Bobbie Kendall's discharge from Nokomis," he said. "Could I please speak immediately with Dr. Rafferty?"

The secretary asked him to hold, and then Dr. Rafferty picked up.

"Hi, Glenda? Jack Kendall here. Dr. Lords just told Bobbie she would be discharged within the hour. Do you know anything about this?"

"Nobody told me. Last I heard, she was planning to stay a few more days to make sure her blood pressure remained stable. How is she?" Dr. Rafferty asked.

"It still fluctuates, but not as much, and she is on IVs from time to time. Is it safe for her to be discharged?"

"I know Dr. Chastain. She wouldn't discharge Bobbie unless it were safe, but it's not like her to call me about taking over."

"It wasn't Dr. Chastain. It was Dr. Lords. I can't reach Dr. Chastain. I think it has to do with my story yesterday. Did you read it?" Jack asked.

"Oh, yes, everybody read it. How are the twins?"

"Dr. Lords said they can be discharged with Bobbie. She said everybody can go home. Of course, Bobbie's thrilled, but she's concerned about the quick change of plans."

"Let's make an appointment to see Bobbie tomorrow. I have two o'clock open," Dr. Rafferty said. "I will contact Dr. Jones, a pediatrician in my office, about seeing the twins right after. In the meantime, if Bobbie or the twins become distressed, call me and bring them into the ER immediately."

"Sounds good. Bobbie's doing much better and looks forward to seeing you."

"Tell her I'm so happy she is doing well and that I will see her tomorrow at two," Dr. Rafferty said.

"Thanks," said Jack as he hung up.

Jack quickly called Nokomis Hospital and asked to speak with Bobbie. A few minutes later, she was on the line.

"Hi, Jack. What did you find out?"

"Not much, but Dr. Rafferty said it's okay to leave. She'll see you tomorrow afternoon," Jack said. "I'm leaving now and will be there in 30 minutes. Don't go anywhere without me."

"I'll ring for the nurse to see if everything is set for me to leave. See you soon," Bobbie replied.

* * *

Jack made the drive to Nokomis in 25 minutes, parked the Mustang, and headed straight for the surgical wing. Dr. Chastain was emerging from an operating room, peeling off her gloves.

"Jack? What's wrong?"

"Bobbie's being discharged. Dr. Lords gave her an hour to leave. Did you approve this?"

Dr. Chastain's eyes narrowed. "No, I did not. She's stable, but I didn't sign off on this. I'll look into it immediately. Call me at my office once she's home."

Jack nodded. "I will. Thank you."

Several minutes later, Jack entered Bobbie's room. She was packed, dressed, and sitting in a wheelchair. Two nurses were fussing over the twins.

"Eli's still asleep. That boy could sleep through an earthquake," one nurse said.

The other smiled at Bobbie. "You've been a model patient. Try to rest when they rest—though I know that's easier said than done."

Minutes later, Bobbie was wheeled toward the front entrance, the twins in special hospital strollers. Jack carried Bobbie's bag while attendants helped load the babies into their rear-facing car seats in the Mustang GT.

Josh saw them heading out. "Why are you leaving? Was it that article?"

"It's the only reason I can think of," Jack whispered. "Did you hear anything?"

Josh shook his head. "No, but let me help you to your car."

"Thanks," said Jack as he handed Josh Bobbie's small suitcase.

"I've got something to tell you," Josh said, glancing around. "I helped your friend Terry with something Sunday morning."

Jack pushed Bobbie toward his Mustang, thinking about what Josh said. He looked up with a puzzled expression. "What's that?"

"He'll be in touch about it soon," Josh quietly said, handing Jack the suitcase. Before turning to leave, he whispered: "I'm working with Nicole and Jane."

"I see. Hey, call me any time," Jack whispered gratefully.

* * *

As Jack drove north along the Tamiami Trail toward Sarasota, he kept thinking about the message Josh had given him: that Terry would be in touch with him soon and that he was working with Nicole and Jane. That was good news. Lard had muscle, but now Jack had some more.

He also kept glancing over his shoulder at the special passengers in his back seat.

"How's everyone doing?"

"We're good," Bobbie said. "Eli's asleep."

Ella stayed alert, making gentle grunts and snorts as Bobbie leaned forward periodically to check on her brother.

"When we get them home, I want to take a lot of pictures," Jack said.

"I have a surprise about that," Bobbie said.

"What surprise?"

"Alex is at the house. He's going to handle all the photography."

Jack smiled. "Perfect. He'll get great shots."

* * *

Jack pulled into Cherokee Estates, punched in the code, and the gates swung open. He drove to his house, tapped in another set of codes and entered his property. Mrs. Laura Kendall stood on the porch with Alex and his camera.

"Look at you!" Laura said, hugging her daughter-in-law gently. "And look at them—oh, Jack, they're beautiful!"

Alex snapped pictures as Jack carried Eli inside, with Bobbie and Laura following behind with Ella. They discussed baby clothes, bottle schedules, and how long Bobbie's two-month maternity leave would actually last.

"Two months?" Laura scoffed. "You'll need three."

Bobbie laughed. "Don't tempt me."

The house was warm, safe, and filled with the sounds

of two healthy babies. Jack was starting to relax when the phone rang.

"Hello?" he answered.

"Jack, this is Jane Willoughby," came the voice on the other end. "You told me to call you at home if something happened. The Joint Commission and the state health inspectors are coming next week, just like I told you. Mike Lard's about to find out what it's like to go into labor."

Jack smiled grimly. "Then it's going to be a very long week for him."

Chapter 26:
Whistleblower Meeting

7 p.m., Monday, Sept. 17, 1984

The Old Hickory Restaurant was just off U.S. 41 in north Sarasota, far enough from Nokomis to stay out of sight. Jack Kendall slid into a corner booth facing the door—always the reporter's habit—while the muffled sounds of conversation and the clinking of glasses filled the dim bar.

Terry Myles arrived minutes later, tall, dark-haired, and athletic. He seemed like someone who could blend in anywhere. He leaned across the table, his voice barely above a whisper.

"Jack Kendall?" Terry asked.

"Right on time. Sit down, Terry," said Jack with a comforting smile. "I'm glad to meet you."

"Nicole told me I could trust you, and I've got a lot to tell you," said Terry.

"That's what I'm here for," Jack said. "Let's discuss it."

"First, you need to know what I found in Mike Lard's office."

Jack reached into his briefcase and placed his recorder on the table. He turned it on, the red light glowing between them. "Not for attribution, I understand," he said.

"You can't quote me," Terry warned, his eyes flicking toward a couple at the far end of the bar. "Mike Lard warned me not to talk with you."

"I just want to set the record straight. Tell me everything."

Terry exhaled. "Early Sunday morning, when he and the others were out of town, I visited Lard's office. In his desk, I found a checkbook for a slush fund—money siphoned from the hospital's accounts. I found several files and documents, and I also found a small bottle of cocaine."

Jack nodded, his pulse racing. He'd expected that based on what he saw himself the week before. "You have proof?"

"I took some pictures and photocopied everything else. Here are some of them." Terry slid a thick envelope across the table.

Jack flipped through them quickly—at least 25 pages of photocopies of ledger pages, the checking register, and pictures of a vial of cocaine.

"I knew it was dangerous. If he caught me, I'd be done."

"This is amazing," said Jack, scanning the copies of the checkbook with payments to names he recognized: Steve Brophy, Charles McMann, John Riggles, Harry Goldfarb, and Jimmy Giles. He didn't immediately recognize Manfred Lords; he wondered if that was Dr. Lords's husband.

Then he noticed another familiar name: Delman Palmer. He was at the party. Nicole said he worked for Riggles, but unlike the others, she couldn't get his photo. However, when

Jack showed her the picture he took of Riggles and Palmer at the party, she confirmed who they were.

"Do you know a man named Delman Palmer?" Jack asked.

"No," Terry said. "I saw his name listed, but I never heard of him."

"Nicole knows who he is. I need to find out more about why he's at the hospital. I heard him talking with Riggles last Saturday night at that party in the C-suite. He is involved with Lard and the embezzlement in some way."

"I'll check into him," Terry said.

As Jack reviewed the documents, Terry began to talk. "My heart was pounding when I saw the evidence in Lard's drawer, especially the cocaine... I'm not sure I did the right thing, but I took it."

Jack looked up at Terry. "You took the bottle of coke?"

"Yes, I figured it has Lard's fingerprints on it."

"What did you do with it?"

"I have it in my car in my floor safe. I need to give it to you when we go outside," Terry whispered. "I have everything I needed to bring them down, if it comes to that."

"Does Nicole know about all this?"

"I gave Nicole copies of everything Sunday night, but I want to discuss with Nicole the complete portfolio of documents, including the two sets of hospital books, that we will share with the press. These should be enough for now, especially with the cocaine vial. She's working late tonight, preparing for the inspection. Your article really shook up the hospital," Terry explained. "I'm really nervous about that and thought you, as a newspaper reporter, would know what to do with the cocaine vial. I didn't want to give it to her."

Jack smiled. "I will have to talk with my editor about what

to do with it, but this is just the beginning, with what you found and the many more people to interview and documents to review."

"Jack, Nicole is the reason I got involved in all this. She told me Lard and the other execs were stealing from the hospital. I figured it was mismanagement, maybe embezzlement. I didn't expect...this."

Jack paused, thinking back to the party from the previous weekend. "Did the cocaine surprise you? Have you heard anything about Lard's parties?"

Terry offered a grim smile. "Oh, I've heard plenty. Private booze-and-drug parties, invitation-only, hosted within Lard's circle. I was never invited, but I knew the guest lists included many executives, a few hip employees, donors, doctors, and, given these documents, many conspirators and collaborators."

Jack was taping the conversation and taking careful notes. "Go on."

Terry leaned forward across the table, his voice low but steady. "At first, I thought it was just bad budgeting—overspending, inefficiency, no plan. But Jack...this isn't incompetence. It's organized theft. I could go over these documents and pictures, one by one, if we had more time."

Jack set down his Heineken, sensing the severity in Terry's tone. "We should do that, but how bad is it?"

Terry exhaled slowly, as if steadying himself. "Lard and his crew—Brophy, McMann, the whole rotten bunch—used hospital money like it was their personal checking account. We're talking luxury homes, diamond jewelry, trips to the Bahamas, Pebble Beach, Augusta." He laughed bitterly. "And that's just the warm-up."

Jack's pen hovered over his notepad. "You're telling me

hospital funds paid for all that?"

"Paid for it and more," Terry said. "Hospital credit cards covered liquor tabs, designer clothes...even private chefs. They melted silver dust from used X-ray film into bars and sold them to coin shops, precious metal dealers, and pawn shops. I have a list of those businesses.

Terry continued. "Donations that were supposed to buy lifesaving equipment? Gone. Sitting in offshore accounts or in local banks to be used to supplement their lifestyles and acquire more front companies to scam the hospital and generate legitimate business to launder money."

Jack's eyes narrowed. "Are there doctors involved?"

Terry's jaw clenched. "That's the worst part. Lard called them 'superstar' recruits. In reality, he was buying loyalty— referrals for inflated salaries, free vacations, and real estate deals. All of it clearly violates anti-kickback laws."

Thanks, I hope I don't get any more corrections, but my books have technical aspects and there is only so much I can check and confirm.

Jack leaned back, tapping his fingers on the desk. "So the people in charge of a hospital—the one place that's supposed to put patients first—are running a racket?"

Terry nodded grimly. "Yeah. And every dollar they steal is a dollar that doesn't go to patient care. That's the part that keeps me up at night, Jack. We're not just talking about money here. We're talking about lives."

Jack nodded and looked at Terry, wondering if this young hospital executive, not much more than a couple of years older than him, understood the importance of what he had discovered.

"I can keep you out of the newspaper, but eventually, if the

FBI, HHS, and state law enforcement start investigating, you'll have to come forward and testify about all this," Jack said.

Terry grimaced, closed his eyes, took a deep breath, and began to explain himself.

"Jack, I've been through so much this year. I lost my wife and two young children in a house fire while I was out of town at a healthcare convention," Terry said, his voice cracking.

"Nicole told me about it. You don't need to explain all of this now. We can talk about it later. I'd like to know how you're doing," Jack said. "I believe your motives for exposing these crimes are to do good."

"Thanks, Jack. Nicole and Jane were right about you. You really care. You're not just in it for a headline or two," Terry said, looking at Jack for reaction.

The reporter half-smiled. "I've been through a lot myself. I lost a wife to murder not too long ago."

Terry raised an eyebrow. "I didn't know. I guess we have more in common than I realized."

"Unfortunately, yes. Listen, there's something else you should know. I've looked into stories like this, where the criminals stop at nothing to protect themselves. You need to take precautions from now on. Be very careful," said Jack.

"I will. Lard told me I would be watched from now on," said Terry, glancing around the bar for any familiar faces. "I have a handgun I keep in my car for protection, and I bought another that's at my house."

"I understand, but just stay alert," Jack replied.

"You mentioned implications. I've also thought about that," Terry said. "Sunday night, while reviewing all the documents and comparing them with the hospital's financial records, I started contemplating what to do."

"I can imagine."

"I wondered, what if I go to the board? Would they even listen? Royster is chairman, and Giles is on the board. Nicole told me Dr. O'Neal and Chris McVay are probably okay, but what if they're not?"

"I still need to talk with Dr. O'Neal. Nicole said he is giving her information. I don't know anything about McVay. She's new, and I've been told she's been to the parties," Jack said.

"I can't be seen talking with Dr. O'Neal or really anybody on the board. But I wondered, what if I went to the authorities? Would they act quickly? Or would Lard cover his tracks before anyone shows up at his door? And what about me? Lard doesn't just let things go. He'd ruin me. Or worse."

"All that is possible," Jack agreed, wondering where Terry was going with his doubts.

Terry said softly, "So, after all those thoughts, I decided the safest way to get it out was to give it to you anonymously. You already wrote the first story, and Nicole practically begged me to give you what I found."

Jack nodded, sliding the envelope into his briefcase. "We'll make sure this sees daylight. Once I finish my interviews, I'll write a story that will nail Lard and Co."

Terry finally offered a genuine smile.

"One piece of advice," Jack said, staring directly into Terry's eyes. "Don't take any more chances. Lie low. Things are about to get very interesting."

* * *

While they talked for 45 minutes, neither man noticed the heavyset figure nursing a whiskey and occasionally getting up to walk past them to the bathroom.

Delman Palmer had been shadowing Terry Myles since he left his house, keeping a steady distance. At the Old Hickory, he slid into a dark corner near the bar, close enough to catch pieces of the conversation between Myles and Kendall. He didn't need every word—he heard enough. Terry was spilling secrets. Worse, he'd handed Kendall a thick envelope and showed him photos.

Palmer's jaw tightened. Lard had warned him about Kendall—the *Herald-Tribune* reporter who wouldn't quit. Now Myles had tied them all together.

When the meeting ended, Palmer waited until Kendall left. He slipped out, got into his car, and drove to a nearby Winn-Dixie on U.S. 41. He got out, walked briskly to the payphone outside the grocery store, and dropped in a quarter.

"Yeah," Palmer said, his voice low, controlled. "Myles talked to Kendall. I couldn't hear much of what was said. He gave Kendall a brown envelope."

There was a long silence. Then a sharp intake of breath. On the other end, Mike Lard's voice rose with anger. "Did you hear anything?"

Palmer hesitated. "I heard him mention Nicole McIntosh. He gave her copies of whatever he gave Kendall."

"Did you hear him mention anything about a vial of cocaine?" Lard snapped. His words came out quickly, almost in a panic. "The vial was in the bottom drawer of my desk. It's gone."

Palmer frowned. "You think he broke into your office? I didn't hear him say that, but they were talking softer at times."

On the other end, Lard's breathing slowed, replaced by a cold, deliberate tone. "Here's what you do. Myles and Nicole—

they're a problem. I want you to back them off. You know what that means."

Palmer's lips curved into a smile. "Consider it handled."

"Let's talk more about them later, but Kendall," Lard added, his voice dropping to a growl. "I want him and that wife of his reminded who they're up against. Scare them. Don't kill them—yet. But give them something to think about."

"Understood," Palmer said. "You know the going rate for silence."

A laugh, quick and bitter, echoed through the receiver before the line went dead.

Palmer hung up the phone and lit a cigarette, exhaling slowly into the night. He felt the familiar adrenaline rush—the job could be dangerous, but it paid well, and he enjoyed the hunt.

*   *   *

Walking to his car, Palmer thought he was so smart. He had followed Myles to the Old Hickory, eavesdropped and reported his findings.

What the thug didn't realize was that his surveillance of Terry and Jack's conversation hadn't gone unnoticed. A tall, casually dressed man sitting at the bar, talking with the bartender and another man, had witnessed the entire scene.

And it wasn't just any patron—it was Ed Kendall. After Terry told Jack the night before that he and Nicole were being watched, Jack had asked Ed to run a quiet cover while he met with Terry.

Ed didn't miss much, and what he'd just seen convinced him Jack's instincts were dead on: the hospital mess wasn't just corruption. It was deadly serious.

As Ed sat quietly at the bar, outwardly just another late-night drinker, his eyes were fixed on the man watching his brother and the hospital whistleblower. He'd followed him in right after Terry arrived and had watched the man hover too close for coincidence.

When Palmer slipped out after Terry and Jack left, Ed settled his tab, tossed a tip on the counter, and followed at a distance.

Palmer drove just a short distance before pulling into the shadowy corner of a Winn-Dixie parking lot. Ed kept his car dark and rolled to a stop among other vehicles, far enough to remain unnoticed but close enough to get a good look. He watched Palmer walk to the payphone, shoulders tense, a hand cupped over the receiver.

Ed stayed in place, watching. He was too far to hear Palmer talking, but he was lively, his free hand making sharp gestures in the air. Whoever was on the other end had him fired up. After a two-minute chat, Palmer clicked the receiver back into place, searched for his keys, and walked toward his sleek black BMW parked in the dim light.

As he approached, Ed slid lower in his seat and pulled out a small notebook. He waited until Palmer opened the door, the dome light flashing just long enough for Ed to catch the license plate. He wrote it down carefully.

When Palmer drove off, Ed stayed put. After giving him a safe lead, Ed eased his car forward and parked near the phone booth. He stepped out, checked both directions, then leaned close to the phone. The metal was still warm from Palmer's hand. Ed pulled out his notebook again and jotted down the number stamped on the inside panel, along with the approximate time Palmer had placed the call.

He stood there for a moment, staring at the digits. A pay phone number might not look like much, but he knew a friend at the telephone office who could tell him the number that was dialed. And that number could lead him straight to whoever Palmer had been calling.

Ed pocketed his notes and returned to his car. He turned back onto U.S. 41 South, toward Jack's house in Cherokee Estates. Jack had been right to ask for backup. The game he and Terry Myles had stepped into wasn't just about exposing fraud—it was something with much higher stakes.

Chapter 27:
Followed

Afternoon, Tuesday, Sept. 18, 1984

Mrs. Laura Kendall drove Bobbie to Dr. Rafferty's office for her
first OB-GYN appointment since leaving Nokomis Hospital.
The twins were sleeping in matching car seats in the back,
their tiny chests rising and falling in perfect rhythm.

On the way, Laura looked over. "How do you feel about
leaving the hospital so suddenly?"

"Honestly, Laura, I was ready to leave," Bobbie said. "I
know it was because of what Jack wrote, but being there was
stressful. Even when Jack wasn't visiting, employees would
come up to me with stories about Mike Lard and the rest of
the management. They're angry."

"You seemed to get special care from the nurses," Laura
said.

"I did get a lot of attention, and they were kind," Bobbie
admitted. "But I'm glad to see Dr. Rafferty. She doesn't have
any agenda."

"You mean like the doctors at Nokomis—Dr. Chastain and Dr. Lords?"

"Dr. Chastain was fine. Dr. Lords was never nice," Bobbie said flatly. "I didn't understand that."

Laura nodded in agreement.

"Here we are," Laura said as she pulled into the medical office building's parking lot. "Now you'll get some good news."

"I hope Jack gets here. He promised to meet us," Bobbie said as she got out of the car and walked to the backseat.

They took out the twins and settled them into their double stroller. They stayed quiet, for now. Bobbie knew that silence could end at any moment. After this appointment, they had a pediatrician's visit scheduled for the twins' first well-baby check.

Ten minutes after they sat in the waiting room, a nurse stepped out.

"Mrs. Bobbie Kendall? Dr. Rafferty will see you now."

Bobbie walked in, followed closely by Laura, who was pushing the stroller. "It doesn't look like Jack is going to make it," she said.

They rounded the hallway's corner, and Dr. Rafferty was waiting by the exam room door with a smile. "I've been looking forward to seeing you all. How are these little darlings?"

"They're doing well," Bobbie said. "Sleeping and eating without too much fuss. Eli is quiet until he's hungry. Ella cries now and then, looking for attention, but nothing major."

"Don't worry. Premature babies," Dr. Rafferty explained as she entered the room, "often have stretches like this in the first few weeks—long, deep sleep cycles, steady feeds, and only brief fussiness."

"They're certainly doing that!" Bobbie exclaimed.

"Have a seat. You must keep a watchful eye because preemies can change quickly, sometimes becoming more restless as their bodies adjust to life outside the hospital." Dr. Rafferty paused, glancing at how calm they appeared.

"Don't let the quiet fool you," she said with a warm smile. "This is a good start, but they'll find their voices soon."

Laura chuckled softly, adjusting the stroller blanket over Ella. "Sounds like we'd better enjoy the peace while it lasts."

"I cleared a half hour of my schedule and spent the last 10 minutes reviewing the notes from your surgery and your stay at Nokomis," Dr. Rafferty said.

"Did you talk with Dr. Lords?" Bobbie asked.

"I had a brief conversation with her Monday after a maternity nurse called me about your discharge," Dr. Rafferty said.

"What did she say?"

"Not much. Just that you'd get better care at home. I sensed she didn't want to talk about your sudden discharge. I didn't comment, but she knows eclampsia can recur within a month of the initial onset. Because of that, we typically don't push mothers and newborns out the door."

"To tell you the truth, Dr. Lords was rude in how she ordered me to leave the hospital," Bobbie said. "I was relieved to go because there is so much tension and stress there, but the more I think about it, the more irritated I get."

"I was disappointed with Dr. Lords," Dr. Rafferty said. "She never returned my call about your post-hospital care. The hospital's medical team was supposed to create a follow-up plan for the twins to coordinate with your pediatrician and me."

"They never told me anything, just that I was discharged. Jack had to call you to set up the appointments," Bobbie said, her voice tight with frustration.

"It might be because they discharged you so quickly," Dr. Rafferty said. "Or it might be...for other reasons."

"You mean Jack's article?"

"I don't want to say that," Dr. Rafferty replied carefully, "but it can be dangerous to discharge a patient after an emergency C-section because of eclampsia and giving her only ten days to recover, and without a plan."

Bobbie felt better getting an acknowledgment that what she experienced wasn't high-quality healthcare.

"Now, let's take a look at how you are," said Dr. Rafferty as she began a pelvic and breast exam.

"The incision is healing fine. Your blood pressure is normal. Have you had any headaches, pain, or vision changes since you were discharged?" Dr. Rafferty asked.

"No, I've been feeling pretty good except for some soreness. I'm thirsty all the time," Bobbie said.

"This was a good first appointment. Given what happened, I want to see you again next week," Dr. Rafferty said. "Call me if you experience any bleeding, unusual pain, or headaches that last more than two or three hours."

* * *

Bobbie's next appointment was with Dr. Barbara Jones, the twins' pediatrician. After 30 minutes in the waiting room, Jack still hadn't arrived, so Laura called the newspaper.

She returned, sat down and said, "Jack's editor said he left ten minutes ago."

Suddenly, a familiar voice filled the room. "Did someone mention my name?" Jack said as he strolled into the office. "Sorry, I'm late. A lot is going on. What did I miss?"

Bobbie gave a relieved smile. "I'm just glad you're here. You missed the drama of my physical exam. I'm fine, but I need to take it easy for the next month."

Jack nodded. "We've got it covered."

Just then, a nurse called out, "Mrs. Bobbie Kendall?"

Jack jumped up. "That's us."

Bobbie slowly stood up and started wheeling the twins down the hall, following the nurse, with Jack and Laura close behind. They entered the exam room. A few minutes later, Dr. Jones arrived.

"Good morning. Well, do I have the whole Kendall family here?" Dr. Jones asked with a smile. "Let me see these two. What are their names?"

"Eli and Ella," Bobbie proudly said.

"These two are amazing," Dr. Jones said after examining them, smiling as she placed each of them back into the warmth of the stroller. "They're doing very well for preemies."

Dr. Jones leaned forward. "Here's what I want you to remember. First, track every feeding, diaper change, and sleep stretch for the next month. It'll help us spot patterns, good or bad."

Bobbie nodded. "I've been doing that already; it's the only way I can keep up with them."

"Second, limit visitor access. Their immune systems are still developing, and even a mild cold could send them back to the hospital."

Bobbie sighed. "Jack's mother will be happy to hear that. She's been shooing people away at the door."

"Good. And lastly, don't ignore your own recovery. Eclampsia is nothing to brush off. If you have headaches, vision changes, or swelling, call Dr. Rafferty or me immediately."

"I will," Bobbie promised. "I'm still getting some headaches, but nothing like before."

"Keep an eye on it," Dr. Jones said. "The babies need you healthy."

"I'll see you next month, Mom, Grandmom, and Dad," she added warmly.

* * *

When they stepped outside, Laura spotted a black BMW idling near the curb. She'd seen that car before.

"Jack, don't look right now, but in a moment glance toward that black BMW on the right by the road. Have you seen it before—maybe parked outside your house?"

As they approached Laura's blue Cadillac, Jack glanced to the side and noticed the BMW. He wondered if it was the same black BMW Ed had identified the night before at the Old Hickory. Ed hadn't yet confirmed the license plate or the phone number the man had called after leaving the bar where Jack had met Terry Myles.

"I'm not sure who it is," Jack said, not wanting to frighten Bobbie until he knew more. "I see a guy in dark sunglasses sitting in it. He does seem to be watching us."

Laura added, "That's the same car. I thought I saw it following us earlier. I meant to mention it."

"Don't act surprised," said Jack. "Let's get the twins in the car. I want you to follow me to the newspaper. We'll see if it follows us."

They loaded the stroller into the trunk and quickly buckled the twins in. A few minutes later, Laura turned to check on the babies and saw the BMW in the side mirror.

"He's coming," she said quietly.

Laura's grip tightened on the steering wheel. She followed Jack as he made a series of turns through downtown, testing whether the car stayed behind. Each time, the BMW mirrored their moves.

When they reached the *Herald-Tribune's* parking lot, the BMW slowed at the corner, its dark windows reflecting the afternoon sun.

Laura cut the engine and turned around to see how Bobbie was doing with the babies. "Are you all right?"

"That man is trying to scare me," Bobbie said, her voice tight, "and it's working."

Jack jumped out of his Mustang and looked to see if the BMW had entered the parking lot. It was driving past slowly.

"Let's get you inside where it's cool," Jack said as he took the stroller out of the trunk and helped Bobbie with the babies, all while keeping an eye out for the BMW. "I'll call Ed. He'll know what to do."

"Do you think this has to do with your Nokomis story?" Bobbie asked.

Jack looked toward the street again. He didn't want to tell her what he really thought, but he was sure Mike Lard was behind this.

"I don't know. Let's get you inside, and we can figure out a plan," Jack said.

As Bobbie pushed the stroller into the newspaper office, she felt reassured knowing whoever had been following them had put himself on Jack's radar. And Jack never took his eyes off a target.

Half a block away, Delman Palmer settled into his seat, a thin, crooked grin curling his lips. He'd made his point, just as Lard wanted. Bobbie Kendall wasn't out of his reach—not here, not anywhere.

Chapter 28:
Shadows at the Gate

3 p.m., Tuesday, Sept. 18, 1984

The newsroom was quieter than usual that afternoon. Jack Kendall leaned back in his chair, his desk cluttered with yellow pads, a coffee-stained mug, and a spread of photographed notebooks and files Terry Myles had slipped him the day before.

His pencil circled a single name on the register: Delman Palmer. Nicole said he worked for Riggles at the hospital. But Jack sensed he did much more, and he was bad news. He hoped Ed would find out more about him.

The phone buzzed. Jack snatched it up.

"Ed? What've you got?"

"You were right about that BMW," Ed Kendall's voice was low, clipped. "Delman Palmer rented it in Miami three weeks ago. Guy's a Cuban Mafia enforcer, out of Hialeah. He's done muscle work for gambling crews, smuggling rings, and construction companies."

"Palmer. This guy works for Lard. Hold on. I've got something," Jack straightened in his chair. He rifled through the stack of copied registers Terry had photographed. His eyes locked on an entry. "Yes. I thought so. Palmer's in here. One check—five grand. Paid straight from Lard's executive account."

"Fits," Ed said. "And listen, Palmer made a call last night after he left the Old Hickory."

"Let me guess," Jack said. "He called Lard."

"Right," Ed replied.

Jack pinched the bridge of his nose. "So Palmer's not just some mystery man. He's Lard's hired muscle."

Bobbie's laugh echoed faintly from the conference room down the hall, where she sat with Eli, Ella, and Laura. Jack turned his chair toward the glass wall, watching his wife cradling one of the twins. His voice hardened.

"This is serious, Ed. Palmer's a gangster. Do you have somebody you can send over to take Bobbie home and stay with her and the babies?"

"I'll do it myself," Ed said without hesitation. "Francis is with me. We'll be there in ten."

*   *   *

Ed's Jeep Cherokee rumbled into the *Herald-Tribune* lot. Inside, Francis adjusted his ball cap, scanning the street before slipping out.

They walked into the newspaper lobby, checked in with the receptionist, and took the elevator to the fifth floor, where they went to the conference room.

Bobbie looked up as he entered. "What's wrong?" she asked, rising instinctively.

"We're your escorts home. Ready to go?" Ed asked with a smile.

Jack saw Ed and Francis and quickly sprinted into the conference room. "I'm sure you all want to go home? The twins are past due for their naps."

Laura glanced at Jack. "They've been napping all along."

Bobbie stood up, frowning, and began to gather their things. "Did you find out about that black BMW?"

Ed glanced at Jack, who nodded. "It's some guy Nokomis hired to keep an eye on his favorite reporters."

"Jack, what are we going to do?" Bobbie asked, concern etched across her face.

"Ed and Francis are going to take you home and keep an eye on things. I have a few more hours of work here, then I'll be home, and we'll make a plan," Jack said.

Minutes later, Ed guided Bobbie, Laura, and the bundled twins into his Cherokee, while Francis ducked into Laura's Cadillac and started it up. Francis pulled out first in the Cadillac, taking the long way around the Tamiami Trail. If Palmer were watching, he'd have to pick one car to follow.

* * *

Ed entered Cherokee Estates, punching in the keycode and driving to his brother's house. He parked under the carport by the front door.

He helped Bobbie carry the twins inside, setting them gently into bassinets near the living room fireplace. Bobbie's

213

hands trembled as she smoothed the blankets.

"You're safe here," Ed said firmly. "Cameras, alarms, the works. Francis'll be here in an hour with Laura's car. You four won't be alone."

Bobbie managed a nod. "Thank you, Ed. I just..." She broke off, clutching the bassinet harder. "I don't want the babies growing up with shadows outside the window."

"They won't," Ed said. But his eyes flicked toward the dark line of trees beyond the iron fence.

* * *

An hour later, the black BMW pulled up three blocks from Jack's gated subdivision. Delman Palmer stepped out, a cigarette between his fingers. He walked past houses and through yards until he found Jack's stately home. He studied the tall iron gate and fence, the cameras fixed at every angle, the motion-sensor floodlights mounted on the corners of the house.

He walked the perimeter once, hands in his pockets, boots crunching over gravel.

"Damn fortress," he muttered. He tugged a small notebook from his coat and scribbled. He snapped a few pictures, shook his head, and left.

He drove to the nearest pay phone.

"Palmer here."

Mike Lard's voice crackled on the other end. "Well?"

Palmer exhaled smoke. "Mike, Kendall's house is locked down—fencing, cameras, sensors. You'd need a five-man strike team to get in. Better bet is to hit him on the move, away from the house."

A pause, then Lard's voice, smooth but edged with fury: "Never mind the Kendalls. Come to my house tonight. Late. I know how to silence both Myles and McIntosh. Killing the messenger isn't enough."

Palmer grinned, tossing the cigarette into the gravel. "Understood." He slid back behind the wheel and drove off.

* * *

Ed sat in Jack's study, eyes fixed on the security monitor. One of the exterior cameras showed a man pacing along the fence line. He leaned forward, jaw tightening.

"Well, Delman Palmer," he murmured, recognizing him from the picture Jack took at the party and when he followed him out of the Old Hickory. "Now we've got you on tape."

He picked up the phone, dialing Jack's direct line at the *Herald-Tribune*. "You'd better get back here soon," Ed said when his brother answered. "Our friend in the black BMW just showed up at your front gate."

Jack gripped the receiver a little tighter. "What's he doing?"

"He's pacing back and forth. He took a couple of pictures. Wait, he looks like he's leaving. Yes, I don't see him anymore," Ed said, relief in his voice.

"If he comes back, call Lieutenant Stevens," Jack said. "Let him know what's happening."

Jack went back to writing the story about what Terry found in Lard's office. He knew it had to be iron-clad to get past the newspaper's careful and methodical lawyer, Peter Gantz. He still struggled with how to report the vial of cocaine that Terry removed. If he reported it, he knew he would eventually need to explain to the police how it came into his possession.

Chapter 29:
Inspections Begin

Morning, Wednesday, Sept. 19, 1984

Early that morning, eight Joint Commission and Medicare state inspectors entered the hospital unannounced and headed straight for the surgery department.

Denise Smith, the surgery director, called Charles McMann in a panic. "I thought you told us the inspectors wouldn't arrive until next week? They're here, and we're unprepared. They'll find all sorts of problems. We can't handle it."

"Now? That's impossible. Premier isn't supposed to start our improvement program until tomorrow," McMann said in disbelief.

"Call me when you find out something."

Smith walked up to one of the inspectors, who seemed to be in charge. "I'm Denise Smith, director of this department. May I ask why you arrived unannounced?"

"I'm Dr. Christy Wells, chief of this team. We've received numerous complaints about patient care and are here to do a complete inspection."

"I see. Is there something I can do to help?"

"Yes, stand by. We will have questions. Why is this patient still on the gurney?" Dr. Wells asked, checking the surgical schedule taped to the wall.

Smith looked at the schedule, wondering how to explain. McMann had told her to make excuses when inspectors asked about problems. But Premier hadn't had a chance to replace the real reports with forgeries. She had to tell the truth.

She responded slowly, her voice strained. "We don't have enough circulating nurses right now. Anesthesia is short two people today. We're calling staff in and doing the best we can with what we have at the moment."

"How long has the patient been waiting?" Wells pressed.

"Forty-five minutes," Smith admitted after she checked the schedule. "This was supposed to be a routine procedure, but we can't move patients until the pre-op checklists and quality reports are done. We don't have the staff to keep up with the paperwork, much less the patients."

Wells and her two associates exchanged a grim look, jotted down notes on their observation forms, and then moved to the sterile processing department. There, the problems deepened.

One inspector lifted the lid on a tray marked *sterile*. Inside, the clamps bore dried blood. A suction tube still had cloudy residue clinging to its walls.

"This tray was cleared for surgery?" Wells asked sharply.

One of the SPD technicians nodded wearily. "It went through the autoclave last night. We were getting ready to send it up."

Another inspector, Dr. Roy Wilson, picked up a scalpel and held it under the light, tilting it slightly. Rust speckled the blade. "This poses an immediate threat of infection," Wilson said flatly, holding it up for the others to see.

A second technician shifted uncomfortably. "We just don't have the time to do it the right way. Two positions haven't been filled for months. I'm on doubles every week. Sometimes we send trays back upstairs half-done because the OR is screaming for them."

"That is unacceptable," said Dr. Wilson. "Give me your name. You won't get into trouble. We need to document who is talking with us."

Dr. Wilson and Dr. Wells interviewed twenty surgery nurses and doctors, along with five SPD technicians, and recorded the names of all individuals who provided information.

By mid-afternoon, Wells, Wilson, and the other six inspectors entered the emergency department. The waiting room was crowded, with families restless and patients coughing into tissues. Inside, Dr. Wilson opened a crash cart and discovered expired vials of epinephrine. Another cart was completely missing atropine.

"Where are your supplies for oxygen therapy?" Dr. Wilson asked.

The charge nurse sighed. "We've been short on masks for weeks. Catheters, IV tubing—it's all hit or miss depending on what came in that morning."

Dr. Rashad leaned against the nurses' station, his white coat wrinkled, his face tired. "We're patching holes every day," he said quietly. "Some nights we don't even have enough staff to cover all the bays. When the ambulances roll in, we pray we have what we need."

Documentation failures appeared everywhere the inspectors examined. In surgery, no data on two-year infection rates had ever been compiled. In sterile processing, the sterilization cycle checks had been skipped for three consecutive months.

Wells closed a binder with a sharp snap. "These aren't oversights. This is systemic. Without records, you don't even know how unsafe your environment is."

"We're doing the best we can," a nurse pleaded.

The staff interviews painted a grim, human picture. A young nurse admitted she had bought gloves and bandages with her own paycheck when the supply room was bare. A surgical tech confessed that they sometimes borrowed instruments from one tray to complete another. In the ER, a resident recalled patients being diverted to other hospitals because critical drugs weren't available.

"It's not that people don't care," said a veteran nurse, her eyes tired but fierce. "We care too much. But management doesn't give us the tools or the staff to do our jobs."

By the end of the first day, the inspectors had cataloged dozens of deficiencies across the three departments. Some were minor. But others were labeled "immediate jeopardy"— findings that, left uncorrected, could place patients' lives at direct risk.

Chapter 30:
Jack's Concerns

Late Afternoon, Wednesday, Sept. 19, 1984

Just as Jack was packing up to leave for the day, the phone rang.

"*Herald-Tribune.* Jack Kendall here."

"This is Jane Willoughby. The Joint Commission and Medicare inspectors started this morning," she said. "I haven't had a chance to call until now."

"Did you talk with them?"

"The state inspectors, contracted by Medicare, began in the OR, and the commission is going department by department, checking logs and interviewing staff and patients," she said. "I was told they will be in maternity tomorrow."

"Whatever memos you see, can you make copies for me?" Jack asked.

"I will. We'll receive a preliminary report when the inspectors leave, likely Friday afternoon. I know Mike Lard will try to keep that away from you, especially if it's bad, but we'll get you a copy somehow," Jane said.

"I'm counting on you. You have my phone numbers. I want to write about it Friday night for Saturday's paper, if possible," Jack said, pausing. "Oh, one more thing: can you have Terry Myles contact me at home?"

"I'll try," she said.

Jack wanted to ask Terry to go on the record with Nicole to reveal everything they knew. He was conflicted about doing this; he didn't ask this of sources lightly. He remembered what had happened—the difficulties and tragic outcomes—when he had asked James Brewster to go on the record and blow the whistle on Granger Phosphate two years earlier.

*   *   *

Jack hopped into his Mustang and drove home, lost in thought. How could he write a story that would expose Lard without revealing Terry or Nicole? Lard already suspected them, even warning them. The dark thought crossed his mind again—James Brewster's murder.

Ed had told him about Delman Palmer's criminal history. He was dangerous, and he was threatening Terry, Nicole, and possibly others at the hospital. When he got home, Jack decided it was time to call Sheriff Bagley about Palmer. Stacy King mentioned that Bagley knew Lard had hired muscle from Miami; it had to be Palmer.

Then his thoughts shifted back to his upcoming stories. How was he going to write the inspection article? And how could he tell the explosive story of fraud with all the allegations and evidence Terry had given him on Monday?

His head filled with questions, he stepped through the door and into his home. Bobbie had news.

"Hey, Jack. WKXY called. They asked if you could do a radio interview on Saturday about the inspection results at Nokomis."

"Who called?"

"Peter Jahns. He left his phone number."

"I'll call him in a few minutes," Jack said, loosening his tie. "Then I need to check in with Terry and Nicole, then call Sheriff Bagley."

"You seem to be in a rush. Have a bad day?" Bobbie asked as she approached him.

"Not really, just the usual. Oh, I've completely messed up, haven't I?" Jack asked.

"You mean you forgot to ask how I am and about little Eli and Ella?" Bobbie teased, looking at him with a pretend sad face.

"I see you're as wonderful as always. How are they?"

"They've had a busy day. I'm going to put them down about seven. Don't forget to wish them goodnight," Bobbie said, turning to go upstairs.

"Now you're really teasing. They have no idea who I am," Jack said.

"They're learning your voice and do know who you are. They can see and smell us," she said. "When I sing to them and when you tell funny stories to them, they know it's us. So please, come up when you are done with your calls."

Jack nodded, then entered the den and closed the door. He wanted to see his babies before they went to sleep, so he decided to start making his calls. He dialed Peter Jahns.

"Could you tell Peter I can do the interview? ... What time do you want me at the station? ... Okay, fine. Tell him I'll be there."

Jack hung up and decided not to wait for Terry to call. He would try his office number directly. Terry answered on the second ring.

"Jack! I was just about to call you. Lard's panicking. The Joint Commission and the state Medicare survey team have been here all day. He's been riding us nonstop to 'get our stories straight.'"

Jack frowned. "Stories straight? Meaning cover up the mess."

"Exactly," Terry said. "He told me in no uncertain terms that if anyone starts talking to the inspectors, their careers are over. He also reminded me I'd be fired if I helped you with any more stories."

"Are you getting cold feet?" Jack asked.

"No, I'm more committed than ever. These inspections are going to give the hospital a black eye. Lard will have to make changes," Terry said.

"What can you tell me about the inspections?"

"Not much. You'll get more info from the nurses or doctors. Maybe after they're done, call me then," Terry said.

"All right. I called for two reasons. First, I've found out several things about this mysterious man, Delman Palmer, and I want you to be careful if you come into contact with him," Jack said.

"Palmer? After you asked me if I knew him, I looked into it myself and found out some things," Terry excitedly said.

"Go on," Jack encouraged.

"He's been seen lingering in the hospital. Everyone avoids him, but he's contacted board members about the importance of staying silent and following orders."

"Mm, um," Jack mumbled.

"I also found out he pressured several managers to falsify information to the Joint Commission and state inspectors. They won't do it, but they're scared," Terry said.

"He's bad news. Stay away from him. We're almost sure Lard hired him from Miami as an enforcer. You need to be careful. This guy's dangerous," Jack warned.

"I'll be careful. Jack, I have to tell you something. There was a man—it must be Palmer—who parked down the street from my house last night. He just sat there for two hours. He knows I saw him. He's trying to scare Nicole and me."

"He's been by my house, too. Just be careful. Have you talked to Nicole? I haven't spoken to her in a week, not since my Sunday story came out, and I want to warn her as well."

"I haven't seen her in a few days. We've been careful not to be seen together after Lard told us not to talk with you. We don't want to raise any more suspicion, but Palmer's been frightening her, too," Terry said.

"Can you get word somehow to Nicole? Ask Jane or Cathy to have her call me tonight?" Jack asked. "I need to talk with her."

"I'll try to get a message through to her," Terry said, pausing. "Jack, what about my story? When are you going to use what I gave you?"

"Soon. So much is happening right now with the inspections and what I've already written. It's complicated," Jack said. "But we will report everything. Be patient."

"If you need to talk with me, don't come over to my house or call there," Terry warned. "Call me directly here—but don't leave any messages. I'll check in with you when I can."

"Thanks."

Jack set the receiver down, exhaled, feeling the tension

settle back in. Palmer worried him more than ever. The man seemed to be escalating—turning his intimidation not only toward Terry and Nicole but also toward board members and hospital staff. Jack had no doubt Palmer was acting on Lard's orders.

At least he'd warned Terry about him. And he'd tried to reach Nicole. Terry didn't know much about the inspections yet, and Jack would need to piece that together with whatever Nicole, Jane, and Cathy could tell him. But what Terry *had* shared about Palmer was deeply troubling, another sign that things were spiraling faster than anyone realized.

* * *

Fifteen minutes later, Jack was upstairs in the nursery with Bobbie, changing Eli's diaper, when the phone rang. "Maybe that's Nicole," he said. "Can you take over?"

"Oh, sure, a likely excuse," Bobbie said with a pretend snarl.

"Jack, Terry asked me to call you," Nicole said. "What do you need?"

"We haven't spoken in a few days, and I just wanted to check in on you."

"I'm doing okay. Doing what I can," she said.

"I want to talk with you about something serious, but I am waiting on the results of the inspection reports. Will they be finished on Friday?" Jack asked.

"Everyone thinks so. Usually, these inspections take three days. They could always come back next week, but we think it'll be Friday."

Jack asked, "Can you get me a copy of the report?"

"I doubt Mike will let Terry or me anywhere near those

reports. We've been excluded from everything since your story came out Sunday, which I thought was great," she said. "Jane is still in the clear; she'll get you a copy."

"Could you make sure to call me on Friday if it comes out, just to touch base?"

"Sure. There is something you should know. Yesterday, when I came home from work, I saw a black BMW idling half a block away. He made sure I saw him. It was Palmer. Do you know anything else about him? I told Terry about some of the things I found out he does in the hospital."

"Yes, I'm sure he's on Lard's payroll. He followed my wife, Bobbie, to her OB-GYN appointment on Tuesday and came by my house later. He's the same guy I saw at the party and the one you confirmed," Jack said.

"I heard he works for Riggles, doing odd jobs, but I didn't know much about him before you told me you saw him at that party. Since then, I've seen him around at the hospital. He has suddenly made himself known to people," Nicole said.

"So that you know, tonight I'm going to report what he is doing to Sheriff Bagley. Meanwhile, stay away from him. Be careful; I'm worried."

"He's only trying to scare me," Nicole said.

Jack thought about how much to tell her. He didn't want to scare her unnecessarily, but she needed to be more cautious. After a moment, Jack asked, "You should contact the Sheriff's Office. You know Lieutenant Stevens, don't you?"

"Jim? Yes, of course. And tell him what? That I'm a whistleblower, and my boss asked Palmer to follow and scare me?" Nicole asked.

"I know. It's pretty thin right now," Jack said. "But I'm going to tell Sheriff Bagley what we know about Palmer."

"Whatever you think is best," Nicole said.

Jack decided to tell her. "My brother found out he's associated with the Cuban Miami Mafia."

"It doesn't surprise me, but I don't think Lard would ask him to hurt me."

"I hope not, but what about Lard? Terry told me he is getting pressured to keep quiet," Jack inquired.

Nicole exhaled sharply. "Lard is angry with me. He pulled me into his office this morning and said, 'You're either loyal to this hospital, or you're finished here.' He's said that to me before, but this time he seemed angrier, if that's possible."

Jack tightened his grip on the phone. "Terry said the same. Listen, I can't stress this enough for you and Terry. You both need to be cautious. I don't have to tell you not to open the door to Palmer if he shows up. I'll find a way to tell the story with what you've given me without revealing your identity or putting you in danger."

"Jack," Nicole said softly, "I might not have been completely honest with you. I understand the risks I face. Palmer is watching our houses, and I know I said he's just trying to scare us. That's not entirely true. He's waiting for orders."

Jack didn't answer right away. His pen hovered over his notebook. He hesitated to tell Nicole what was on his mind. He sensed that the more bad news Lard received from the inspections and the press, the more dangerous he would become.

"Nicole, I'm going to tell Sheriff Bagley that Palmer followed us and staked out our house, and I'm worried about what he might be doing to you. But you need to talk with Lieutenant Stevens at the Sheriff's Office. Lard and Palmer are threatening you and Terry. You've got to involve law enforcement to push them back," Jack said emphatically.

"I thought about it, but once I do so, Lard would use that as grounds to fire me. I need to be here at the hospital as long as I can to provide a voice for the nurses, employees, and patients," she said.

Jack didn't respond. He realized she was determined to expose Lard and the corruption at Nokomis Hospital, no matter what it cost. While he couldn't sway her, he could tell Bagley to watch Palmer. He had a bad feeling about this guy.

"Stay safe, Nicole, and call me when the inspection is done," said Jack. "Bye for now."

"Don't worry! Bye," she said.

* * *

Jack was upstairs again, helping Bobbie put the twins to bed. He was holding Ella, and Bobbie was holding Eli. He was telling them a bedtime story about little Sami the Star and how he felt all alone until other stars floated into his neighborhood. He wasn't alone any longer.

Just then, the phone rang. "I'd better get it, Bobbie. Can you finish the story?"

"Finish it? I have no idea how *Sami the Star* ends!" Bobbie exclaimed.

"Make it up. I always do. Besides, at 12 days old, they have no idea what you are talking about!" Jack chuckled as he bolted into the hallway and grabbed the phone.

"Jack, this is Jane calling again from the hospital. Something has happened."

"Tell me," Jack asked.

"I just heard Harry Goldfarb died. They found him dead

from an overdose of crack cocaine in his car," Jane said.

"Oh, sorry to hear. I had wondered what happened with him after he overdosed at that hospital party," Jack said.

"I'm calling because the word is that his death was suspicious. I heard he was going to expose Lard."

Jack immediately thought of Delman Palmer. "You think Lard had him killed?"

"After Harry recovered from his stroke, people said he was a changed man," Jane said. "I don't know for sure, but I think Lard is responsible. Everyone is talking about it."

"Have you or anyone at the hospital told the Sheriff this?"

"No, should I?"

"I think so. I'm sure deputies will investigate Harry's death. Maybe this is a good time to let them know about Lard's parties and how Harry and Cora Billingly almost died at one of them," Jack said.

"I'll think about it."

"Please let me know if you do. I'm going to write about Harry's death, and it would be helpful if the detectives learned about the parties from inside the hospital."

Jane didn't respond.

"Thanks for calling about Harry, Jane," Jack said, hanging up.

Five minutes later, Jack went back to the nursery to watch Bobbie rock the twins to sleep. They had two rocking chairs, so theoretically, they could soothe both twins at the same time. As soon as Jack sat down, the phone rang again. He sighed, shook his head at Bobbie in apology, and hurried to take the call in another room.

"Hi, Jack, this is Cathy. Do you have a few minutes?"

"Yes. I'm trying to help Bobbie get the twins asleep. How

are you and everything in maternity?" Jack asked.

"Amazingly, everything remains the same. The board will vote to close maternity, but not until these darlings are discharged. The supplies we obtained before the inspections have been helpful. At least we can keep our people and provide top-quality care until the last minute," Cathy said.

"Have you heard anything about mental health? That was one of the departments I thought was on the chopping block, especially with the merger coming up," Jack said.

"I talked with my friend, Pat Baltimore, the director of the behavioral health department. She said Lard plans to close her department on November 1. The word is that after National buys Nokomis, it will consolidate services into its Charlotte County hospital," she said.

"Do you have anything in writing on that?"

"After your foundation story, management doesn't do memos anymore. Let me ask Pat if she has anything."

"Could you ask her to call me?"

"Sure, and thanks so much for keeping the pressure on management."

"You heard about Harry Goldfarb?" Jack asked.

"Yes, he died under suspicious circumstances," Cathy said.

"What else do you know?"

"Harry's wife is so upset," Cathy said. "I heard she called the police about it because Harry had been clean since his overdose."

"Thanks for calling, Cathy," Jack said. "I've gotta get back to the twins. Let me know how the inspections go."

* * *

Before returning to the nursery, Jack had to call his brother. He knew he had another story and needed help.

"Ed, I have another assignment for you," Jack said.

"What's that?" Ed asked.

"Harry Goldfarb, environmental services manager at Nokomis Hospital, has died. He was the one I told you about who overdosed on crack last month at that hospital party," Jack said.

"Sure, I remember. What do you need?" Ed asked.

"I want you to get Goldfarb's death certificate and talk with detectives. I have two sources saying something unusual happened, and his wife allegedly spoke with the police. It might be the Venice Police Department, but call Lieutenant Stevens first."

"Sure will. How are Bobbie and the twins?"

"Everything's good, but I want you to talk to Stevens. Tell him everything you know about Delman Palmer," Jack said. "Tell him about how he followed Bobbie from her OB-GYN's office and how he came by to stake out my house. I think he might have been involved with Goldfarb, and he's threatening Nicole and Terry. They need protection. I'll tell Bagley, but you talk with Stevens."

"Right away. Talk with you soon," said Ed, hanging up.

*   *   *

It was nearly 7 p.m., and Jack needed to finish his next phone call quickly. Bobbie was still upstairs settling Eli and Ella, and he had promised to say goodnight to them.

He dialed Sheriff Tom Bagley, who answered on the second ring. "Jack? Everything all right?"

231

"Not really," Jack said, lowering his voice. "Sorry to call you at home, Tom, but I need to report something."

A pause. "Go ahead."

"It's about a man by the name of Delman Palmer," Jack began. "He followed Bobbie and my mother yesterday to an OB-GYN appointment for the twins. Then, when I met them there, we spotted him, and he followed us over to the *Herald-Tribune*."

Bagley exhaled slowly. "Who is Palmer? And why are you so worried?"

"You don't know? I'll explain in a moment, but the situation didn't end there," Jack continued. "Later, after Ed and Francis escorted Bobbie home in Cherokee Estates, Ed spotted him on the security camera walking in front of my house, taking pictures. Ed thought he was staking us out."

"That's a hell of a pattern," Bagley muttered. "So, who is this guy?"

"Palmer works for Mike Lard at Nokomis Hospital—unofficially, anyway. He handles Lard's dirty work."

"Lard's upset you wrote that story? And you can prove Palmer works for Lard?" Bagley asked, cautious.

Jack scratched the back of his neck, thinking hard. How could Tom not know about Palmer? He knew Lard had hired Miami muscle—Stacy King at Sarasota Memorial had told him as much.

"Tom, I've been told you know something about this, so c'mon, tell me," Jack prodded.

"I can't talk about ongoing investigations," Bagley replied. "What do you know about this Palmer?"

"Ed's been digging, and he found Palmer has Miami Mafia ties and a criminal record."

Bagley didn't respond right away. "Why would a man like that be following your wife? Your mother?"

"Because of Nicole McIntosh and Terry Myles," Jack said quietly. "They work at Nokomis Hospital and are giving me information about corruption at the hospital—embezzlement, fraud, Lard's deals. Palmer has been threatening both of them. Nicole told me she was scared, but she doesn't want to report it. Terry told me that Palmer had shown up at his house twice. Now he's turned his attention to my family."

Bagley's tone hardened. "All right. Let me look into this."

"Good," Jack said, glancing toward the stairs where he could faintly hear Bobbie talking to the twins. "Tom, this guy isn't bluffing. He's dangerous."

"I hear you," Bagley said. "I'll take care of it."

Jack nodded to himself, grateful but still uneasy. "Thanks, Tom. I've got to get upstairs."

"Go," Bagley said.

Jack hung up, paused for a moment, and took a breath. Then he headed upstairs to kiss Eli and Ella goodnight. He was sure they had already fallen asleep.

As Jack climbed the steps, a familiar dread crept up his spine—the memory of James Brewster, the brave phosphate engineer who'd trusted him...and paid for it with his life.

Now, with Nicole and Terry caught in the crosshairs—and Palmer circling his own family—he felt the same fear tightening around him. He had sworn he would never again put a source in harm's way. But the truth was sinking in with cold clarity: it might already be happening.

Chapter 31:
Bad News

5 p.m., Friday, Sept. 21, 1984

Charles McMann didn't want to deliver more bad news to Mike Lard. However, as COO, he was the designated contact for Medicare inspectors and Joint Commission surveyors.

"Mike, I have the summary of findings and deficiency reports. We've been cited for 42 Medicare infractions and 15 JCAHO violations," McMann said, trying to move past the worst part quickly. "There was nothing I could do. They all said it would have been worse if we hadn't resupplied."

"Why did they surprise us? Unannounced visits aren't supposed to happen," Mike grumbled.

"We were told both Medicare and the Joint Commission had a high number of patient and employee complaints," McMann replied softly. "The number and severity warranted the surprise inspection and survey by both agencies, the chief inspector, Dr. Christy Wells, told me."

"God damn squealers," Mike said. "Have you notified

Premier that we don't need them next week?"

"Yes, but they weren't too happy about it. They charged us a $5,000 cancellation fee for the emergency prep contract," McMann said.

"So, what exactly did we fail?"

"We got hit pretty hard," McMann admitted. "Surgery is shut down for a week while we clean SPD. We have 10 days to submit a correction plan, three weeks to fix the SPD and surgery—the major violations—and 60 days to complete everything else. We will get the preliminary report on Friday."

Lard had nothing to say about the seven-day pause for the surgery and sterile processing departments. Once he started hearing reports from departments on Wednesday, he accepted the punishment. He knew it was risky to make the hospital look worse than it was, but his goal was to convince the board that the merger was the only viable option.

"Tell Tonya to come in. I want to issue a statement to the press. I'm sure Kendall will hear about it," Lard said solemnly. "We've got to get ahead of this. I don't want National to back off on their handshake agreement to merge because of bad publicity. We also need to strengthen support for the board to approve this plan. Otherwise, we're going down."

June beeped him on the intercom. "Mike, John Riggles is here and says it is urgent."

"Send him in," Lard said. "John, I hope you have good news. Today has been all bad."

"More bad than good. Palmer said he briefed you earlier about the Myles-Kendall meeting on Monday night. He will be focused on locking down Terry and Nicole this week to prevent more leaks," Riggles said.

"How so?" Lard asked.

"He's been following them after work since Tuesday and then staking out their houses at night for a few hours, going back and forth, making it clear to them that he's there," Riggles said. "They used to speak regularly and meet at McIntosh's house, but they stopped doing that this week. Palmer also found out how they exchange information."

"How's that?" Lard asked.

"They put notes on the front tires of their cars when it's time to meet. We can use this information later, if we need to take action," Riggles explained.

"Good; what else did he find?"

"A few other things, but let me tell you first what we found out about Dr. O'Neal. He's likely to oppose the merger. He somehow got the draft memo you wrote."

"How did you find that out?"

"We have a few doctors in O'Neal's group who support what we are doing and told Delman," Riggles said.

"O'Neal is a disappointment, but word is out in healthcare circles about the proposed merger," Lard said, shaking his head. "You can't keep secrets for long in our industry. I expected Kendall to hear about it eventually. He's written about the foundation transfers. I'm sure he's planning to write about the merger and whatever Terry gave him."

"Palmer and I talked about it. We think he will," Riggles said. "He hasn't published anything yet, and it's been a week since that first story."

"Do we know if Nicole has any documents at her house?" Lard asked. "And if Terry plans on giving more documents to Kendall?"

"We don't know, but Delman asked if we want him to break into their houses to look," Riggles said.

Lard poured himself a scotch and motioned for Riggles to move closer.

"I've spoken with Delman about a way to take care of Terry and Nicole. It's best you not know about it," Lard said.

"What about Kendall?" Riggles asked.

"We might have to take care of him, too," Lard said, swirling his liquor in his glass before taking a drink. He paused. "It depends on what he writes."

Chapter 32:
Dirty Instruments

5:15 p.m., Friday, Sept. 21, 1984

Jack was at home when the phone rang.

"This is Jane. Did you hear about the preliminary reports the Joint Commission and Medicare inspectors gave us?"

"No. I've been calling everyone. You're the first to call back. What happened?" Jack asked, taking out his notebook.

"They're still briefing the departments and McMann. I left when I got the reports. Come by my house, and I'll give you copies," Jane said.

"I'll be right there. See you in 15 minutes," Jack said.

From the other room, Bobbie heard the phone ring and Jack's short discussion. "I thought coming home early was too good to be true. Are you going into the newspaper after?" she called out.

Before leaving, he went into the downstairs baby room.

"Yes, but don't worry. I'll ask Ed and Francis to come over."

"Call me when you get to the paper. I want to know everything," Bobbie said, rocking the twins in their bassinet.

Jack nodded. "I'm going to be late tonight, maybe midnight. I have to call Rick to let him know what's coming."

Bobbie smiled. She knew what he had to do: a deadline story that needed to explain, be precise, but most importantly, be accurate.

"Rick, I've got it—the inspection report. I'll be there in about an hour," Jack said.

"Is it bad?" Rick asked.

"Nokomis got slammed. Send out a photographer. You might be able to get shots of the inspectors as they leave. See you soon."

Jack picked up his car keys and rushed out the door. Five minutes later, he was traveling south on U.S. 41, headed to Osprey, a small town just north of Nokomis.

* * *

Jack knocked on Jane Willoughby's door at 5:30 p.m. A few seconds later, she opened.

"Come in. I have everything ready for you," she said.

"How are you?" Jack asked, noticing she seemed nervous.

"I'm fine. Things are getting a little weird at work, but I'm managing the best I can. We all are. I want to tell you about a person I've been working with on this. She has more details on these inspection reports."

"Who is it? Someone I know?" Jack asked.

"Yes. Call Cathy Leesay. She serves on the quality assurance committee across various departments. Ask her about sterile processing," Jane said.

"I've met Cathy. She's the charge nurse in the neonatal unit. Will she go on the record?"

"Ask her. She knows they plan on closing her unit, and she's looking for another job. Still, what she's doing is dangerous. Here's her number," said Jane, handing him a slip of paper. "You remember the threats we've received? It is getting worse, but I don't want to discuss that."

"All right, just be careful," Jack said. "I'll call Cathy, and then I have to call Nokomis for a comment, then write this story."

"Good luck, and nail those bastards," she said.

* * *

Jack hurried to the *Herald-Tribune* office, sat down at his desk, and read quickly through both inspection reports. He couldn't cover everything tonight, but there was enough.

Fifteen minutes later, he called Cathy. She picked up on the first ring.

"Hi Cathy, this is Jack. Can you talk?"

"Have you read the report?" she asked cautiously.

"Yes. It seems the most significant findings are the dirty instruments and the surgery shutdown. That'll be my lead. What are your thoughts?"

"Not for attribution, but you can quote me as an anonymous source. Is that what you say?" Cathy asked.

"That's right, but Jane said you are looking for another job anyway. Can't you go on the record?" Jack asked.

"You do want me to get another job?" Cathy asked, laughing nervously.

"All right. Talk to me."

"Both reports are damning. Closing the surgery department for a week will hurt financially, since that's where we've been generating most of our revenue," she said. "It will make it harder to fix our problems within 60 days. Otherwise, we could lose accreditation. This could cut off all our Medicare and Medicaid funding."

"Would that be a death blow?"

"Bankruptcy and bond defaults, I would expect," Cathy said. "Are you going to call Terry? He's still at work. I talked with him. He knows more about the financial implications."

"I can try. He told me not to call him, saying he would call me instead," Jack said.

"He's under a lot of pressure."

"What about Nicole?"

"The same. Let me highlight a few other things," Cathy offered.

Jack spoke with Cathy for another twenty minutes. He thanked her, then dialed Tonya Creating's direct line at Nokomis Hospital.

"Tonya, this is Jack at the *Herald-Tribune*. Do you have a comment or a statement about the inspection reports?"

"We expected your call. I was just going to FAX it to you. Are you at the newspaper?" Tonya said, sounding surprisingly cooperative.

"Yes. Would it be possible to talk with Mike?" Jack inquired, holding his breath.

"He has said all he wants to say in the statement, which is two pages long," Tonya said. "He's in meetings right now."

"All right, thanks, Tonya," said Jack, hanging up.

He had one last call to make. He dug out Rose Blatt's

home number.

"Rose, it's Jack Kendall with the *Herald-Tribune*. Can I get a quick comment? The Joint Commission has issued its interim inspection report on Nokomis. They have suspended surgeries until improvements are made in sterile processing. Medicare also cited the hospital in a long list of deficiencies, including incomplete records, supply shortages, and insufficient staffing. What do you think?"

"That doesn't surprise me. When a hospital is bleeding cash, corners get cut. And at Nokomis, they've been cutting for years," Blatt said.

"Thanks, Rose. I'm on deadline. Let's talk longer next time," Jack said, hanging up.

After spending thirty minutes organizing his notes and reviewing the reports again, highlighting key passages, Jack wrote a quick account for Saturday's paper about the very negative reports issued by the Joint Commission and Medicare inspectors. He would follow up with more detailed articles in the coming days.

NOKOMIS HOSPITAL CITED FOR DIRTY INSTRUMENTS; SURGERIES TEMPORARILY HALTED

Jack Kendall
Herald-Tribune Staff Writer

NOKOMIS, Sept. 22, 1984 — Patients at Nokomis Hospital waited for operations that never began this week after federal and national inspectors uncovered dirty surgical instruments, missing supplies, and what they called a "widespread pattern" of unsafe practices across the hospital.

Medicare officials and Joint Commission surveyors arrived early Wednesday morning, prompted by months of staff and patient complaints. By Thursday, elective surgeries had been suspended for at least seven days, pending changes in sterile processing and operating room staffing.

The suspension is a rare and drastic measure, inspectors acknowledged, taken only when lapses pose an "immediate threat" to patient safety.

SURGERIES CANCELED, PATIENTS LEFT WAITING

Surgeons told the *Herald-Tribune* that more than a dozen surgeries had been abruptly canceled in recent months when trays of "clean" instruments arrived contaminated. Blood-stained clamps, suction tubes clogged with residue, and even a scalpel flecked with rust were found in sets prepared for spinal fusions, brain surgeries, cleft palate repairs, and appendectomies.

243

One patient reportedly lay under anesthesia for nearly an hour while surgical staff scrambled to find sterile replacements. Another case, a young boy scheduled for cleft palate repair, was sent home when a tray was deemed unsafe to use.

"We're doing the best we can with what we have," said one surgical nurse, who requested anonymity for fear of retaliation. "But the truth is, we don't have enough people or clean equipment to keep up."

Rose Blatt, a healthcare professor at the University of South Florida in Tampa, stated that financial losses exceeding $10 million over the previous two years could have led to lapses in patient safety.

"When a hospital is bleeding cash, corners get cut. And at Nokomis, they've been cutting for years," Blatt said.

INSPECTORS FIND WIDESPREAD FAILURES

The Joint Commission team's preliminary report identified 15 standards "out of compliance" across multiple departments, including surgery, emergency, maternity, sterile processing, maintenance, and environmental services.

In sterile processing, inspectors confirmed what staff had long warned: chronic short-staffing, skipped sterilization checks, and inexperienced technicians left trays improperly cleaned and incomplete. The department employed 20 staff members just three years ago. Today, after layoffs and departures, only 11 remain—many without state certification.

In the emergency department, inspectors found long waits for patients, missing IV tubing and catheters, and expired drugs still stocked on crash carts. In surgery, two years of infection-control data were missing.

"These are not paperwork oversights," one inspector told the newspaper. "They are systemic breakdowns that put lives at risk."

HOSPITAL RESPONSE

In a statement issued Friday night, hospital spokesperson Tonya Creating blamed "unexpected turnover" and staffing shortages.

"Quality control is paramount to Nokomis Hospital," the statement read. "We are committed to safe, high-quality care and implementing new protocols to strengthen patient safety."

CEO Mike Lard, in a Wednesday morning memo to medical staff, sought to project calm. "The State of Florida has arrived at Nokomis Hospital. Please support your hospital," he wrote. A follow-up memo on Thursday promised quick fixes: "Rest assured, this hospital will become better and stronger within a week. We will have great news to announce to you shortly afterward."

However, behind the public reassurances, staff members said the hospital was struggling to maintain basic operations. Nurses admitted to buying gloves and bandages out of their own pockets when supply shelves were bare. Surgical techs said they sometimes borrowed instruments from one tray to complete another operation.

"It's not that people don't care," another nurse told the *Herald-Tribune*. "We care too much. But management doesn't give us the tools or staff to do our jobs."

A TROUBLED HISTORY

This is not the first time Nokomis has faced questions about its standards. Last year, state inspectors fined the hospital $10,000 after a morgue refrigeration failure left a woman's body decomposed beyond recognition, preventing her family from holding an open-casket funeral.

Other Joint Commission citations in recent years have included an elevator left inoperable for three months and MRI patients being wheeled outdoors past dumpsters to a rented trailer in the parking lot.

For a hospital already losing an estimated $500,000

per month, the current suspension could be devastating. Medicare and Medicaid reimbursements account for nearly 80 percent of Nokomis's revenue. Losing accreditation could effectively close the hospital.

NEXT STEPS

Hospital leaders said they will submit a corrective action plan to Medicare within a week and have hired Unity Sterile, an Alabama-based management firm, to take over the sterile processing department immediately.

Lard downplayed the severity of the inspection report, calling the findings "no surprise" and "easily correctable."

But inspectors left no doubt: Nokomis has 60 days to correct its deficiencies or face termination of its accreditation and federal funding.

And for patients, families, and staff caught in the middle, the consequences are immediate. Surgeries are halted. Care is delayed. And trust, once broken, will not be easily restored.

Chapter 33:
On Air at WKXY

Morning, Saturday, Sept. 22, 1984

The crisis spread from sterile hallways and newsprint into living rooms across Sarasota County on Saturday, when *Herald-Tribune* reporter Jack Kendall appeared on WKXY's morning show with host Peter Jahns.

"Jack, the phones are lighting up," Jahns said as the red light blinked in the cramped studio. "Our listeners want to know—how serious is this? Are patients in danger?"

Kendall leaned into the mic, his voice steady. "Peter, the inspectors' findings are serious. They used the phrase 'immediate jeopardy.' That means they believe patient lives could be at risk if the problems aren't fixed quickly."

"Let's get into the details," Jahns pressed. "Dirty instruments? How does that happen? It sounds almost unthinkable."

"It does, and yet inspectors found clamps and scalpels with dried blood and even rust," Kendall said. "Staff told me they're so short-handed that trays are rushed upstairs without full sterilization. Surgeons told me they've had to cancel or delay operations. Imagine waiting hours for surgery, only to be told the tools aren't safe to use."

"What about the ER?" Jahns asked.

"I've seen that up close. Shortages of supplies and staff," Kendall replied. "Ambulances diverted, patients waiting twice as long as they should. It's not what people expect when they come to a community hospital in crisis."

"I understand you spotted these problems first-hand two Friday nights ago when you rushed your wife, Bobbie, into the Nokomis Hospital ER for an emergency C-section."

"That's right, Peter. We have two lovely twins, a boy and a girl. Our OB-GYN, Dr. Jennifer Chastain, and her team performed magnificently. But what I saw outside this excellent maternity unit—and what the staff told me—led me to investigate. This community and the hospital's employees deserve better."

"You mentioned community. What does this mean for the community?"

Jack paused, then replied: "If Nokomis can't fix this in 60 days, it could lose accreditation. And if that happens, the hospital may not survive financially."

Jahns glanced at the clock, then wrapped up. "Jack Kendall, intrepid, Pulitzer-prize-winning reporter at the *Sarasota Herald-Tribune*, thank you for shining a light on this. I know we'll be hearing more."

Kendall exhaled as the mic went silent. The story was unfolding faster than he could type or speak. And behind the scenes, darker forces were stirring.

*　*　*

Jack drove home after his radio interview, a little after 11 a.m. He went straight into the nursery to see how Bobbie and the twins were doing.

"They've been angels this morning," Bobbie said softly, adjusting Ella's blanket. "Eli's been wide awake, though—already watching every move I make."

Jack leaned against the crib, smiling. "That's our boy. Always curious."

She looked up at him. "So—how did it go on KXY? I didn't get a chance to listen."

"It went fine," Jack said. "Peter asked tough questions, but nothing I couldn't handle. I told listeners what we know about the inspections without giving away more than I should. People deserve the truth."

"And now?" Bobbie asked, brushing a lock of thick blonde hair from her face. "Are you going to bury yourself in the Nokomis story all weekend?"

Jack sighed. "I have to. Between the inspectors' findings, Terry's revealing photo-documents, and the merger memo, it's all moving fast. I'll try to work here at the house, though—so I can spell you with the twins."

She smiled faintly. "Good. Just remember, they need their dad, too."

"What about you?" Jack teased.

"Of course!" Bobbie exclaimed with a big, tired smile.

He kissed her cheek, then Eli's forehead. He sat on the rocker, trying to relax, but had expected Lard to call all morning to go berserk over the article.

At noon, the phone rang.

"Good story this morning. This is Joel O'Neal. I wasn't planning on calling you, but I heard you on the radio and knew you had asked to talk with me."

"Hi, Dr. O'Neal. I'm glad you called. I've got a million questions to ask, but you start," Jack said, waving goodbye to Bobbie as he rushed into the kitchen to get a notebook.

"Things are getting way out of hand at the hospital and on the board. I want to share some information and be available to you. I can talk with you if you need background information," Dr. O'Neal said.

"I don't have anyone on the board, so I am very interested in what you are being told," Jack replied.

"Yes, well, Nicole told me you are a good journalist and that I could trust you. I have something to share with you about that."

"What do you have?"

"I have a copy of a draft memo from Lard about how he's been secretly talking with National about merging and how it would be best for the hospital, especially now," Dr. O'Neal said.

"Is the board going to vote on a proposal?" Jack asked.

"We have an emergency meeting set for this Thursday. It had been scheduled for October 10, but Lard moved it up—I think because of your story from the previous Sunday."

"I see. What's on the agenda?" Jack asked.

"He's recommending we sign a letter of intent for the merger. He believes this will help the hospital overcome its current difficulties. If I give you the memo, will you write a story ahead of the meeting?" Dr. O'Neal asked. "I'd like the public to know about it."

"You bet. Can I come get this memo now?" Jack asked.

"Come to my house, and we can talk," Dr. O'Neal said.

Chapter 34:
Reality Check

Morning, Sunday, Sept. 23, 1984

Rick Wise drove to Jack's house early Sunday morning with a copy of the newspaper. He also had a copy of Lard's Saturday press release about the Medicare and Joint Commission inspection reports.

Jack was in the kitchen, making coffee, when he heard the buzzer ring from the front gate to Cherokee Estates.

"It's Rick. We have to talk about Lard's press release. Buzz me through," he requested impatiently. "It won't take long."

Rick parked in the driveway and walked to the front door. Jack waited for him, holding a yellow legal pad and his own copy of the Sunday paper.

"You're talking about that fictional account Lard wrote, and we blindly published about the inspections?" Jack asked. "I can't believe we ran that this morning. Here's my notes on it."

"Me neither," Rick said. "I have my own notes. Let's go into your study."

Jack nodded, motioning his editor to follow him inside. "Whose idea was it to run it verbatim?"

"Don't ask. It was a mistake," Rick replied.

"And you want me to fix it," Jack said as they entered the downstairs study. "Take a seat," he offered, sitting behind his desk.

"Jack," Rick said, rubbing his temple, "Lard wrote this release as a love letter to himself. I want you to take it apart in Monday's paper."

"I see, a point-counterpoint? Fine. Lard blamed everything and everyone but himself—Medicare's new payment system, competition, suppliers, and even inflation," Jack disbelievingly said.

"Of course, none of that explains blood, bone, and rust on scalpels labeled sterile," he said, shaking his head.

"Exactly," Rick said, tapping the paper. "He's trying to turn systemic failures into excuses. I want you to remind readers of what the inspectors actually found. Dirty instruments, missing infection data, expired crash cart meds. Bring it back to patients waiting six hours for surgery, nurses paying for gloves out of their own pockets. Lard can't hide behind Washington or Sarasota Memorial."

Jack nodded slowly, his reporter's instinct firing. "How long?"

"Twenty inches. Make it sharp, factual, cutting," Rick said, leaning forward. "Lard's statement is self-gratification. Your story is accountability. Hit it hard. Make the readers see through him."

Jack smiled. He knew precisely what Rick meant.

* * *

Rick had hardly closed the front door when Bobbie shot Jack a glance—part sympathy, part exasperation.

"My parents are here, and I thought we'd spend time together," she said softly, shifting Ella on her hip. Eli was sleeping in the bassinet nearby, his tiny fists curled against his blanket.

Jack rubbed the back of his neck. "I know, Bobbie. I didn't expect Rick to assign me anything today. He wants a counter to Lard's statement for Monday's paper."

At that moment, Mr. and Mrs. Jackson entered the living room. Mr. Jackson, tall and slender in a polo shirt, briefly nodded at Jack while examining a model bridge on the bookshelf. Mrs. Jackson smiled warmly, her teacher's voice gentle yet precise. "We don't want to monopolize your Sunday, Jack. We just enjoy seeing you two, now four, together."

Jack offered an apologetic grin. "I'm sorry about all this. I swear I'm not trying to dodge family time. It's just—this story keeps twisting, and every time I think I can put it aside, something new lands."

Bobbie adjusted Ella's blanket and sighed. "I get it, Jack. Just...don't let it swallow you whole. We're still here."

Mr. Jackson cleared his throat. "Jack, I built bridges for forty years. The lesson was always the same: if you don't anchor them, they fall apart. Your work matters, and you have to meet deadlines, but don't forget that the anchors"—he looked toward Bobbie and the babies—"are what keep you steady."

Jack met his father-in-law's steady gaze, then bent down to kiss Ella's head and gently tapped Eli's cheek. "I'll be back before dinner. I promise."

With a quiet nod from Mr. Jackson and a gentle smile from

Mrs. Jackson, Jack grabbed his notebook, already imagining the first lines of Lard's rebuttal in his head.

* * *

ANALYSIS: CEO'S STATEMENT VS. REALITY INSIDE NOKOMIS

Jack Kendall
Herald-Tribune Staff Writer

NOKOMIS, Monday, Sept. 24, 1984 — When Nokomis Hospital CEO Mike Lard issued a two-page statement that ran unedited in Sunday's *Herald-Tribune*, he sought to assure the community that inspectors' findings were "isolated" lapses and that his staff remained "committed to excellence." Yet interviews with nurses, technicians, and physicians—as well as the inspection report itself—paint a far more troubling picture.

DIRTY INSTRUMENTS NOT "ISOLATED"

Lard characterized the discovery of blood-stained and rusted surgical instruments as isolated incidents. But inspectors found multiple trays labeled "ready for use" with visible debris, dried blood, and residue in suction tubes. One inspector wrote that conditions in sterile processing "constitute immediate jeopardy" for patient safety—the most serious category of risk under Joint Commission rules. Technicians admitted the department has been short-staffed for months and that trays are frequently rushed upstairs before proper sterilization.

STAFFING SHORTAGES BEYOND NATIONAL TRENDS

Lard blamed understaffing on "national shortages of nurses and technicians." However, staff interviewed by inspectors described a deeper problem: unfilled positions that management has refused to post or fund, forcing existing employees to work double shifts. Nurses reported that two RNs were often missing on nearly every surgery shift. Emergency physicians told inspectors they sometimes had to "pray the staff will be enough when the ambulances roll in."

SUPPLY PROBLEMS NOT JUST A VENDOR ISSUE

The CEO suggested that a vendor's bankruptcy caused supply shortages in the emergency department. However, ER staff reported that shortages of oxygen masks, IV tubing, and basic medications existed before the vendor collapse. "We've been patching holes every day for months," said one physician. Inspectors found crash carts stocked with expired drugs and supply closets that had been empty for weeks. Additionally, Baxter withheld supplies for nearly a month due to non-payment of previous shipments.

DOCUMENTATION FAILURES GO DEEPER

Lard highlighted documentation lapses as correctable with "modernized reporting systems." But missing or incomplete records span two years of surgical infection data, three months of skipped sterilization cycle checks, and absent quality-improvement audits. Inspectors concluded that Nokomis lacks a functioning system to track patient safety—problems far larger than paperwork alone.

FINANCIAL PRESSURES REAL, BUT NOT THE WHOLE STORY

Medicare's Prospective Payment System has indeed squeezed community hospitals nationwide, reimbursing them at fixed per-procedure rates. It is also true that larger regional hospitals draw more profitable patients. Yet staff interviews indicate that mismanagement—not just reimbursement formulas—contributes to Nokomis's crisis. Nurses spoke of buying gloves and gauze with their own money. Surgical techs admitted they borrowed instruments from one tray to another to complete operations. These are not signs of a system stressed only by external pressures; they are signs of internal collapse.

THE STAKES

By law, Nokomis has 60 days to correct its deficiencies or risk losing accreditation. That would cut off Medicare and Medicaid reimbursements, which make up 80 percent of its revenue. For a hospital already losing $500,000 a month, it would be a mortal blow.

Lard concluded his statement by promising Nokomis will "endure" and "adapt." For patients and staff, the more pressing question is whether it can survive long enough to do so.

Accompanying Jack's analysis of Lard's statement was an editorial written by Publisher David Lindsay Jr.

EDITORIAL: NOKOMIS PATIENTS DESERVE BETTER

The inspection findings at Nokomis Hospital are not minor lapses. They are failures that put patients at risk: dirty instruments labeled sterile, missing infection-control data, empty supply closets, and an emergency room stretched beyond capacity.

CEO Mike Lard's statement cites Medicare payment pressures and competition from larger hospitals. Those challenges are real, but they do not excuse basic breakdowns in sterilization, staffing, and safety protocols. When nurses are forced to buy gloves out of their own pockets, the problem is not with reimbursement formulas—it is leadership.

Nokomis now has 60 days to correct dozens of deficiencies or risk losing accreditation and Medicare funding. The hospital's survival is at stake. More importantly, so is the trust of this community.

The *Herald-Tribune* believes Nokomis must do more than paper over problems with memos and outside consultants. It must confront the truth: patient safety has been compromised, and accountability starts at the top.

* * *

After finishing his story, Jack arrived home three hours later, the smell of sesame chicken and fried rice filling the car. He gently pushed open the front door with his elbow, carrying a paper sack of cartons.

Bobbie looked up from the bassinet, where Eli and Ella lay on their backs, gazing at a colorful mobile. "You actually made it home," she teased, relief softening her grin.

"Bearing gifts," Jack said, lifting the bag. "The finest Chinese cuisine Cherokee Estates has to offer."

"Come look at your babies," coaxed Bobbie. "They missed you. Give Mom the food."

Jack handed the four small take-out bags to Mr. and Mrs. Jackson, who unpacked the food—lo mein, sweet-and-sour pork, and vegetables glistening in sauce—and soon the dining room filled with the comforting clatter of chopsticks against cartons.

"I hope everyone likes Chinese. The House of Chong is famous in Sarasota," Jack said.

"I'm glad you came home now," said Mrs. Jackson. "We were just talking about what to make for dinner. This is perfect."

"Have the twins eaten yet?" Jack asked as he sat down at the table.

"Eli has, but Ella is fussy. I'll get to her when she's ready," Bobbie said.

"Look at them—bright eyes, strong little hands. You'd never guess what a rough start they had," Mr. Jackson said, finishing unpacking the food.

Bobbie reached for Jack's hand across the table. "We're lucky," she said quietly. "After the eclampsia scare, I still can't believe we all came through it."

Mr. Jackson nodded, spooning rice onto his plate. "Healthy kids, a roof over your heads, and a man who finally knows when to bring dinner home. That's success in my book."

Jack chuckled, passing egg rolls around. "I'll take that endorsement. And for the record, deadlines or not, this beats the office's lunchroom any day."

For a moment, the stories, the hospital intrigue, and the headlines faded, replaced by warm food, the twins' babbles, and the easy rhythm of a family gathered around a table.

Chapter 35:
Evil Plans

Late Night Sunday, Sept. 23, 1984

In the quiet of his paneled study, CEO Mike Lard poured two bourbons and handed one to Delman Palmer.

"You saw the papers," Lard said. "Kendall keeps writing. Myles and McIntosh continue feeding him information. The stories are out, and there may be more, but I don't want anyone testifying. We need...a solution."

Palmer grunted, swirling the glass. "We tried scaring them. There is only one other way."

Lard's lips curled into something colder than a smile. He lowered his voice. "Nicole first, then Myles, like we discussed last week. Then clean up his place, and hers. Everything they gave Kendall—find it, and take it back. Even if Kendall has documents, that evidence might not be admissible without the people who provided it."

Palmer leaned forward, his bulk filling the chair. "And Kendall? We do nothing?"

"Not yet," Lard said, eyes narrowing. "Frighten him. Remind him he's not untouchable. A rattled reporter makes mistakes. If he gets in your way, silence him for good."

"Right," Palmer said. "He's not the pope, a judge, or a cop. He's a fucking journalist!"

"I totally agree. Take him out if necessary. After the jobs are done, I want you to get lost until you hear from me. I'll transfer your going rate to that account in the Bahamas."

The ice clinked as Palmer drained his glass. "Consider it done."

Outside, the cicadas droned in the wet Florida night, as Nokomis Hospital's crisis veered from failing instruments, supply shortages, and corrupt executives into something darker, more dangerous—a campaign not to fix the failures, but to bury the truth with intimidation, and perhaps worse.

Chapter 36:
Ethical Dilemma

Morning, Monday, Sept. 24, 1984

Jack spent most of Monday morning juggling calls tied to the growing storm at Nokomis Hospital. Health lawyers, consultants, and federal regulatory experts all had opinions, but their consensus was clear: Nokomis faced not just scrutiny but possible collapse.

On the far side of Jack's desk, Terry's photocopies of the corruption at Nokomis sat in a thick manila envelope. Jack had written a draft of the investigative story, but he wasn't yet happy enough with it to give it to Rick for a first read.

Seven days after his interview with Terry, Jack finally told Rick what he had learned from the young hospital accounting manager. He had to disclose the cocaine vial Terry had taken. Rick was surprised and reminded Jack that, technically, he was holding stolen goods, even though it was evidence meant for an article.

"You should have told me sooner," Rick said with a stern

look. After a moment, he suggested placing the vial and its contents in a secure container inside the newsroom's safe and informing Peter Gantz, the newspaper's general counsel.

Rick paced once around his desk, then stopped. "I'll loop in Gantz, but we need to tread carefully. This puts the paper in a delicate spot."

A half-hour later, Jack and Rick were sitting in Peter Gantz's office as the newspaper's general counsel thumbed through legal books and case summaries. Gantz adjusted his glasses, cleared his throat, and began running through precedents on newspapers publishing documents obtained illegally—not by the papers themselves, but by sources.

When Gantz mentioned the 1971 *Pentagon Papers* case, Jack and Rick exchanged a quick, knowing grin. They were in good company.

"If Daniel Ellsberg could walk out of RAND with a classified report on the Vietnam War and hand it to *The Washington Post* and *The New York Times*—and neither paper faced criminal charges for publishing it—then we're not exactly plowing new legal ground here," Gantz said, tapping the file with a practiced calm. "Your situation is cleaner, actually. Terry isn't dropping state secrets; he's exposing corporate crimes."

He sat back, folding his hands. "But we do need transparency. An editor's note explaining the circumstances covers us ethically. I want readers to understand how the material came into our possession without compromising Terry."

Jack nodded. He felt the weight of that comparison—the gravity of what he held. He wasn't Ellsberg, but Terry had taken a similar leap of faith. Now it was Jack's responsibility not to squander it.

Once Gantz finished, he told Rick that Jack should continue

drafting the exposé and that the documents and the cocaine vial needed to be surrendered to law enforcement. On Wednesday morning, Gantz, Jack, and a security guard would hand-deliver everything to Sheriff Bagley.

"There are several steps we must take before this article is published," said Gantz. "The first is, you need to explain to Terry Myles that he could be arrested for breaking into Lard's office and stealing his private papers, regardless of whether they reveal crimes."

Rick nodded. "If memory serves me correctly, Ellsberg was prosecuted for stealing the Pentagon Papers."

Jack added," But the charges were dismissed due to government misconduct. There is a gray area here."

Gantz rose from his chair and circled the desk, his expression tightening with the weight of what lay ahead. "Jack, when we're ready to publish, I need you to sit down with Myles and explain the legal exposure he could face. He stole documents from Lard's office. Even if those papers reveal crimes, that doesn't shield him from what a prosecutor might argue." He paused, letting the implication settle. "If Myles understands the risks and still agrees—and if Mr. Lindsay and I sign off—we'll run the story."

Jack nodded. "That's fair."

Rick leaned forward in his chair, fingers laced, the impatience in his voice unmistakable. "Good. Now, in the meantime, go write the story."

There it was—marching orders. Jack was to do what he did best: finish the exposé. Lard's drug use, the shell companies funneled through friendly executives, the embezzlement records, and the hidden causes behind the financial losses, layoffs, and outsourced services all had to be pulled into one coherent narrative.

But before he started, one question still haunted Jack—the same one he had avoided for days: how to tell the truth about Terry's thefts in a way that served the story without needlessly exposing the source who trusted him.

* * *

Just before lunch, Jack called Bobbie to check on her and the twins, then asked Tom Justice if he'd like to make a quick run to the Main Bar for sandwiches and a beer. They were heading out when Rick's voice cut through the newsroom din.

"Hey, Jack, before you leave, I'd like to talk with you for a few minutes," Rick called from behind his desk.

Jack looked at his watch, then waved Tom on. "I'll meet you over there in a few minutes. Grab us a table," he said before walking over to the city editor's desk.

Rick leaned back in his chair, arms crossed. "I spoke with Peter again, who explained the situation with Mr. Lindsay. We need you to draft the exposé as soon as possible—tonight, if you can. Twenty inches. We can add the finer points later. But we need something on paper that you and I can discuss before I sit down with Gantz and figure out what we're comfortable running."

Jack rubbed the back of his neck. He still hadn't decided how to explain that Terry had obtained the evidence of embezzlement by breaking into Lard's office. Above all, the trickiest item to explain was the cocaine vial.

"All right. I'll get you a draft. It won't be ready for prime time, but it'll give us something to talk about, and you'll know the highlights."

Rick gave him a quick nod. "Good. That's all I'm asking. Just get it started, and we'll refine the edges together. You've got a good story, Jack. It needs to be told. Now we need to put it in black and white."

Jack exhaled slowly. He knew what that meant—a long afternoon ahead. But he also knew Rick was right. It was time to write.

*   *   *

Jack slid into a side booth at the Main Bar, a favorite lunch establishment for the legal, business, and tourist crowds on Main Street near the County Courthouse, where the smell of grilled onions and peppers hung heavy in the air.

Tom Justice was already there, sipping a draft beer and half-reading the *Herald-Tribune's* sports page.

"I ordered us beers, but I wasn't sure you'd show up," Tom said, folding the paper. "Rick pushing for that secret Nokomis exposé? You haven't told me much about it. What's up?"

Jack exhaled and set his notebook on the table. "That's the problem. I don't know how to write it without crossing an ethical line."

"Well, I don't think a political reporter is the best source for advice about ethics," Tom said, smirking.

"Tom, this is serious. I've had this evidence for a week, and I had to tell Rick about it today. Now, he's asking me to write a draft of the story," Jack said, shaking his head. "I'm not ready."

"What's the big deal? You've written many scoops before. What's so different about this one?"

"Between us, it's my inside source, Terry Myles. He broke

into the CEO's office, took nearly 36 pictures, and photocopied 100 pages from a second set of hospital financial ledgers. But that's not all. He swiped a vial of cocaine that was in CEO Mike Lard's desk," Jack said, his eyes bulging and his mouth open in disbelief. "We haven't had the vial tested yet, but Terry believes it will have Lard's fingerprints on it."

Tom blinked and shook his head in surprise. "And you worry that because it's stolen evidence...you report it, even possess it, you're laundering a crime?"

"Correct, Sherlock," Jack teased his best newspaper friend.

Tom leaned back, rubbing his chin. "You're worried about ethics. I get it. But look, Jack—Lard isn't running a church bake sale. I read your story. He's running a hospital that's bleeding patients and money while he snorts coke in his executive suite. That vial? That ledger? They're the truth. The only reason you have them is that your source dug deep enough to find them."

Jack took a big sip of his Heineken. Just then, the waitress came over.

"What can I get you two hotshots?" asked Sherry, a longtime server who was a legend at the restaurant for her good looks, sharp tongue, and refusal to go out with customers.

Jack looked up at her with a big smile. "Give me my usual Italian sandwich. Tom, do you want to split a hummus plate?"

"Sure thing. I'll have a Reuben. Sherry. My, my. You sure are looking good today!" he exclaimed in his usual flirtatious style.

"If I had a dollar for every time I heard that!" she shot back, flipping her long blonde hair as she turned to bring the order to the grill.

Tom and Jack watched her as she snaked her way through the patrons waiting for a table.

"Okay, Tom, pay attention to me. My problem is attribution. If I build a story around stolen goods, I give Lard an escape hatch. He'll claim he's a victim, and everything I've received from my source is tainted, refutable," Jack said, stopping for a second to take another sip. "Can't you see? Lard's lawyers, maybe the police, could make what Terry and I did seem dirty and underhanded. Rick told me to get the draft in and let Gantz decide what can be printed—but I keep asking myself: where's the line between exposing corruption and enabling a burglary?"

Tom finished another sip and pointed his finger at Jack. "You report it as what it is: whistleblower evidence. You don't glorify how Terry got it, but you also don't ignore the facts. Put the hospital's failures first. Make the ledgers and the cocaine a supporting fact, not the headline. That way, the story's about Lard's corruption, not Terry's midnight stroll through his desk drawers."

Jack finished his beer. "I see. I frame the story as corroboration. The ledgers prove what the staff already told me. The cocaine indicates excess and a pattern of behavior. I haven't told you yet about the cocaine party in the hospital C-suite that I witnessed last Saturday night, the night after Bobbie was admitted."

"What's that? Coke party in the hospital?" asked Tom with a puzzled look on his face.

"Never mind that right now," Jack said, holding up his hand. "And if anyone asks how I got the evidence..."

"You say a source," Tom cut in. "Period. Let the lawyers worry about the chain of custody. Your job is to tell the public why their hospital's circling the drain and who's driving it there."

Sherry returned with the sandwiches, running off to another table before Tom could make another flirty remark.

"Don't look so disappointed," Jack teased. "Let's eat. I have to get back to the office. You've given me something to think about."

Jack took a big bite of the Italian, a thick sandwich served on a toasted bun with salami, ham, provolone cheese, tomatoes, chopped peppers, and onions, with a house-made blend of oil, garlic, and spices. So good; he never grew tired of them.

Five minutes later, the two reporters finished, leaving two tens and a five-dollar bill on the table for Sherry.

Tom grinned at Jack as they stood to leave. "And if you need help with this story, I'll do anything—short of gunplay."

"What do you mean? You run at the first sign of trouble," kidded Jack, recalling two years earlier when he was warned that the murderous Gordon Gecht had returned to Sarasota to settle a score with Jack, and Tom immediately excused himself.

"You've had enough shootouts for one career in Bogotá and at your house, and I'm too good-looking to get caught in one of those," Tom joked.

Jack chuckled, the tension easing from his shoulders. "Fair enough. But I might need your healthcare regulatory contacts in Tallahassee. Something tells me this story's not going to end quietly."

* * *

After lunch, Jack sat at his desk and started working on the exposé again. He typed another suggested headline: "Nokomis Hospital Scandal: Theft, Lies, and Drugs."

Then he quickly rewrote the first ten paragraphs. The

sentences were blunt, but that's how he felt. He'd fill in the blanks later and refine the rough edges, but this connected the layoffs, supply shortages, outsourcing, and departmental closures to possible thefts, embezzlement, and financial losses.

Tom's words echoed in his mind: "Don't make it about Terry's break-in—make it about Lard's corruption."

Jack leaned back in his chair, staring at the blinking cursor, and looked over his initial rough draft and the notes of the story. The documents Terry smuggled out of Lard's office would serve as confirmation, not a centerpiece. The real weight of the story would rest on testimony from nurses, surgeons, and inspectors—the voices of people living in the mess every day.

He pulled Terry's photocopies closer, spreading them across his desk like a crime scene board. It was all there—ledgers with revenues, expenses, kickbacks, shell companies, and phantom vendor payments.

Jack jotted down a note to himself: Focus on patients first. Keep it human.

The cocaine vial presented a tougher problem. How should he mention it? Should he mention it? Yes, he needed to include it, even if it wouldn't make it into the final story. The Sheriff's Office needed to know this cocaine vial was important.

Jack picked up the photograph of the small glass vial and examined it closely. The actual vial was kept inside the newsroom's safe, but he wondered if Lard's fingerprints were on it. How would he explain this to Lieutenant Stevens?

Tom's advice returned: *"A source gave you evidence of executive drug use. Period."*

Jack nodded and typed: "An anonymous source provided the *Herald-Tribune* with evidence linking hospital executives to drug use, corroborating accounts from multiple staff."

The sentence was clean and direct, without implicating Terry for taking the vial or himself for being on the floor during one of the drug parties. He considered writing about that specific situation in a later column, after the investigation was complete.

By late afternoon, the newsroom around him hummed with phones and typewriters, but Jack was lost in his own thoughts. Each sentence felt like a step onto a wire, but Tom's advice steadied him: truth first, process later. This wasn't about how evidence had landed in his lap. It was about exposing the rot at the center of Nokomis Hospital before more people died.

Two hours later, he finished and looked over his second draft.

NOKOMIS HOSPITAL SCANDAL: THEFT, LIES, AND DRUGS

Jack Kendall
Herald-Tribune Staff Writer

For years, Nokomis Hospital has portrayed itself as a community institution—an indispensable part of Sarasota County's healthcare system. But new evidence reveals a darker picture: a culture of corruption at the top, where drug abuse, financial manipulation, and criminal ties have eroded the hospital's stability and jeopardized patient care.

At the center of the scandal stands Chief Executive Mike Lard, whose leadership has now been linked to both embezzlement and cocaine use.

Photocopies of a hidden set of hospital ledgers reveal funds siphoned off for personal and political purposes. At the same time, a vial of cocaine found in Lard's office suggests addiction at the highest level. Sources close to the investigation say Lard is not alone—other executives have also been implicated in using hospital resources for personal gain.

The scandal also reaches beyond the hospital's walls. Records show that Lard and his associates maintained ties with Delman Palmer, a convicted felon whose presence in Nokomis's boardroom raises troubling questions about organized crime's role in local healthcare. Palmer, known for his violent history, has surfaced repeatedly in connection with hospital contracts and debt restructuring deals.

The corruption comes amid mounting regulatory pressure on Nokomis Hospital. Recent inspections by both Medicare and the Joint Commission uncovered serious deficiencies in the surgery, sterile processing, and emergency departments.

Inspectors reported dirty surgical instruments, inadequate staffing, missing reports, and shortages of basic supplies. Medicare officials warned that continued violations could result in reduced reimbursements or even termination from the federal program—a potentially devastating financial consequence for any community hospital.

These inspection failures, combined with evidence of embezzlement and drug abuse, have put Nokomis in free fall.

Patient volumes are already declining, and rival hospitals have begun to advertise aggressively, highlighting their high quality and superior patient satisfaction ratings.

For a facility once seen as a pillar of South Sarasota County healthcare, public trust is vanishing as quickly as its revenue.

Chapter 37:
Wait Until Dark

7 p.m., Monday, Sept. 24, 1984

Nicole McIntosh waited at her house for Terry Myles. Although she found the typewritten message about the meeting time—8 p.m.—unusual, Terry wrote that he needed to see her. She hadn't spoken with him in several days because Mike Lard was threatening them, and Delman Palmer was watching them.

She was nervous already because her husband, Pete, was out of town on business. He was usually home when Terry stopped by.

Earlier that afternoon, she'd met with her friend and lawyer, Della Mason, to discuss filing a federal whistleblower lawsuit. She also wanted to share her fears of retaliation by Lard.

Della asked for copies of all the documents, and Nicole gave her the ones Jack had provided, as well as the ones Terry had given her from Lard's office.

But she hadn't told Della yet that Terry was helping her expose Lard and the others. She would, but she also hadn't yet explained her whistleblower plan to Terry. She thought she'd do that when he came over.

While waiting, she called Jack Kendall at his office to leave a message about meeting with Della and collaborating with Terry.

"Jack, this is Nicole McIntosh. I wanted to share a few things with you while I wait for Terry Myles to arrive. I'm glad you finally got to speak with him off the record. I hope he told you about his visit to Mike Lard's office. I have some other things hidden and will give them to you when I can," she said.

"Oh, by the way, I decided to talk with Della Mason today about your suggestion that I become a whistleblower," Nicole said. "I haven't told Terry that I've discussed this issue with Della, but I will mention it to him tonight. Thanks for your help."

*　*　*

Delman Palmer arrived at Nicole McIntosh's house at 7:30 p.m., parking a few blocks away to avoid attracting attention. He knew the layout of her yard and home; he had watched her many times. He sat in the dim glow of the dashboard, his pulse steady as he observed the house. The stolen handgun sat beside him on the passenger seat, cold and ready.

After a few minutes, he stepped out of the car, pulling his jacket's collar up against the cool night air. He circled the block, staying in the shadows, and slipped into her backyard. The pool shimmered under the faint porch light, its calm surface contrasting with the violence he had planned.

He approached the sliding glass door by the patio, crouching low. Pulling a screwdriver from his pocket, he inserted it into the gap between the frame and the latch. A slight twist, a little pressure—*click*. The lock released. Delman slid the door open just enough to slip inside, closing it quietly behind him.

The house was silent, except for the faint hum of the refrigerator. Moving carefully, he crept through the living room and then into the kitchen, his gloved fingers brushing against the cool marble countertops. Everything was quiet; no sign of her. He moved through the dining room and toward the hallway leading to the bedrooms.

Nicole McIntosh was in her bedroom, preparing for the next day. She had just finished dinner and planned to relax with some TV before Terry arrived. She looked at the clock. It was 7:40 p.m., still twenty minutes before she expected Terry.

The hairs on her neck stood up as she heard the faintest creak from the hallway. She turned and saw a large man fill the doorway. She gasped.

"Good evening, Mrs. McIntosh."

Delman's voice was low, his tone edged with menace. He stood there, calm yet purposeful, his eyes sweeping the room.

Nicole's heart pounded. "Palmer, how'd you get in?" she demanded, stepping back to the dresser.

Delman ignored the question. "Come with me," he ordered. "We're going to wait for Terry in the kitchen. We need to have a little talk about what you two have been doing."

Nicole hesitated, her mind racing for a way out. But Delman stepped forward, pulling back his jacket just enough to reveal the gun at his waist. He wasn't giving her a choice.

Palmer led her into the kitchen, his grip firm on her arm. He kept the gun hidden but close, his gloved hand resting on the handle.

"Where are the documents?" he asked, his voice calm but insistent. "I know Terry gave them to you. Where are they?"

Nicole swallowed hard. "I-I don't know what you're talking about."

Palmer heard a car pull up in the driveway. He exhaled sharply, realizing Myles came early, and he didn't have time to search her house. He shook his head. "Wrong answer."

He tugged his gloves tighter, a slow, deliberate motion that sent ice through Nicole's veins. Before she could react, he drew the gun, aiming it squarely at her.

"Tell me where the documents you stole from Lard are."

She could only say his name and plead for mercy. "Delman, don't."

He shook his head. "You had your chances."

Tears filled her eyes. "No, I..."

A single, muffled shot rang out.

Nicole crumpled to the floor, her body limp, her blue eyes wide with shock, a tear sliding down her cheek. She exhaled softly. Her heart stopped.

Palmer didn't notice, nor did he pause. He set the scene. He took the murder weapon. He knew exactly where he would put it next.

Without a trace of hesitation, Delman stepped over Nicole's body and disappeared out the back door and into the night.

* * *

Terry Myles sat in his car in the driveway, looking at the note Nicole had left for him. He found the timing strange; they had agreed not to meet now that Jack had all the documents. He felt she had something to tell him, but still, something about it nagged at him.

Then he noticed the house was dark, except for the porch light. There was no light in the living room, where Nicole usually kept the TV on.

Frowning, he jumped out of his car and approached the front door. As he reached for the doorknob, something felt wrong. He remembered what Kendall had told him about being cautious. A chill ran down his spine. He went back to his car and retrieved his small Raven-25 handgun.

He returned to the front door, but it was locked. He rang the doorbell, yet no one answered. Frustrated, he went around to the back and saw that the sliding glass door was open. Something was definitely wrong. He considered leaving and calling the police, but he felt compelled to investigate further. He stepped inside the house, which was eerily quiet. A faint light shone from the kitchen, and he headed toward it. Then, he saw her.

Nicole's lifeless body sprawled on the kitchen floor, blood pooling beneath her. His friend. Could she be dead? His hand trembled as he reached out to feel her wrist for a pulse. Nothing. She was gone.

A wave of panic washed over him. His breath hitched, and he staggered backward, his hands trembling. Then he wondered...was the killer in the house? Was he next? He checked his pocket pistol. It was there. He took it out.

Turning, Terry rushed through the house to his car. He opened the front door and looked around for anyone nearby. He needed to get away, just in case the killer was still close. He would call the police once he reached home.

Behind him, a neighbor looked through their window, watching the entire scene.

Chapter 38:
The Wrong Man
8 p.m., Monday, Sept. 24, 1984

When Terry got home, the first thing he did was check all the doors to make sure they were locked, and there was no sign of a break-in. He examined his closets and every place someone could hide.

He sat at his kitchen table, his handgun from the car resting nearby. He struggled to decide what to do. Should he call the police? Or Jack Kendall or his parents for advice?

What should he do? His friend Nicole was dead. His wife, Jill, and his two children, Jonathan and Elise, were gone. He felt that familiar heaviness and pressure start to build in his head. Another migraine? Stress brought it on. He needed to relax. Breathe.

He needed to do something. Minutes passed as he sat at the kitchen table. He knew he should call the police, but he was frozen, incapable of moving.

Suddenly, it was too late for that. Police sirens echoed

through the night. He wasn't surprised; someone must have seen him leave Nicole's. He still sat, frozen; his mind raced with thoughts of his family and Nicole. His future seemed meaningless now. He should have called the police from Nicole's house as soon as he saw her body.

* * *

Lieutenant Jim Stevens drove his squad car to the house and parked it. He approached the front door with two deputies by his side. He felt heavyhearted because he knew Terry—through Nicole and his wife—and believed it was best for him to make the arrest.

"Terry Myles. This is the Sarasota County Sheriff's Office. Open the door. We have a probable cause to arrest you for the murder of Nicole McIntosh," Stevens said.

There was no response. The door was locked. Stevens told a deputy to break it down. They entered the house with weapons drawn.

"Terry, are you here?" he said, holding a .38 Special revolver at his side. He wasn't sure of Terry's state of mind, so he automatically followed police procedure.

"Phillips, go to the back door and wait," Stevens said. "Turk, follow me."

The two deputies looked into the living room. The house appeared empty and quiet. There was a light down the hall. Carefully, they moved to the kitchen, where they found Myles sitting at a table.

"Terry Myles," said Stevens in a formal voice, "you are under arrest for the murder of Nicole McIntosh. You have the right to remain silent. Anything you say can and will be used against you in court. You have the right to an attorney. One will be provided for you if you cannot afford to hire a lawyer. Do you understand these rights?"

Terry didn't move or react. He didn't say anything. He sat, frozen, at the kitchen table. Stevens saw a handgun lying on the table.

"Please stand up and raise your hands above your head," Stevens said as he moved over to pick up the handgun.

"Turk, get him up and cuff him," Stevens said as he opened the back door. "Phillips, come in."

"Do you have anything to say?"

Terry remained silent, tears forming in his eyes, not even acknowledging that Jim Stevens, a new friend he had met upon moving to Venice, was arresting him.

"No? Well, you are coming with us," Stevens said unemotionally. "Maybe you'll talk downtown."

Chapter 39:
"Theft, Drugs, and Murder"

10 p.m., Monday, Sept. 24, 1984

Jack was home, winding down for the night, when the phone rang. "Sorry to bother you. I know it's late. Before I start—how are you and your family?" Sheriff Tom Bagley asked.

"We're fine, Tom. What's going on at ten o'clock?" Jack said, sensing trouble.

Bagley hesitated just long enough for Jack's pulse to quicken. "I've got something to share... We arrested Terry Myles for the murder of Nicole McIntosh."

Jack felt the words hit him like a punch.

"What? Nicole is *dead*? And Terry—Terry was arrested?" he said, his voice catching.

"Yes," Bagley said softly.

Jack took a deep breath, then exhaled. "That's impossible."

He flashed back to what he knew about Nicole and Terry,

including the conversations and meetings he'd had with them—especially the last one with Terry at the Old Hickory, when Delman Palmer showed up, and Ed followed him to make a phone call to Mike Lard. None of it pointed to murder. None of it pointed to *Terry*.

"Tom...how could you arrest him? You knew I was working with Terry on the hospital corruption story," Jack said, frustration rising with each word. "There's been a terrible mistake. Terry wasn't hiding anything—he was my source. He was working with Nicole, trying to blow the whistle on the hospital."

Bagley didn't respond.

"Who's running this investigation?"

"Lieutenant Stevens. He took the call, and he's in charge. Jack, it looks open and shut. The evidence is quite strong," Bagley said, his tone neutral but heavy.

"Not with what I know—which you knew, too!" Jack shouted, realizing he was stepping over a journalistic boundary by taking Terry's side. "I told you about Delman Palmer. Why don't you arrest him? He did it!"

Bagley exhaled. "I figured you'd say something like that. Everything you told me about Palmer is correct, but we couldn't find anything on him, and Mike Lard denied he hired him, saying he didn't know him."

Of course he would say that!" Jack snapped. "Palmer was at one of Lard's coke parties; I saw him; I took his picture there!"

"Look, Jack, calm down. You can come to the station, read the arrest report, talk to the detectives. But I think one of your young reporters is already on it."

Jack still couldn't understand what had happened. Nicole murdered? Terry the killer?

"Tom, listen," Jack said. "I interviewed Terry a week ago at the Old Hickory. He wasn't violent. He wasn't desperate. And Nicole—Terry cared about her. I told you then, and I'm telling you now: they were working together to expose what the CEO was doing at Nokomis Hospital."

He paused, lowering his voice. "I know more about their investigation than anyone."

Bagley chuckled gently, trying to cut the tension. "You always end up in the middle of *something*, don't you, Jack? I'll tell Jim what you said. He'll likely want a statement."

"I'll come in," Jack said, standing now, energized by a sudden surge of clarity. "And I'll do more than give a statement. I'm going to write a story that'll shake this whole damn mess up."

* * *

Jack explained everything to Bobbie and told her what he needed to do. She had overheard him, and she nodded. "Go. We'll be okay," she said.

He jumped into his Mustang GT and sped to the *Herald-Tribune*. He entered the nearly empty newsroom, which was staffed only by a few copy editors, Katie North, and the new night editor, Patrick McGreeley.

"Katie, did you hear the news over the scanner?" Jack asked, slightly out of breath.

"Yes. I picked up the report and already interviewed Lieutenant Stevens," Katie said, glancing up from her computer. "I've been working on the story since eight thirty."

"Good. This whole thing is a big mistake, a tragedy," Jack said, sitting down at his desk.

"Kendall, what are you doing here?" Patrick called out from across the room.

"I'm not writing anything for the morning. I'll talk with you and Rick about it tomorrow!" Jack shouted back. He was still upset about losing one source and having a second source clearly framed.

He pulled out his recorder, inserted a cassette, and turned it on to listen to Terry's interview at the Old Hickory. He had listened to it several times and had it transcribed by an intern, but he wanted to hear Terry's voice once more.

The weight of Terry's words lingered in the air. When he discussed Nicole, it was with respect, admiration, and even love—loving appreciation, not romantic love.

She had been nice to him when he arrived earlier in the year, after the death of his wife and two children. He'd hesitated to make friends at first, but slowly came to rely on her for support, especially as he became aware of the corruption at the hospital.

Jack typed a few paragraphs before stopping to stretch. Nicole's face flashed across his mind—the sharp-eyed vice president of nursing, the compassionate and dedicated professional who'd been silenced for knowing too much. Her personality wasn't just a tragic footnote. It was part of the story.

Jack scribbled in his notebook: *Nicole was a wonderful person; her murder was an act of desperation, a pattern of intimidation, and driven by a need to cover up crimes.*

But it still felt unreal. Nicole McIntosh, Terry's friend—and Jack's—was dead, murdered in her own home. The exposé of Nokomis Hospital, which Nicole believed in more than anyone else, was about more than financial greed, thievery, and misconduct. It was now about saving an innocent man being framed for murder. After listening to the thirty-minute recording once again, Jack started typing furiously, writing another draft of the story he had started Monday afternoon.

The new headline read: "**Nokomis Hospital Scandal: Theft, Drugs, and Murder.**"

It was blunt, but that's how he felt after hearing the news about Nicole and Terry. He'd fill in the gaps later and smooth out the rough spots, but this tied Nicole's death to the embezzlement, Lard's cocaine addiction, the top executives' drug issues, and the proposed merger between Nokomis and National.

He wrote about the fraudulent financial documents Terry had discovered in Lard's desk, including the damning evidence of Lard's cocaine use, shown through the coke vial. He also described how Nicole McIntosh had the courage to stand up against corruption.

He typed the story of meeting Terry at the Old Hickory, obtaining evidence of Lard's corruption, the vial of cocaine, and how Ed had identified Delman Palmer entering the bar, spying on Jack and Terry, then leaving to call Mike Lard at a nearby Winn-Dixie public phone.

As Jack furiously wrote, he couldn't shake the image of Nicole, a dedicated nurse, murdered for her integrity. Now, Terry Myles, the man who had risked everything to expose the truth, was behind bars. The stakes were higher than ever, and Jack knew he was on the brink of uncovering something even more sinister.

He suddenly glanced at his phone. He hadn't noticed the flashing red button, which indicated a message was waiting. He picked up the receiver, punched in his security code, and listened.

"Jack, this is Nicole McIntosh. I wanted to share a few things with you while I wait for Terry to arrive. I'm glad you were able to speak with him off the record last week. Did he tell you about his visit to Mike Lard's office? I hope so. I have some things hidden and will give them to you when I can.

"By the way, I decided to talk with Della Mason today about your suggestion that I become a whistleblower," Nicole said. "I haven't told Terry that I've discussed this issue with Della, but I will mention it to him tonight. Thanks for your help."

Jack sat there, stunned. The message. It was Nicole.

He heard a voice calling him. "Jack, Jack, Jack?"

Turning, he saw Katie North.

"Are you all right? What are you listening to?" she asked.

Jack blinked, gasped, and said, "Katie, listen to this. It's Nicole McIntosh. She recorded this message tonight. Just minutes before she was killed. Listen."

He tapped a few buttons to increase the volume and play the recording through the speakerphone. Katie immediately realized this should be part of her story for the morning paper.

"I don't know, Katie," said Jack slowly. "It could clear Terry, but it also confirms he was at the scene of the crime."

"This also is evidence that they were friends, and she wasn't worried about him—at all. In fact, she was expecting him and showed they were working together," Katie said. "Let's talk with Patrick about it."

"You're right, of course," said Jack, "but I'd like to write this story in a different context than as part of his arrest."

"It has to be part of my story," Katie insisted. "Let's talk with Patrick. I'm sure you could write something else. This is strong evidence we can't bury right now."

"All right. Let's both make copies of this recording, but do with it what you feel best. Let me know if you need my help," Jack said.

Katie walked over to explain Jack's phone message to Patrick. He agreed it should be included in her story, glancing at Jack, who stayed out of the conversation. Jack was still a little annoyed with Patrick, who was responsible for publishing Lard's two-page press release in Sunday morning's paper.

While Katie and Patrick worked through revisions, Jack sat at his desk for another hour, bouncing between two pieces—the corruption at Nokomis and Nicole's recording.

Katie called Lieutenant Stevens, informed him about the tape recording, and asked for his comment. She and Patrick consulted with Jack to put the quotes in context.

As they polished their story on Nicole and Terry, Jack reviewed his own draft. When Patrick finally asked him to look over Katie's piece, he read it carefully. It was solid journalism—tight, fair, and well-sourced. Still, he couldn't shake the feeling that Terry was being framed, a victim caught in the crossfire of something far bigger.

He glanced at the clock. It was now Midnight. He walked over to Katie's desk. "I'm leaving now."

She softly replied, "Thanks for your help. We'll talk tomorrow. Let me know what you need. I'm here to help."

Jack nodded. He had calmed down while working on the story, but he needed sleep or at least a break. He'd originally come in upset and mad about Nicole's murder and Terry's arrest, and to take another swing at his exposé—draft number five or six; he'd stopped counting.

Exhaling, he shut down his computer, watching his reflection fade from the darkening screen. Tomorrow he'd revisit the Nicole recording and go through the latest version of the Nokomis story, line by line. He knew it ran hot with emotion, but that was where he was. And if it were ever going to see print, it would have to survive the scrutiny of Rick Wise, Peter Gantz, and Mr. Lindsay.

"This is just the beginning. I've got to get to the bottom of this," he muttered as he grabbed his coat and walked toward the door.

Nokomis Hospital Scandal: Theft, Drugs and Murder
By Jack Kendall *Herald-Tribune* Staff Writer

Nokomis Hospital, once considered a bedrock of Sarasota's medical community, is now at the center of a spiraling scandal involving stolen funds, drug abuse by executives, a brutal murder, and a proposed merger that could decide the institution's fate.

Photographs and internal records obtained by the *Herald-Tribune* reveal that senior hospital officials maintained a secret set of ledgers, documenting off-the-books accounts used to funnel money through shell companies and cover up kickbacks. Those same offices also contained a vial of cocaine bearing fingerprints linked to CEO Mike Lard, according to sources familiar with the investigation.

The revelations follow the killing of Nicole McIntosh, the hospital's vice president of nursing, who had been an anonymous source with this newspaper. McIntosh had told colleagues she feared for her safety after speaking out about irregularities in Nokomis's books. Her death has shaken both staff and patients, adding a chilling layer to a story already marked by greed and betrayal. Sheriff's investigators have not ruled out a connection between McIntosh's murder and the financial scandal.

The corruption is unfolding amid regulatory collapse. A recent inspection by Medicare and the Joint Commission identified "serious and systemic deficiencies" in three critical areas: surgery, sterile processing, and emergency care.

Inspectors reported that soiled instruments were labeled as "ready for use," the department lacked infection-control data, and the department experienced chronic understaffing and shortages of basic supplies, including IV tubing and oxygen masks. "These conditions constitute immediate jeopardy," the Joint Commission wrote in its report.

Experts say the combination of financial misconduct and operational breakdowns has left Nokomis on the brink of collapse. "A hospital cannot survive when both its finances and its patient care are compromised," said Rose Blatt, a healthcare finance professor at the University of South Florida.

"Medicare reimbursements are the lifeblood of a community hospital. If those payments are cut off, Nokomis will collapse almost overnight."

Perhaps anticipating that collapse, Nokomis's board of trustees has abruptly accelerated its vote on a proposed merger with National Healthcare Corp., a for-profit chain based in Nashville.

The meeting, originally scheduled for October 10, has been moved up to September 27—two weeks earlier. Sources close to the board say the change was influenced not only by inspections but also by this newspaper's ongoing investigation and the murder of McIntosh.

The accelerated vote raises urgent questions about who would benefit if National absorbed Nokomis. The hospital is losing roughly $500,000 a month, and insiders warn that the merger could lead to sweeping layoffs, service cuts, and the sale of assets. "This isn't about saving patient care—it's about salvaging what's left for the executives," one longtime nurse told the *Herald-Tribune*.

For patients, the stakes are clear: the community hospital they have relied on for decades may soon vanish. For staff, the uncertainty is even darker. With fraud, drugs, and murder now shadowing its halls, Nokomis Hospital is no longer just a place of healing—it has become the scene of a crime story still unfolding.

Chapter 40:
Official Statement

Tuesday, Sept. 25, 1984

Nicole McIntosh's murder, Terry Myles's arrest, and Katie North's article sent shockwaves through the community. These events transformed Nokomis Hospital's scandal from a bureaucratic crisis into a community tragedy.

Once a respected force for good within the community, Nokomis Hospital now stood at the center of an ever-widening storm—one that involved financial fraud, patient safety lapses, and, now, murder.

As Jack had expected, Lieutenant Jim Stevens asked him to come to the Sheriff's Office with the tape recording of the message Nicole left on his machine that Monday night.

The tape placed her alive only 15 minutes before the coroner estimated her time of death, and just as a neighbor claimed to have seen Terry enter and leave her home with a handgun.

Reluctantly, Jack handed over the original but kept a copy, knowing it might be the only way to safeguard the story.

Stevens also wanted Jack to make an official statement and talk about the case with him and Sheriff Bagley.

Inside the Sheriff's Office, the air was heavy with tension. Stevens sat across from Jack at the table, while Sheriff Tom Bagley leaned against the wall with his arms crossed. Next to Jack was Peter Gantz, the *Herald-Tribune's* attorney, silent but alert.

Transcript of the Conversation at the Sheriff's Office

Stevens: "Mr. Kendall, let's start with the tape. Why do you think Nicole called you and not the police?"

Jack: "Nicole trusted me. She knew I'd listen, and she knew I was working on the story about Nokomis. She was worried her information might disappear if it went through official channels."

Stevens: "Did she mention who she was afraid of?"

Jack: "Yes. She said she was in danger from CEO Mike Lard. He'd been pressuring her to keep quiet, threatening that he'd fire her and ruin her career if she kept talking with me. She also suspected a man was following her, an employee and convicted felon, a man named Delman Palmer. Ed and I warned you about this criminal."

Bagley: "And what about Myles? You've been in touch with him. Did he ever mention harming her?"

Jack: "Absolutely not. Terry leaned on Nicole. She was the only person who stood by him after he lost his wife and children in that fire in Philadelphia before he moved here earlier this year. You know Terry, Jim. Nicole believed in him, and he needed her. He had no reason to hurt her. They both told me separately that Delman Palmer, whom I knew worked for Nokomis, was watching and following them, trying to intimidate them into silence. I don't know why you didn't look into Palmer. Ed told you about him; I told Tom about him. I wish you could have stopped him before this happened. I have much more to say about him if you want."

Stevens: "I can't talk about Palmer right now. Let's focus on Myles. The neighbor puts a gun in his hand and identifies him inside her house just minutes before the murder. That doesn't sound like they were friends."

Jack: "You'll have to ask him why he had a gun. I don't want to speculate. He told me some things about having two guns, one in his house and one in his car. All I can tell you is this: Terry and Nicole were both sources. They were good people. They gave me documents, photos, and testimony about what was happening at Nokomis. Neither of them wanted this exposed more than the other. They were working together. If Nicole's dead and Terry's in cuffs, you should be asking who benefits from shutting them both up."

Peter Gantz raised a hand gently. "That's all Jack can say for now. He's provided you with the tape. The rest will come out as our investigation continues."

Before leaving, Jack stopped to question Bagley. "Tom,

292

I'm very disappointed. I told you all about Palmer and the threats to my family and me, and to Nicole and Terry. I don't understand what happened."

Bagley sighed. "We looked into Palmer; that's all I can say now."

Jack moved closer and whispered, "A knowledgeable source told me you know about Palmer, and you know he is dirty and involved, but you didn't do anything. Is this true?"

Bagley backed away. "Jack, I can't talk about the details of this investigation. It's complicated, but we are looking at all aspects of this case," he said. "I promise I'll tell you when I can."

Jack left the Sheriff's Office feeling empty. He'd answered carefully, but it wasn't enough. Perhaps he'd hoped Stevens might thank Jack for his statement and tell him they would reopen the case.

At least Bagley had hinted they were still looking at the case. They know something isn't right about Palmer and Nicole's murder. Jack knew Terry Myles wasn't a killer; the grief-stricken man had finally regained purpose by exposing Nokomis's corruption. Nicole had been his partner in that fight, not his enemy.

As Jack drove away, the bigger picture became clearer: Nicole had called him because she planned to blow the whistle on Nokomis and was afraid for her life.

He also didn't understand why Stevens didn't ask him more questions about Palmer, his investigation into Nokomis, and how he was working with Nicole and Terry. The Sheriff's Office also had all the documents about hospital corruption that Terry had given him. He knew Stevens, and it wasn't like him to keep his thoughts so guarded. But this was an official interview, on the record. Surely, he must have doubts now.

Terry had been framed—Jack was sure of it. The tougher part was figuring out how to prove it before Terry went to trial and the actual killers escaped—or attacked again.

* * *

Back at the newspaper, Jack was at his desk, waiting for his computer to boot up. The phone rang.

"This is Josh Lucas, the security guard at Nokomis Hospital," the caller said in a low, steady voice. "We met the night your wife came into the ER."

"Yes, of course, Josh."

"I've been meaning to contact you. Odd things have been happening for months, but Nicole's murder? That was the last straw."

Jack immediately straightened in his chair. "Go on."

"Don't quote me, but top management told us guards to give Delman Palmer access to every floor and department. He has passcards that open anything—surgery, sterile processing, the pharmacy, and even medical records. No questions asked," Josh said.

He paused. "And here's what really gets us: Palmer carries a gun inside the hospital. Management looks the other way."

Jack felt the weight of the words. He wasn't surprised Palmer had a gun, but based on what Ed had discovered, Palmer was a convicted felon. Police would be very interested if he had a handgun.

"Have you told the police this?" Jack asked. "Lieutenant Stevens is running the investigation."

"Not yet. We only talk among ourselves."

"What do you talk about?" Jack pressed.

Josh hesitated, then whispered. "I can tell you this much. A few nights back, I was patrolling the employee garage. Saw Palmer out by the rows where staff park. That's Nicole's section. He didn't see me, but he was there, walking away quickly. I don't know what he was doing, but it didn't feel right."

Jack scribbled in his notebook, the name underlined twice: *Palmer by Nicole's car.*

Josh cleared his throat. "And there's one more thing. Two weeks ago, late one night, I saw Mr. Lard in the west wing service corridor. With him were Palmer and that contractor, Riggles. The three of them were huddled by the loading dock, talking low. Palmer was holding a duffel bag.

"When they spotted me, Riggles snapped. He said, 'This area's closed. Move along.' I did as I was told because Mr. Lard was there, but Riggles has no authority over me. I'll tell you this: it didn't look like any hospital business I've ever seen."

Jack listened intently. "You should tell this to Stevens. He needs to know."

"I know, but this will likely cost me my job if I have to testify."

Jack smiled. "Don't worry about that. I don't have to tell you that if you testify, Lard won't be CEO for long."

"You're right. I'll call the lieutenant right away," Josh said, his voice now full of confidence.

"Thanks for keeping in touch. Let's talk again," Jack said, hanging up.

He sat at his desk, reflecting on how the day had gone so far. He felt discouraged about Nicole's death and Terry's arrest, but he also believed the truth would eventually emerge. He needed to dig deeper to bring it to the surface.

Chapter 41:
Lard Pushes Merger

Late Morning, Tuesday, Sept. 25, 1984

Mike Lard shut his office door and let out a slow breath. For a week now, he had felt the floor shifting beneath him—rumors spreading through the hallways, state inspectors showing up unannounced, and Jack Kendall poking into the hospital's finances.

Worse still, Kendall's articles—fed to him by disloyal staff who Lard felt didn't grasp either the pressures of managing a modern hospital or his vision—had sparked inquiries from state and federal agencies. What had started as a manageable public relations issue was now threatening to ruin the deal he desperately needed.

He had to find a way to redirect the narrative. And he had a plan.

Despite the negative publicity, National Healthcare still wanted Nokomis. They needed a second hospital in the profitable Sarasota County healthcare market to satisfy investors, and Lard had spent months convincing them that Nokomis was the right acquisition—lean, strategically located, and ready for modernization.

National's executives had been shaken by the headlines, yes, but not enough to walk away. They had lawyers who could manipulate facts and settle disputes, even if it meant paying a few million dollars in fines. As long as Lard could keep the situation under control, they were willing to keep the deal moving forward.

The merger had to proceed quickly. If National signed the letter of intent before anyone connected the dots—regarding the foundation transfers, the phony companies, the siphoned money, and the rest—then everything could be integrated into the new corporate structure. New ownership, new oversight, and new financials. A fresh start for everyone, including him.

That was the plan—survival, disguised as strategy.

Lard checked his watch, picked up the phone, and punched in a few numbers. "Tonya, come in for a moment. Bring your notepad."

Tonya Creating slipped into the office with her usual professional calm. Lard appreciated that about her—steady, composed, and loyal enough not to pry into what didn't concern her.

"You needed me, Mike?" she asked.

"Yes. Close the door." He waited until the latch clicked. "I need a press release drafted this afternoon. The board meeting scheduled for October tenth—we're moving it up. September twenty-seventh."

Tonya blinked. "That's two days away."

"I'm aware." Lard gestured toward a chair. "Make sure the release emphasizes scheduling conflicts among board members. Call them vacations. You know the drill. Keep it vague but reasonable."

She sat, pen poised. "All right. What's the message once the meeting's moved? Why the urgency?"

Lard leaned back, clasping his hands over his stomach. "The board will vote on the letter of intent with National. I want that included, but delicately. No details. Just that the board will consider strategic partnership opportunities. Nothing more. We will also have other agenda items to improve efficiencies."

Tonya nodded, already forming language in her head. "So, emphasize efficiency and alignment. Tighten the timeline as a benefit."

"Exactly," Lard said. "We don't want speculation. This is about modernization, keeping pace with growth in the region, and positioning ourselves for long-term success." He paused, letting the rehearsed lines roll off his tongue. They sounded almost true when said confidently enough.

Tonya glanced up. "And if Jack Kendall calls?"

Lard forced a smile. "Tell him what we always tell him— we're committed to transparency and patient care. That's all. And I know he will ask for an interview. I don't want to speak with that jackal, so tell him I'm in meetings."

Tonya wrote a few final notes. "I'll have a draft to you in an hour."

"Good." He dismissed her with a nod. The moment she stepped out, the smile evaporated.

He knew this wasn't about modernization. It wasn't even about the hospital anymore. It was about staying one step ahead of Kendall, O'Neal, law enforcement, the regulatory agencies, and anyone else who thought they could unravel what he had built.

By next month, the merger would be in motion, and, with luck, the mess underneath would be someone else's problem.

And Mike Lard would still be standing.

* * *

By midafternoon, Jack was convinced that the story at Nokomis Hospital wasn't just about embezzlement and a suspicious murder—it was about Mike Lard and his criminal conspirators' self-preservation.

Jack chuckled at the press release Tonya had sent him via facsimile. Dr. O'Neal had already warned him that Lard was moving the board meeting to Thursday and had provided Jack with an internal memo about it. With both documents in hand, Jack hammered out a preview story for Wednesday morning's edition.

The headline was direct: "**Nokomis Board to Vote Thursday on Merger with National Healthcare.**"

The story cited Tonya's press release, but Jack also used the internal memo, in which Lard portrayed the deal as a visionary step.

"This merger with National Healthcare will reduce healthcare costs, open new markets, and ensure the survival of our hospital for years to come. It will create a national model that focuses on keeping people healthy through high-quality, affordable, and accessible care to more patients."

O'Neal didn't buy it. Neither did Jack. Katie's article about Nicole McIntosh's murder had already raised questions about Terry's arrest and why the hospital whistleblower was killed. Every day, the paper dug deeper. Jack suspected Lard was rattled, and if National Healthcare was reconsidering its deal, his best move was to secure a board vote before the story got further out of his control.

Jack had interviewed Dr. O'Neal at his home last Saturday. The cardiologist had said other factors were involved in the merger.

"Mike's painting this as a lifeline, but he's hiding the real motive, and National wants more than just a second hospital in Venice," he'd explained. "National's multi-specialty group is a direct competitor to mine. You think they'll keep independent practices like ours around after the ink dries? Not a chance."

"So you'll oppose the merger?"

"Absolutely. National isn't about care—they're about control. I've heard enough stories from colleagues in Fort Myers and Venice. They poach patients, they squeeze out independents, and frankly? Some of their practices skirt the law. Call it what it is—corruption."

"Thank you, Dr. O'Neal, for providing this memo and for your willingness to go on record with your thoughts," Jack said as the interview ended.

*　*　*

On deadline later that afternoon, Jack called Fort Myers healthcare consultant, Rick Matts, who had been following National Healthcare's growth for several years before it began acquiring hospitals in Southwest Florida.

"Thanks for talking with me again about investor-owned healthcare," Jack began.

"Jack, National is writing a playbook for investor-owned hospitals—shady billing, free rent, and other perks for doctors," said Matts, his voice carrying the weight of someone who'd grown tired of corruption and self-dealing, which had become popular for many investor-owned hospital chains and the doctors on their medical staffs who became investors.

"What kind of perks?"

"First, they let physicians invest in diagnostic centers, labs, and imaging units tied to their hospitals. That way, doctors profit twice—once from the admission, and again from the ancillary service," Matts said. "Then there's HHS investigations—kickbacks for referrals. Admit a patient, order a scan, and you get a slice of stock."

"They seem to get support on Wall Street for their business strategy," Jack commented.

"They sure do. Last year, National's stock was trading at $30 per share. Now it's up to $45."

"National is growing very fast, especially in Southwest Florida. Why?"

"Their growth is explosive. One hundred fifty hospitals and climbing. Why here? Look around. We live in a major retirement market, and they've figured out how to game Medicare reimbursements, squeeze insurers, and still look clean on paper," Matts said. "They even avoid most federal taxes. It's slick, I'll give them that. But ask yourself: are they in the business of healthcare, or the business of making money off the sick?"

"Thanks, Rick. You always come through, night or day," Jack said as he concluded the interview.

*　*　*

It was nearing 5 p.m. The newsroom was getting busy as reporters returned from assignments and copyeditors began reviewing early stories and checking the wire services.

Jack went over to talk with Rick about his story. "Rick, I'll have that preview story done soon about Nokomis moving up their meeting."

"I wished you had it earlier for the *Journal*, but I know you've been busy meeting with Bagley and Stevens," Rick said.

"I had other interviews as well, but I don't think anybody else will get them unless Tonya sends the press release to them, and I doubt she will. Lard wants to keep this as contained as possible. Besides, Dr. O'Neal gave me an internal board memo, and he is the only board member who will talk to the press," Jack said. "I've got one more interview with Professor Blatt, then I'll finish it."

"Good enough," Rick said, looking back at his computer screen.

Jack walked back to his desk and called Rose Blatt, a reliable healthcare finance expert.

"Hi, Rose. This is your daily checkup call from your favorite healthcare reporter," Jack said, teasing his source. "Guess what this is about?"

"Nice to hear from you again. What is it today? More on the Nokomis fiasco?" she asked.

"I'm writing about the proposed merger between Nokomis Hospital and National Healthcare. We've discussed the rumor, but the Nokomis board is scheduled to vote on a preliminary agreement tomorrow."

"I see. The pressures for small nonprofit hospitals like Nokomis aren't unique, Jack. Nokomis is losing half a million a month. They're $25 million in debt. Bondholders and staff are panicking," she said.

"So Lard's move makes sense on paper?"

"On paper, yes. National swoops in, pays off some liabilities, and brings in capital. But remember—these for-profits don't do charity," the professor said. "They'll close unprofitable units, cut staff, and refocus everything on revenue streams. ER, psych, indigent care? Gone. The irony is, the very services the community relies on most are the ones least likely to survive a merger."

"And Lard's role?"

"If National promised to cover illegal transfers from the hospital foundation, that's not a merger—that's a bailout. He's not saving Nokomis. He's saving himself," Blatt said.

"Thanks again, Rose. Talk with you next time."

"Anytime," she cheerfully said.

Jack clicked off the receiver and dialed Nokomis. He had left several messages earlier for Lard and Creating, but neither had returned his calls, and it was nearly 6 p.m.

"Tonya, this is Jack Kendall calling again," he began. "I'm on deadline and left messages for you and Mike. Call me back with an interview, or I will have to say neither of you returned repeated phone calls."

Just as Jack was finishing his story and getting ready to leave at 6:30 p.m., Creating returned his call. "I'm sorry, Jack. Mike is unavailable, and the board needed to meet early because of vacations," she said. "We're ready to present the board with the good news. You're welcome to attend the meeting tomorrow." She hung up without waiting for a response.

Jack didn't need to talk with Lard, since he had included his memo in the story, but he did want to know the real reason why the meeting had been moved up.

As for the story, he knew what was really happening with Nokomis: a hospital on the verge of meltdown, a corrupt CEO on the brink of arrest, a national chain with a shady history, ready to participate in the cover-up—willingly or not—and a vote coming up that could alter the course of healthcare in Sarasota County.

He leaned back in his chair and tapped the keyboard to send the story over to Rick. He doubted the story would change anything Lard wanted to do. However, it was sure to make the meeting livelier.

Just then, the phone rang.

"Jack, this is Jane Willoughby. I have something to tell you about Nicole."

"I'm glad you called. I've been thinking about you and Cathy. How are you doing?" asked Jack, realizing he hadn't checked in with any of Nicole's friends since her death.

"I've been thinking about telling someone at the Sheriff's Office what Nicole told me last week," Jane said. "She told Cathy, too. She was standing with me."

"What did Nicole tell you?" Jack asked.

Jane said, "She told me she was afraid of Mike Lard and Delman Palmer. Lard had threatened to fire her and silence her because he thinks she's working with you and Terry to expose the illegal activities at the hospital."

"I knew that, but she told you?"

"Yes. She also told Cathy and me that if anything happened to her, she had a cassette tape that would reveal everything Lard had done and what she and Terry were doing to expose the crimes," Jane said.

"Do you know where this cassette is?" Jack asked calmly, even as his body flared with emotion and his mind flooded with questions.

"She didn't tell me. I will try to find out," Jane said.

"You should immediately inform Lieutenant Stevens at the Sheriff's Office. He's conducting the investigation," Jack said.

"Will this help Terry?" she asked.

"Absolutely. It points the finger at someone other than Terry," said Jack. "You should also inform Terry's lawyer about the existence of this cassette tape. Please let me know what you do."

"I will," Jane said, hanging up.

Jack leaned back in his chair and thought. *Another recording? Stevens can't ignore this.* Then, a more pressing thought crossed his mind: *Where would Nicole have hidden this tape?*

* * *

The next morning, Jack's piece, based on a leaked memo from CEO Mike Lard and confirmed by board member Dr. Joel O'Neal, warned *Herald-Tribune* readers that the deal was being rushed through in the shadow of federal inspections and Nicole McIntosh's murder.

NOKOMIS HOSPITAL MOVES UP MERGER TALKS WITH NATIONAL HEALTHCARE

Jack Kendall
Herald-Tribune Staff Writer

NOKOMIS, Wednesday, Sept. 26, 1984 — In the wake of mounting financial troubles, a federal inspection report that cited serious patient-safety violations, and the shocking murder of Vice President of Nursing Nicole McIntosh, Nokomis Hospital has moved up a critical board meeting to vote on a proposed merger with National Healthcare Corp., a Nashville-based for-profit chain.

Initially scheduled for October 10, the vote will now take place on Thursday, according to a hospital press release and a confidential memo from CEO Mike Lard, obtained by the *Herald-Tribune*. In the memo, Lard told board members the merger is "the hospital's best opportunity to preserve clinical services and ensure future viability" amid what he called "unrelenting regulatory and financial pressures."

Dr. Joel O'Neal, a board member and long-standing member of the medical staff, confirmed the contents of the memo. "They're moving fast because of the bad publicity and because they don't want staff or the community asking too many questions," O'Neal said. "This is being pushed through before anyone can stop it."

Contacted by the *Herald-Tribune*, Spokesperson Tonya Creating explained that the hospital had to move up the meeting date because of board member "vacations." Creating added, "We're ready to present the community with the good news."

The merger proposal comes just days after Medicare and Joint Commission inspectors cited Nokomis for dirty surgical instruments, understaffing, and overall poor quality. The citations temporarily shut down elective surgeries at the facility. Sources indicated that the hospital is already losing over $500,000 per month, raising doubts about its ability to survive without a bailout.

According to the memo, Lard argued that affiliation with National Healthcare Corp. would "stabilize operations through scale efficiencies, better vendor contracts, and access to capital markets."

Critics, however, worry that a for-profit takeover could also mean additional cuts beyond maternity, behavioral health and emergency services.

"I am opposed to this takeover. This isn't just about saving Nokomis Hospital," Donald Tusk, one of the hospital's biggest donors, said. "It's about who controls the mission of this hospital. Will decisions be made locally for the good of our community, or in a corporate boardroom hundreds of miles away?"

The memo obtained by the *Herald-Tribune* also revealed that Lard met privately with National Healthcare executives earlier this summer. Several physicians said they were not informed of the talks until word of the proposed merger began circulating last week.

Creating didn't respond to questions about whether Nokomis needs an infusion of capital to avoid bankruptcy. But according to the memo, Lard told board members, "We must act decisively and without delay to protect our institution from further erosion."

Chapter 42:
Letter of Intent

Morning, Thursday, Sept. 27, 1984

Chairman David Royster called the board meeting to order. The room buzzed with talk, filled with employees, hospital supporters, and concerned citizens.

Mike Lard's agenda was also full: cutting maternity services and signing a letter of intent to merge with National Healthcare Corp.

All of this was supported by reports that Nokomis Hospital was losing market share to Sarasota Memorial to the north and National's three for-profit hospitals to the south.

"Mr. Chairman, before we get started, may I have the floor to ask a question?" asked Dr. Joel O'Neal, continuing without waiting for permission. "There has been a newspaper report that the reason for this merger is that the hospital is losing money. Management has not provided us with financial statements this year, so I want to know if this is true."

Before Royster could answer, Mike Lard cut in.

"No, we are not losing money, Dr. O'Neal, but our projects' declining market share and rising supply and vendor costs indicate negative growth in 1985," Lard said. "Mr. Brophy will give the board a more detailed summary after I present proposals for votes."

"I'd like to express my disappointment that these proposals did not go through the finance and planning committees," Dr. O'Ncal forcefully complained. "All we got was a brief memo several days before this meeting. There was no chance to discuss or debate."

Lard ignored Dr. O'Neal's criticism and began presenting a report on the financial losses caused by the hospital's NICU services.

"The issue of financial instability was raised," began Lard.

Donald Tusk, standing up in the front row, interrupted in a loud voice. "Excuse me, Mike, I'd like to say a few words before the board does its normal thing and approves whatever you say."

"Donald, I appreciate your enthusiasm for our hospital, but you are out of order," Royster said, tapping his gavel on the table.

"I also would like to talk," called out Valerie Paremi, a significant donor and former retired heart surgeon from Detroit. "I came to the meeting because I was told Mr. Lard will propose a merger with National Healthcare. I object to even starting discussions. As a community hospital, joining National could potentially save us 1% to 2% on our supply and vendor costs. However, we would transfer much more of our revenue to out-of-state investors."

Royster raised his voice. "I am sorry, Valerie, but you are not even on the board."

"We have a right to speak," Tusk said. "I've donated millions to this hospital to build it up. I will tell you right now: if the board votes to cut maternity services, eliminate alcohol and drug rehabilitation when some of our own executives have these problems, or merge with National—*any* one of these three—I will withdraw my support."

The dozen wealthy donors at the meeting erupted into applause. Another dozen nurses, doctors, and staff in the maternity ward also clapped in support of the affluent donors.

"We are a vibrant, heavily endowed, independent non-profit hospital," Tusk said. "We do not need to sell out to a for-profit chain that will make decisions from another city."

"If we face financial problems or lose market share, we need outside help to prevent it, and that should be in the form of hiring a management consulting firm," Paremi said.

Dr. O'Neal raised his hand to speak. "Mr. Chairman, I move to reject Mr. Lard's proposal to sign a letter of intent with National and instead hire Coopers and Lybrand Consultants to evaluate our problems," he said.

Royster shook his head. "Dr. O'Neal, I don't recognize you or your motion. Donald and Valerie, I appreciate your support, but our management team has already investigated this matter. I move that we allow Mr. Lard to continue his presentation."

Lard felt he had said enough. He nodded to board member Jimmy Giles, who motioned to approve the letter of intent to merge with National. Manfred Lords seconded it. Five other board members agreed, and the board approved the motion to begin official merger negotiations by an 8-6 vote, with McVay abstaining.

"Thank you, Mr. Chairman," Lard said.

Boos erupted from the audience. Several donors stood up and exited. Donald and Valerie remained, shaking their heads in disbelief.

Jane Willoughby, Cathy Leesaw, Josh Lucas, and Valentina Rubenko stared in shock at how quickly the vote on the negotiation was taken. Would Nokomis be sold and the crimes hidden?

As the people left the board meeting, General Counsel Gus Lessem pulled Charles McMann aside.

"Some of the board members are getting nervous. Did you know there's talk about hiring an outside lawyer to review some of our contracts before the board approves the merger?"

"They need to vote on that, and the best they can do is tie," McMann said.

"Giles told me Donald Tusk has agreed to pay out of his own pocket for the review," Lessem said. "We may need to make the next vote appealing for McVay and Dr. O'Neal."

"That can be arranged," McMann said.

Chapter 43:
Deadly Secrets at Nokomis

Morning, Friday, Sept. 28, 1984

After Harry Goldfarb's overdose at the hospital cocktail party in early September, he spent two weeks in the ICU recovering from a stroke that paralyzed the left side of his face. Several days after he was discharged, he was found dead in his car with crack cocaine and several used needles beside him, even though he had sworn he had quit using and turned his life around.

Ed spoke with his Sheriff's Office source and discovered they had investigated Harry's death and considered it suspicious. Many people told deputies that Harry planned to report Lard's hospital-sponsored coke parties. Still, no suspects were identified, and the case was marked "unsolved" and closed administratively.

Sheriff's detectives also investigated Cora Billingly's overdose at Lard's penthouse suite party. They questioned Lard about the parties, but he denied supplying any drugs to guests.

Detectives also investigated why Cora left for California. She told deputies she was getting a divorce from Billingly, but she wouldn't provide any other reason for her departure or how she got drugs at the party.

Jack called Cathy to ask if she had heard anything more about Harry and Cora.

"Off the record. Everyone at the hospital thinks Lard had something to do with Harry's death, but, of course, no one knows for sure," Cathy said.

"What about Cora?" Jack asked.

"Funny you should ask that. I heard Cora left Carl and moved to California to stay with her sister," Cathy said. "I heard her overdose was traumatic for her. She needed to get away from him and her decadent life here."

"Hmm," said Jack. "Didn't McMann's wife, Mary, also leave him to move to California? I wonder if that's a coincidence."

"I don't know. I didn't know Mary that well either. I just heard the stories about them," Cathy said.

"Could you ask around and find out how I can contact them?"

"I'll try, but they didn't hang out with us nurses. You know we're always working," Cathy said without a trace of humor.

Jack thanked Cathy, then dialed Ed's number. His brother answered directly.

"I found out where Goldfarb was buried. Guess what? Nokomis paid for his funeral, wake, and reception, plus hush money to keep the parents quiet," Ed said.

"Do you have his parents' phone number? Give me his wife's, too, if you have it," Jack requested.

Jack called Goldfarb's parents, but they refused to talk. He called Anna, Harry's wife, and had better luck.

"Harry was murdered. I told the sheriff's detectives the hospital tried to bribe me to keep my mouth shut. I told them what I thought," Anna said. "They thanked me, but said they had no evidence to pursue. They seemed to believe the story that he was a drug addict and had fallen off the wagon. My Harry was killed because he knew too much."

"Mrs. Goldfarb, I'm going to pursue this story and see where it goes," Jack said. "I know several facts about what happened with Harry that the detectives don't. May I call you again?"

"Yes, Mr. Kendall. Please get to the bottom of this. Harry was a good man. He just had a drug problem," Anna said.

Jack interviewed several hospital employees and others about Nokomis's plan to shutter mental health, drug, and alcohol programs before the merger with National became final.

It was ironic, Jack thought, that the hospital was shutting down local inpatient drug and alcohol programs while its top executives were addicted to cocaine and alcohol.

On Sunday, September 30, two stories appeared in the *Herald-Tribune*.

NOKOMIS HOSPITAL TO CLOSE BEHAVIORAL HEALTH PROGRAM, LAY OFF 100 WORKERS NOV. 1

Jack Kendall
Herald-Tribune Staff Writer

NOKOMIS, Sunday, Sept. 30, 1984 — Nokomis Hospital's 30-bed inpatient psychiatric unit, which treats hundreds of patients with mental health, alcohol, and substance abuse problems each year, will close Nov. 1, hospital officials said.

On Oct. 24, Nokomis will stop accepting inpatients. Any remaining patients will be transferred to other hospitals a week later, said CEO Mike Lard in a statement.

Lard said emergency services for mental health and substance abuse will still be provided.

"We have signed an affiliation agreement with National Healthcare for inpatient and outpatient mental health, alcohol, and drug abuse patients," Lard said. "This will smooth our transition to National's programs in Port Charlotte once the merger is completed."

On Thursday, the 15-member Nokomis Hospital board of trustees narrowly approved a letter of intent to merge with 30-hospital National Healthcare Corp., an investor-owned company based in Nashville, Tennessee.

National operates three hospitals in Southwest Florida, including a 100-bed hospital in Venice, a 300-bed facility in Fort Myers, and a 250-bed hospital in Naples.

Pat Baltimore, Nokomis's director of behavioral health, said she was told of the unit's closure on Friday. She said her last day, and that of her 100-employee staff, will be Nov. 1.

"We will do our best to help our dedicated employees find new positions, whether with National or another hospital," Baltimore said. "I am concerned, however, that our community will lose a vital resource, one that saved many lives in the ten years I have been here."

Melinda Turner, a former drug counselor in the hospital's drug and alcohol unit, said mental health services in the community would worsen because there would be no inpatient services for more than 20 miles for people who are treated in the ER.

"We need the services. We used to get 80% of our admissions from the ER. They will still show up, and where will they go for drug and alcohol treatment services? We turn them away and make things worse for them and the community," Turner said.

"For many people, Nokomis Hospital is quite literally the starting point for recovery," she said.

However, with Nokomis set to close its inpatient acute substance abuse and addiction unit on Nov. 1 and its crisis center on Nov. 15, patients seeking services will have nowhere locally to go, sources said.

"People are going to die without these services," said Amanda Heiter, a substance abuse nurse. "If they close these services, South Sarasota County has no other outstanding programs for 20 miles. This closure will devastate the entire community. We had so many people who were clean and sober for years. Now, without a convenient place for them, many will relapse. We need this service. They can't shut this down."

Heiter previously worked at the Nokomis inpatient unit but transferred to the hospital's outpatient recovery unit last year. Both units will close within 45 days.

Since 1970, nearly 50 public state psychiatric hospitals have closed nationwide following the repeal of the U.S. Mental Health Systems Act in 1981 and as care was shifted to private psychiatric hospitals, outpatient clinics and halfway houses.

"This move to deinstitutionalization was based

partially on the need to eliminate suffering, but the result has been increased homelessness and incarceration for people with psychiatric or behavioral health problems," said Rose Blatt, a healthcare professor at the University of South Florida in Tampa.

Dr. Joel O'Neal, a cardiologist on the hospital board, opposed shutting down the behavioral health department. He said a group of board members is working to reverse the closure of mental health services, which he argued is prompted by the proposed merger.

"We are still looking into the reasons for this merger. Many leading citizens and supporters of the hospital feel we don't need National Healthcare. Other options should be pursued," Dr. O'Neal said.

Lard also said Nokomis's ambulance company will be merged with National Healthcare's company after the merger.

"This will expand ambulance services for the people of South Sarasota County, improving response times and reducing costs," Lard said.

Jack also quickly finished typing a sidebar about Harry and Cora, describing what he knew about the cocaine parties Lard held most Saturdays and some Wednesdays.

He had begun the story several days earlier, interviewing Josh Lucas and Dr. Rashard on background, but he delayed telling it because he needed a hook to connect it to the larger issue at the hospital. Sadly, Harry's death provided that.

NOKOMIS EXECUTIVES WINED, DINED, TOOK COCAINE AND QUAALUDES AT PARTIES IN THE HOSPITAL'S PENTHOUSE SUITE

Jack Kendall and Katie North
Herald-Tribune Staff Writers

NOKOMIS, Sunday, Sept. 30, 1984 — Nokomis Hospital CEO Mike Lard hosted lavish parties in the fifth-floor penthouse suite, where employees and guests feasted on plump shrimp and rare roast beef, sipping expensive wines and liquor, while others snorted cocaine and took quaaludes, sources told the *Herald Tribune*.

The expensive parties, estimated to cost more than $5,000 each, were paid for by a particular executive payroll account, one unknown to most board members.

At the Sept. 8 party, one employee and the wife of a contractor overdosed and were treated in the hospital's emergency department.

Harry Goldfarb, the hospital's vice president of environmental services, suffered a stroke and was hospitalized for two weeks. Two days after being discharged, he was found dead in his car of an apparent overdose.

Sheriff detectives investigated Goldfarb's death, conducting interviews with both friends and hospital officials. While the circumstances surrounding the death raised suspicions, the investigation yielded no viable leads or suspects for arrest.

However, based on new evidence, Lieutenant Jim Stevens said the Sheriff's Office has reopened its investigation.

"Nokomis Hospital offered me money to stay silent about Harry's death, but he was killed because of what he knew about these parties and the corruption at the hospital where he worked for five years," said Anna Goldfarb, Harry's widow.

Tonya Creating, Nokomis's director of public relations, denied that any money was offered to Mrs. Goldfarb. She refused further comment.

Cora Billingly, the wife of contractor Carl Billingly, overdosed on quaaludes and liquor. After recovering, she left her husband and moved to California to live with her sister. When contacted by the *Herald-Tribune*, she declined to comment about the parties or her overdose.

"I have something to say, but only after my divorce is finalized," Cora Billingly told the newspaper.

Many Saturday nights, Lard hosted the decadent parties, which sometimes featured prostitutes, strippers, and live music, said several hospital officials familiar with the events.

Hospital officials declined interview requests, citing ongoing investigations. Spokesperson Creating released a statement.

"Nokomis executives regularly held sophisticated gatherings for senior management, doctors, trustees, and business partners. These events were intended to foster professional relationships and advance hospital business initiatives.

"We categorically deny any insinuation that attendees engaged in unlawful behavior. Such assertions are entirely baseless and without merit," the statement said.

However, according to the *Herald-Tribune*, photographs and audio recordings showed hospital ER doctors and nurses transporting Harry Goldfarb and Cora Billingly from the fifth floor of the executive suite into the elevator, where they were treated for overdoses in the hospital.

CEO Mike Lard, Board Chair David Royster, and construction contractor John Riggles were also among those pictured behind Goldfarb and Billingly on the stretchers.

A two-minute audio recording of hospital and contract employees revealed that party attendees used cocaine, crack cocaine, and marijuana, and drank alcohol to excess.

The *Herald-Tribune* identified the people speaking in the recording with the help of coworkers who knew the employees.

EDITOR'S NOTE: As part of a Sheriff's Office investigation, the *Herald-Tribune* voluntarily provided copies of photographs, audio recordings, and documents gathered during the party, along with a statement detailing how the evidence was obtained.

The *Herald-Tribune* chose to cooperate with law enforcement in accordance with its commitment to public accountability and community safety.

Editors determined that the materials gathered during their investigation—particularly photographs and recordings from the party—could help clarify the circumstances surrounding Harry Goldfarb's and Cora Billingly's overdose and support the broader inquiry into drug activity linked to the hospital.

While the decision was not taken lightly, newsroom leadership emphasized that the evidence was obtained lawfully and that sharing it aligned with the paper's responsibility to serve the public interest without compromising journalistic integrity.

Chapter 44:
Della Visits Terry

Afternoon, Friday, Sept. 28, 1984

The clank of the heavy door echoed as Della Mason stepped inside the visitation room. She wore her usual legal outfit—dark suit, leather briefcase—but her eyes betrayed her true feelings.

Terry Myles sat across the table, hands folded, looking more like a tired bookkeeper than an accused murderer. He rose when she entered.

"You're Nicole's friend. My father told me," he said quietly, searching her face.

"I was," Della answered, sliding into the chair. "That's why I didn't want this case. I told my partners I had no business defending you."

"Then why are you here?"

She paused, unclasping her briefcase and taking out legal papers. "Because your father wrote a check, my firm couldn't ignore. Twenty thousand buys a lot of votes at the table."

She leaned in. "But I'll be honest, Terry—I came in wanting you guilty."

Terry nodded. "I figured as much."

"Then I started digging. I read Kendall's articles about the quality problems and corruption at Nokomis Hospital, and I learned how you and Nicole were trying to expose it. I asked myself a question the sheriff's detectives and prosecutors overlooked: what motive would you have to kill your collaborator and friend?"

"That's what I've been trying to tell people," Terry pleaded.

"I read Jack's statement about the message he received from Nicole minutes before she was murdered. I listened to the recording. It didn't sound like she feared you; it sounded like she feared Mike Lard and his employee, Delman Palmer."

"Jack knows how I felt about Nicole," Terry said, feeling stronger for the first time in days.

"But the final piece of information that sealed it for me is the phone call I received from Jane Willoughby," Della said.

"The cassette tape? You have it?" Terry asked.

"No, we're still looking for it, but Jane told me it exists. And if it contains what she believes is on it, I can use that as evidence of your innocence," Della said.

Terry straightened, his voice firm. "And Delman Palmer's guilt! That's what I've been trying to tell anyone who'd listen. It wasn't me. Nicole was close to blowing it open, and Palmer made sure she couldn't."

Della studied him for a long moment. "I don't trust people easily, Terry. But I trust patterns. And the pattern here says you're being framed." She gathered up her papers. "So I'll defend you. Not because of your father's money. Not even because of you, even though I don't really know you. It's because

322

Nicole deserves the truth—and so does this community."

Terry's throat tightened. "Thank you, Della. That means more than you know."

"Don't thank me yet," she said, standing up and snapping her briefcase shut. "We have a pre-trial hearing in two weeks. Until then, I want every detail you've got—dates, names, scraps of paper. If Lard, Brophy, McMann, Riggles, Palmer, and others are involved, I'll find out. When I do, this whole house of cards will come crashing down."

Terry leaned forward, his voice low but steady. "If we can expose them... then maybe Nicole didn't die for nothing. She was my friend, too."

Della studied him for a long moment. Behind the exhaustion in his eyes, she saw something else—a man weighed down not only by confinement but also by a grief he hadn't yet learned how to bear. As she looked at him, she realized they both had lost a friend. There was something else, too—a quiet echo of something Nicole once hinted at, something Della had never quite understood.

* * *

Della Mason spread her files across the table in the *Herald-Tribune* conference room. She looked different than she had in previous meetings—less guarded, more determined. Jack and his brother Ed leaned forward, ready to hear what she had.

"All right," she began. "I visited Terry this morning. I told him this, and I'm telling you the same. I don't trust easily. However, after a week of following up on leads, my investigators are convinced that Terry Myles was framed. I believe the net is starting to close around Lard."

Jack raised an eyebrow. "We've found out a lot. What've you got?"

Before Della could answer, Ed leaned in. "Let me start by telling you what we've got. I haven't even told Jack this additional detail yet. We just found out."

Jack coughed. "What are you holding back?"

"Remember the guy in the black BMW who tailed Bobbie to the *Herald* last week and then showed up outside your house in Cherokee Estates while I was watching it? We just found out that the BMW Palmer used was rented by a shell company in Miami that is a front for a Cuban outfit that the feds have tied to drug smuggling, protection, intimidation, and contract hits."

Jack winced. "Are you telling me the feds knew about Palmer and his ties to this Cuban drug gang? Bagley hinted the Sheriff's Office knew something about Palmer. I wish you had found this out before you talked with Stevens, which raises a big question. Why didn't the feds or Bagley act on your tip about Palmer *before* Nicole was murdered?"

"I don't know. You'll need to ask Stevens or Bagley. My sheriff's source is mum about that," Ed said, shaking his head. "However, it's possible the feds targeted Palmer as part of a larger investigation and asked Bagley to leave Palmer alone."

Jack's mouth dropped open. "And they *weren't* tailing Palmer? You're telling me the feds and sheriff's detectives let a violent enforcer roam free while Nicole was out there begging for help?"

Ed shrugged his broad shoulders.

Jack's voice sharpened. "If the feds told Bagley to stand down, then someone needs to explain why an innocent woman ended up dead because they were too busy protecting their own damn investigation."

Della tapped her pen. "We know Palmer and Riggles have connections in Miami. Riggles handles construction contracts; Palmer does the dirty work. Lard contracts with Riggles and the Cuban Mafia in Miami for muscle."

"I'm confident the Sheriff's Office was aware of this. They will answer for it before this is all over. I will make sure of that," Della said firmly.

Jack looked at Della, his eyes still burning. "We will get to the bottom of this, believe me. I want Bagley to explain how he could let the feds do this."

He stood up, went to the window, and looked out over U.S. 41. Talking about Palmer, Jack's old pain resurfaced. Guilt over not acting sooner to save Becky in Bogotá, not trying harder to protect Brewster, and now, not alerting law enforcement early enough about the danger Delman Palmer posed. Did his failure contribute to Goldfarb and Nicole's murders?

Ed watched as Jack grew quiet. He understood what his brother was thinking.

"Jack, don't blame yourself for Nicole," Ed said. "If anyone is to blame, it's me. I passed all the information about Palmer to Stevens. I even informed my source in the Sheriff's Office of the importance of finding Palmer. I should have pushed harder and followed up."

"No, I knew about all this, believe me, I knew," Jack said, staring out the window. "I don't have any excuses. It was my responsibility."

Della frowned. She sensed Jack and Ed's discomfort. "Here is something neither of you knows. One of my investigators told me deputies looked but couldn't find Palmer. They knew he was dangerous. He must have gone underground to a safe house days before Nicole was killed. He is a professional killer. You both did what you could."

Jack took a deep breath, went back to the table, and sat down. "I don't know. The feds must have known about him and should have kept tabs on him. We need more information about why he wasn't found."

He scribbled "talk with Bagley about the feds" in his notebook, then turned to Della. "Did you speak with Josh Lucas?"

"Your security guard source?" Della nodded. "We interviewed him. He confirmed Palmer was in the employee garage the night Nicole was killed—lurking near her car. No reason for him to be there. And he's been seen before. A week earlier, Lucas caught Palmer, Riggles, and Lard talking in a locked supply area. He heard voices and opened the door with his master key. He said they acted like they were caught. None of them belonged there."

Jack's pen froze mid-sentence. "That's important. If Palmer had unfettered access and Lard signed off on it, that puts all three in the murder conspiracy."

"Exactly," Della said. "Add in the unexplained payouts in Lard's register, the Miami ties, and the BMW surveillance of your wife—it's not just corruption. It's intimidation. They're making moves on anyone who gets close. We can use all this in court to establish reasonable doubt, if nothing else."

Ed chuckled grimly. "Sounds like a playbook I've seen before. You don't put muscle on a hospital accountant or on a reporter's family unless you're scared the story's true."

Jack leaned back, jaw tight. "Then maybe we can stop them. We just need to prove all of this before Palmer surfaces to kill again."

Della snapped her folder shut and looked from Ed to Jack. "He's not going to kill again. That's why I'm involved now. Nicole's gone. Terry's staring at life in prison. Palmer's still loose. And unless we act quickly, Lard can still play his remaining cards. So—Jack, you write. Ed, you work with my team and dig. And I'll fight this in court."

Jack leaned back, pen poised over his notebook. "Ms. Mason," he said gently, "I like your enthusiasm. Ed will work with your team. I'll write—but it's journalism for the *Herald-Tribune*, not a brief for the defense."

Della blinked, then nodded slightly. "Of course. My apologies. I just...appreciate this meeting. And so does Terry."

Jack softened his tone. "I get it. We're all chasing the same truth, but I have to keep a line between what I print and what happens in the courtroom. That line protects the people who read my stories, and it protects you, too." He set the pen down. "As long as we respect that, I'm happy to share what I learn, and I'll expect the same."

Della allowed herself a faint smile. "Fair enough."

"Good," Jack said, sliding his notebook back toward himself. "Now, let's figure out how to keep Lard from stacking the deck."

As Della stood up, she exhaled. "I hesitate to say this, but have you thought about asking for protection?"

"You mean for me?" asked Jack.

"Yes, Palmer followed your wife and staked out your house. He did that for a reason," Della said.

"To frighten us," Jack said. "You don't know me well, but we're prepared. We've faced danger like this before. Ed's detectives go with Bobbie if she needs to see the doctor or step out for any reason. We have protection around the clock at our house. Don't worry."

Chapter 45:
Jack Visits Terry

Monday, Oct. 8, 1984

The weekend was restful. Jack and Bobbie remained at home, looked after the twins, swam in the pool, and chatted with friends and family on the phone. Monday morning, Jack's top priority was to visit Terry at the county jail.

Jack stepped in front of the metal detector and emptied his pockets into a tray as he easily walked through the electronic scanner without trouble. A deputy signaled him to move forward, and the heavy steel door groaned open. Fluorescent lights lit up the dull gray walls. The air carried a faint smell of bleach and coffee.

Terry Myles sat on the other side of the glass partition, his prison jumpsuit wrinkled, his face lined by exhaustion. But his eyes—they burned with urgency.

Jack picked up the handset. "You holding up?"

"I've been better," Terry said with a bitter laugh. "But I need you to hear me, Jack. I didn't kill Nicole."

Jack let the words hang. "I believe you. We've been talking with everyone. I gave two statements to the police. They have everything they need to dismiss the charges. I don't understand why they haven't."

"Why haven't you written that story you promised me at the Old Hickory two weeks ago?" Terry asked. "Don't you think it would help?"

"The Sheriff's Office knows everything, but it's complicated. I'm still pushing for us to publish that story. My editor and publisher asked me to come in and talk with you one more time. So, tell me again, what happened that night?"

Terry leaned forward, took a deep breath, and pressed the handset more tightly. "As I mentioned, I received a typewritten note from Nicole saying she wanted to talk. We hadn't spoken in a week because Palmer was tailing us, and Lard was making threats. I wanted to speak with her, but it felt odd to meet this way. Still, I thought maybe our plan had shifted."

"And you went to her house?"

"Yeah. I thought Pete would be there; he usually was. When I arrived, everything was dark, and the front door was locked. That's when my gut told me something was wrong. I grabbed my handgun from the car—same one I always keep in a floor lockbox—and went around back. The sliding glass door was open. I went inside."

Jack's voice was steady. "And?"

Terry swallowed hard. "She was on the kitchen floor. Shot. No pulse. I froze—then started searching the rooms, thinking maybe the shooter was still there. Nothing. The whole house was quiet."

His voice cracked. "I panicked, Jack. I bolted. Thought I'd call it in from home, but then...how would it sound? Me, at the scene, with a gun, when half the town knows I was close to her, a married woman? With her husband out of town? Who would believe me?"

"Let me get this straight," Jack said, leaning in. "You took a handgun from the car inside the house, found Nicole, never fired a shot, and left with the same gun?"

"That's right."

"What gun was it?"

"My Raven .25. The one I always keep in the car," Terry replied.

"But Nicole was killed with a .38-caliber revolver," Jack said. "Do you own a gun like that?"

Terry's eyes widened. "Yes. I keep one at the house. Wait— was it *my* gun that killed her? Is that why they think I did it?"

"It must be," Jack said. "I don't know the full evidence the police have, other than the eyewitness who saw you enter and leave the house with a gun, which had to be your Raven. Della must know, but she didn't tell me anything. But if they found a .38 in your home..."

Terry rubbed his forehead. "No wonder they arrested me. Palmer must have stolen my .38, used it on Nicole, and then planted it back in my house."

"I'll tell Della," Jack said. "She'll at least have a theory to explain how the detectives got this wrong."

Jack studied him for a moment. "So who do you think did it?"

Terry didn't hesitate. "Palmer. Who else? He's been threatening Nicole for days. Threatening me. And I don't think she ever believed Lard would actually send him to do something like this." He lowered his head, shutting his eyes. "She trusted too long."

Jack didn't say it aloud, but he'd seen corruption turn desperate men into killers before. Cornered criminals rarely behaved rationally.

He took a breath. "Terry, I've got a tough question—but I have to ask it. Making sure you don't pay for this is what matters now."

Terry looked up, wary.

"We need to publish the story about what you found in Lard's office," Jack continued. "Everything I know—how Lard siphoned money from the hospital, insurance, Medicare... the secret ledgers, the bank transfers, the payoffs. We reveal all of it. And we explain how you uncovered the evidence. It shifts the spotlight. People will start to see Lard's and Palmer's involvement in this."

Terry stiffened. "That's a big risk, Jack. Mentioning the break-in? You're talking about tying my name to it. I thought we agreed you'd report what I *found*, not how I found it."

"I remember. But then they arrested you," Jack said quietly. "I can write around the break-in. Keep the focus on the documents, not the method. The paper's lawyers will review the story. They won't let anything through that puts you in more danger."

Terry swallowed hard. "I don't know..."

"I've already turned over the things that help us," Jack added. "Nicole's phone message from that night. Proof that you were working with her to expose Lard. Everything shows you had no reason to kill her—and every reason to protect her. If I keep the story clean and factual, the documents will speak louder than any accusation."

Terry was silent for a long moment. Then he nodded. "All right. But one condition—talk to Della first. If she thinks it won't hurt my defense, then go ahead."

Jack paused. There was one last issue to talk about with Terry, one that Peter Gantz had insisted he mention.

"Terry, you should consider one more possibility. I'll talk to Della, but you need to understand that what you did in breaking into Lard's office could be seen as theft by a prosecutor. You might be charged later with a crime."

Terry smiled. "That is the least of my worries. If it comes to that, I have a good attorney and a hard-working investigative reporter who'll put what I did into context. I'm not worried."

Jack listened carefully, nodding in agreement.

Taking a deep breath, Terry rested the phone against his shoulder, sagging for a moment before lifting it again. "And Jack... promise me something."

"Anything."

"Don't let Palmer get away."

Jack met his eyes through the glass, his voice steady. "I won't. Not while I've got the newspaper behind me—and blood in my veins."

* * *

After leaving the jail, Jack ducked into a payphone at the adjacent courthouse. He dropped in a quarter and dialed.

"Della Mason," came the crisp voice on the other end.

"Della, it's Jack. I just spoke with Terry. He okayed me to publish the story about how and why he took the evidence of the crimes at Nokomis Hospital from Lard's office, but only if you agree. He also understands he might be charged with theft for stealing those documents."

A pause. Then: "I can defend him against theft based on Nokomis Hospital's own crimes. If it helps point the finger where it belongs, I won't stop you. Just make sure the piece sticks to facts. Don't taint the jury pool."

"You have my word. Only the truth."

"Then go ahead, Jack. Print it. I'll talk with Terry again in the morning, and we should meet again if anything comes up from it. As you know, sometimes newspaper articles do some good."

"Sometimes?" Jack asked with a chuckle. "We can discuss the value of journalism another time. Just let me know if there's anything we need to discuss before the hearing. Now, I've got some writing to do."

* * *

By midafternoon, Jack was hunched over his computer. He rewrote, cut, and tightened the story, and then he did it all over again. It was at least his tenth version. But finally, he was happy. The story tied everything together.

Nicole's murder. Palmer's shadowy presence at Nokomis Hospital. Lard's cocaine use and financial rot. And the damning embezzlement that was revealed in the secret ledgers.

The headline read: "**Nokomis Hospital Scandal: Secret Files Expose Theft and Corruption**"

Jack sat at his desk, looked it over one last time, closed his eyes, then punched the send button on the keyboard. The story electronically shot over to his editor.

"Rick, you got my story," Jack called out across the newsroom.

Rick nodded, adjusted his glasses, and read in silence. Ten minutes later, he walked over to Jack.

"It's tight, it's bright, and it's going upstairs to Gantz for review. Stand by."

An hour dragged on, then another thirty minutes. Rick was called upstairs several times. Jack knew Peter was questioning him about some of the story's facts and details. He wondered if Peter would allow Delman Palmer's name to be used. Palmer was a real person, but he had disappeared days before Nicole was murdered. Jack was at peace with the possibility that Rick and Gantz might decide not to include Palmer's name until he was found and arrested. That was fine. He knew Peter would scrutinize every line and phrase for potential libel risks.

By 8 p.m., Jack was starting to worry. He had called Bobbie several times to explain what was happening. She told him to hang in there.

At last, Rick returned from the publisher's office, holding the proof. "Peter objected to using Delman Palmer's name, and we had to tweak a couple of parts, but they signed off. Mr. Lindsay thought it was great, some of your best work. It's running on the front page tomorrow."

* * *

Jack grabbed the phone and dialed Della. He wanted to call Terry at the jail, but it wasn't allowed.

"It's done," Jack said. "Terry's story hits the streets in the morning. Bring a copy with you when you see him in the morning. Tell him not to lose faith. Tell him I believe the story should raise many doubts about your arrest and point the finger at the real criminals."

There was a long silence. Then Della said, "Jack, Terry believes in you. You kept your promise, just as Nicole told me you would. Thank you for Terry and for Nicole."

Chapter 46:
Secret Files, Public Reckoning

Early Morning, Tuesday, Oct. 9, 1984

For the first time in many nights, Jack slept peacefully and woke up at five-thirty, only when he heard the faintest sound from one of the babies. He got up and checked on them, and they were still sound asleep. Bobbie hardly moved in her bed. She had been up twice earlier for feedings. He quietly went downstairs and stepped outside the front door.

Walking out into the crisp early October air, Jack nearly ran across the lawn to grab the morning paper. He wanted to see the headline. He unwrapped the paper, slipping off the rubber band, and there it was.

NOKOMIS HOSPITAL SCANDAL: SECRET FILES EXPOSE THEFT AND CORRUPTION

Jack Kendall
Herald-Tribune Staff Writer

NOKOMIS, Tuesday, Oct. 9, 1984 — Nokomis Hospital's troubles deepened with the disclosure of secret financial ledgers that point to systematic theft and mismanagement at the highest levels of the institution.

The documents—obtained last month by a hospital accountant arrested in connection with the murder of Nicole McIntosh—show two sets of books.

The official ledgers reveal the hospital's declining financial health. At the same time, the hidden records detail unauthorized transfers, inflated vendor payments, and unexplained withdrawals linked to hospital CEO Mike Lard and his top managers.

The revelations come as Nokomis reels from a cascade of crises: a Joint Commission and Medicare inspection that cited life-threatening safety lapses, mounting federal scrutiny over Medicare billing practices, and now, the murder of McIntosh, a respected nurse who had spoken out about patient-care failures.

Sheriff's investigators arrested Terry Myles, a hospital accounting manager and widower, in connection with McIntosh's death. However, Myles has told the *Herald-Tribune* that he is innocent and that the real threat to the hospital—and possibly Nicole's true killer—comes from a shadowy figure, a hospital contract worker whose influence reaches across multiple departments.

Together, the hidden ledgers, increasing inspection failures, and a proposed merger with for-profit National Healthcare Corp. raise questions about whether Nokomis

Hospital has become less a community institution and more a stage for personal gain, corporate gamesmanship, and violent cover-ups.

Interviews with hospital staff and internal sources describe a culture in which a private contract worker, whose name has been withheld because no charges have been lodged, was granted unrestricted access to every floor of Nokomis Hospital, despite having no medical training.

A security guard, who requested anonymity but has provided the Sheriff's Office with the same information as this newspaper, confirmed that the contract worker carried a firearm on the premises—an extraordinary breach of hospital protocol—and was seen in closed-door meetings with Lard and construction contractor John Riggles.

At the same time, evidence has emerged that Lard and other senior executives may have been using cocaine inside hospital offices.

Myles recovered a small vial containing the drug during an after-hours entry into the CEO's office. The vial, along with photocopies of the hidden ledgers found in Lard's desk, now form part of the evidence reviewed by law enforcement and attorneys for the *Herald-Tribune*.

"This isn't a case of one or two nights of bad judgment," said one hospital employee who asked not to be named. "Decisions about money, staffing, and patient care were being made by people who were impaired—and the community is paying the price."

The timing of these revelations is significant. Lard moved up a board meeting—initially scheduled for October 10—to last Thursday, September 27, when trustees voted 8-6 on a preliminary merger agreement with National Healthcare, which nationwide owns 150 hospitals, including one in Venice and two others in nearby Lee and Collier counties.

In a memo to the board obtained by the *Herald-Tribune*, Lard argues the merger will "reduce costs, expand markets, and secure Nokomis's future."

But critics, including Dr. Joel O'Neal, a cardiologist

338

and hospital board member, contend the move is a smokescreen. "This is about hiding the financial mess, not fixing it," O'Neal said. "National has a history of rewarding doctors with perks and kickbacks to generate admissions and referrals. The merger won't protect this community—it will bury the truth."

For bondholders, employees, and patients, the stakes could not be higher. If Nokomis fails to correct 15 major deficiencies, the Joint Commission could revoke accreditation. If the hospital loses accreditation, Medicare and Medicaid reimbursements would cease, resulting in a loss of more than 80 percent of the hospital's revenue.

The merger with National may be the only lifeline left for Lard and his inner circle. Still, it comes at a cost to transparency, accountability, and, potentially, justice in Nicole McIntosh's murder.

At the center of the scandal are photocopies and pictures Myles took earlier this month inside Lard's office. The documents show two sets of hospital ledgers: the official books presented to the board and auditors, and a second set that reveals the diversion of foundation funds into secret accounts controlled by Lard and his inner circle.

"These are classic hallmarks of embezzlement," said Keith Tillis, a Sarasota-based CPA who reviewed the documents for the *Herald-Tribune*. "You've got parallel records, hidden transfers, and unexplained expenses categorized under vague terms like consulting fees or community programs. That's exactly how executives conceal their crimes."

According to Tillis, the ledgers were designed to mask losses and enrich the executives. "If you see allocation entries without supporting invoices or receipts, that's money walking out the door," he said. "It's the same kind of scheme that bankrupted smaller hospitals in the 1970s, and in most cases, it's theft, plain and simple."

Tillis added that Lard's attempt to push Nokomis into a merger with National Healthcare may be directly related to these financial irregularities.

"A merger would bury these losses inside a much larger corporate balance sheet," he said. "That's a tactic we've seen before. It's not about saving the hospital—it's about covering tracks."

[**Continued, Page A4**]

[**Continued, Page A4**]

* * *

The night before Terry's hearing was peaceful at the Kendall house. A gentle lamp softly lit the living room. Jack sat on the sofa with Ella against his chest, her tiny fists clenched under her chin. Bobbie rocked gently in the chair across from him, Eli asleep in her arms, wrapped snugly in a pale-blue blanket.

"You're still keyed up," Bobbie murmured, keeping her voice low so she wouldn't wake the babies, "ever since that story ran today."

Jack brushed a fingertip through Ella's soft hair. "Hard to shut off after a story like that. It's finally making the sheriff look beyond Terry." He nodded toward the folded *Herald-Tribune* on the coffee table, headline blaring about Nokomis Hospital's hidden ledgers.

Bobbie looked down at Eli, his lips twitching in sleep. "I read it while they napped this afternoon. It's good, Jack. You made people see the mess for what it is."

"Maybe," Jack said, voice low. "But the evidence against Terry isn't just smoke. Someone swore they saw him at Nicole's place right after she was shot. He admitted being there. And the murder weapon—registered in his name with his fingerprints on it—ends up at his house. Hard to walk a jury past that."

"You think Palmer and Lard set him up?"

Jack exhaled slowly. "No doubt in my mind, but the prosecution can make the jury see things that aren't there.

340

Ed's guys are uncovering connections between Palmer, Lard, and contractor Riggles. But then you have the fifty grand sitting in Terry's account—the same amount missing from one of the hospital's books—that's going to be tough for Della to explain."

Bobbie shifted Eli to her shoulder, patting his back until he gave a tiny sigh. "I wish I could attend the hearing tomorrow."

Jack smiled, then looked at Ella's small face and the perfect curve of her ear. "I'll tell you all about it. I keep wondering how Della will present everything. A few of the recent developments have cheered me up. You know, new evidence is coming in every day, and people are calling the newsroom, asking why the hospital board's silent. Even Stevens is finally moving like there may be more than what he thinks is the truth."

Ella stirred, letting out a thin cry. Jack stood carefully, rocking her until she quieted. He glanced at Bobbie, a tired smile crossing his face. "One step at a time, right?"

Bobbie smiled in return. "You're stealing my line. Jack, step one: get some sleep before tomorrow's hearing. And step two: make sure these two grow up knowing their dad fought for what was right."

"I promise." Jack bent and kissed Ella's soft forehead. "Sleep, pearly girl," he whispered.

"You need to sleep as well. Tomorrow will be the big day," Bobbie said.

Chapter 47:
Preliminary Hearing

Morning, Wednesday, Oct. 10, 1984

It was a sunny fall morning when Judge S. John Launer gaveled the hearing in session.

"The purpose of this examination is only to determine whether a crime has been committed. If so, are there reasonable grounds to believe that the defendant participated in the commission of that crime? If that's clear, we may proceed. Mr. Burger, you may open for the prosecution," Judge Launer said.

Sarasota County District Attorney Hamilton Burger Jr. stood up and glanced at Della Mason, who sat next to defendant Terry Myles, dressed in an orange shirt and pants.

"Your Honor, this present case is elementary and straightforward. And, if we can avoid endless and purposeless cross-examination, this preliminary hearing can be quickly resolved," Burger said in his opening remarks.

"We will prove beyond a shadow of a doubt that Terry Myles did willfully turn on his co-worker Nicole McIntosh when she discovered he was embezzling money from Nokomis Hospital," Burger continued.

"He tricked her into meeting him at her house, and while her husband was out of town and she was alone, he shot her with his gun, which was found at his house when Sarasota County sheriff's deputies arrested him.

"We ask, Your Honor, to find the evidence we will present at the hearing as sufficient to bind Terry Myles over for trial in the premeditated murder of Nicole McIntosh," Burger concluded as he glared at Della and returned to his seat.

The two lawyers knew each other very well. They'd learned about their family histories from an early age. Della was the daughter of George Mason, the brother of the well-known Los Angeles defense attorney, Perry Mason. Hamilton Burger Jr. was the son of LA District Attorney Hamilton Burger Sr.

Now retired, the elder Mason and Burger Sr. had faced each other many times during their careers. Coincidentally or not, Perry's niece and Hamilton's son had moved to Sarasota, renewing their family rivalry in the Sunshine State.

"Do you wish to make any statement, Miss Mason?" the judge asked.

Della smiled and stood up. "Yes, Your Honor. Mr. Burger has presented a rather imaginative story about what happened the night my friend Nicole McIntosh was brutally murdered. I will present to the court what happened that night and what Terry Myles did and didn't do," she began.

"Terry and Nicole were friends. When Terry moved to Florida after experiencing the unfathomable loss of his wife and two young children in a tragic fire, Nicole was one of the first people who befriended him.

"Once Terry found out what was happening at Nokomis, he confided in Nicole about critical and sensitive accounting discrepancies in the hospital books going back years.

"The embezzlement he uncovered troubled him because he is very ethical and honest. Despite his pain from losing his family, as he saw how hospital staff and their families were being affected and how patients were being short-changed by mismanagement from the hospital's top executives, he chose to help Nicole, his friend, who was hearing from nurses about how supply shortages and unusual decisions were impacting patient care.

"I will present witnesses who will tell the court how Terry and Nicole worked together to expose crimes they believed were happening at Nokomis Hospital.

"While it is not my job to name or even point fingers at those who are truly guilty, the evidence and facts will point to high-ranking individuals at the hospital who worked to frame Terry to cover up their crimes," Della concluded as she sat down.

"Mr. Burger, call your first witness," said Judge Launer.

"Lieutenant Stevens, would you come to the stand?" Burger said. "Would you please state your name, what you do, and what you did on the night in question?"

"My name is Jim Stevens, I am a lieutenant with the Sarasota County Sheriff's Office. I was called to investigate the death of Nicole McIntosh on the night of September 24th, a Monday," the officer said.

"What did you find?" Burger asked.

"Miss McIntosh was shot three times in the chest by a .38 caliber revolver. She was dead when I arrived, at approximately

8:55 p.m."

"Did you talk with any witnesses?"

"Yes. There was a neighbor, Mr. McGillicuddy, who heard the shots and saw a man run out of the house and get into a dark-colored 1981 Chevrolet and race off."

"Was there anything else he saw?"

"He saw the Pennsylvania license plate, SPA1495."

"How could he see it so clearly?"

"The car was right under the streetlight."

"What did you do next?" Burger asked.

"I asked DMV for the name and address of the owner," Stevens said.

"Go on," Burger prodded.

"Terry Myles owns the car," Stevens explained. "We went to Mr. Myles's house."

"Was he there?"

"Yes. The car described by Mr. McGillicuddy was there. We knocked on the door. No one answered. We called for him several times, then entered the unlocked house and found him sitting at a kitchen table."

"What happened next?"

"We asked him if he was Terry Myles. He didn't respond. He just sat there, staring at a picture on the table," Stevens said. "We asked him to stand up and face us. He did so, and that's when we saw it."

"Saw what?" Burger asked.

"Blood. There was blood on the left sleeve of his shirt."

"Did you test the blood?"

"Yes, later. It was Mrs. McIntosh's."

"Did you ask if he killed her? Mrs. Nicole McIntosh?" Burger asked.

"Yes. Myles just stared at me and said nothing," Stevens said. "We arrested him on suspicion of murder and brought him down to the jail for processing."

"Thank you, Lieutenant Stevens," Burger said. "Your witness, Miss Mason."

Della slowly stood up, glanced at her notebook, and approached Lieutenant Stevens.

"Sir, did Mr. Myles ever say anything about the murder?" Della asked.

"Yes, after we booked him, we brought him into a room for questioning," Stevens said.

"What did he say about the murder?" Della asked.

"He said he went to Mrs. McIntosh's house for a meeting she called. The front door was locked when he arrived, so he went around back and entered through a sliding glass door. He said he called her name several times, but there was no answer. The defendant then walked into the kitchen and said he found her lying on the floor," Stevens replied.

"What did he say he did then?"

"He bent over to take her pulse. He said she was dead."

"Is it possible that is how he got blood on his sleeve?"

"Well, yes, it is possible. But it was Myles's gun we found at his house, with his fingerprints on it."

"We will get to that later. So, your testimony is that it is possible when Terry Myles bent over to see if Della was still alive with multiple gunshots into her chest, he got blood on his sleeve, just as he said?" Della asked.

"Yes, it is possible," Stevens said.

"Why didn't you ask him if he had killed her before you arrested him?"

"We asked him many questions at his house. He didn't

346

answer any of them."

"He didn't, or he couldn't?"

"What do you mean?" Stevens asked.

"Is it possible he was in such a state of shock at seeing his friend lying on the floor with a gunshot to her chest, with her mouth and eyes wide open, and thinking of his own family dying in that fire seven months ago, that he couldn't speak?" Della asked.

"I don't know. It's possible. He did seem disoriented and confused," Stevens said.

"Lieutenant Stevens, you testified that when you got to Terry's house, you found him sitting at the kitchen table staring at a picture. Do you know who was in that picture?" Della asked.

"It looked like him and his family."

"Lieutenant Stevens. Do you know me?"

"Yes, you are my wife Julie's sister."

"Did you know Nicole McIntosh?"

"Yes, I did."

"Would you say she was an honest, ethical person who cared deeply about people, especially those at her hospital?" Della asked.

Burger stood up. "I object. Miss Mason is precisely doing what her uncle used to do. She is trying to distract Your Honor with extraneous, incompetent, and irrelevant information. Terry Myles is on trial, not the decedent."

"Overruled. Sit down, Mr. Burger. I'm sure you will have the opportunity to object to something more substantial. Please continue, Miss Mason," the judge said.

"Will you answer the question?" Della asked again.

"Nicole was one of the best people I ever knew," Stevens

replied.

"Did you ever hear her lie, cheat, or steal, or could you ever envision it happening?"

"No, never."

"Your Honor, I would like to introduce this audio cassette into the record and play it for all to hear," Della said.

"Objection. What is the basis of this tape?" Burger asked.

"Miss Mason?" the judge asked.

"This is an authenticated recording that Nicole McIntosh made with Jane Willoughby, Nokomis Hospital's director of maternity services, on September 12. Nicole discusses her fears of retaliation from management for exposing crimes at Nokomis Hospital and explains how Terry Myles is assisting her in gathering evidence," Della explained.

"We object. We need time to listen to the evidence," Burger said.

"Overruled. This is a preliminary hearing. There is no jury. Let's hear it," Judge Launer said. "Mark it as Exhibit 1 for the defense."

Della handed the cassette tape to the court clerk. He inserted it into the court's tape machine and pressed play.

* * *

"This is Nicole McIntosh. I'm recording this tape on September 12, in case I am unable to speak for myself. If this is the case, I most likely will be dead. Jane Willoughby is standing next to me to witness what I'm saying.

"I'm incredibly fearful of what I'm doing, working closely with Terry Myles, who has become close friends with me and my husband, Pete. I'm afraid because Mike Lard has threatened me. He has told me to stop talking with Jack Kendall about problems I see and hear at the hospital.

"I believe, and so does Terry, that Mike Lard, Steve Brophy, Charles McMann, and their associates are embezzling hospital funds.

"Reporter Jack Kendall at the *Herald-Tribune* has evidence that Lard and his cronies are using stolen hospital money to build luxury homes, selling or leasing buildings to the hospital at inflated prices, and holding expensive parties in the penthouse suite where cocaine and other drugs are being used.

"This is just a sample of what is destroying the hospital and hurting the community and patients.

"Mike Lard also has threatened Terry Myles if he doesn't stop talking with Kendall," said Nicole, pausing.

"A man by the name of Delman Palmer has been following me from work to my house. Terry told me the same thing. I haven't told my husband about this because he wants me to stop collecting information.

"Finally, if I die, I want this recording used to prosecute Mike Lard and to aid in finding the person who killed me," Nicole said.

The tape ended.

A hush fell over the court. One, two, three seconds passed.

Then Judge Launer spoke. "This is a powerful testimony from the grave. Miss Mason, are you prepared to authenticate it?"

"Your Honor, Jane Willoughby is here and can testify to the authenticity of the recording. I have an affidavit here with everything you need if that will suffice," said Della, handing it to the judge.

"Without objections, I will enter this affidavit as Exhibit 2," the judge said. "Mr. Burger?"

"Let me see that," he growled. "Yes, I suppose this will suffice. Your honor, I would like to object to the theatrics of the last 15 minutes. Defense counsel could and should have turned over this evidence before the hearing started."

"Do you wish to make any further statement or withdraw the charges against Mr. Myles?" Judge Launer asked.

"No. We have plenty of evidence to prove Mr. Myles's guilt," Burger said.

"At this time, would you like to redirect, Mr. Burger?" the judge asked.

"Yes, Your Honor. We wanted to save the court from a lengthy pretrial hearing, but we have no choice but to present our full evidence," Burger said.

"Very well, go ahead," Judge Launer said.

"Lieutenant Stevens. Did you search Mr. Myles's house? If so, what did you find?" Burger asked.

"We found a .38 caliber handgun in a bedroom drawer," Stevens said. "It is registered in Mr. Myles's name."

"Did you test the gun?" Burger asked.

"Yes. Three shots were fired very recently. Ballistics tests showed it was the murder weapon," Stevens said.

"Were there fingerprints on it?"

"Yes. The defendant, Mr. Terry Myles."

"Miss Mason?" said Burger.

"Lieutenant Stevens, did you test Terry to determine if he had gunpowder on his hand?" Della asked.

"Yes"

"Did he?"

"No."

"How do you explain that?"

"He wore gloves."

"Did you find any gloves?" Della asked.

"No," Stevens said. "He could have disposed of them."

"Why didn't he 'dispose' of the murder weapon?"

"I don't know."

"Isn't it possible that he never fired the gun?"

"We believe he did."

"Do you have any witnesses showing he did?" Della asked.

"No," Stevens said.

"Thank you, Lieutenant Stevens. That's all," Della said.

"Mr. Burger, do you have another witness?" Judge Launer asked.

"I would like to call Al Stephensen, manager at Nokomis Bank," Burger said.

Stephensen was sworn in.

"Did you review Mr. Myles's checking and savings accounts, and what did you find?" Burger asked.

"Yes. On September 8, Mr. Myles had $82,000 in his checking account," Stephensen said.

"When was the last deposit?"

"There was a $50,000 deposit on September 7."

"Was it a cash deposit?"

"Yes."

"Is that unusual?" Burger asked.

"For him, yes, based on his activity. Since he opened the account six months ago with $25,000, all that was deposited was his bi-monthly paycheck—nothing else," Stephensen said.

"Thank you. You may step down from the stand," Burger said.

"Not so fast, Mr. Burger," Della said. "I have a few questions."

"Why, go ahead, Miss Mason. I didn't think you had any questions for this witness," Burger replied.

"Mr. Stephensen, did you see Mr. Myles make this $50,000 deposit?" Della asked.

"No, I didn't," Stephensen said.

"Do you know who did?"

"No, I don't."

"So, it could have been anybody?"

"Yes, anybody with the correct account number," Stephensen said.

"Thank you, Mr. Stephensen," said Della.

She walked back to the defense table and winked at Burger.

The prosecutor glared at her again. "Your Honor, the state now calls Mr. Steve Brophy to the stand."

Brophy was sworn in.

"Mr. Brophy, who are you, and what do you do?" Burger asked.

"I'm Steve Brophy, CFO of Nokomis Hospital," the witness replied.

"Did you review the withdrawals from the environmental services account over the past month, and what did you find?" Burger asked.

"There was a $50,000 cash withdrawal that was unaccounted for," Brophy said.

"What does that mean?"

"That somebody representing the hospital went down to our bank and withdrew the money."

"Was it authorized?"

"No."

"Do you have any idea who could have done that?" Burger asked.

"We believe it was Terry Myles. He had access to the account," Brophy said.

"I object," Della said. "Mr. Myles was a lower-level accounting manager with no authority to withdraw."

"Mr. Burger?" the judge said.

"We believe the testimony of the hospital's CFO is more authoritative than the speculation of defense counsel," Burger said.

"Overruled," the judge said. "Mr. Burger, is that all for Mr. Brophy?"

"Yes, your honor. The prosecution rests," Burger said.

"Miss Mason, would you like to cross?" the judge asked.

"Yes, of course, unless Mr. Burger objects?" Della replied, irritated.

"You testified Mr. Myles was authorized to withdraw. Do you have a written authorization?"

"No."

"You said the withdrawal was unaccounted for," Della asked. "What do you mean?"

"There was no reason cited for the withdrawal."

"Who else has authority to withdraw funds?"

"Uh, I'm not sure what you mean," Brophy said.

"Let me rephrase the question. Has anyone ever directly withdrawn money from the bank from the environmental services account?"

"I don't know."

"Who else has authority to withdraw money from that account?" Della asked.

"I don't know."

"Then, is it possible that you, or Mr. Ward, or Mr. McMann could have withdrawn money from that account and deposited it in Mr. Myles' account?" Della asked.

Mr. Burger stood up. "I object. Another one of Ms. Mason's tricks. This question calls for speculation from the witness."

"Sustained. Ms. Mason, the witness cannot answer hypothetical questions about what others might have done. Please stick to facts within the witness's knowledge and rephrase."

"I'm sorry, Your Honor. I'll rephrase. Does Mr. Ward, Mr. McMann, or do you have authority to withdraw money from that account?"

"Um, yes, I suppose we do," Brophy said.

"Now, do you know of a hospital contract employee by the name of Delman Palmer?"

"Who?" asked Palmer.

"Do you know John Riggles?"

"Yes."

"Are you aware that Delman Palmer works for John Riggles?"

"No."

"Have you ever met Delman Palmer?"

"Not that I remember," Brophy replied.

Mr. Burger stood up. "I object to further questions. Miss Mason is again going on an irrelevant fishing expedition."

"Overruled. Miss Mason, may I ask where you're headed with this?

"Your Honor, I am trying to establish that Mr. Brophy has met Delman Palmer and knows he works for Mr. Riggles and does odd jobs for Mr. Ward."

"Very well. If you can tie this to the issues before the court, you may proceed. The witness will answer the question. Please rephrase," Judge Launer ordered.

"Mr. Brophy. Is it correct that Delman Palmer works for

Mr. Riggles and does jobs for the hospital and Mr. Ward?"

"I don't know," Brophy said.

"Your Honor, this line of questioning will be tied directly to our defense. I'm establishing relationships between key individuals, and I intend to return to this when the defense presents its evidence."

"Do you have any more questions for this witness?"

"No, Your Honor."

"Would you like to begin your defense or wait until Tuesday morning?" Judge Launer asked.

"I would like to call Jane Willoughby to the stand," Della replied.

"Ms. Willoughby?" Judge Launer said.

"I'm coming," Jane said.

"Do you swear to tell the whole truth and nothing but the truth?" the court clerk asked.

"I do."

"Jane. Can you swear and certify that the cassette recording you heard earlier in court is authentic and that of Nicole McIntosh?" Della asked.

"Yes. I was there when Nicole made it," Jane replied.

"Can you tell me the basis for which Nicole said she was fearful of management, and which managers she was afraid of?"

"The day she made the tape, and even before, she talked about how Mike Lard, Steve Brophy, and Charles McMann were stealing from the hospital," Jane said.

"Objection. The gentlemen she mentioned are not on trial," Burger said.

"Miss Mason, do you have any basis for making such an accusation?" Judge Launer asked.

"I am prepared to introduce several documents into evidence to show Lard, Brophy, and McMann's complicity in embezzling money from Nokomis Hospital," Della replied.

The courtroom erupted in gasps, claps, boos, and murmurs as spectators conversed. The three executives remained silent, staring icily ahead at the judge.

Judge Launer rapped his gavel on the table for quiet. "What evidence do you have?"

"I have the two years of financial statements showing Nokomis Hospital lost $10 million. It also shows Mr. Lard and Mr. Brophy got the hospital's foundation board to transfer $10 million to cover up the losses," said Della, handing it to the judge.

"Hmm, mark this as defense Exhibit 3," Launer said.

"I have a financial statement for the same year showing Medicare and private insurance company payments of $25 million, but only $20 million goes into the hospital's financial statement," she said. "Five million is missing."

"Mark this as defense Exhibit 4," Launer said.

"Your honor," Della Mason said. "Exhibit 5 is a tape recording of Nicole's call to Jack Kendall at the *Sarasota Herald-Tribune* on Monday night, September 24, minutes before she was killed. It proves that Terry and Nicole were friends and were working together to expose Mike Lard's financial misdeeds at the hospital. It, in fact, points to Mike Lard as the only person who would profit from Nicole's death."

"Objection!" shouted Mr. Burger as he quickly stood up. "I move to have that last sentence stricken from the record!"

Judge Launer said, "Upheld. Recorder, strike Miss Mason's last sentence. Miss Mason, you know better."

"Sorry, Your Honor. May I play the tape?"

"Yes, you may," Judge Launer said.

"I object again, Your Honor, very strenuously. This is unfair to the prosecution that Miss Mason gets to play recordings before this court without providing them to me first," Burger said.

"Your Honor, Sheriff Bagley has told me that reporter Jack Kendall submitted this original tape recording to his office more than a month ago. It is not my fault, Mr. Burger is unaware of it," Della said.

"I agree. Play the tape," Judge Launer ordered.

Della clicked on the player. "Jack, this is Nicole McIntosh. I wanted to share a few things with you while I wait for Terry to arrive. I'm glad you were able to speak with him off the record last week. Did he tell you about his visit to Mike Lard's office? I hope so. I have some things hidden and will give them to you when I can.

"By the way, I decided to talk with Della Mason today about your suggestion about being a whistleblower," Nicole said. "I haven't told Terry that I've discussed this issue with Della, but I will mention it to him tonight. Thanks for your help."

At the end of the tape, Della remained silent to let the impact of Nicole's words sink in. This second recording, spoken minutes before her death, clearly stated she'd invited Terry to her home, and she had no fear of him.

"Miss Mason, do you have any further witnesses?" Judge Launer asked.

"I'd like to call Jack Kendall to the stand to corroborate the tape and what he did with it," Della requested.

"Mr. Burger?"

"Hold on, Your Honor," Burger said as his assistant whispered in his ear that the prosecution had made a mistake.

The tape had been in Bagley's office all along.

"We stipulate this tape is authentic. There is no need for Mr. Kendall to take the stand," Burger said.

"Your Honor, I reserve the right to call Mr. Kendall, Jane Willoughby, and other witnesses tomorrow morning," Della said.

"Do you want a recess before lunch?" Judge Launer asked.

"We have one more exhibit critical for our case, Your Honor. We hope to have it by tomorrow," Della said. "We have one more witness today, and then I'd like to request a recess until the morning, if that pleases the court?"

Judge Launer asked, "Is this a witness who can testify to the significance of these exhibits here?"

"Yes, Your Honor. I'd like to call Christine McVay to the stand," Della said.

The people in the courtroom gasped again. Judge Launer tapped his gavel. "Now there, calm down," he ordered.

Christine McVay, the tall, well-dressed CPA with Beloit Associates, one of Lard's personally recruited trustees to the board, stood up.

As she approached the stand to take the oath, she felt Mike Lard's stare pierce right through her.

"Can you tell the court your name, what you do, and what you know about these financial transactions we just discussed?" Della asked.

"My name is Christine McVay. I'm a partner with Beloit Associates, an accounting, tax, and consulting firm. I've been on the board less than a month," she said.

"Was the hospital's board ever informed that it had lost $10 million in 1982 and 1983, ending December 31, and that the foundation had transferred $10 million to cover its losses?"

Della asked.

"I was never told," McVay replied. "I was shocked when I learned of this, but it didn't come as a surprise. My experience on the board, which I have previously discussed with Mr. Lard and Mr. Brophy, is that management provides us with very little information about the hospital.

"When I joined the board, I was told to approve whatever came across my desk, not ask questions, that it was management's decision, and that the board was to say 'yes.' I was told this was how it had been for years," McVay explained.

"Did Mike Lard ever tell you this?" Della asked.

"Yes, he did, on several occasions during my recruitment," McVay replied. "One was just two Saturdays ago at one of his penthouse suite parties. I told him I needed more information. He said Steve Brophy would give me a fuller report to help me make decisions."

"Did Brophy ever do that?"

"No," McVay said. "It's why I abstained from the vote on the preliminary agreement to merge with National Healthcare. I am new to healthcare, and I wanted background information and a committee meeting where I could ask questions."

"You are a trained accountant and a board member. What do you make of Exhibit 3, which shows $5 million in missing Medicare and private insurance payments?" Della asked.

"I believe that financial statement screams out for an audit."

"Where do you believe this money is?"

"I cannot say for sure, but I believe it must be in another account controlled by the hospital or the executives," McVay said. "They can do what they want with hospital funds."

"Steve Brophy testified that Terry Myles embezzled $50,000 from the hospital's environmental services department, withdrew it in cash, and deposited it into his account. Do you find this believable?" Della asked.

"Objection, your honor. The state has allowed Miss Mason considerable latitude to explore the financial transfers of hospital revenue, as it is in the public's interest to know how executives spend money. Still, the court should not allow unfettered attacks on other witnesses," Burger complained.

"Objection overruled," Judge Launer said. "You opened this door when you had your witness testify about where he thought the $50,000 went."

"Do you want me to repeat the question?" Della asked.

"No. In my opinion, Terry Myles could not have withdrawn $50,000 from the hospital's account. It doesn't work like that. There has to be a specific account with the money available for him to do that," McVay replied.

"Thank you, Ms. McVay," Della said. "Mr. Burger, do you have any questions?"

"Your honor, in light of this new information, the state requests a 24-hour postponement so we can look into the allegations that Miss Mason tossed out from right field," Burger said.

"I concur," Judge Launer said. "It is now almost noon. Hearing adjourned until 10 a.m. Thursday."

Della walked back to the defense table and patted Terry on the shoulder. "This was a good day," she whispered in his ear.

Terry leaned over and whispered, "How will you find those documents I took from Lard's office? Kendall only has a fraction. You couldn't find the film, photos, or documents at my house. Whoever stole my gun, shot Nicole, and planted the gun back at my house also must have stolen the evidence."

"You told me you gave copies to Nicole, right?" Della

whispered.

"Yes, but the police couldn't find them at Nicole's house. Pete didn't know where she put them," Terry said louder.

"Jack Kendall has a new clue and thinks he can find them with Pete's help. He will find them tonight with his brother and one of my detectives," Della whispered.

* * *

Mike Lard left the courthouse with McMann and Brophy. They didn't like what they'd heard in court, especially the implications that they'd committed crimes based on the testimony and the financial records and documents Della Mason introduced.

"We need to contact our lawyers and stay ahead of this," Lard growled.

"What evidence do you think Mason will present tomorrow? Those documents and tape recordings strongly suggest we're in trouble," Brophy said.

"We can dispute the documents in court, but I think I know what Mason and Kendall are looking for," Lard said. "Kendall's story revealed the checking register I use to pay your bonuses and where my coke vial went. But I'm sure Myles copied many, if not all, of our secret files."

"You were right about that, boss," McMann said. "Palmer searched their houses and offices for those additional documents. Where else could they be?"

"I'm going to call Palmer in Miami and have him come back to tail Kendall," Lard said. "I'm sure he and his detective brother are working with Mason and have a good idea where they are. Why else would she tell the judge she'll have more evidence in the morning?"

"Don't tell us what Palmer will do. I can only imagine," McMann said.

Chapter 48:
Thor's Pool

Wednesday Evening, Oct. 10, 1984

Jack drove with Ed to Pete McIntosh's house just after sunset to look for Terry's complete file of the executive payroll account.

Sheriff's detectives had already searched for the documents and pictures Nicole had hidden in her house, but could not locate them.

But Jack had a new lead: a letter Nicole had mailed him that the newspaper's mailroom had misplaced for a week. The letter contained more evidence of corruption at the hospital, but it also gave Jack the information about where she'd hidden the secret files at her house.

She'd ended the two-page letter with a cryptic clue. "What is rectangular and can be found where the Kon-Tiki sails?"

Jack told Pete this over the phone, and Pete immediately grasped his wife's meaning.

"Kon-Tiki is another name Nicole used for our pool. I'll explain when you get here," Pete said.

When Jack and Ed arrived, Paul Drake Jr., one of Della's investigators, was already waiting for them outside.

"Pete's around back," Paul said.

They walked together around the back to the 15-meter swimming pool and patio.

* * *

Thirty seconds later, a black BMW drove past Pete's house and parked on the next street, out of sight from the streetlights, to remain unseen from anyone in the house.

Delman Palmer reached over and took out his .357 Magnum from the glove compartment. He checked to make sure it was loaded and put the gun in the pocket of his hoodie.

Dressed in black, he exited the car and walked toward Pete's house. He noted Jack's dark green Mustang GT parked in the driveway alongside another vehicle he didn't recognize.

* * *

Pete waited for Jack, Ed, and Paul by the pool. He sat in a chair, thinking about his wife, Nicole. He had built the pool for her. There was little he wouldn't have done for her.

"Hi, Pete," called out Jack as he rounded the corner of the house. "Thanks for letting us come over to look one more time. You think we can find the documents here?"

"I never thought to look outside," Pete replied.

"We always thought the same. Someplace dry," Jack said.

"When you mentioned that she said 'Kon-Tiki' in her note, I knew she meant to look by the pool," Pete said.

"Why Kon-Tiki?" Ed asked.

"She loved the Kon-Tiki story about the Norwegian who sailed across the Pacific on a balsa wood raft. She used to float on a blow-up lounger and talk about Thor Heyerdahl's expedition. Nicole always thought differently," Pete said, his voice trailing off.

"You said the pool. Do you think she meant the copies are in the pool?" Jack asked.

"Not exactly," Pete said. "There are only two places where she could store these documents in a waterproof container, just like Thor stored water on the Kon-Tiki."

Pete looked around the pool patio. "It could be in the storage locker with the other pool toys, or it could be inside the skimmer over there by the ladder," he said, pointing to the far side of the pool.

"You three look for it. I'm going inside for a few minutes," Pete said. "I'll bring out some beers, and we can talk then."

Palmer heard voices in the backyard. He quietly moved along the side of the house. He peeked around the corner and saw Jack Kendall and two other men. It didn't matter— he was there to recover documents and kill Kendall.

"I can't imagine Nicole put the documents here in this skimmer. If she did, she must have waterproofed them somehow," Jack said.

He removed the plastic cover. Inside was a basket. The pump was operating, and water was rushing through the basket, which appeared small for the skimmer box.

"Ed, can you turn off the pump? I want to pull up the basket," Jack said.

"Sure," said Ed. "Give me a second."

Ed found the electric switch and turned it off. The pump stopped. Jack lifted the basket and saw a thin plastic box to the side.

"Hey, there's something down there," said Jack, reaching for it.

Palmer noticed that Jack had discovered something, probably the evidence Lard wanted him to find. He hadn't come across anything in Terry's house during his two searches, the last time when he planted the murder weapon.

Jack smiled when he looked inside the plastic box and saw two film rolls.

"What is it?" Ed asked.

"Looks like the film. Terry said he took some pictures before he photocopied everything," Jack explained. "We need a screwdriver to get them out. The documents must be elsewhere."

"Where else could they be?" Ed asked.

"I'll look in the storage locker," Paul said, opening the lid. He took out some floaters, life vests and toys. "Hey, looks like she has a plastic first aid kit underneath all this junk."

Jack rushed over to see. Paul pulled out the kit, unclicked it open, and pulled out more than 100 photocopied documents.

"You did it, Jack!" exclaimed Paul. "Della will be able to present this as evidence that could clear Terry. If this is everything, it will get him off."

"Not so fast, dudes," said Palmer as he approached with his .357. Just stand there, don't move, and I will take those boxes from you."

"Delman Palmer," Jack said.

"You think you're so smart, don't you, Kendall? Mike Lard knew all along you would lead us to the only evidence linking him to the crimes," Palmer said, stopping about 10 feet from the three men.

"I want you to toss the box on the grass beside the pool gently. Now. Do it," barked Palmer.

"Is that the gun you used to kill Nicole?" Jack asked, hoping Pete would hear and call the police.

"Smart boy, aren't you? Myles killed her with his own gun. Don't you know? I'm going to kill you, just as I did Nicole, with my own gun. Then there will be nobody to testify against Lard, me, or anyone," Palmer bragged, confidently planning to kill them all.

Pete was in the kitchen when he heard an unfamiliar voice. He looked out the window and saw Palmer pointing a gun at Jack, Ed, and Paul.

An active duty Marine before going to law school, Lieutenant Pete McIntosh quickly assessed the situation. Jack warned him that the man who killed Nicole might come looking for evidence she had hidden in the house.

Although seething with anger, knowing that the man in his backyard likely had killed Nicole, Pete calmly went to the master bedroom. He unlocked his gun box, took out his M9 Beretta, slid a clip in, and returned to the kitchen, where a door led back to the pool area.

"I'm only going to tell you one more time, Kendall," said Palmer. "Toss those boxes on the grass by me."

Jack noticed Pete coming out of the kitchen door from the corner of his eye. "I don't think so," he said.

"Drop your weapon, or I will fire!" Pete yelled.

As Palmer turned with his gun raised, Pete didn't hesitate. He opened fire and emptied his clip of eight rounds into his wife's killer.

"You bastard, you shit, you murderer! You killed my Nicole! Now you die!" Pete yelled as Palmer shuddered and fell backward into the pool.

Blood poured out of Palmer's multiple entry wounds, coloring the pool red, then pink as it diffused.

Jack stared at Palmer floating in the pool for several seconds. He took a deep breath and looked over at Paul, then Ed.

"You guys good?" Jack asked.

"Yes," exhaled Ed. "Just another close call with my big brother."

"This was a little closer call than our hike at midnight in the Blue Mountains of Jamaica," Jack quipped.

"Was that Delman Palmer?" asked Paul. "The mob hitman from Miami?"

"The *late* Delman Palmer," Jack replied, glancing over at the corpse. "He got what he deserved."

"Della was right about Riggles. He hired Palmer, but not for construction work—for murder," Paul said.

Jack looked at Pete, who had moved over by the pool to stare at Palmer, floating face-up in the water with a surprised expression on his frozen face.

"It serves this bastard right," Pete said. "Thanks for letting me kill him. I only wish I had another clip."

"Thanks? No, thanks to you for going along with the plan," Jack replied.

"What plan?" asked Ed. "You knew Palmer would be here?"

"I thought he might. I suspected Palmer was following me. Meet retired Lieutenant Pete McIntosh. He's one of the best Marines in town—besides Colonel Hanks, who outranks him," Jack said with a relieved laugh.

Pete just stood there. He appreciated Jack's comments, but he was not in a celebratory mood. Jack walked over and put his hand on his shoulder.

"You did what you needed to do," Jack said. "Let's go inside and call the Sheriff's Office."

"Say, you promised to bring us some beers. I'm ready for one," Ed said.

"I'll have two," Paul quipped with a big smile.

"They're on the kitchen counter. Come in, and we can have them while we wait for the police," Pete said.

"Ed, can you call Lieutenant Stevens? He'll be so happy to come out and see for himself that they arrested the wrong man," Jack said.

"Did you all hear what I heard Palmer say about Lard?" Paul asked. "I quote, 'Mike Lard knew all along you would lead us to the only evidence that can link him to the crimes.'"

"Exactly right. I have it all on tape," Jack said.

"You were recording?" Ed asked.

"Of course, always," Jack said. "I turned it on as soon as we came back here. It's Delman's confession, Lard's ticket to jail, and Terry's freedom."

Chapter 49:
Charges Dismissed

Morning, Thursday, Oct. 11, 1984

Jack and Katie North's story on Thursday morning about Delman Palmer's confession before Pete killed him nearly made the hearing before Judge Launer unnecessary. The proceedings didn't last more than 10 minutes.

Della asked Judge Launer to dismiss all of Terry's charges.

"Mr. Burger, do you have any objections?"

"No, Your Honor. The state concurs and has filed papers doing so," Burger said.

"Terry Myles. Will you stand?" said Judge Launer.

Terry stood up, and Della rose beside him.

"Ladies and gentlemen of the court, after new information came to light about the circumstances surrounding the death of Nicole McIntosh, the prosecution has agreed to drop the murder charges against the defendant, Terry Myles," Judge

Launer announced. "Therefore, the court hereby dismisses the charges in this case with prejudice. Mr. Myles, you are free to go. Court is adjourned."

A collective sigh of relief filled the courtroom. Terry turned to Della and hugged her. More than a dozen of his coworkers who attended the hearing smiled and put their hands together, nearly clapping. Terry's parents hugged each other.

Sitting in the front row behind the defense table, Jack patted Terry on the back. Terry turned, and they shook hands.

Then, Jack turned to Pete McIntosh and said, "We *will* nail the son-of-a-bitches who caused this." Pete solemnly nodded.

* * *

Terry Myles was a free man. He was released from custody after a series of events, starting with his late friend, Nicole McIntosh, who provided audio evidence that they were working together to expose the crimes at Nokomis Hospital.

His pictures and photocopies of Mike Lard's checking register and notebook with details of the crimes—copies that Nicole had the creativity to hide in the pool skimmer and first aid kit before she died—provided further evidence of his innocence.

But it was Jack Kendall's foresight and plan to trap Delman Palmer into a confession that led to the charges being dropped and evidence linking Mike Lard to Nicole's murder.

Walking out of the courtroom, Katie asked Della for a few comments.

"Miss Mason, what do you have to say about Terry Myles and the outcome of this case?" Katie asked.

"We said from the beginning that Terry Myles was innocent.

Now, we know what happened. Delman Palmer stole Terry's gun, shot and killed Nicole, then brought it back to Terry's house and planted it for the police to find," said Della. "Now, it's up to Sheriff Bagley, Lieutenant Stevens and his detectives to arrest the people behind Delman Palmer's actions."

Katie asked Terry how it felt to be vindicated.

"I can't tell you how happy I am to have friends like Della, Jack Kendall, Jane Willoughby, and especially Nicole McIntosh, as well as everyone at Nokomis Hospital who believed in me," Terry said. "I also want to thank my parents, who stood by me and never doubted my innocence. Now, I want to go home."

"He will go home. I'm going to drive Terry there myself. He deserves to sleep in his own bed," Della declared.

"We'll meet you there, son," said Mr. Myles, his wife beside him with tears in her eyes.

Katie saw Sheriff Bagley standing by. "Sheriff, what about this investigation? What went wrong?" she asked.

"Nothing went wrong. The truth came out," Bagley said in his deep voice. "I want to say that Sarasota County was correct in dropping all charges against Mr. Myles and releasing him from custody. There was nothing personal against him. We got it wrong, but now we will pursue the truth until all the guilty are behind bars."

"What about the evidence against the hospital administrators we heard in witness testimony?" Katie asked.

"We will investigate this thoroughly, but the documents and tape recording of her suspicions that Jack and Ed Kendall—along with Della's investigator, Paul Drake Jr.—found hidden at her house were instrumental in clearing Terry and uncovering her true murderer," Bagley said.

"Anything else you want to add?" Katie asked.

"Well, Miss North, we have determined that Pete McIntosh's shooting and killing of Delman Palmer was an act of self-defense. Pete should be declared a hero for saving Jack, Ed, and Paul," Bagley opined.

"Will there be charges against Terry Myles for taking the secret files from Mr. Lard's office?" Katie asked.

"We don't believe so. What Mr. Myles did wasn't for personal gain. He secmed to be trying to expose crimes, not commit them. That's all for now," Bagley said, turning to face the television reporters and cameras.

Katie hurried over to face him. "Sheriff, one more question. What are you going to do now? Will you investigate the allegations against Mike Lard, Steve Brophy, Charles McMann, John Riggles, and any others?" Katie asked.

"Stay tuned. We'll be moving quickly, and we might have a few surprises," Bagley said with a smile.

Chapter 50:
Jack Confronts Bagley

Morning, Friday, Oct. 12, 1984

Jack left home and drove straight to the Sheriff's Office, his jaw locked, the steering wheel creaking under the pressure of his hands. By the time he walked into Tom Bagley's office, he'd rehearsed what he wanted to say—but every version felt too soft compared to the anger burning in his chest.

Bagley looked up from a stack of paperwork. "Jack. Didn't expect to see you this morning."

Jack shut the door behind him. "Tom, we need to talk."

Bagley caught the tone and slowly leaned back. "All right. What's going on?"

Jack didn't sit. Couldn't. "Terry's case has been dismissed. Now's the time to ask why Delman Palmer wasn't brought in for questioning?"

Bagley blinked. "About what?"

"Don't do that, Tom," Jack snapped. "You knew. I came to you, and Ed briefed Stevens. We told you Palmer had ties to the Miami Mafia and was employed by Nokomis Hospital. We told you he was threatening Bobbie and me. That he was going after Terry and Nicole. And nothing happened. Not a damn thing."

Bagley rubbed his eyes. "Jack—we couldn't..."

"No." Jack's voice cut through the room. "I want an answer. Why wasn't he watched? Why wasn't a deputy even told to drive by his place? Tom, Palmer followed my wife and my mother to an OB-GYN appointment. He trailed us to the *Herald-Tribune*. He staked out my house in broad daylight. He threatened two of my sources—one of whom is now dead. How much more 'concrete' did you need?"

Bagley let out a long breath, the kind that said he'd been carrying something he had no interest in sharing. "You know how this office works. We need probable cause. Something solid. Not just suspicions and rumors."

"Rumors?" Jack stepped closer, voice low but more dangerous than when he'd shouted. "You had documentation. You had witness statements. You had Ed giving you every detail he dug up. Tom, Nicole and Terry needed help. They weren't rumors—they were terrified."

Bagley winced. "Look...I passed what you and Ed told me along to Stevens. He said he didn't have enough to act."

"Stevens?" Jack nearly laughed. "Stevens made up his mind on Terry as soon as he found that murder weapon at his house. He didn't want to chase down this scumbag despite what we told him."

Bagley shifted, jaw tight. He opened his mouth, closed it, then scratched his cheek, then his chin. Folded his arms.

Unfolded them. Hemming. Hawing. Searching for an answer he didn't want to give.

"Tom," Jack said quietly, "enough. Just tell me."

The sheriff finally met his eyes. "All right...but this is off the record. Not for publication."

He waited for Jack's nod.

"We were told—directly—by the DEA not to touch him. Not to question him. Not to surveil him. Palmer was under their investigation, and they didn't want us screwing up their operation."

The admission hit Jack like a slap in the face. "So you backed off?"

"I didn't have a choice," Bagley said. "They made it clear. Any interference could compromise a federal case."

Jack stared at him. "A federal case," he repeated slowly. "Meanwhile, a woman who trusted me—a woman who begged me not to use her name because she was scared—was left completely unprotected."

"Jack—"

"No." Jack raised a hand. "You could've warned me, warned her and Terry that you couldn't protect them. Instead, everybody stayed quiet to keep the DEA happy."

Bagley didn't respond. He didn't have to. His silence told the truth.

Jack exhaled sharply. "I promised you this was off the record, and I'll keep that promise, but I'm not going to pretend you did your job."

"My hands were tied," Bagley said.

"What I know is that you bowed to pressure. I'd like to write everything I know about Nicole's death, but I won't because of my promise as a journalist and our relationship.

I just hope this doesn't happen again, but now I see you can be influenced."

Jack noticed Bagley looked tired—older than he had been a few minutes ago. The sheriff rubbed a hand over his face, the gesture slow and defeated, as though the weight of the whole mess had fallen on him.

Without saying another word, Jack turned and walked away. The door clicked shut, leaving Bagley alone with the knowledge of what he could have done but chose not to.

Chapter 51:
Busted Execs

Morning, Saturday, Oct. 13, 1984

Bobbie settled deeper into the couch in the living room, a blanket over her lap. The incision still tugged, but she was stronger now—strong enough, at least, to finally ask the question she'd held back since Friday.

"Jack...what happened after the arrests? You never told me everything."

Jack exhaled. "I was so tired last night, I'm sorry, I just crashed out. Grandma's got the twins. We've got time. And you deserve to hear the whole story."

"Finally, I get some attention!" Bobbie happily exclaimed. "Start from the top, and all of it."

Jack nodded. "All right. Let me get my notes. I'll bring us more coffee." He stood up, picked up their cups, went into the kitchen and poured the brews.

He returned, handed Bobbie a fresh cup of cappuccino, then went into the study to grab his notebook and small tape recorder.

"You're going to love this," he said, sitting beside her. "Katie recorded this for me. This is the moment they arrested Mike Lard."

He pressed play. Lieutenant Stevens's voice crackled through the speaker: *"Mike Lard, you are under arrest for murder-for-hire, embezzlement, money laundering, fraud, and possession of cocaine..."*

Bobbie's eyes widened. "Murder-for-hire. They nailed him. Good."

"Oh, it gets better," Jack said, flipping a page. "Listen to what he shouted as deputies dragged him out."

"Print this. I'm innocent. I never stole a dime... Arrest the board. Not me. I am a victim of my own success and healthcare reform. My competitors set me up!"

Bobbie shook her head slowly. "He's delusional."

"Katie North thought so too," Jack said, smiling faintly. "She filled in for you magnificently. She asked, 'Mr. Lard, did you order Delman Palmer to kill Nicole McIntosh?'"

"And?" Bobbie asked.

"He slumped and said, 'No comment, on advice of my attorney.'"

Bobbie exhaled. "Good. Jack, I know it is early to talk about me going back to work. But when I do, I am going to ask Rick if I can interview Lard in prison. Do you mind?"

"I think that would be great. It'll be your beat again, and you'd do a great job dealing with that sick and conniving man. Want to hear more about what happened yesterday?"

Bobbie eagerly nodded.

Jack turned a page. "Brophy and McMann were arrested next. Katie tried to get a comment. McMann ignored her. But

Brophy said, 'Tell Mary I'm sorry.'"

Bobbie frowned. "At least he had enough shame left to say that."

"Mary left him and moved to California. I think—at least I hope—I told you. As for John Riggles...deputies searched everywhere." Jack paused, his voice heavier when next he spoke. "A few days later, they found his body in a back alley in Miami. Throat slashed."

Bobbie closed her eyes. "So the man who hired Delman Palmer, the enforcer, got silenced too."

"Looks that way. No suspects either. With Riggles dead, the only link prosecutors have to tie Lard to Nicole's murder is the money trail."

"And Palmer's confession you got from him by the Kon-Tiki!" Bobbie added.

"So you *were* reading my stories!" Jack kidded.

Bobbie smiled, but didn't respond, so Jack turned a few more notebook pages. "The day after the arrests, trustees David Royster and Jimmy Giles surrendered voluntarily. Released on bail."

Bobbie leaned forward. "So the entire leadership collapsed."

"Pretty much," Jack said. "Bobbie, do you want me to continue? This is a lot for you right now."

"I want to hear everything. You promised me," Bobbie said, her eyes expressing worry that Jack might stop. They hadn't talked—really talked—about work for some time, and she missed it. "It's a lot, but I need to know. I can rest later."

Jack smiled and clicked on a new recording. "Here's Professor Harlan Oates from UF Law. By the way, I had him for my Constitutional Law class."

"You've told me like six times. You loved that class," Bobbie replied with a chuckle. "I think you told me you took it because of your father."

Jack turned off the recorder. "Yes, he wanted me to take over his law practice. I also took a business law class. Both those courses were more fun thinking about them later than actually attending," he said with a chuckle, turning the recorder back on.

Oates's voice emerged: *"It's such a brutal case of unabashed greed... They stole money, gutted programs, drained resources, laid off employees, and sullied the image of honest hospital executives."*

Bobbie whispered, "He's right."

"He's *always* right. Now, the amazing part. The IRS showed up," Jack said.

"So soon?" Bobbie said, equally amazed.

"I suppose when they can collect money, they can act quickly," Jack observed. "I have no idea. I could never reach them by phone. Jane called me about it. I called board member Christine McVay for confirmation."

"She's come a long way," Bobbie commented.

"Yes, overcome a lot, I'd say. Anyway, they hit the hospital with a potential revocation of tax-exempt status unless the board paid a $2 million penalty."

He handed Bobbie a printed sheet. "Here were the violations: excessive compensation...self-dealing contracts...misuse of tax-exempt bonds for luxury suites and for-profit groups."

Bobbie skimmed it. "This is...astounding."

"Chris, who I heard will be appointed the new board chair, said they'd pay the fine. No choice."

Jack glanced at another transcript. "Then the executives' attorney, Woody Woodward, held a press conference. This guy is priceless. I'm surprised he wasn't busted along with the rest, from what I heard."

"What for?" Bobbie asked.

"He was at many of the parties and those golf outings. He must have been smart to avoid the indictments. I'm sure he handled many of these fake transactions. Still, he was seen numerous times driving around town with Lard and McMann, hitting strip clubs and drinking whiskey straight from the bottle — at least, that's what sources told me."

Jack quoted Woodward: "The money they received was loans and bonuses."

Bobbie snorted. "Of course he said that."

"Chris Rollie from the State Attorney's Office shut that down quickly," Jack said. "I love this quote he gave me.

"The money was over and above their salaries. No documentation supports their claims... They used hospital credit cards to buy jewelry and other personal items over $100,000...diverted hospital money to buy a warehouse and flipped it at inflated prices...drunken cocaine parties... conspiracies hatched in drug-addled stupors..."

Bobbie covered her mouth. "This was happening while people were losing their jobs."

Jack nodded. "And while patients had surgeries delayed and potentially botched from infected instruments."

"And while you and I were in that hospital," Bobbie said, recalling the stressful days she spent in Nokomis. "I was relieved to be discharged, but then to find out why they kicked me out... I'd half a mind to report Dr. Lords for complying with Lard's discharge order."

Jack nodded. "Me too." He turned another page. "Rollie also said they used hospital funds for luxury homes, diamond rings, and golf trips to Scotland and Hawaii. Severe alcohol and drug issues. Brophy testified how they drove around town drunk, boasting, 'They'll never prove it.'"

Bobbie shook her head again. "They thought they were untouchable."

"And for a while, they were."

Jack listed the most significant charges:

- Money funneled through fake corporations
- Over $10 million stolen through phony companies
- Properties resold to the hospital at inflated prices
- Rigged construction bids with $3 million in kickbacks
- $17 million illegally transferred from the foundation
- Brophy's gambling debt
- Lard's, McMann's, Goldfarb's, and Dr. Wickman's addictions

"And then Owen Sharks from the IRS," Jack said. "I very much like the quote he gave me:

"The financial resources of nonprofit hospitals make them ripe for insider transactions... They failed the community."

Bobbie swallowed. "So many people hurt."

"And not just at the top," Jack added. More than a dozen others at the hospital or who worked as contractors or for affiliated companies were also arrested. For example, James Richter—a lower-level manager—submitted $60,000 in fake invoices, spent it on cocaine, and collected paychecks from both the hospital and the phony companies."

"Wow."

"And Dr. Stan Wickman, the radiologist I mentioned earlier? He pleaded guilty to defrauding Medicare, illegally melting the radiology film, and selling cocaine. He turned state's evidence for a lighter sentence."

"That was the most ridiculous thing I think I ever heard a radiologist doing," added Bobbie.

"It was Lard's brilliant idea to fund the cocaine parties," Jack said, shaking his head. "You can ask him about that."

"I'll put it on my list," Bobbie quipped.

Jack flipped the last pages. "Two days after the arrests, Brophy pled guilty to theft and agreed to testify. Said he hoped Mary would take him back after his five-year sentence."

Bobbie gave a soft, sad nod. "He must love her."

"And finally," Jack said quietly, "Lard faces the death penalty for hiring Delman Palmer to murder Nicole McIntosh. Stevens told me they are still investigating Goldfarb's overdose, but they don't have any clues other than what his wife told me. Even if not convicted of those murders, he could still get up to 30 years and a $2 million fine."

Bobbie whispered, "All that power...and he threw it away."

"This is what addiction and greed do to people," Jack mused.

"Does the hospital get anything back now that they are caught?" Bobbie wondered.

"Yes, good question. I didn't write about this, but Rollie told me Nokomis has applied to recover money stolen under the asset forfeiture rules. Same for Medicare and Medicaid. I'm not sure how much, but it should total in the millions," Jack said.

"Another question. The Harry Goldfarb death. Are you going to pursue that? You promised his wife," Bobbie asked.

"There are several loose ends I want to follow up on: Harry, and the DEA asking Tom to stand down on the Palmer investigation," Jack said.

"Anything else to share?" Bobbie asked.

Jack moved over to sit beside her, taking her hand. "June Powell—Lard's former secretary—said it best."

He read the last line: "Sadly, many people have to pay for a few bad guys."

Bobbie leaned her head on his shoulder. "I'm glad you wrote it all, Jack. I'm glad people know the truth."

"It's almost over," Jack said.

"I know. Then will I have you all to myself?" Bobbie asked, leaning over to him.

"Nearly all," Jack said, kissing her lips three times.

"I do have one thing to do."

"What's that?" Jack asked.

"You'll see."

Chapter 52:

Terry's Party

Afternoon, Saturday, Oct 20, 1984

Bobbie's idea for a gathering had started small—"just a few friends to celebrate Terry's release," she'd said. By midafternoon, however, thirty people were spread through the house and patio, balancing glasses of wine, cups of iced tea, and paper plates from the buffet table.

Jack watched from the sliding door for a moment, taking it all in. It was a perfect mid-October day. The sun slanted across the backyard, casting a shadow on the edge of the pool and making it shimmer like glass.

It had been nine days since Terry Myles walked out of the county courthouse a free man. Now here he was, standing near the hibiscus with Della Mason at his side, laughing at something Ed Kendall had said. Ed surprised everyone by bringing a special friend, given that he usually kept his girlfriends out of the limelight.

At Jack's suggestion, Terry and Della were honored guests. The two had grown close over the past month and were rumored to be on the verge of announcing their engagement.

The crowd was a mix of newsroom colleagues and law enforcement allies, hospital staff, and old friends: Tom and Susan Justice with their toddlers, Rick and Tiffany Wise corralling theirs, Katie North perched on the deck rail with a notebook, even at a party.

Laura Kendall knelt near the twins' playpen, cooing at Eli while Ella kicked at a soft rattle. Bobbie's parents, George and Martha Jackson, had flown down from Hartford and now mingled near the buffet, with George offering quiet nods while Martha listened to Dr. Rashad talk about hoped-for changes at the hospital. Keith and Barbara Tillis chatted with Susan Swartz.

Hospital staff dotted the crowd—Josh Lucas from security, Dr. Joel O'Neal, Jane Willoughby, Cathy Leesay, Valentina Rublenko, Dr. Jennifer Chastain—along with Sheriff Tom Bagley and his detectives, Lieutenant Fred Nicholas, Lieutenant Jim Stevens, Detective T. Paul Perry, Detective Patrick Duffy, with their wives.

Pete McIntosh, Nicole's widowed husband, stood off to one side, hands folded, until Christine McVay, the new board chair, surprised everyone by greeting him warmly.

Jack wanted to make Pete another guest of honor, but Pete shook his head when Jack mentioned it earlier in the week.

"I appreciate it, Jack," Pete had said quietly, his hands wrapped around a coffee mug at his kitchen table. "But this isn't about me. Nicole was the brave one. She's the reason we're standing here. I'd rather be part of the crowd—raise a glass to her, let everyone else have their moment."

There had been no bitterness in his voice, only a steady respect for the woman he'd lost. Jack understood. Some honors are too heavy to accept when they belong to someone who isn't there to share them.

Later, Colonel John Hanks walked up and introduced himself to Pete. The two Marines chatted about the recent events and reminisced about their time at Parris Island and Camp Lejeune. They didn't talk about their deployments.

When the last of the wine and iced tea had been poured, Jack tapped a spoon against his glass. Conversations stilled, and faces turned his way.

"I just want to thank you all for coming," he began. "Today isn't only about clearing a man's name—though we're grateful Terry's finally free. It's about the people who made sure the truth came out."

He turned toward Terry, who shifted uneasily but managed a smile. "Terry Myles never stopped believing the facts would win out," Jack said. "And Della Mason—she took this case when it looked impossible, and when her heart had every reason to stay clear. She fought hard for justice, and for a friend she lost."

"Della, her private investigators, Paul Drake Jr., my brother Ed, and young Katie North at the *Herald-Tribune* worked hard to expose the lies."

"Hats off to Della," said Jack, nodding respectfully toward the successful, young defense attorney.

Della raised a hand, half in protest, half in thanks, but the group applauded anyway. Jack grinned and let the moment settle.

Then his voice softened. "Now, I'd like a moment to honor someone who isn't here."

Everyone quieted.

"Nicole McIntosh was an honest, decent, and brave woman. On a personal note, I met Nicole two years ago when I started reporting on healthcare. She was always friendly and helpful to me, but never more than during the support she gave me after Bobbie delivered our little ones under trying circumstances on September 8.

"Little did she or I know what would happen in the weeks after she bravely revealed her suspicions about her fellow executives. She knew the dangers of exposing the criminals, but she told Terry and me everything. She stood up for what was right when she could have looked away, and she paid for it.

"The documents and photographs that Ed, Paul, and I discovered hidden at her house were crucial in clearing Terry, identifying her real murderer, and bringing Lard to justice.

"But if it weren't for Pete's quick thinking and straight shooting, we wouldn't have survived Palmer's attack."

Jack lifted his glass toward Pete. "You've shown courage none of us can quite imagine. Because of you, Palmer didn't get the chance to silence anyone else. Our door is always open to you."

The group applauded. Terry looked embarrassed but waved his hand in thanks.

Jack raised his wine glass high. "Now, I'd like to salute a very special person. Here's to Nicole, and may we honor her by keeping this place and each other safe. Let's have a moment of silence to remember her."

Glasses rose all around the yard, catching the last of the afternoon light.

Chapter 53:
Rewarded

Friday Night, Nov. 2, 1984

Jack Kendall leaned back from his workstation and keyboard, the green type glistening on the VDT. For the first time since Nicole McIntosh's murder, the words before him didn't feel like exasperation or sadness gripping his heart. They felt like sunlight after a long storm.

Rereading the opening paragraph, a faint smile tugged at the corners of his mouth. He'd written a lot of stories about Nokomis Hospital—fraud, secret accounts and ledgers, a woman's life cut short, a drug-related murder, and a web of lies spun by Mike Lard and his criminal associates.

Tonight, though, the story was about someone who'd survived it all and was ready to rebuild.

He glanced at the photograph Alex Mahoney took of the event: Terry Myles, shaking hands with board chair Christine McVay, a half-surprised grin breaking through his usual reserve.

A month ago, Terry had been sitting in the county jail,

staring down a murder conviction. Now, the same community that once doubted him had voted to make him CEO of the very hospital where his ordeal began. Jack felt a quiet satisfaction—not just as a reporter, but as someone who'd watched Terry fight his way back.

He punched the "send" button on the keyboard, nodded his head and stood up. "Rick, you got it," he declared.

For once, the Nokomis story wasn't about scandal or death; it was about a man cleared by truth, ready to put a broken institution back together.

NOKOMIS HOSPITAL HIRES TERRY MYLES AS CEO

Jack Kendall
Herald-Tribune Staff Writer

NOKOMIS, Saturday, Nov. 3, 1984—Terry Myles went from beating a false murder charge to becoming one of the nation's youngest hospital CEOs.

At a special Friday night meeting, the newly formed board at Nokomis Hospital hired Myles, a former hospital accountant, as president and CEO, an astonishing turnaround for the young executive.

A few weeks ago, Myles, 32, was in jail facing murder charges. Now, he's spearheading a massive hospital turnaround effort.

At his trial, new evidence surfaced proving that Delman Palmer, not Myles, was responsible for the murder of former Nursing Vice President Nicole McIntosh.

Palmer was later killed after he attempted to murder Jack Kendall, Ed Kendall, and Paul Drake Jr. to recover damaging evidence showing corruption at Nokomis

Hospital.

"I am extremely humbled by the board's trust in me. I will do my best to ensure Nokomis once again becomes the hospital we all think it should be, a place where rich and poor can seek healthcare services," Myles said.

Myles was hired in February as an accounting manager for budget in the hospital's finance department. He previously held a similar position at Philadelphia Medical Center, a 600-bed facility.

The board also announced it will reinstate behavioral health and cancel the plan to terminate maternity services.

"All 200 employees laid off over the past year by the previous management will be rehired as we in-source contracted services, including housekeeping, janitorial, food service, maintenance, and security," hospital Board Chair Christine McVay said in a statement.

The new board also issued a letter of apology to the community for blindly following former CEO Mike Lard.

A statement from the newly formed 15-member board said, "The former board members who supported the previous hospital administration have either resigned or are facing criminal charges for doing wrong to this community."

"There are no appropriate words to dismiss the damage the old board did. We can only pledge to be as transparent and dutiful as possible," the board said.

Chapter 54:
"Bunch of Bozos"

Tuesday, Nov. 20, 1984

Jack wrote several follow-up stories in the days and weeks after the arrests. Each one added more nails to the coffin of the old Nokomis Hospital. The newly appointed board, after hiring Terry as CEO, knew they faced a tough job of rebuilding the community's trust after Lard and Co. had done so much to destroy it.

FORMER NOKOMIS TRUSTEES ROYSTER, GILES SENTENCED

Jack Kendall
Herald-Tribune Staff Writer

Former Nokomis Hospital trustees David Royster and Jimmy Giles pleaded guilty Monday to fraud and insider dealing against the nonprofit hospital.

Because both cooperated with prosecutors in the investigation of the former hospital administrators, Judge Launer sentenced Royster to five years and Giles to three years. They were also fined $100,000 each and required to pay restitution to the hospital.

Royster and Giles, the only two hospital trustees charged with crimes, admitted to conspiring with former administrators Mike Lard, Steve Brophy, and Charles McMann. Per the indictment, these administrators approved projects with expenses they knew were false and financially benefited from the crimes.

"These charges against these outstanding executives are fabricated to distract the public from who committed the real felonies," said Woody Woodward, attorney for the executives. "The board knew what was going on and approved it. They are a bunch of bozos who have ignored this hospital for ten years."

Chris Rollie, the state assistant district attorney in charge of the prosecution, stated that the trustees had concealed the crimes in exchange for kickbacks from the projects.

"They persuaded a majority of the rest of the board, who were willfully ignorant, to look the other way," Rollie said. "Most trustees were recruited because they are rich and could donate money to the hospital and not ask questions."

Others familiar with the Nokomis board of trustees had similar opinions.

"There were clear warnings that the board should have recognized as financial stress," said Jennifer Crum, a 15-year hospital volunteer. "After all the disclosures, the trustees now claim they were unaware of it. No, they chose to ignore it. They let it happen."

Teddy Mack, a retired firefighter whose wife died at the hospital after a long illness, said he was often surprised by how the board conducted business.

"Nobody opened their mouths after management

made a motion to approve. It was automatically done. Not only did I never hear disagreement, but I never heard a discussion. It was utterly ridiculous," Mack said.

And David Vandermeer, a former hospital construction manager who resigned in 1979 after Lard brought in Riggles and others who participated in the fraud, said "rubber-stamped" is a kind word to describe how the board acted.

"The board was like a bunch of sheep eating shrimp and scallops at the meeting. They would raise their hand to vote 'yes' for everything Lard asked," Vandermeer said.

However, Vandermeer said that after Dr. Joel O'Neal and Christine McVay were appointed to the board, some other trustees started questioning management.

"I wouldn't say they opposed what Lard was doing, but they understood what Dr. O'Neal and later Ms. McVay wanted done," Vandermeer said.

One problem was that CFO Brophy would cut 30-page reports down to one page or several paragraphs.

"They were left in the dark for many years, but that doesn't excuse not asking for more information," Crum said. "Dr. O'Neal and Ms. McVay pushed the issue much more, but came late in the game."

Bob Roberts, one of the longest-serving trustees for 10 years, summed up the problem.

"The top administrators, Lard, Brophy, and McMann, were like my sons. I loved them, and they were good to me, especially after my wife died," said Roberts, who recently turned 83.

Roberts stated that some trustees lacked the financial skills to understand a $40 million hospital operation.

"I'm the guy who went to the hospital for a board meeting once a month," said Steve Sandburg, a retired teacher. "I looked at what management gave me, but I'm a layman. What do I know?"

Chapter 55:
Bobbie's Interview

Six Months Later

Bobbie Kendall had been eager to interview Mike Lard at Florida State Prison in Raiford since returning from maternity leave. After three months back at the *Herald-Tribune*, she was grateful to feel like herself again—chasing stories, digging into records, pressing people for facts and truth.

Being a cop reporter suited her, and today's interview with the infamous former CEO of Nokomis Hospital promised to be her biggest interview since the twins were born.

The four-hour drive north to Raiford—passing cattle fields, prairies, wetlands, pine flatwoods, horse farms, and stretches of two-lane road—felt shorter than she remembered. It was partly because she had brought photographer Alex Mahoney, who kept a steady stream of commentary about lighting, lenses, and possible headlines.

"Are you going to ask him if he's ready to confess?" Alex asked as they neared the prison gates. "He still claims he's innocent. Keeps blaming McCann and the 'lousy board members.'"

"I'll ask him something like that," Bobbie said. "Everyone except Lard, McMann and Billingly took plea deals. The evidence against the three of them was overwhelming."

"So what's the point unless you think he'll finally talk?"

Bobbie looked out the window at the razor wire curling above the perimeter fences. "Call it intuition. Maybe motherhood changed me—my instincts feel sharper. Lard's final appeal to the Supreme Court was denied. Ten years before he even sees a parole board. Men like him don't like being powerless."

"You think he's ready to crack?"

"I think he's ready for an audience."

As Bobbie stopped at the security guard station, she held out her press pass and driver's license through the cracked window. A guard, unsmiling and broad-shouldered, verified their names on his list.

"You're cleared. Visitor parking is straight ahead. Follow the yellow line," he said, waving them through.

The prison grounds stretched wide: squat brick buildings, towers with tinted glass, guard catwalks, and the long, low concrete blocks that housed everything from close-management units to death row.

Raiford—known officially as Florida State Prison—was old, grim, and unmistakably designed to keep prisoners from leaving. Bobbie had covered enough court cases to know its reputation: violent, oppressive, and steeped in history. Executions were carried out here. A cold feeling swept through her; the place seemed to harbor ghosts.

Alex grabbed his equipment bag as Bobbie checked her purse for everything she needed: notebook, tape recorder, two pens, and—at Lard's request—a box of Mars Bars.

Getting inside was a bureaucratic obstacle course—metal detectors, a hand-held wand, a shoe check, a fingerprint scan, temporary badges, and another round of questioning from a sergeant who clearly didn't care for reporters.

"Jack warned me about this place. It seems way worse," Bobbie muttered as they followed the escort officer down an echoing corridor.

"That's the way it's designed," Alex whispered back.

They were brought to the warden's office, where Ward Cleaver—a tall, silver-haired man with a firm handshake and a calm, almost pastoral demeanor—stood waiting.

"Bobbie Jackson Kendall," Cleaver said warmly. "Jack's wife. We've spoken on the phone. How was your drive?"

"Long, but fine," she said. "We go to Gainesville at least twice a year. Jack graduated from UF."

"I know Jack and his UF connection," Cleaver said with a nostalgic grin. "He interviewed me years ago. Came up here to witness the Spenkelink execution in '79. Sharp guy. I'm sorry he couldn't come along."

"He wanted to, but one of us has to stay with our twins."

"Twins—congratulations. Children are a blessing. My wife and I have five." He chuckled. "Most days, I still can't believe we survived it. Planning on more?"

"I don't think so," Bobbie said. "But you never know."

Cleaver motioned for them to follow. "Lard's in the medium-security compound. White-collar section. Very different from the close-management wings. Fewer fights. More rules followed. These guys have college degrees, investment portfolios, and egos bigger than their cells."

Bobbie raised a brow. "How's Lard adjusting?"

"He's not the worst I've seen," Cleaver replied. "Reads constantly. Volunteers in the library sometimes. Thinks he's still on the board of something." Cleaver lowered his voice. "But don't let your guard down. Men like Lard are slippery. Their remorse comes and goes with their self-interest."

Bobbie smiled. Cleaver resembled Jack's description—grandfatherly. She glanced at him as they walked and wondered how he could bring himself to come to work here every day.

They passed through another set of locked doors and into a quieter hallway lined with bulletin boards, inmate notices, and a small chapel. Cleaver paused.

"You've been searched, and the Mars Bars are fine. But a few rules," he said. "No promises, no talk of special treatment. Ask your questions, get your pictures. And don't antagonize him. Lard is cooperative—until he isn't."

He led them to a small interview room next to the prison library. "Guard's right outside," he said. "Good luck. And tell Jack I said hello."

Bobbie stepped inside, pulse quickening. The room smelled of disinfectant and stale air. A metal table, two metal chairs. A window with wire mesh, though it looked out only onto a cement walkway.

She wondered what Lard's attitude might be and if he would give her some news. Otherwise, she felt Wiseman would give her little space, and she'd have to turn the story into a simple Q&A.

Mike Lard sat waiting, hands folded neatly on the table, orange jumpsuit crisp, hair trimmed. Alex lifted his camera.

"How are you doing?" Bobbie asked politely.

"My doctor says I'm healthy. Had my teeth fixed. I've read all of *War and Peace* and *The Brothers Karamazov*," Lard said with a sly grin.

"Not *Crime and Punishment*?" she teased.

He ignored the jab.

Bobbie continued. "Those are all good books. Long, but you have a lot of time. Are you adjusting to being in prison?"

"I'm in A.A. and Narcotics Anonymous. Don't tell anybody. I don't want it known that I have a drug and alcohol problem. It could hurt my job chances when I get released," Lard said.

Surprised at his answer, Bobbie followed up. "What are you going to do when you get out?"

"Run for political office. What else? I'll have a good resume and dynamite references," Lard sarcastically replied.

She smiled and jotted down the quote. Looking up, she asked, "What about the U.S. Supreme Court refusing to hear your appeal?"

"We expected that. I still feel the charges against us were based on vague and unenforceable statutes," Lard replied with a poker face.

"Now that you have exhausted your appeals, are you ready to acknowledge your crimes? Lawyers say remorse could help you with early release when you are up for parole," Bobbie asked.

"What crimes? The board approved everything I did," Lard insisted.

Bobbie turned her lips to the side, disappointed in Lard's answer. She knew the interview was slipping away from her.

"Don't you feel guilty about the people you laid off and those lives that were turned upside down? The layoffs, your subordinates who died or are serving time?" Bobbie asked directly.

"Yes, in a way, but I had a plan to turn everything around," Lard pleaded, his voice bitter.

"Well, how do you feel about Nokomis being sold to Sarasota Memorial?"

"They did what they needed to do. It was my plan, actually, but the board just sold to a different company. Single, independent hospitals stand no chance against health systems with their purchasing power and deep pockets," Lard said, sounding like his old CEO self.

Bobbie asked a series of questions about the embezzlement, fraud, cocaine parties in the C-suite, board manipulations, appeals, rulings, statutes, and his denials. He avoided everything with smooth, practiced arrogance.

Once she felt comfortable with Lard, Bobbie's questions became more pointed. Her voice grew steadier. Alex's camera clicked consistently.

It was time, she felt, to ask about Nicole McIntosh.

That's when his mask slipped.

And then, Lard—cocky, careless, convinced he could talk his way into early release—started to confess in bits. First accidentally. Then indirectly. Finally, in a reckless, self-important ramble that became the core of Bobbie's story.

"What about Nicole McIntosh? Anything to say to Nicole's relatives?"

"Nicole...who? Is she the nurse who worked 18 years for me? How is she doing?" Lard replied with mock disgust.

"Mr. Lard, you know perfectly well that Nicole McIntosh was murdered by Delman Palmer, who was hired by John Riggles and paid for under an account controlled by you and Mr. Brophy," Bobbie said in a stern voice.

"That's what they said at my trial. I don't know anything about that," he said.

"You don't think having Nicole McIntosh killed was a mistake?"

"Yes, killing Nicole shouldn't have happened," he said plainly. "I don't know who did it, but it was a mistake."

"Your mistake?" Bobbie quickly asked.

"Those were all mistakes. I regret doing that. Yes, I'm guilty of knowing about all those things," Lard said offhandedly.

Alex caught the moment perfectly—the crease of Lard's forehead, the tension in his jaw, the faint tremble of something that might have been honesty, or might have been calculation.

Bobbie had her front-page story: "Mike Lard regrets McIntosh killing, says he knew about it." She also knew Nicole's husband, Pete, and their relatives would appreciate it.

But Bobbie wanted a more direct quote, so she pressed her luck.

"Mr. Lard, are you saying you knew about Nicole's murder before it happened?"

"Yes. I don't know who did it, but it was a mistake."

Bobbie watched Alex snap photos as Lard confessed. They both knew they'd struck gold.

"Do you mind if I take a sip of water?" Lard asked.

"You don't need to ask," Bobbie said as she continued to write in her notebook. She glanced at her recorder to make sure it was still working.

"You don't understand. I have to ask permission for everything here, even to take a crap," Lard said. "You don't mind, do you?"

Bobbie looked up and changed the subject. "Any regrets?"

"Regrets—now that is a loaded word. I don't regret stealing

the money; I loved having it. My wife loved it."

Was this another confession? Bobbie needed a good follow-up question, but he continued his line of thought.

"I do regret what I did to my family and how I let them down: my wife, my son, and my daughter. I'm sorry for that. They deserved better," he said.

"Your wife and children love you. They would want you to tell the truth now so they can be proud of you again," Bobbie said.

"I let them down. I'll tell you this, Bobbie Kendall, for the record. I wanted it all: money, power, family, drugs and sex. I wanted too much. I know." He paused, looking over to Alex.

"But if I had to do it all over again, I'd probably do it all the same—except for three things."

Alex snapped multiple pictures of Lard looking directly into the camera.

Bobbie watched him, still hoping for a full confession. "What three things?"

"First, I regret allowing the hire of Terry Myles. He was a mistake. Second, I also regret bringing Dr. O'Neal and Christine McVay on the board. O'Neal wanted to grow his cardiology practice, and I was putting him in a position to do that before he betrayed me. McVay...I don't know why she turned on me. I was giving her everything she wanted."

Lard paused and looked directly at Bobbie.

"What about the third regret?"

"You should know. You're married to him. I regret talking with Jack Kendall. I should have known better. I let him walk around inside my hospital, talk with my employees, stir them up, write those stories."

"What you should have known is not to get Jack mad,"

said Bobbie, pausing. "Thanks for explaining that. What I want you to know is that your hospital saved my life by being so close when I developed eclampsia. You had a wonderful staff, even though you took them for granted."

"I'm glad my hospital did some good. You were saved. Your twins are healthy. I am *not* a monster. I know what we did for the 12 years I was there. We saved a lot of people and did a lot of good with our hospital," Lard said.

*   *   *

The drive back to Sarasota was quiet. Alex organized his film while the countryside rolled past. Bobbie stared out the window, replaying the interview, marveling at how quickly a routine assignment had turned into a bombshell.

By morning, the *Herald-Tribune* had the story splashed across A1:

Mike Lard Regrets McIntosh Killing, Admits Knowledge of Cover-Up.

In his cell, Lard read the article twice, studying the photos. He thought Bobbie and Alex had done good work. He believed his "regret" would be seen as remorse by the parole board someday.

That was another mistake Lard made.

Epilogue

Three years later

On a peaceful Saturday afternoon in mid-November 1987, Jack and Bobbie played in the backyard with their energetic twins. The toddlers were active, and outdoor activities were always enjoyable.

Jack played catch with little Ella and Eli, tossing the soft rubber ball underhand. He smiled as he watched them take turns snatching and throwing it back. Like their father, they were natural athletes.

Ella always caught the ball, but sometimes she'd run to give it to Bobbie, who would laugh and tell her to throw it back to Daddy. Eli was also a good catcher. He had a strong left arm and threw the ball back quickly, although not always accurately.

Over the past three years, Jack and Bobbie had been busy raising twins and working at the newspaper. It was a relief to enjoy a peaceful, everyday life after Bobbie's eclampsia led to an emergency C-section at Nokomis Hospital.

While life remained steady for the Kendall family, some things had changed. Terry and Della got married. Pete McIntosh tried to pick up the pieces after Nicole's death, but he chose to move back to his hometown of Chicago.

Under the leadership of Board Chair Christine McVay and CEO Terry Myles, with unexpected help from former General Counsel Gus Lessem, Nokomis Hospital successfully fended off a takeover attempt by National Healthcare. Instead, Nokomis entered into an affiliation agreement with Sarasota Memorial Hospital, preserving its semi-independence and financial stability.

Lard, McMann and Billingly remained in prison. Brophy was released after two years for good behavior. He rejoined Mary in California.

Jack had gotten used to working the 9-to-5 and returning home to spend time with the twins. He regularly covered healthcare and environmental issues and wrote a twice-weekly column on social and public interest topics.

Katie North went back to the court beat. She helped Jack and Bobbie with special projects. Bobbie was completely emeshed again as the newspaper's chief police reporter.

Grandma Laura and the babysitters looked after the toddlers during the day. As they grew older, Bobbie slept more.

Young Ella and Eli developed their personalities. Ella talked more than Eli, but Eli showed greater creativity and the ability to imitate both his parents, especially their fondness for writing in notebooks.

Eli had already written a book of stories that he'd created for his babysitter, Diane, who drew pictures to illustrate his ideas and visions. Ella used her tape recorder to sing songs and tell stories.

This afternoon, while Jack and Bobbie watched the twins play outside, the patio phone rang. Jack walked over and answered it.

"Jack, Rick Wiseman gave me your number. This is Mary, Ed France's daughter. He may have told you my son, Steve, is getting help from a drug rehabilitation program in Sarasota."

Jack remembered that Manatee County Commission Chairman France had told him the story a few weeks earlier.

"Yes, Mary. Go ahead," Jack said.

"Breakthrough kidnapped Julie, my 16-year-old daughter. You wrote about them once. Can you help?"

Afterword

I covered the healthcare industry for newspapers and magazines from the early 1980s to 2022.

Over the years, I have observed that many hospital administrators, doctors, nurses, advanced practice providers, consultants, and frontline healthcare workers are dedicated and hardworking.

However, I also discovered some unscrupulous healthcare owners and executives, many of whom the Department of Justice rightly labels as criminals, who ruthlessly laid off hardworking employees and cut vital programs that communities rely on, all to boost profit margins and annual bonuses, and fatten their bank accounts and retirement plans.

Tragically, some of these criminal healthcare executives were caught up in their circumstances because of drug, alcohol, or gambling addictions. Others were simply greedy and believed they were above the law or the community's needs.

My novel, *Nokomis Hospital,* is entirely fictional. However, some of the names, places, and situations are composites of real healthcare criminals and characters, based on my own experiences writing about them, reading articles from fellow healthcare journalists over the years, reviewing closed case reports from the U.S. Department of Health and Human Services' Office of Inspector General, or watching documentaries.

- 30 -

Healthcare Fraud:
You Pay for Their Greed

Healthcare fraud affects everyone, whether it's through inflated medical bills that burden patients, taxpayers funding government health programs that are drained by fraudulent claims, or employees facing layoffs due to embezzlement of hospital funds.

What was once a hidden cost of doing business in healthcare has evolved into a multibillion-dollar criminal enterprise that impacts the financial well-being of millions of Americans.

In 2026, U.S. healthcare spending is expected to reach $6 trillion, accounting for approximately 18% of the nation's gross domestic product—a significant increase from previous decades. For comparison, U.S. healthcare spending in 1996 totaled $1 trillion, accounting for 14% of the country's GDP. By 2033, healthcare spending is expected to reach 8.6% and 20% of GDP.

Each year, personal healthcare costs average $13,500 annually, further straining household budgets. On average, health insurance premiums and out-of-pocket expenses make up 17% of an individual's yearly income.

In comparison, the federal government directs 28% of its budget to healthcare programs for veterans, the elderly, people with disabilities, and low-income families. State governments, facing rising costs, now allocate 25% of their budgets to healthcare, highlighting the significant financial pressure on public resources.

WHERE DO HEALTHCARE DOLLARS GO?

75% of healthcare spending covers legitimate hospital care, physician services, and medical treatments.

15% is wasted due to inefficiencies, mismanagement, and unnecessary administrative costs.

However, 10%—nearly $500 billion—is lost to fraud, abuse, and outright theft, according to government estimates.

This level of fraud surpasses even the savings-and-loan scandal of the 1980s, which cost taxpayers only $5 billion.

It's unclear exactly how much money is pocketed by corrupt executives, physicians, and con artists working within legitimate healthcare institutions. Fraud experts estimate that 25% of stolen healthcare funds are deposited directly into criminals' personal bank accounts. At the same time, most of the money is funneled into fraudulent corporate schemes that boost profit margins at investor-owned and even nonprofit hospitals.

THE COST TO YOU

Healthcare fraud costs each American between $196 and $996 annually, depending on the scam detected and prosecuted. If just $350 of this fraud each year were invested in a conservative retirement fund, a 40-year-old worker could save $50,000 by retirement—money that would otherwise be lost to fraudulent schemes and enrich criminals.

HEALTHCARE FRAUD:
A NEVER-ENDING EPIDEMIC

Despite efforts by the FBI, federal watchdog agencies, private insurers, and whistleblowers, healthcare fraud has surged over the past 30 years. Some of the most notorious fraud cases include:

National Medical Enterprises (1990s): Executives paid doctors and bounty hunters to admit patients into psychiatric hospitals, defrauding insurance companies and the government of hundreds of millions. NME, formerly Tenet Healthcare Corp., paid the government $379 million in fines and penalties to resolve criminal and civil False Claims Act charges that it provided unnecessary treatment to thousands of patients in its psychiatric hospitals.

Columbia/HCA Inc. (2000): HCA, now known as HCA Healthcare Corp., agreed to pay the United States $631 million in civil penalties and damages related to false claims the government alleged it submitted to Medicare and other federal health programs from 1987 to 1997, the Justice Department said. Current Florida Sen. Rick Scott was CEO of Columbia/HCA during this period of fraudulent activity. Scott was never personally charged with a crime. Still, he was forced to resign by the company's board in July 1997 and later invoked the Fifth Amendment 75 times during a civil lawsuit deposition related to his time at the company.

"Health care providers and professionals hold a public trust, and when that trust is violated by fraud and abuse of program funds, and by the payment of kickbacks to physicians on whom patients and the programs depend for honest medical judgment, healthcare for all Americans suffers,"

Robert D. McCallum, Jr., Assistant Attorney General for the Civil Division, said.

University of Pittsburgh Medical Center (2023): Settled for $8.5 million over fraudulent billing practices in cardiac surgery. The DOJ alleged that Dr. James Luketich, chair of cardiothoracic surgery, "regularly performed as many as three complex surgical procedures *at the same time*, failed to participate in the key and critical portions of his surgeries, and forced his patients to endure hours of medically unnecessary anesthesia time."

Michael J. Ligotti, D.O., 48, of Delray Beach (2023): Sentenced to 20 years in prison for defrauding insurance companies and government healthcare programs. The DOJ said Ligotti "engaged in a massive multi-year scheme to bill health care benefit programs for fraudulent tests and treatments for vulnerable patients seeking treatment for drug and/or alcohol addiction."

Alexander Baldonado, M.D., 69, a Queens, New York, gastroenterologist (2023): Convicted for performing unnecessary procedures and inflating Medicare billing. He received "tens of thousands of dollars in illegal cash kickbacks and bribes in exchange for ordering laboratory tests, including expensive cancer genetic tests, that were billed to Medicare by two related laboratories," said the Department of Justice.

RECENT FRAUD SCHEMES

Telemedicine Fraud: In a $2 billion scheme, 11 defendants used telemedicine to bill Medicare and TRICARE for unnecessary medical equipment and prescriptions. Kickbacks were paid to corrupt telemedicine companies, defrauding taxpayers.

This scheme involved a network of telemarketers who

targeted vulnerable populations, such as the elderly and disabled, convincing them to purchase unnecessary medical equipment and prescriptions. The fraudulent claims included falsified doctors' orders and diagnostic tests, with kickbacks paid to telemedicine companies.

Pharmaceutical Fraud: A $150 million scheme involved illegally repackaging HIV medications through "buyback" programs, endangering patients with compromised drugs.

Hospice Fraud: Shiva Akula, the owner of Canon Healthcare LLC, was sentenced to 20 years in prison for billing $42 million in fraudulent hospice services. On May 15, 2024, U.S. District Judge Lance Africk sentenced Akula, 68, of New Orleans, to 240 months of imprisonment, three years of supervised release, and $2,300 in mandatory special assessment fees for his extensive healthcare fraud scheme.

The fraud involved billing for medically unnecessary hospice services and manipulating billing codes to increase profits. This large-scale scheme spanned several years and was implemented across multiple locations.

Durable Medical Equipment Fraud: Operators of a medical supply company stole $14 million by submitting fake repair and purchase claims.

These cases show how fraud is deeply rooted at every level of the healthcare system—from corporate executives at billion-dollar hospital chains to small-time criminals operating in local clinics.

SOARING SALARIES

In the 1980s, it wasn't considered criminal for a hospital CEO to earn $100,000 to $150,000 annually or for a corporate healthcare CEO to take home a $1 million compensation package.

By 2023, those figures had skyrocketed. Today, the average hospital CEO earns over $450,000 annually, with top for-profit healthcare CEOs raking in $1 million to $10 million compensation packages:

Jeffrey Balser (Vanderbilt University Medical Center): $6.8 million

Marc Harrison (IHC Health Services): $6.6 million

Albert Bourla (Pfizer CEO): $30.5 million in 2022

THE HUMAN COST

Some healthcare executives undoubtedly earn their pay through hard work and strategic leadership. However, too many cross the ethical line, prioritizing greed over patient care.

While only a fraction of fraudulent executives are ever caught, fined, or jailed, the actual victims of healthcare fraud include:

Employees who dedicated their careers to hospitals and clinics were only to be laid off due to fraud-induced budget shortfalls.

Trusting board members whose reputations were ruined when the frauds they unknowingly endorsed were exposed.

Patients who suffered or even died due to fraudulent medical procedures and overbilling scams.

Communities were left without adequate healthcare when hospitals collapsed under the weight of corruption.

FICTION MIRRORS REALITY

Nokomis Hospital reveals a story of fictional executives driven by greed, addiction, and corruption—and the actual situation is much worse.

In the real world, fraudulent executives gamble with lives,

divert hospital resources for personal luxuries, and exploit the trust of the communities that depend on them. Their actions don't just drain funds—they destroy livelihoods.

Employees who dedicate their prime years to hospitals and healthcare companies often pay the highest price. Many are betrayed and laid off to balance budgets drained by executive misfeasance and malfeasance.

The board members of nonprofit hospitals, often well-meaning but overly trusting, also become collateral damage. When fraud is exposed, their reputations are shattered, their institutions are plunged into scandal, and entire communities are embarrassed. As funding dries up, once-thriving hospitals decline.

The result? A flawed system in which a corrupt few profit while millions struggle to afford care.

As real-life scandals unfold, one truth remains: healthcare fraud isn't just about money—it's about people. Until meaningful reforms take hold, the cycle of greed and deception will continue, leaving behind a trail of shattered institutions, ruined careers, and lives lost to corruption.

It is our collective responsibility to remain vigilant, speak out, and report healthcare fraud to the relevant authorities. Only then can we start to restore a system intended to heal, not exploit.

- 30 -

How to Contact Jay B. Greene

Visit my website, review my books, and sign up for my newsletters at **www.jaybgreene.com**

By subscribing, you'll get:

- Early sneak peeks at upcoming books.
- Bonus chapters, deleted scenes, blogs, exclusive children's stories, short stories and newspaper articles I wrote over the years.
- Insider updates on my novels, including the investigative reporter Jack Kendall mysteries and the family space opera Tim and Peggy Smith Space Adventures.
- Special offers and giveaways.
- Author insights, personal notes and healthcare policy blogs.

Love My Books?
Leave a review and share it with your friends!

Your reviews on Amazon, Barnes and Noble or independent bookstore websites help other readers discover the series, and they mean the world to me as an author.

Thanks again for reading, and I hope you'll join Jack Kendall on his next thrilling adventure!

Pursue the Truth, **Jay B. Greene**

Other Jack Kendall Mysteries

Mountain Crossing—Investigative reporter Jack Kendall is devastated after witnessing a suicide while on assignment. His life begins to unravel further when his wife, Becky, disappears, leaving behind only a cryptic letter. Driven to uncover the truth, Jack's investigation discovers Becky's connections to a dangerous global cocaine ring. With help from Sarah, an enigmatic woman linked to his wife's disappearance, Jack ventures into Jamaica's dangerous Blue Mountains. Guided by haunting dreams of a mysterious angelic figure, Jack confronts perilous secrets about Becky's hidden life. This gripping debut in the Jack Kendall Mystery series is a compelling tale of love, betrayal, and survival.

Other Jack Kendall Mysteries

Becky—Becky Kendall and Michelle Talley have fled their traumatic past in Jamaica, taking control of $5 million in drug profits. But they are pursued by Gordon Gecht, a ruthless enforcer determined to reclaim the money he believes is rightfully his. When estranged husband Jack Kendall arrives in Bogotá to uncover the truth about Becky, he gets caught in a deadly game of betrayal and survival. As old wounds resurface and trust becomes hard to find, Jack races against time to expose Gecht's crimes. *Becky* is a tense journey through danger, resilience, and the relentless pursuit of justice—set against the gritty backdrop of 1980s Colombia.

Other Jack Kendall Mysteries

Bone Valley—In the third book, Jack exposes the dark underbelly of Florida's phosphate industry, where corruption, environmental ruin, and murder collide. An anonymous tip leads Jack into the heart of Bone Valley's phosphate mines, where toxic spills devastate communities and powerful corporations bury the truth. Partnering with police reporter Bobbie Jackson, Jack uncovers a string of murders tied to an industry willing to kill to protect its secrets. As a Category 5 hurricane approaches, Jack faces relentless threats, including a vengeful enemy from his past. Can he survive long enough to reveal the truth? *Bone Valley* is an unflinching thriller about justice, greed, and the high stakes of environmental disaster.

Jack's Next Adventure
Breakthrough Lies

Breakthrough Lies— When sixteen-year-old **Julie France**, granddaughter of a powerful Manatee County Commissioner, is seized from her home and forced into Breakthrough—a controversial teen drug rehabilitation program—her desperate mother turns to investigative reporter **Jack Kendall** for help. Inside the Sarasota facility, Julie's younger brother, Steve, already confined there for a month, faces humiliation, isolation, and emotional manipulation in the name of "tough love." When program enforcers claim that Julie must also be admitted to protect her brother's recovery, she becomes the next victim of Breakthrough's coercive methods.

Breakthrough Lies, the fourth Jack Kendall book is a gripping, emotional thriller about power, family, and the dark side of institutional control—based on the chilling reality of one of America's most notorious youth rehabilitation programs.

About the Author

Jay B. Greene was born, raised, and still lives in Sarasota. He studied environmental science and journalism at the University of Florida. His passion for storytelling led to a 40-year career covering healthcare, government, crime, and the environment for newspapers in various states. Greene is the author of *Mountain Crossing, Becky,* and *Bone Valley*, the first three books in the Jack Kendall Mystery series. He also wrote *Danger From Space* and *Flight to the Stars*, the first books in the Tim and Peggy Smith Space Adventure trilogy. In 2026, Jack will return in *Breakthrough Lies*, and Tim and Peggy will conclude their space adventures in *Children of the Stars*.

www.ingramcontent.com/pod-product-compliance
Lightning Source LLC
Chambersburg PA
CBHW020541120726
47903CB00001B/73